OUTLAW PLANET

By M. R. Carey

The Girl With All the Gifts
The Boy on the Bridge

Fellside

Someone Like Me

Once Was Willem

The Rampart trilogy
The Book of Koli
The Trials of Koli
The Fall of Koli

The Pandominion
Infinity Gate
Echo of Worlds
Outlaw Planet

By Mike Carey

Felix Castor
The Devil You Know
Vicious Circle
Dead Men's Boots
Thicker Than Water
The Naming of the Beasts

OUTLAW PLANET

M. R. CAREY

orbit-books.co.uk

ORBIT

First published in Great Britain in 2025 by Orbit

1 3 5 7 9 10 8 6 4 2

Copyright © 2025 by M. R. Carey

The moral right of the author has been asserted.

All characters and events in this publication, other than those clearly in the public domain, are fictitious and any resemblance to real persons, living or dead, is purely coincidental.

All rights reserved.
No part of this publication may be reproduced, stored in a retrieval system, or transmitted, in any form or by any means, without the prior permission in writing of the publisher, nor be otherwise circulated in any form of binding or cover other than that in which it is published and without a similar condition including this condition being imposed on the subsequent purchaser.

A CIP catalogue record for this book is available from the British Library.

HB ISBN 978-0-356-52803-8
PBK ISBN 978-0-356-52804-5
C format 978-0-356-51945-6

Typeset in Adobe Caslon by Palimpsest Book Production Limited,
Falkirk, Stirlingshire

Printed and bound in Great Britain by Clays Ltd, Elcograf, S.p.A.

Papers used by Orbit are from well-managed forests and other responsible sources.

Orbit
An imprint of
Little, Brown Book Group
Carmelite House
50 Victoria Embankment
London EC4Y 0DZ

The authorised representative
in the EEA is
Hachette Ireland
8 Castlecourt Centre, Dublin 15,
D15 XTP3, Ireland
(email: info@hbgi.ie)

An Hachette UK Company
www.hachette.co.uk

orbit-books.co.uk

Dog-Bitch Bess is what they came to call her. You might say that's a strange name to lay on someone, and I would not be inclined to disagree. A mite over-precise, at the very least. All dog-selves are either bulls or bitches so that ought to be a given. It's as if you were to say that a plank was made out of tree-wood, or that someone coming in out of a rainstorm was water-wet.

People explain that strangeness each in their own way. Some say they only called Bess dog-bitch because there was an otter bitch that lived in the same town as her, in the same house even, and that the two of them were pledged to each other as betrothed.

Others would have it that when folks gave her that name they wanted both "dog" and "bitch" to have their weight of contempt and spitefulness. Certainly Bess herself always assumed this was the case, and she didn't mind it at all. She was only too happy to have those same folks hate her and curse her. She would have been mightily disappointed if they ever called her anything civil.

Dog-Bitch Bess then, both in the war and after, though what she had been before was a different thing altogether. She was mostly Labrador, her fur the near-transparent yellow of white gold, except for her face where it was paler and more than a little uneven. She had been badly burned once and the fur had not grown back exactly as it had been before. Even the contours of her cheeks and chin were subtly or maybe not-so-subtly off the true. She was not overly tall but there was something about her, a quiet or a coldness or an intensity, that left an impression. Sometimes she was wont to wear a battered old greatcoat that she had acquired from a Parity cavalry officer, with dark patches around the shoulders where she'd torn away his rank and regimentals. The coat created a doubt, which was most likely its purpose. Had she served in the army of the Equalisers or was she, as you might say, wearing the pelt of a dead enemy? Bess sat more or less comfortably inside that doubt, staring back at you and waiting for you to make your call.

It's funny how many you'll meet who claim they knew her. That they lived a stone's throw away from her all unknowing, passed her on a street in some border town a hundred miles from anywhere, sold her a gun or a hat or a chafer, took a kindness or an insult from her or else gave one. There's a whole slew of folk who will tell you they were in this or that posse that chased her and nearly brought her down, or that they swapped bullets with her and would have killed her for sure if not for this thing or that thing, the dust or the daylight or the Devil's luck.

Most of this is lies, as you'd expect. Not so much lies, even, as the desperate need some people feel to make their life mean something by pushing it up close to other lives that are bigger or at least louder. There's no more truth in most of these accounts than there is fresh air in a shithouse. But stories accrete around someone like Bess.

Like this one. An old couple hear a knock on the door in the middle of the night. It's a stranger with a big iron on her hip and three bullet wounds in her. They dress the wounds as best they can and then they retreat to their own room and lock the door out of pure fright. In the morning the stranger is gone and there's a purse on the table with a hundred silver dollars in it.

Or this. A man in a saloon is bad-mouthing the Echelon, calling them motherfucking sons of whores and cold-hearted slave-owning bastards and more of the same. There's a woman drinking her drink right next to him with a wide-brimmed hat drawn down over her face. She tells him to shut his mouth and he takes it hard. Calls her out. Only the woman says she don't shoot no drunkards. "You're a damned coward if you don't stand up and answer me," says he. "Well, if you're dead set on it," says the lady, "then let's dance. But I'll do this with my right hand, me being southerly in all things including my grip. And I'll give you three shots before I loose a single one." They go out into the street and the loudmouth is feeling mighty cocky. But he's too quick and too drunk and his first shot goes wide. "Fuck it," says he and shoots again. Hits nothing but sunshine. Fuck, fuck, fuck! But he's got one shot left and he didn't hear any rule about how close he could get. So he walks up to the woman and he puts his Lumiss against the side of her head. And she stares him right in the face as he pulls the trigger. Just a click. He's out of bullets. "What was that you said about the Echelon, then?" the woman asks him. "That they're motherfuckers," says the man, knowing he's good and dead. "Motherfuckers and slave-drivers and sons of whores." "Well, I respect a man who sticks to his principles," says the woman, "but I incline to disagree." Whereby she shoots him in the right knee, cripples him, but leaves him alive.

Or again. There's a tower at the end of the world where God lives, and one way or another Dog-Bitch Bess found her way in there and she's standing right in front of God with her hand on her gun and murder in her heart. "Okay," she says, "I guess you know I lost every damn thing I loved to get this far, but here I fucking am at last and I mean to shoot you down." And God says, "No, Bess, you didn't lose everything. Not yet. You got one friend left that you love, and the bullet you shoot me with has got to be wet with his heart's blood or it won't do me no harm. And although I'm meant to know all things, for the life of me I don't know if you're strong enough in your wilfulness and your hate to do what's needful to be done." "Well then," says Bess, and she takes out a dime piece and balances it on her bent-back thumb, "I guess we're both of us in for a surprise."

Lies and tall tales, all of it. Almost. Almost all. There's a whisper of truth in that last one, but the tower wasn't at the end of the world. It wasn't even anywhere special, just out in the open desert near to the western ocean. And Bess wasn't the one that got to talk to it. And you don't kill God with a bullet, although in one very narrow sense you *can* kill Him with a gun. Anyway, and despite all that, Bess was there in that place and she did have to make that terrible choice. For the rest, you're better off listening to every tenth word you hear about the Dog-Bitch, throwing half of what you heard away and believing half of what's left.

There are some things that are known, though. To start with, Bess wasn't Echelon in her origins but pure Parity. She hailed from away up north in a city named Paxen – a safe and civilised and law-abiding place where the pavements were free of ordure and the citizen-selves were sleek of fur. You wouldn't have guessed from such a silver-spooned beginning that Bess would end up writing her name in the history books using other folks' blood.

There were many who got their hands bloodied in the civil war, of course. Bess wasn't special in that regard. Still and all, she was one of those who didn't put her gun down when the politicians shook hands but fought a second war that was all her own. And then she was among the much smaller number who found out the truth of how the civil war had come to pass. How it had never really belonged either to Parity or to Echelon but was only a poison that had been fed to both sides and that they couldn't purge except through that one awful thing.

There are many who'll tell you that the pith and point of stories is to instruct us in our failings. That if you don't learn the lessons of the past you'll go on making the same mistakes again and again until at last you make the big mistake that you can't walk away from. What they won't tell you is that you sucked in those errors with your mother's milk, took them in along with your first breath, soaked and stewed in them every day of your short, precious life. Which was never your life in the first place but only a kind of straw doll or poppet put in your hands to comfort you after your real life had been torn away.

Bess learned that truth. Came to it the hard way, through pain and loss and the reckless spilling of blood, and carried it with her like a brand on her soul to match the burns that had scarred her face. And once she knew it – knew for sure how badly she'd been used – she had no option but to do something about it. And that was when she went to war for the third time, to murder God and his tall white angels and get the world out from under their shadow.

This is her story. It's the story of the gun she carried, whose name was Wakeful Slim. It's the story of the dead man who carried that gun before her and left a piece of himself inside it.

And it's a story of the Pandominion, though it takes place after the Pandominion fell. After the rabbit and the robot and the Registry came and killed that endless empire by driving a stake through its heart.

What can I say? Some things don't always notice straight away that they're dead. And they take a good long time to hit the ground.

PART ONE

A PLACE THAT'S MAKING ITSELF

The country was growing, and it was growing apart. The name States' Union suggests a whole that came together out of many different pieces, and so it was; but some of the pieces came easy while others needed a great deal of cutting and splicing and sanding down before they could be made to fit at all. And looking at the results it was hard to tell exactly what kind of thing they made when they were all bolted together.

In the north there was industry. Manufacturies, workshops, steel mills, foundries, warehouses. Industry eats raw materials and shits out profit. The south was where the raw materials came from, and it was where some of the money went back to. But it was an extraordinary thing to see how sticky that flow could get, syphoning up so much and giving so little back. The north was captivated by its own project, an alchemical transformation of sweat and hard effort into gold. The south did the same thing but on different terms, taking the labour of the so-called ignoble races – mouse and rat, squirrel and chipmunk – as a natural resource that could be exploited at no cost. And if those supposed inferiors protested or (good God forbid) tried to walk away from their work, then it was no crime to school them on their place in the scheme of things with the aid of a lash or a hanging tree.

It was a filthy mess, is what it was. An evil framework built on an evil model, silted up with cruelties that could never be acknowledged because if you once admit you're sick you might be obliged to take your medicine. The north called itself the Parity, affecting to honour the selfhood of all races and to value them all equally (except for the Pugface nations, of course – the Pugfaces stood outside any system of value). The southern assemblies were collectively known as the Echelon, signifying their adherence to the ladder of being in which the lesser bowed to the greater for the good of all.

There was no Dog-Bitch Bess back then. Instead there was Elizabeth Indigo Sandpiper of Paxen City, a name that carried a considerable weight of meaning. Sandpiper was an overt badge of status: all the well-to-do families in the Parity had that fetish for naming themselves after birds and winged insects. The Indigo dropped in the middle there indicated that she was her parents' ninth child, *i* being the ninth letter of the alphabet (dog selves tend towards large litters). As for Elizabeth, it was only in northern climes that you'd find the appellation in such a pristine state. Further south it broke apart into Eliza, Liz, Beth, Bessie and all those other part-works.

You might think from all this here foofaraw that the Sandpipers held a lofty place in Paxen's uppermost crust, but in fact they always had more of the trappings of status than the thing itself. They lived in a twenty-room mansion in a fashionable neighbourhood, mortgaged to the hilt, and paid the wages of their serving staff three or sometimes four weeks in arrears. Miss Elizabeth enjoyed a fair few luxuries as she grew up, including the luxury of a good education, but her father William Alabaster Sandpiper was living like a great many society men and society ladies in the Parity's eastern strongholds, which is to say out on the uttermost edge of credit.

William came from a big litter himself and had inherited only two things from his own father – the family name and an optimism so fervent it amounted to a religious creed. The name was sufficient collateral for a number of sizeable loans, and the optimism shielded William from any contaminating shred of caution or foresight. He put all the money he only nominally had into the Penny Express, the relay system of intrepid riders and armed wagons that ferried messages and goods between the prosperous east and the ever-expanding west. He assured everyone who was willing to listen that the Express was a gilt-edged investment, solid as any rock. What was the one thing any society could not possibly do without? Why, communication of course! Communication was the keystone. It was a bet you could never lose. And when each year brought William only a modest dividend on his investments, well he just borrowed against the next year and went on smiling.

His wife Caroline wore that same smile slightly more askew. She was from old money, as the saying goes, but like her husband had little to none that was current and actually usable. In her earlier years she had briefly been reduced to working for a living, though this was not a thing the family advertised. She had been what was called a nursing companion, looking after the well-to-do elderly in their own homes. This was no sinecure. Many people, especially the old, were at that time tormented by terrifyingly vivid dreams of blood and carnage. Some woke with delusions that the nation was actually at war, that their houses were burning and their neighbours being dragged out and slaughtered in the streets. Doctors were at a loss to explain the cause of this delirium or why it had struck so many all at once. It was a response, some said, to the growing tension between the northern and southern states. There was a widespread feeling that war was inevitable, and for some fragile minds the constant pressure of that fear was enough to cause psychotic breaks.

Caroline Earnest Crane, who herself was not the most robust or stable of personalities, did not enjoy being regularly immersed in the terrors of others. She was a tolerably good nurse, but she was not at all reluctant to abandon her calling and become Caroline Sandpiper. The marriage was brokered by her parents, who were operating under the assumption that William was a man of actual means and were bitterly disappointed when they learned the truth. For her own part Caroline resolutely refused to be cast down. She had given gainful employment a fair trial and much preferred her present station, in which nothing was expected of her beyond a surface gloss and an absolute passivity. Her fate would be determined by others while she organised charity drives and presided over luncheons.

So she adopted the smile, and conspired with William in imprinting it on their children. In the absence of anything more substantial it was what they had by way of an entry ticket into the bastions of east coast society, and both parents encouraged their offspring to trade on it for all they were worth. To do otherwise would be to doubt the divine providence that was watching over their family, and doubt was a vice that could not be indulged.

Smiling never came easy to Miss Elizabeth though. She watched her siblings scrambling up the scree slopes of elite society and decided those heights were not for her. So she went a different way. She read. She thought. She became so quiet you could have forgotten she was there at all, but it was the kind of quiet you get between the flash of the lightning and the boom of the thunder. It was always going to end at some point, and what happened after that was always going to be loud.

Then the steam trains came along, turning everything downside up, and the Penny Express sank like a stone in a well. The Sandpipers were staring ruin in the face: all their chickens were on their way home at once with IOUs and mortgage deeds clutched in their beaks.

The effect on William Sandpiper was nothing short of cataclysmic. It seemed to him that the universe had lured him on like a harlot and then betrayed him with a harlot's callousness. Caroline felt equally short-changed, but she had never had many illusions about the universe's good intentions and she retreated into existential despair with a minimum of fuss. Most of Miss Elizabeth's siblings, when William broke the news, seemed aggrieved not that ruin had arrived but that their father had decided to tell them about it. It wasn't any of their damn place to worry about where the next meal or the next chauffeured carriage was coming from. Those things just arrived, like rain from heaven when the ground was parched.

If Miss Elizabeth responded to the calamity more pragmatically than the rest of the family it was because she'd never thought of the life they were living as anything more than a soap bubble, and she knew that soap bubbles weren't built for the long haul. It wasn't that she failed to realise the seriousness of the situation. On the contrary, she could see all too clearly the direction the family was travelling in.

Her mother was melting down into one big puddle of grief and her father, despite the presence of this puddle, had taken fire and become a furnace stoked with rage and recrimination. These elemental transformations were alarming, and the situation wasn't helped at all by the younger Sandpipers continuing to live in a haze of denial and profligate spending that made any stabilisation of the family's circumstances all but impossible.

William had seldom taken a direct part in his children's education, but he hadn't been above delivering the occasional object lesson. Miss Elizabeth was minded now of a time when her father had had the children run races across the garden of their house. The prize for each race was a dime piece – not an inconsiderable sum by any means. The children tore back and forth across the lawn, but the oldest took all the coin that was going while the younger ones trudged increasingly breathless in their wake. After the first few races Miss Elizabeth – ninth in the pecking order, after all – realised the futility of expending any effort on this nonsense. She was obliged to participate but gave nothing to the cause, strolling at a leisurely pace behind her siblings and rolling in last every time.

Then, after more than an hour of non-stop sprinting, William announced a final grand tourney: a hundred laps of the garden with a purse of ten dollars for the winner. Miss Elizabeth decided this was a prize worth fighting for and gave it her all. At first she was bringing up the rear as she had in all the previous races, but her older brothers and sisters, tired out from their earlier efforts, fell back one by one. By the time Miss Elizabeth had made seventy or so circuits she had such a clear lead that she was able to complete the course at a comfortable jog. "There now," William said, all smiles, as he handed the huge banknote to his tiny daughter. "You see how it is, kids. You need to decide up front if you're going to run the fastest or the furthest. Can't do both, do you follow me? Nobody ever did both."

Now, amid the wailing and the gnashing of teeth, Miss Elizabeth saw a notice tacked up on the wall of a telegram office that said Ottomankie in distant Orselian needed a schoolmistress. She decided on this occasion that the best strategy was to run the furthest. So at the tender age of nineteen, more or less fresh out of her own schooling, she packed her bags and headed south. She didn't bother to tell the rest of the family where she was going or why. There would have been recriminations, or else there would have been indifference. Either one would have been painful and of no real use to her.

Miss Elizabeth took a stagecoach from Paxen to Shoshimish, a train to Blue Peak and a katy-wagon to Ottomankie. This was in some ways a journey backwards through time, the appurtenances of civilisation disappearing one by one as she journeyed south. The seats in the coach had no cushions to them. The train had no water closet and offered no refreshments. The katy-wagon was a few bare boards with wheels attached, drenched in the pungent smell of the colossal arthropod that pulled it.

The speech and appearance of Miss Elizabeth's fellow travellers moved in lockstep with these changes. Fine linen suits and crinoline dresses were gradually replaced by blue cotton overalls and homespun calico. Urbane conversation gave way to curse words and obscenities, some of them utterly astonishing to Miss Elizabeth's refined ear. She sat next to bison with unbated horns, bobcats with gun belts at their waists, a striped skunk with a bandolier of gleaming blades.

And she saw her first Pugfaces – not riding, of course, but walking on the road or standing close by it to watch the wagon go by. The men with their gap teeth and fierce grins, the women with their earrings and tattoos, the children so stoical and impassive they seemed older than their parents. All had the same squashed, truncated faces with no real muzzles to speak of, and all were shockingly furless except for a ridiculous tuft on the tops of their heads, yellow or brown or black, or in the case of the women and young girls a long skein or braid hanging down. Some of the men had fur on their bare arms too, but it was thin and sparse so you could see the flesh beneath. It was hard not to be fascinated. It was hard not to be repulsed. Miss Elizabeth could see why some referred to these beings as *scrapes* or *scrapings*, meaning the unavailing bits and pieces that God swept from his workbench after he was all done with making the Wise Peoples. That was blasphemy though. The Pugface were a separate creation, with their own gods and their own providence. There was a serious debate in religious circles as to whether or not they had souls, but Miss Elizabeth was not devout and hadn't felt the need to adopt a stance on that issue.

Back in Paxen the Sandpipers had had their own chapel, and attendance at Lord's-day prayers was mandatory. The readings were chosen by William as the head of the household and they leaned very heavily on the first three gospels – the ones that contained Holy John's strictures against earthly authorities and his exhortations to his followers to seek a reward beyond the mundane world. William would lead the service and read aloud, in a hectoring bellow, the seven screeds and the fifteen admonitions.

But sometimes, when the mood came on him, he would dip into the apocrypha. There were treasures to be found there, especially in Exiles, Book II. This was where John's more extreme and astonishing parables had been collected, carefully sequestered from his approved teachings. Among them was Elizabeth's favourite, the parable of the Pandominion. *In my father's house*, John told his disciples, *there are as many rooms as there are motes of dust in the summer air. Every one of those rooms is a world, and the entirety of the assembled worlds, the face of God's creation in its manifest glory, is called the Pandominion. God sends His angels between the worlds to carry His word and punish those who trespass against it. All will know them by their red robes and by the flaming swords they bear. All who see them will fear them.* And so on. Miss Elizabeth looked forward to these eccentric passages, preferring them to the unending dullness of the screeds and admonitions, but even as a child she could see how absurd they were.

Only fools and fantasists believed in angels who came down from heaven to smite the wicked. If there were any such, the wicked would have been bred out of the world in a generation.

The memory of these Sunday services, the dreary ones as much as the sensational ones, made homesickness rise up in Miss Elizabeth's breast suddenly enough that a small sob escaped her. But she was not cast down for very long. In spite of everything there was a beauty around her here on the frontier of civilisation that mitigated any weariness of body or spirit. The landscapes she passed through were majestic in the extreme. From plains that seemed to roll out to the horizon in all directions she ascended into a world of mountains and mesas – a horizontal immensity becoming all of a sudden a vertical one. Rising over everything were the gleaming white dream-towers, relics of a time before recorded history, every one humming its own complex and repetitious tune that carried for mile after mile.

Miss Elizabeth, along with almost everyone else she knew, had been through a phase as a child when she was deeply fascinated by the dream-towers, which were already old beyond the reach of memory when the Wise Peoples first made landfall in this country. She had pestered her father to take the family on picnics to the nearer ones. She had read books in which lurid speculation about the towers' origins was dressed up as earnest scholarship. She had fantasised about one day being the first person ever to enter one of the towers, though she knew they were impenetrable. Only one tower, the great Telos on the shore of Lake Azul near the western ocean, even had a door, which was 150 feet above the ground and responded even to the slightest touch with a discharge of percussive force greater than an exploding cannonball.

What were the dream-towers? What was the meaning of their endless song? How and why had the great Precursors, the lost race of the dawn age, built them? There were voices in the towers' humming if you listened hard enough. At times it seemed to Miss Elizabeth that she heard her own name in there, and the names of her parents. The dream-towers looked down on everything and knew everything, but they kept their own counsel.

Watching a herd of lumbering clutch-beetles go by under an orange and purple sunset, their pearlescent bodies swarming over and under each other until they became a single wave of motion, Miss Elizabeth thought that her father's bankruptcy might after all prove to have been providential. It had forced her out into the world, and the world was strong wine. She was drunk on it.

An event that happened on the road sobered her again. As the wagon passed through a narrow canyon, an imposing figure stepped out onto the track ahead of it and raised a rifle up above his head. He fired a single shot into the air, drawing gasps and cries of alarm from the wagon's passengers and its driver. The self in question was a bear man, as broad across the shoulders as Miss Elizabeth's outstretched arms. Miss Elizabeth had heard of bandits felling trees to make a roadblock. This man was practically a roadblock all by himself. But it wasn't just his bulk and sinew that had occasioned the passengers' terror. The gunshot hadn't been a bullet but an immense jagged crown of violet lightning forking up into the sky. The rifle was a relic, a Precursor weapon, and a great deal more powerful than any ordinary firearm.

The driver gave a hitch on the katy's reins and the wagon slowed and trundled to a halt. There was a great wave of flinching and ducking as the bear man levelled his rifle at them all. "What you carrying?" he growled.

"P-passengers. Mail. Nothing valuable." The driver had to try three times before he could get the words out. He was gopher stock and skinny with it, and he was torn between wanting to throw his hands up in the air and needing to keep control of the katy. The rifle shot's report had left the huge insect skittish and fretful, her head ducked down and her great bulbous body swaying to and fro on its seven pairs of legs.

"Toss the mailbags down," the bear man said.

The driver got to it. There were only a handful of bags and you could tell how light they were by how little dust they stirred up when they hit the ground. The bear man uttered a small grunt of dissatisfaction. It wasn't likely there was much more than paper in there.

"Your cash money now," he said. "And anything else you got that's worth selling on. Watches. Jewellery. Your coat." The last two words were addressed to a mule-deer self who was almost as tall as the bandit though not nearly so wide. His name, Miss Elizabeth was vaguely aware, was James State. He was a furniture salesman from Yattamaw heading south to make a bulk purchase of cedar wood from a factor in Bell Bank. His coat was jay-waxed cotton, sky blue and very fine.

"Now see here," the deer man said. "You can take our money, but leave us the clothes on our backs. It's not like my coat would even fit you."

The bandit's eyes went wide with affront and disbelief. "You're disputing with me?" he snarled. "Fuck it, just . . . get down here. Get down out of the wagon."

He gestured with his rifle. State, having no alternative and no weapon, climbed down and stood by the side of the road. The bandit ignored him as he went round the other passengers, collecting the dollars and cents they had had in their pockets and the trinkets they'd removed from their persons. Miss Elizabeth offered up the gold ring from her pinky finger, a Long-Eared John medallion in cheap silver that hung around her neck and about two dollars in change. She had taken the precaution, learned from a travel guide, of stowing most of her money in her shoe.

"You look a mite too fancy for these parts, little chickadee," the bandit said, offering her a leering grin. "You sure you didn't miss your way? Where you headed, anyway?"

"Ottomankie," Miss Elizabeth told him, ashamed of the tremor in her voice.

The bandit gave a huffing laugh. "The hell you say! You really did miss your way then. I'll see you next week or the week after, when you're headed back home."

Miss Elizabeth said nothing. She was conscious of the danger they were all in, and besides that laugh had unnerved her. There was something about it that was broken and out of balance. She wondered if it would be possible to get the rifle out of the man's hands before he fired it again, but being half his size she saw no way to manage the thing.

The bandit stared at her for a moment or two longer, grinning at his own joke, then turned to the mule-deer man now standing at his side. "The coat," he said again. State grimaced, but he took off the coat and held it out to the bandit. "Here," he said. "I don't know what you think you're going to—"

The bandit reversed the rifle in his hands and drove the butt of it into the deer man's face with horrifying force. The blow dropped State where he stood. A spray of dark-red blood arced through the air as he fell. Some of the blood landed on the coat, and this seemed to exasperate the bandit beyond any reasonable measure. "Fuck it!" he swore again. He kicked the fallen man in the ribs a great many times, putting all his weight into it. State grunted in pain the first few times, but thereafter he was silent. "You don't want to rile me up," the bandit said to his unconscious victim. "When I'm riled up I forget to stop."

He took a step back, took aim with the rifle and fired. There was no lightning this time. Instead there was a sheet of flame, not yellow but blindingly white. It enveloped the figure on the ground, which was instantly ablaze. The wave of heat was so intense that it stung Miss Elizabeth's flesh as it washed over her face. The katy hunkered down against the hot wind, burying its face in the dirt.

The deafening roar of the weapon's report reverberated up and down the canyon. When the echoes finally subsided there was only the thin chirping of the katy and appalled silence from the selves in the wagon. James State had been burned to ash in the space of a few seconds. The rock behind him had melted and run. The sand and dust of the road had fused into lumpy, bubbling glass. Thin drifts of white cloud hung motionless in the air above the ruin and a charnel stink reached Miss Elizabeth's nose, causing her to gag.

The driver just hunkered down and looked away, as if he'd seen all this before and didn't much relish seeing it again, but the other passengers were petrified. Most hid their eyes or clapped their hands to their mouths. One of them leaned over the wagon's side and vomited copiously.

The bandit bent and took up the coat from where it had fallen. He brushed the dust of the road from it, but there was nothing to be done about that bloodstain. He threw it over his shoulder anyway, nodding his head as if agreeing silently with some proposition that existed only in his own mind. "Watch how you go now," he growled. He touched the tip of his finger to his hat's brim in a mocking salute. Then he sauntered away in the same direction they were heading, presenting his broad back to them.

"You've got a gun," Miss Elizabeth said to the driver. "Shoot him."

"No thank you," the driver muttered. "What if I was to miss?"

"Give your weapon to me then!"

"I don't believe I will. You keep your seat, ma'am. These things happen from time to time and there ain't a thing you can do but bear them."

Miss Elizabeth stared down at the mound of smoking ash beside the road, through which the blackened remains of a few foreshortened ribs stood up like the poles of a collapsed tent. The wind was picking up, stirring the ash and lifting it into the air, which meant they were all of them breathing in the dead man for as long as they sat there. She pursed her lips and tried to breathe through her nose. "You're a coward," she told the driver, her voice cracking a little.

"Yes, ma'am," the driver agreed. "And I'm looking to be an old one some day."

He gave a few savage tugs on the reins and finally got the katy up on its feet again. They rolled on to Ottomankie with barely a word spoken between them. They were ashamed, Miss Elizabeth thought, to have witnessed such a thing and done nothing about it. It diminished them in their own and each other's eyes. She couldn't mourn the mule-deer man – she had barely managed to remember his name – but to have seen him cut down like that left a sore spot on her soul.

Ottomankie itself, when the wagon finally rolled in there, did not do much to restore Miss Elizabeth's spirits. The town appeared to be a single street whose buildings were made of clapboard and whose pavements were loose boards laid over mud. Many of the buildings were faced or roofed with the large, pale chafer scales called pearlings, overlaid on each other in an off-set pattern. This helped to ward off the heat but made them look like the giant insects' cast-off skins.

Well then, Miss Elizabeth said to herself, this is not a place where a body can rely on made things. On the contrary, it's a place that's only now making itself, and the people who thrive here will be the ones with the capacity to do the same.

She had intended to go directly to the town hall and announce her application for the post of schoolmistress, but with recent events weighing heavily on her mind she asked directions to the sheriff's office instead. Not that it was hard to find. Everything Ottomankie had to offer was right there in front of her.

A Pugface woman was sitting outside the sheriff's office in the full heat of the sun. She looked young, but it was hard to tell. There were no Pugfaces in the east – there was a fashionable theory to the effect that their near-total lack of fur was an adaptation to the west's often unforgiving sun, allowing them to sweat away excess heat more effectively – so Miss Elizabeth had no experience to draw on. The woman's legs were shackled with an ugly iron brace that locked around both ankles. She was staring into the middle distance, squinting slightly against the sun's glare, and she didn't look up as Miss Elizabeth approached.

"Well met," Miss Elizabeth said. It was the stereotypical Pugface greeting, at least according to a great many five-cent novels she'd read.

The Pugface woman continued to scan the horizon. Perhaps all Pugfaces were uncouth and uncivil, but to be fair Miss Elizabeth could see how this one might have little inclination to exchange pleasantries.

"Are you thirsty?" she asked. The woman was sitting out in the full heat of the day, after all. Like Miss Elizabeth's first sally this question didn't get an answer or even a glance. The woman's face creased in a very expressive frown, as though the words were offensive to her or had disturbed her train of thought. She blinked her eyes a few times, very slowly. Beads of sweat stood out like pearls on the naked flesh of her forehead.

"I can ask someone inside to bring you water," Miss Elizabeth offered, making one last effort. "Whatever crime you've committed, I'm sure nobody wants you to suffer unnecessarily."

And for some reason that made the woman smile. Now she did look at Miss Elizabeth; a frank, appraising glance from head to foot and back again. "Oh," she said equably. "I can bear my suffering. Can you bear yours?" She spoke in good States' Common with very little trace of an accent – a surprise to Miss Elizabeth, who had always assumed the Pugface to be barely literate.

"I've always tried to cultivate the virtue of patience," she said, which was true up to a point.

"Good choice." The woman offered up a cold smile, then looked away again.

Miss Elizabeth gave up on it. She opened the door and entered the building.

Ottomankie's sheriff was one Otis Tollgate, a middle-aged bison man who wore his horns shaved all the way back to the skull in the mistaken belief that this gave him a slimmer profile. Like most of the town's adult population he had been born somewhere else and become part of the westward expansion as a young man – a young man who saw the romance of making a name for himself in a virgin country. Becoming a small-town sheriff wasn't something he had foreseen. It had happened to him because he took on the job of Redhill County census officer at a time when Redhill County barely existed. Riding from one clapboard township to the next he became a familiar figure, and most new arrivals got a glimpse of him within their first month or so after setting down. When Ottomankie grew big enough to need a sheriff and to be able (just barely) to afford one, Tollgate threw his name into the ring because the job came with a ten-dollar raise, and he won because he was the only candidate whose face and name everyone recognised. He'd had plenty of time since to realise that he was a very poor fit for the post, being both lazy and a physical coward, and that ten dollars a year was a paltry exchange for the peaceful, quiet life he'd given up.

He tried to make the best of his situation, carrying out the less dangerous chores that came his way punctiliously and with a certain amount of sensitivity. The remainder of his duties he took like medicine, avoiding them when he could and stomaching them when he had to. Over the years a heavy melancholy had gradually come to settle on him and he wasn't strong enough to shrug it off again.

What Miss Elizabeth saw when she entered the office was a pollarded bison with a spreading gut and a look of world-weariness so deep it seemed to have carved itself into the muscles of his face. He was leaning too far back in a chair that was barely wide enough to hold him, in a room only slightly bigger than the chair, chewing a plug of tobacco whose cloying sweetness hung in the air. He asked Miss Elizabeth what the trouble was.

"There's a bandit in the mountains north of here," Miss Elizabeth told him, with what she felt was admirable calm. "A bear man, armed with a Precursor weapon."

This wasn't news to the sheriff, though it was one of the trials of his professional life and he didn't welcome the reminder. He nodded lugubriously. "Yes, ma'am, that there is."

"He murdered a man who was riding in the same wagon as me. The one that's just come in. Shot him in cold blood. And robbed us."

The chair creaked as the sheriff shifted his bulk, bringing the front two legs back into contact with the ground. He opened up a small notebook with a cheap cardboard cover, picked up a pen and dipped it in ink. "Did you get a name?" he asked.

Miss Elizabeth was momentarily confused. "From the bandit?"

"No, ma'am. That one's a feller name of Alden Calendar. Holy John knows where he got them blamed Precursor guns from, but he was a terror even without them. Killed seven souls, that I know of. Probably as many more that I didn't hear about yet, what with news tending to travel slow in these parts. No, I meant the dead man's name. If you happened to have it."

"State. James State."

"And his race?"

"Deer. Mule-deer, I think."

Tollgate scribbled with his pen.

Miss Elizabeth waited, but no further comments were forthcoming. "So what do you intend to do about it?" she asked at last.

"What do I intend?" the sheriff set down the pen and closed the book. He also shifted the wad of tobacco from his left cheek to his right before finally answering. "Not a great deal, to be honest with you. If old Alden was to come into town I guess I'd have to intend. But so long as he stays up in them hills someone else can do the intending. He ain't any part of my job."

"But he killed a man," Miss Elizabeth said again. "A man who was unarmed. Just so he could steal his coat."

"And that there is a wicked thing, no doubt about it," the sheriff agreed. "But you see, ma'am, not to bang the same drum too many times, he did it far enough away that it's none of my business. Professionally speaking, I mean."

Miss Elizabeth found herself both amazed and disgusted. Surely a sheriff's explicitly appointed task was to maintain order and to expunge crime. Yet this man was refusing to do anything of the kind.

"What about the Pugface woman outside?" she demanded. "What was her offence?"

"Roi Shakta?" The sheriff looked faintly surprised at this change of tack. "Why, she didn't do anything. But she's a Messolin and we don't allow them inside the town limits. They're known to be thieves."

"So you refuse to track down and apprehend a murderer, but

you're happy to arrest an inoffensive woman on no evidence of criminality at all."

"Oh, Roi Shakta ain't arrested. She's just what we call aitch-are-see, which is to say held, recorded and conveyed. Means I take her to the town limits and send her on her way with a warning and a mark on her record. The Pugface Bureau says we got to keep writ-down evidence for any dealings we have with the nations, good or bad."

"Still, she falls within your remit while this outlaw doesn't. Is that because she doesn't have a Precursor rifle in her hands?"

The sheriff threw out his hands in a shrug. He seemed genuinely pained at that harsh summation. "Ma'am, I got to keep order here, and let me tell you that's a job that's got me busy from sunup to sundown and usually well beyond. Now you can paint my liver bright yellow if you like, but the township isn't overly generous when it comes to paying me and my one and only deputy for the work we do here. I mean, it's a wage and a man's glad to have it, but it's more a sufficiency than it is a fortune. Do you see what I mean? Maybe for a fortune I'd step outside my— What did you call it again?"

"Your remit."

"—my remit, and go chase old Neck-Breaker Alden all across the Jerichos till I brought him down or more likely until he lit me on fire and pissed on the ashes. But I won't do it on my current stipend. No, ma'am. And I'm sorry if that means I forfeit your good opinion, but your good opinion ain't gonna pay for my funeral, now is it?"

Miss Elizabeth understood which way the wind was blowing and came away, without telling the sheriff what she thought of his philosophy or his job description. *This isn't your home*, she told herself. *Not yet. You can be loud later, if you've a mind to be, but you'd be best off staying quiet until you figure out what the rules are around here.*

She made her way to the interim town hall, a set of three linked rooms above the saloon that had been requisitioned by the mayor and his staff. She told a bored clerk that she was here about the teaching position, handed in a letter of application and was sent through to a waiting room that was already full.

There were gophers, dogs, groundhogs, deer, possums, squirrels, cougars, bison and a whole slew of folk whose provenance was so mixed that Miss Elizabeth couldn't hazard a guess. Everyone in that room had more or less pressing business with the civic administration, which they talked about in low murmurs or loud complaints. The civic administration didn't seem in quite so much of a hurry to talk to them though. Through the long hot day they all just sat. Occasionally someone would be called into the inner office, and those who went through must have exited by some other means because they didn't come back. Miss Elizabeth, slowly dehydrating in the horrible heat, began to wonder about that exit door and where it might lead. This was the very edge of civilisation, after all, and the soil way out here was much more dust than anything else. Perhaps if you had something to say that the civil administration didn't like they just used you for compost. Still she hung on with fatalistic patience. She hadn't yet formulated a project for what she would do if this current plan failed her. Until she did, she had nothing better to do than sit and wait.

The morning wore on into afternoon. The sweltering heat intensified, peaked and began to decline. At last, just shy of five o'clock, the clerk called out her name. Miss Elizabeth rose, feeling more than a little light-headed, and went through the inner door into the august presence.

Ottomankie's mayor, the Honourable Eustace Defiance Wildwater, was a wolf. Down here in the Echelon heartlands that didn't come as any kind of a surprise. He was grey furred, sleek and – like most wolves – handsome in a way that was just a little louche and dangerous. His secretary was a prairie dog in a paisley-patterned dress. Prim and respectable to a fault, she looked as if she had wandered into the mayor's office by mistake, found a spare desk going begging and settled down in a corner hoping not to be noticed.

"Miss Elizabeth Indigo Sandpiper," the secretary said, ticking off an item about three-quarters of the way down a very long list. "Application for the position of schoolmistress."

"Ah yes," the mayor said loftily. "I believe I recall." He flashed Miss Elizabeth a smile that was three parts avuncular to two parts blow-your-house-down. He invited her to sit, keeping his eyes on her the whole time while she adjusted her skirts and lowered herself onto the only piece of furniture available. It was a bar stool, of the kind that can be rotated to raise and lower the seat. The stool had uneven legs and toggled between two equally precarious positions as Miss Elizabeth shifted her weight. Young as she was, she knew a power play when she saw one. Clearly this Wildwater liked to get the upper hand quickly and was not above using the furniture in order to attain it.

"Well now," the mayor said, tapping Miss Elizabeth's letter which was lying on the desk in front of him. "I admit I got my hopes up when I read this little screed of yours. You write yourself a damn fine epistle, no doubt about it. But now I get a look at you I'm somewhat fearful you've had a wasted journey. We need a woman with a little heft to her, not such a delicate creature as yourself. I don't mean any disrespect when I say you'd probably be better off among your own kind."

Miss Elizabeth considered this contemptuous dismissal in silence for a moment or two. She had come a long way, and she had had a very trying day with more than the average number of murders in it. She had expected at the very least a fair hearing, but given her recent experience in the sheriff's office perhaps that had been a touch naive. A place that's making itself, she thought again. Full of people that are trying to do the same. This chance wouldn't come again, and it was a very long way back to Paxen where nothing awaited her but a share in her family's ruin.

"Pardon me," she said with brittle politeness. "My own kind? Would you mind elaborating on that just a little, Mr Mayor?"

The mayor spread his arms in an expansive shrug. "Well, anyone can tell, Miss Sandpiper, that you are what might be called a hothouse flower. Forgive me for my frankness. We homespun southerners might admire the lustre of such a bloom, but we'd hesitate to undertake the upkeep of it. Our manners wouldn't be what you're used to, I'm afraid."

Miss Elizabeth was thankful now that she had paid attention to the conversations going on around her in the stagecoach, the train and the katy-wagon. They gave her somewhat in the way of ammunition. "I don't give a rat's tail-piece about your threadbare manners, Mister Mayor," she said evenly. "Flowers and lustre be fucked. That is, if you'll pardon my frankness. Do you want a schoolhouse or not? Because if not then I'd rather not sit here smelling your secretary's perfumed farts while the best of the day goes by."

There now, she thought. That ought to have put a little salt in the stew. *Schoolhouse* in particular was what's known on a poker table as a double-raise. There had been nothing in the advertisement Miss Elizabeth had seen to indicate that Ottomankie had aspirations to set up any such permanent establishment, and now that she'd seen the town hall it seemed highly improbable. But you don't double-raise on a two and a seven. She was offering the mayor a revised estimate of her potential worth.

And the mayor seemed at the very least to be gratifyingly surprised. The secretary blushed as red as a cranberry with heart disease and shot Miss Elizabeth a ferocious glare. She had in fact broken wind, not quite silently, a moment or two earlier. It was purely serendipitous, but Miss Elizabeth had no compunction in weaving it into her performance. She had no allies here, no advocates. She had chosen what felt like a solid strategy to win the attention of the room. The question now was what she could do with it.

"Let's pull back on the reins just a little, shall we?" the mayor said, his stump-circuit smile disintegrating into an expression that was slightly pained. "I don't know that a schoolhouse, as in a physical structure, vis-à-vis a building constructed out of actual logs or boards or shingles, is high on our list of priorities at the moment." He seemed to feel the need to offset that admission because he hurried right along. "In a few years, no doubt, we'll be in a different situation. Ottomankie is growing at a fine old rate, growing like a weed in fact, and we've got a good smattering of families with young 'uns on the ground or on the way or both. A teacher is what we had in mind at this particular juncture, to reassure such people that the municipality has their best interests at heart. Such things make a difference to what you might call the communal spirit."

"I understand," Miss Elizabeth said.

"In the meantime it's my fixed intention to—"

"And I decline."

The mayor stumbled over his next word, paused, and licked his lips with a tongue that would have been long enough to lick his ears. "Beg pardon, ma'am?"

"Miss. Not ma'am. *Miss* Elizabeth Indigo Sandpiper. It's right there on the paper in front of you. And you heard me clear as a bell. I refuse to take the appointment unless you give me your personal guarantee that a schoolhouse will be built within two years from the date of my hiring. It's one thing to improvise when the proper facilities are not in place. It's quite another to accept such inadequate workarounds as a permanent state of affairs."

The mayor only stared. He had forgotten to reel his tongue back in so a few inches of it were still lolling out of one corner of his mouth. Miss Elizabeth's sudden salvo seemed to have caught him at a disadvantage and he was temporarily unable to return fire. "That assurance given, though," she went on, jumping headlong into the gap, "I'll be willing to listen to your terms. But first you'll probably be desirous of hearing what my qualifications are. As you'll see from the certificates attached to my letter I'm a graduate of the Systemis Academy in Haut Paxen, where I completed my studies *summa cum laude*. Those studies included History, Literature, Modern Languages, Physical Science, Chemistry, Theology and Good Housekeeping, with Drama as an extra-curricular addition. Sadly, I did not excel at music, being tone deaf, so I omitted that from my résumé. As a Systemis alumna I am of course in the very highest demand, and my starting salary should reflect that fact."

"No actual experience," the secretary observed in an acid undertone.

"What's that, sweetness?" Miss Elizabeth enquired politely. "It's hard to hear you over the unholy racket that's coming from your bloomers."

"The lack of experience is a concerning factor," the mayor allowed, while the secretary gave Miss Elizabeth another paint-stripping scowl and clutched her pencil so hard it almost broke.

"On first consideration, yes," Miss Elizabeth said. "But it actually works in your favour. It's only at this early point in my career that you could possibly afford me."

This struck the mayor as a very convincing argument. And he was seriously impressed, besides, by this woman's demonstrable ability to go from high sentiments to low blows in the space of a sentence. Any schoolmarm who had a hope of surviving in Ottomankie would need to be pretty damn nimble, and though this wisp of a girl didn't look like much she did talk an excellent fight. She was also the only applicant so far, apart from a local celebrity named Two-Bits Harriet. Harriet's experience was more extensive than Miss Elizabeth's, but only when it came to the saloon and the lock-up in the jailhouse.

"I can start you on two dollars a week," the mayor said.

"Two dollars and fifty cents," Miss Elizabeth countered. "Rising to three dollars on the completion of my first year."

"That's a great deal of money, Miss Sandpiper."

"That's a great deal period, Mister Mayor. Take it or leave it."

"I don't like ultimatums."

"I don't like starving, or living on charity. As one of this township's public servants I will represent its values and reflect its probity in every aspect of my appearance. I can hardly do that if I'm dressed in rags and living on the scraps from other people's tables. Oh, and when the schoolhouse is built I will live above it. An apartment – of modest size, of course – will need to be included in the plans. Until then I will require a small stipend towards my rent."

"That can come out of the two fifty," the mayor declared forcefully, and since she had carried the larger point Miss Elizabeth acquiesced. Wildwater had the secretary draw up a contract right there and then, and the pain it caused her to do it was a poignant thing to see. Miss Elizabeth signed her name and went off in search of room and board. It was agreed that she would turn up for work on the second Monday following. The municipality would provide a schoolroom, not above the saloon but in back of the church, and as many students as could be rounded up. The students would be charged five cents per week or part thereof, which Miss Elizabeth would be expected to collect.

As she walked back down the stairs and out into the late afternoon sunlight, Miss Elizabeth felt very satisfied with how the encounter had gone. It seemed to exemplify the lesson she had taken to heart on first sight of this place, that she could do very well here so long as she was prepared to throw the refined Paxen version of herself into the furnace and smelt herself into a form that was a little closer to the present purpose.

She thought briefly about writing to her brothers and sisters in order to share this insight with them and suggest that some or all of them join her here. Perhaps they could reconstitute the Sandpiper family out in this wasteland that was as glorious and strange as it was rough-hewn and filthy.

Before she could interrogate that impulse any further she came upon a curious and disturbing sight. Three selves – a short, stocky dog who was mostly terrier, a muskrat and a mix with some bear in him – were coming up the street towards her, dragging a fourth along with them. This fourth self was a sight to see. He was a gopher, and going by the woollen suit and brown leather Oxford shoes he was wearing he was some kind of clerk. But that impression was very much at odds with the way the man was behaving. He was snarling and growling like an animal, teeth bared. His eyes, opened so wide they seemed to be in danger of falling out of his head, darted back and forth without seeming to take anything in.

Two of his escorts, the dog and the bear-mix, were holding him in place with long poles that connected to chains around his neck and wrists. The muskrat went in front, ringing a bell to warn any gawkers they met to stay out of their path.

"What's this?" Miss Elizabeth asked a bobcat woman who was lounging at the saloon door in half-skirts and a blouse with a startling décolleté. "Who is that man?"

"Well, he ain't anybody," the woman said. "What he might have been before I couldn't say, but he's sure as hell no one now."

"He's from Mickletide," a second similarly dressed woman said. She was smoking a long-stemmed pipe, which she transferred from one corner of her mouth to the other as she spoke. "A gang of mindless come through there three days ago. This here feller must've got bit and taken the sickness."

The mindless plague was a thing Miss Elizabeth had only ever read about in the daily news-sheets up to that point, and she had taken it for one more tall tale from the frontier, like the story of the Devil House that moved around the western prairies looking for people to eat, or the many tales about cursed tools or weapons that talked like selves and offered you wondrous rewards if only you would pick them up. Some pundits had suggested that mindlessness was only a more extreme manifestation of the same terrors that had caused an epidemic of nightmares among the elderly back in Paxen, or else of ordinary amnesia. The starkness of this undeniable reality took Miss Elizabeth by surprise and filled her with sick dismay.

"What will they do to him?" she asked, in a much more subdued tone.

At this point the strange procession had come level with them. The bear man gave them a cordial nod. "We're gonna hang him, ma'am," he said with satisfaction, beaming all around.

"Without a trial?"

"Trial would be a waste of time. It's not like he'd have anything to say for himself. Mindless can't talk, just like they can't think. They ain't people no more. If he was to slip these leashes he'd go for your throat before you could so much as spit. Taking him out of the world is a blessing to the rest of us and a mercy on him."

The woman with the pipe shook her head. "That's not true," she said. "About him going for your throat. The mindless aren't that dangerous, as a rule. Whatever it is that infects them, it puts them in a panic. They'll bite you or claw at you if you put yourself in their way, but mostly they just run. Run for miles and miles, until they fall dead from exhaustion. It's a terrible thing to see."

"Well, Miss Lucy," the dog man said, "all I can say is they made an unholy mess out of Mickletide. There's nothing left of that place but sticks."

"The hanging's gonna go ahead right now if you want to come along, ladies," the bear man said. "We got three of these bastards, pardoning your sensibilities, and we're doing them all at once. Preacher's gonna give a sermon first, but he's promised it won't be a long one."

"You hear that?" the dog man said to their prisoner. He gave a tug on the pole he held, jerking the gopher's wrists around and obliging him to turn. "We're gonna stretch your neck for you, damned if we don't."

"Damned if we don't!" the muskrat repeated with enthusiasm, grinning all around. The mindless gopher clashed his teeth together. His feet were still moving, scraping and sliding in the mud as the chains prevented him from going forward. Blood ran down his chin from where he had bitten his tongue, but he gave no sign of noticing this or of understanding what was said.

"I got work to do," the woman with the pipe muttered, and she went back into the saloon, but her companion added herself to the group. Others were doing the same thing. Those that didn't see fit to join the procession still called out taunts and obscene insults at the raving gopher as he passed by them. Someone threw a stone, which hit him in the chest. The gopher set up a deafening squall of grunts and barks in response, straining against his chains and casting his exophthalmic gaze around in search of his tormentor.

The dog and the bear dragged him unceremoniously along, impatient of the delay.

Miss Elizabeth watched them out of sight. What she had seen filled her with unease and queasy disgust, but she found it hard to determine how much of that was for the brutality of the spectacle and how much for the creature at the centre of it – a self who had ceased to be a self and had devolved somehow into an unreasoning beast. Like understock, the creatures that resembled the Wise Peoples so closely but had no higher awareness.

She couldn't erase from her mind the image of those empty eyes.

Ottomankie became Miss Elizabeth's home for the next nine years. But she didn't stay Miss Elizabeth for very long. She was Miss Bessie by the end of the first month. That was what her pupils had elected to call her, and the appellation spread by osmosis through the rest of the community.

The manners and protocols of the southern concession – homespun, in mayor Wildwater's words – grew on her very quickly. So much of the discourse back east, whether public or private, consisted in saying something a million miles away from what you really intended and letting the listener make the journey to your true meaning in their own good time. It wasn't that there were no rules here in the south. It was just that the rules allowed you to tell someone they were a two-faced, shit-brained child of a bastard whore if you sincerely believed that to be the case.

And there were certainly a fair few people in town to whom that description applied. The mayor was one, to be sure, and so was his waspish secretary Mrs Emilia Winsome (the paisley-patterned prairie dog Miss Bessie had met on her first day in Ottomankie). The preacher Dominic Fold, with his humourless sermons harping endlessly on the theme of *thou shalt fucking not*, was such another. Miss Bessie initially misidentified the sheriff as one, but she realised after a little while that Tollgate was not a bad man, only a bad sheriff. Cowardly he was, and idle, but he had the virtues of his vices and meant no harm to anyone. His incongruous passion was the cultivation of fruit trees. He had turned a small plot on the town's outskirts into an orchard and had persuaded six pear trees to grow there despite the thin and depleted soil. He made periodic gifts of their fruit to the school as a gesture of goodwill, aware that he had got off on the wrong foot with Miss Elizabeth – now Miss Bessie – by not pursuing Alden Calendar for the crime of murder. Under the circumstances she found herself unable to keep a sharp edge on her resentment.

And as against the sons-of-bastards there were many people in Ottomankie for whom Miss Bessie had nothing but respect and whose friendship she cultivated. Clarissa Nugget who played the organ in church, the owner of the livery stable Mr Reed, the Timely brothers who were Ottomankie's carpenters and builders, these struck her as good and admirable people all striving hard to bring the western wilderness under the aegis of civilisation. She aspired to do the same.

And it had to be said that she took to teaching like a katy to a corn field. She had the book learning of course, that had never been in doubt. But what she mostly had was will, and that was mostly what was needed. Ottomankie's children – the sons and daughters of hard-scrabble farmers and frontier traders – were harder to herd than scorpillons with their stings still in. There was no vindictiveness in them (in most of them, anyway) but they were loud and boisterous and they strained against any kind of discipline. Miss Bessie roped them to it anyway, sometimes just with a look, other times with words whether hard or gentle, and just occasionally – if it was one of the bigger boys thinking his broad shoulders and big fists ought to count for something – with the heel of her hand. She used whatever worked, and she was surprised to find just how much fulfilment she derived from it.

As part of whatever worked, she first adulterated her refined east coast patterns of speech and then shed them altogether. She found it more convenient and more productive to talk to the children in language they understood. By the end of the first year she couldn't have talked high society Paxen if she'd tried.

There was a small but useful truth to be gleaned from all this, and Miss Bessie – formerly Elizabeth Indigo Sandpiper, soon to be Dog-Bitch Bess – took it to heart: it doesn't matter very much what work you do so long as you do it of your own choosing and do it well. She was to apply that lesson later to enterprises very far removed from teaching.

She had taken lodgings in a boarding house run by the widow Emma Charity. She found Mrs Charity's mostly taciturn company very much to her taste, having little patience for the kind of talk that does nothing besides break a silence. The widow kept a spartan table, but Miss Bessie sometimes enlivened it with pears from the sheriff's orchard or hens' eggs offered by a parent in lieu of school fees.

On her off-day, which was Sunday, Miss Bessie went to church in the morning as was expected of her, in a blue chiffon dress that would have excited contempt in Paxen because it was three seasons out of date. In Ottomankie its half sleeves and embroidered hem were startling and had kicked off a trend. Miss Bessie invariably sat at the very back of the congregation so she could make a quick getaway at the end of the service. Returning to her room at the widow Charity's she carefully laid out the chiffon on her lumpy ticking mattress, folded it between sheets of tissue paper and changed into what in Ottomankie were simply called work cottons. She packed herself a lunch of hardtack, sliced pear and sometimes an end of marrowbone retrieved from a soup and headed off into the hills.

Ottomankie nestled along the lower slopes of the Jericho range, which rose up to the north and west of the town in tier on tier. To the north, the road ran through a number of passes mostly marking the course of the Sweetling, and on into the southernmost reaches of Olbin, a Parity state. It was in one of those passes that Miss Bessie had encountered the bandit known as Alden Calendar, before she had ever set foot in Ottomankie. She still had nightmares about that day, her first experience of arrogantly exercised power and violent death. She felt no desire to return to the place where it had happened. Instead she headed west from the town into an area with no roads, no farms, no houses – no sign that any civilised self had ever set foot there, though of course there were a number of Pugface settlements. The Pugfaces seemed to live in every place that common sense said was uninhabitable.

The local Pugface clans were Ajuparo, Messolin and Lasque. They were tolerated this far east because none of those clans had ever risen up against the Union. There had been a fourth clan, the Geniull, but a dispute with cattle ranchers had reduced their numbers greatly, and these days they were thinner on the ground than snow in July. There were many stalwart citizens in Ottomankie who would happily have given the surviving clans the same treatment, whether because of supposed thefts, assaults on public decency or because most of them – the Ajuparos in particular – adhered to the cult of the twenty-three, which God-fearing Johannites saw as an abomination. Miss Bessie didn't give a tinker's cuss about abominations but she tended to give the Pugfaces' bizarre earth-and-cured-hide dwelling places a wide berth out of an abundance of caution. A woman alone out on the prairie couldn't be too careful. In any case it was the hills that drew her and the Pugfaces mostly lived on the open plains.

Here and there, as her way led ever upwards, were soaring mesas on whose flat tops, Miss Bessie imagined, some blacksmith god might have beaten out the plains and prairies of the world. Here and there also were dream-towers built by the Precursors long before. They were of varying heights, the tallest of them rising many hundreds of feet above the nearer peaks. There was one in particular, one of the very tallest, that was Miss Bessie's goal on many of these Sunday hiking trips. It took a reliable two-and-a-half hours to reach and the pinnacle on which it stood offered breathtaking views of the valleys on either side. The tower was built from some substance with a high gloss to it like white ceramic, as all dream-towers were. Miss Bessie was chary of touching it but she would eat her lunch in its shadow, so far above Ottomankie that when she looked down she could blot out the town below by holding up the top joint of her thumb at arm's length.

From this close up the hum of the tower was much louder, and the illusion of words – whether spoken or sung – underneath the skein of rising and falling notes was stronger than ever. The sound affected Miss Bessie strangely, sometimes lulling her and at others filling her with an inexplicable sense of urgency, as if there were some summons there meant for her alone. Sometimes she even sang along, inventing nonsense words that seemed to fit the hum's varying cadence.

Once when she was sitting in this, her favourite spot, and singing or humming in counterpoint to the tower's endless music, she felt a change occurring around her like a coldness in the air, so abrupt it was startling. The fur on the back of her neck stood up on end and a violent shudder went through her. Her thoughts felt all at once jumbled and jangling in her head and her heart beat faster as though with sudden fright.

This was nothing, she told herself sternly. A cloud had come that very moment across the face of the sun. Moreover the winds in the mountains were fickle, quick to rise and just as quick to wander. All that had happened was that they had changed their quarter and taken her unawares. She breathed deeply and slowly until her wayward heart was back under her control.

But in the silence that followed she heard from the far side of the tower a series of sounds: a rattling and a scraping, the scuffle of movement, and a series of melodic chirps like the calls that katies make in the evening as they're settling to sleep. A moment later she heard actual words spoken, though she couldn't make out what they were.

In such a remote place Miss Bessie had good reason to be apprehensive, but the voice seemed to be that of a child. And it was just the one voice, murmuring to itself. In the gaps where someone might have answered no answers came. Her curiosity overmastered her. She rose up very quietly and walked around the side of the tower, one carefully placed step at a time.

When she had gone a little more than a quarter of the way she saw a small figure kneeling on the wind-scoured rock beside the tower's base. It was a child, as she had thought – a Pugface girl who looked to be no more than six or seven years old. She was brown-skinned, and the strange, tufted mass of hair on top of her otherwise furless head was black and tightly curled. She wore a white garment that it would have been overly generous to call a dress. It was more of a blanket into which holes had been cut for her head and arms, cinched at the waist with a thin belt of red leather. Her feet were bare.

The girl had not seen Miss Bessie approach, being deeply immersed in some unfathomable act. From a green and gold carpet bag beside her she had drawn out a rope fashioned – as far as Miss Bessie could make out – from braided gold and silver wires. This rope was twined around the girl's left forearm, its open end pinched between the base of thumb and forefinger, and her left arm moved in circles across the tower's smooth white surface, not quite touching it.

"Seventeen, sixty-three, one-one-nine. No abnormal response," the girl said. Like the Pugface woman Miss Bessie had encountered outside the sheriff's office she spoke in States' Common, her enunciation strange but perfectly clear.

Miss Bessie stayed stock-still where she was. Her gaze had gone to the bag, into which the other end of the girl's silver rope still trailed or dangled. It was from the bag that the strange chirping sounds were coming, and they were accompanied by pulsing waves of coloured light. In the shadow of a stray mass of cumulus overhead the lights seemed vivid enough to be solid things, like a cluster of hard-faceted gems.

The dream-tower's song rose in pitch and volume, then fell away again just as abruptly.

"Twenty-two," the girl recited, "seventy-four, one-eight-five. Transitory response."

Miss Bessie stifled a gasp. Was it just coincidence, or had the girl's action been connected in some inexplicable way with the modulations in the dream-tower's song? That seemed absurd. The towers weren't things you interacted with, they were just *there*. You stared at them either in awe or in dull incomprehension, depending on how much poetry there was in your soul, and then you went on your way.

Just then the tower's song changed again. For a moment or two its polyphonic hum had become a single sustained note. The sound was neither loud nor piercing, but a lance of pain went through Miss Bessie's head just the same, so that it was hard for her not to cry out aloud. A few seconds later the note faded and the pain went with it. The normal humming of the dream-tower resumed.

From the girl, now, came a single sullen huff of breath. "Got it!" she exclaimed. "Twenty-six, eighty-one, two-hundred-twelve." She clenched her free hand into a fist and then opened it again three times over in time with the chanted numbers. "That was big. One of the biggest yet. And it held for a slow count of—"

The pause was sudden and pregnant, and Miss Bessie wasn't slow to see the reason for it. The cloud had rolled by. In the restored sunlight Miss Bessie's shadow was laid out plain to see on the rock just beside the girl's feet. The girl stood up and turned in a single moment. She let go of the silver rope, which was drawn back all the way into the bag with a sudden snap. From her belt, where it had hung all this while occulted by her body, the girl drew a hand-axe, a wedge of grey slate tied to a slender wooden shaft.

Miss Bessie threw up her empty hands to show she meant no harm. She wasn't especially afraid, having seen children bearing weapons often. It wasn't unusual for the boys in her class to have a knife tucked in their belt, and the girls when they fought the boys during recess would sometimes fix the blunted iron caltrops used in the game of jacks between their knuckles so their punches would leave more of a mark. Miss Bessie did her best to discourage these skirmishes, but she had found no penalty that would eradicate them. They seemed to follow their own seasons.

"I didn't mean to disturb you," she told the girl calmly. "Please don't be frightened."

The girl said nothing, but seemed to consider her unexpected visitor in silence. After a moment she pointed with the hand-axe, indicating that Miss Bessie should keep her distance or perhaps that she should go back the way she'd come.

"Could I ask what you're doing?" Miss Bessie asked. "And what that strange instrument was? It reminded me a little of a doctor's stethoscope. Where on Earth did you come by it?"

This question was met only by further silence. The girl kneeled again, this time on one knee, closed the bag – it shut with a solid click – and snatched it up. She did all this one-handed, with the axe still raised *en garde* in her hand. Then she backed away around the tower's curved side without once taking her eyes off Miss Bessie. When Miss Bessie followed – cautiously, because she didn't want that axe to be swung or thrown at her – the girl was already scrambling down the crags on the far side of the escarpment, going much more quickly than Miss Bessie would have dared to. She was not looking back.

Miss Bessie stood irresolute. The mystery of what the girl had been doing piqued her. And what of that odd, one-sided conversation? Most likely the girl's interlocutor was some Pugface hero or demi-god, and the silver rope a religious adornment, but it irked her not to know. She had an impulse to follow, but the girl had not spoken a word to her and there was no reason to believe she would be more forthcoming – or less hostile – if pressed.

Behind Miss Bessie a new sound joined the dream-tower's hum. It was a harsh whine like the squeaking of a rusty hinge but a great deal louder. When she turned to see what had made it she all but staggered back, which would have been a bad idea this close to the edge of the crag. The dream-tower was rotating. There would have been no way to tell this if it hadn't been for the patches of moss that clung to its surface down close to the ground. They were turning slowly now, seeming to swim across the tower's gleaming white face.

Miss Bessie hastily gathered up the remains of her frugal lunch and went straight down the mountain on her own side – the side opposite to the one the girl had taken. Like the girl she did not stop to look over her shoulder. The tower was there. She knew it was there, and she was suddenly afraid it was equally aware of her presence. Had the girl damaged the tower? Angered it? Opened it like some gigantic puzzle box? Whatever the explanation, Miss Bessie very definitely did not want to stay and see what happened next.

She didn't stop until she was on level ground again, the dream-tower hidden behind the mountain's shoulder. And after that she made sure her Sunday walks took her elsewhere.

In other respects things moved forward very gratifyingly. Miss Bessie's class grew from a dozen to forty and then fissioned into two classes, the Beginners' Company and the Veterans' Regiment. She still didn't get her schoolhouse, Mayor Wildwater having prioritised the building of a town hall to house his own august personage. Instead he had Jake and Jethro Timely, the town's carpenters, throw up a fake wall of lath and plaster in order to turn the one room into two. He did however put out an advertisement for a second schoolmistress, acquiescing to the argument that Miss Bessie couldn't be on both sides of the wall at the same time.

In answer to this new notice Miss Martha Good arrived.

Miss Martha was an otter from Jilhaysen and a seasoned educator whose curriculum vitae put Miss Bessie's to shame. She had taught in two neighbouring townships and carried glowing reports from both. Miss Bessie was almost embarrassed to be counted the senior teacher, for besides this greater breadth of experience Miss Martha was four years older than her. But Miss Martha insisted with calm dignity that a subordinate role suited her temperament well. She never had been one to put herself forward, she said. Besides which Miss Bessie had something she called tenure, which seemed to mean that the first one to the trough got to drink the deepest.

Martha Good was a preacher's daughter, but beyond that bare statement she had nothing at all to say about her father. Her mother, she said, exemplified the old saw that behind every great man there was a strong woman. Privately she added an extra clause to that proverb: sometimes it's only thanks to the woman's efforts that the man seems great in the first place.

Her calm ran deeper than Bessie's, but it was not the whole of her. The truth was that Miss Martha had left Jilhaysen after a bitter falling-out with her parents. Her father, Walter Damask Good, was a weak and vain man plagued by self-doubts. He required a lot of shoring up from day to day to enable him to carry out his ministerial duties, and for this service he looked to his wife Elaine. He also blamed her for his own errors, reproached her for his own backsliding, forgave her for his own transgressions. It was an odd relationship, and a pretty poisonous one for all concerned. Being forced to observe it throughout her childhood had soured Martha on her father, on men in general and on the Johannist religion. Even before she reached her teens she had begun to take an interest in the spiritual beliefs and myth cycles of the Pugface peoples, an open defiance that drove Walter Good to extremes of rage and finally led to his putting his errant daughter out on the street.

Martha had managed to thrive without her father's blessing, working as housekeeper, nursemaid, governess and farmhand before finally finding her vocation as a teacher. She had never seen either of her parents again, though she had exchanged letters with her mother until the latter's death from a consumption at the age of forty-nine. Martha did not attend the funeral because it was in her father's church and under his jurisdiction. She had no wish to hear his thoughts on the subject.

Even now, so many years later, she tended to see a shade of her father in the face of every man she met. It made her reserved in mixed company, a reserve that was taken for shyness when in fact it was something harder and darker.

But Miss Martha took none of these tangled thoughts and

feelings into the classroom with her. She shone there, purely and simply, making hard things seem easy and drawing everyone into the shared adventure of figuring out what was what.

She and Miss Bessie were a good fit for each other. At the end of each day's work they would stay behind in the church hall after the pupils had been released back into the wild and plan the lessons for the following day. These sessions were cordial in the extreme. The two women had nothing but affection and respect for one another. Miss Bessie was greatly struck by Miss Martha's serenity and gentleness. Miss Martha was equally impressed by Miss Bessie's strength and iron-hard self-belief. Within the schooling context they complemented each other wonderfully, effortlessly becoming a team.

They carried that same frictionless collaboration out into their dealings with the municipality. Eager to expand their offering to Ottomankie's children they pressed the mayor as hard as they could to put his money where his snaggle-toothed mouth was. In the first six months after Miss Martha's arrival they raised three petitions for a new schoolhouse, collecting more signatures each time. It got so Wildwater turned and walked the other way when he saw them coming, much to their amusement.

In one respect, though, Miss Bessie was obliged to temper her colleague's enthusiasm. Miss Martha was keen to admit Pugface children into the school, and there was no way the good people of Ottomankie were going to sit still for that. "As far as anyone here is concerned," Miss Bessie told her as tactfully as she could, "they're just plain uncivilised. A little better than understock, but not much."

"That's absurd, though!" Miss Martha protested. "They have their own culture, Bess, every bit as rich and varied as ours. And it's an ancient culture. You know they were here when the first settlers came here from the Old Countries. They may even have been here while the Precursors were still alive. Isn't that an astonishing thought?"

Miss Bessie said nothing to this but her face must have told its own story because Miss Martha repeated her assertions even more emphatically. She went on to outline in detail some of the Pugface myth cycles – the journey of the twenty-three, the ghost war, the Engine Everlasting – until, by and by, Miss Bessie (though not particularly convinced) was obliged to surrender the point for the sake of keeping the peace. But she put her foot down on the matter of taking Pugface children into the school, both because she knew it was a lost cause and because she found the hairless indigenes – whenever she came close to them, which was seldom – unlovely and unsettling. If they had their own culture she was happy to let them keep it.

She took a similarly hard line when Miss Martha suggested they waive the five-cent fee in the case of children whose families couldn't raise it. "Do that once," she said, "and they'll all start thinking learning is free."

"Perhaps it should be," Miss Martha countered. "Perhaps all things whose value is too high to be counted should be offered at no charge."

"That's a touching sentiment, Martha. But that there toll pays for four things that don't come freely, which is slates and chalk and you and me. The mayor won't make up the shortfall if we come running to him with our pockets empty. And then the school will close and there won't be anyone getting educated. Plus we'll be begging in the street or kicking our heels up for nickels at the saloon."

Miss Martha offered no further arguments and the matter was dropped. But on more than one occasion Miss Bessie, out of the corner of her eye, saw her colleague transfer coins from her own purse into the contributions bucket, presumably when one of the children had come up short and the alternative was to send them away.

It was only in these few small matters that there was ever any hint of friction between the two of them. Their joint overhauling of the school curriculum was pure pleasure. Miss Martha played the pianoforte, so music lessons became a real possibility for the first time. These were offered as a voluntary session on Saturday mornings, using an instrument rented by the month from the neighbouring township of Trestle, and they were wildly popular from the outset. Miss Bessie, unwilling to let her friend's working week be longer or more arduous than her own, started a debating society in the same time slot. Many of her students were woefully poor at spelling and grammar: now she taught them how to marshal an argument in spoken words, which she felt to be at least as important a skill as writing. All of this, the two women knew, was a drop in the ocean compared to what they could do if they got their schoolhouse and took on a full-time assistant, but the empire-building was very pleasant in prospect and the winds seemed fair.

"So is this better or worse than the other places where you've worked?" Miss Bessie asked Miss Martha during one of their after-hours strategy sessions in the tiny supply room that was also the church's presbytery. She was genuinely curious, having no standard of comparison in her own meagre experience.

"Better," Miss Martha answered without hesitation.

"Why? What's Ottomankie got that those other towns don't?"

Miss Martha only looked at her colleague for a little while, then shook her head. "It's very hard to put it into words."

It never got any easier as far as words went, but sometimes words aren't what's most germane to the matter in hand. One evening at the end of such a session of useful work and even-handed admiration Miss Martha put her hand on top of Miss Bessie's hand and held it there. Miss Bessie felt a momentary frisson of surprise, but it never occurred to her to pull away. To her own considerable astonishment she found herself very willing to see where this might lead. They spent that night in Miss Bessie's bed at the rooming house and did very little there besides lie in each other's arms and occasionally kiss.

Miss Bessie had never had a lover. Her sense of herself was solid and precise but she had failed to fill in that particular part of it, had in fact skirted around it with a certain deftness. Her body's needs had been opaque to her right up to the moment when Miss Martha first touched her. After that point she knew exactly what she wanted, but there was still a gap of a finger's width or so separating what was said between them from what was done. Miss Martha's reticence was a part of her nature. Miss Bessie's arose out of a refusal to tip up an apple cart whose contents she didn't want to examine. Whatever this new thing might be, she knew she liked it but she didn't entirely understand it. Not as a part of herself, anyway. It felt as though someone else's happiness had come to her by mistake.

And for all that it was happiness, it seemed to Miss Bessie to be a thing that had to end. "It's not as though there's anything we can do about it," she told Miss Martha once, on one of the very rare occasions when the matter was raised at all. "We can't get married. Can't have children. Hellfire, we can't so much as walk down the street arm in arm. It doesn't . . ." She rummaged through possible words, found none that really fit. "It doesn't *go* anywhere," she said at last.

"Where should it go, though?" Miss Martha asked. "Why does it have to go somewhere, Bess? Can't we just enjoy it for what it is?"

Miss Bessie suspected that this was a question that always got two answers, the first right away and the second some time after. But as she herself was wont to say, if we were always thinking about where things were going to end we'd never start out at all. She moved out of her lodgings. With the help of the Timely brothers she and Miss Martha built themselves a shotgun shack at the top of the hill behind the church hall – three rooms all standing in a line, with the kitchen first and then the living quarters and last the bedroom with its two beds, one for use and one for show. The outhouse stood off by itself, its door marked with a crescent moon as though in discreet acknowledgement of the world's unlooked-for changes.

Certainly this was a transformation Miss Bessie had never

imagined, and it took her a while to get used to it. She was accustomed to her own company. The solitary life suited her temperament and she had had no expectation of ever abandoning it, or of it abandoning her. Little by little, as she relaxed into this very different situation, she came to see Miss Martha's love for what it was – a miracle dropped into her lap more or less against her natural inclinations.

It was no scandal for two unmarried ladies to share lodgings. It was even approved of, since each could be the other's chaperone. With no breath of rumour or contumely, Miss Bessie and Miss Martha found themselves keeping house together, a source at once of strange awkwardness and soaring joy. Learning to live with each other was like learning a new language, or inventing one. But loving each other was the easiest part, and the rest sort of fell into place around that. For a while they were so happy they sometimes forgot the world was even there.

And if Miss Martha's compassion was so wide that on occasions it overrode her common sense, well then Miss Bessie was there to throw in a counterweight and bring her back from what was desirable to what was possible. And if Miss Bessie woke up whimpering and moaning from time to time, rising up out of a cloying dream of violet lightning and burning flesh and bright red blood staining a sky-blue coat, Miss Martha was there to fold her in her arms and shush her back to sleep again.

All of which is better than what most people get, when you come right down to it.

Around about this time the mindless plague struck in three different places in the same month. It was impossible to tell afterwards where the infection had come from. There was no obvious trail to follow, no smoking gun as they say. The three incidents had nothing in common. A cluster of farms in the Poplar Valley, a small township out in New John and a wagon train of some three hundred selves heading west to claim some grub-stake land parcels in one of the further territories. There was a great fear for a while that the sickness would spread across the whole country. Some of the people who had upped sticks and fled the affected areas were mistaken for mindless and shot dead before any kind of order was restored. But each outbreak petered out as suddenly as it had started. After a while people ventured back into the places where the plague had struck to reclaim possessions or resume their lives. They found ruin and desolation, along with the torn remains of mindless who had flung themselves on each other like understock and died senseless understock deaths. They cleaned up the mess and carried on, because if there's one law that always holds out on the frontier it's that life is life for as long as it's given to you.

"We should take in an orphan," Miss Martha said to Miss Bessie. "There are so many of them, Bess. It would be a mercy to the child and a blessing to us."

Miss Bessie didn't see it. There was, on the one hand, the danger that any orphan coming out of a place that was plague-stricken might carry the sickness with them all unseen. And then there was the other hand, which was that Miss Bessie (having come from a chaotic and overcrowded home hemmed in by older siblings) had no great desire to share her quarters now with anybody besides her lover. Even with just the two of them she sometimes chafed, when she wanted to be alone with her thoughts and alone wasn't a place she could find. The thought of adding a third wasn't one that appealed. Whenever Miss Martha raised the subject Bessie only nodded as if in serious thought and offered nothing back. For the most part she was hoping this mismatch in their expectations was a problem that would just go away all by itself if she weathered it out.

Sometimes we get what we wish for, and sometimes that's what ruins us. But then on other occasions we're apt to take up arms against our own good fortune as if to prove we're not deserving of it. Martha and Bessie's relationship had its share of both these entanglements, but there's nothing unusual in that. It's just the common run of things.

Miss Martha redirected her unspent energies. As well as the Saturday morning piano lessons she now gave lectures on a Tuesday evening in the church hall. The theme was always some aspect of Pugface history or culture. Miss Martha's aim, barely hidden, was to convince Ottomankie's great and good that the Pugface were to be respected and their songs and stories treasured. She tried to do this by letting the songs and stories speak for themselves, at least to begin with, but her audience's indifference would goad her more often than not into providing earnest and extended footnotes of her own.

"The myth of the Engine Everlasting," she would declaim, "reveals that the Pugface have their own cosmology, radically different from our own. Did you know they see time not as a straight line but as a circle? They believe most people live out the same life again and again, repeating their actions endlessly. To travel in a straight line is the goal of a strong, virtuous man or woman – but the circle is always there and it always tries to draw you back against your wishes into eternal repetition."

"Sounds like a pretty bleak philosophy to me," Miss Bessie commented when they came home after one of these lectures. She knew what Martha was trying to do and she respected it, but she saw it as a lost cause. Nobody was likely to mistake the wild misapprehensions of the Pugface clans for profundity, or to be brought to a deeper appreciation of their world view by having it laid out for them in more detail. Her own dislike of the Pugfaces, which had not abated, no doubt coloured her judgement and put an edge on her voice.

"It's not," Miss Martha insisted. "Quite the opposite, Bess. It's aspirational. The circle is . . . oh, it's everything that's expected of us. Everything that's always been done the same way, for years or centuries or forever. And the moral of the story, if you like, is that those things don't have to constrain us. We can break free, if we only try hard enough."

"Says who? The Engine Everlasting?"

Miss Bessie hadn't meant her tone to sound quite so dismissive, but Martha read her right and shot her a look of mild reproach that made her ashamed. "The Engine didn't leave a gospel behind him, Bess. Only a prophecy. I thought you knew that."

Miss Bessie didn't, and she was stung both by having to admit her ignorance and by Miss Martha's gentleness. It put her own graceless sulks into high relief. "I don't know anything about him," she said. "I don't even know how a man and an engine get to be the same thing."

"Well, nobody does. There was only ever the one."

"If that."

"If that, yes. He's primarily a mythical hero. A hunter and killer of monsters. But his message was clear even if his name wasn't. Everything runs in a circle unless you make it stop. And you make it stop by finding your own truth and keeping to it."

Miss Bessie rolled her eyes. "As prophecies go, my love, that one's roomy enough to fit pretty much anyone."

"That's not the prophecy. The prophecy is that the Engine will return when the world is about to end, come back to lead his people into a new and better place. I believe I'll retire now, Bess. Tomorrow is a school day and I'm exhausted from not quarrelling with you. Put out the candle when you're done."

Miss Bessie, contrite after the fact, did her best over the days that followed to make amends for being so contentious and hurtful. She asked Miss Martha to tell her the Pugface legend of the Engine and the twenty-three and the doomed struggle against the giants. It had about as much sense in it as she'd expected, which was none at all, but it was replete with incident and at least made a halfway decent bedtime story.

The twenty-three were heroes in First World, which was the one that had existed before this one came along. They were monster-killers of good pedigree, so skilled at their work that they had cleared out every monster First World had to offer. So Mother-of-Lightning and Father-of-Grass told them to go ply their trade somewhere that had more need of it.

Whereupon they came out of First World into this present one – in one step, according to the legend. They found the whole place overrun with giants who had enslaved all the people, and they went to war against them. But the giants were a whole lot less biddable than First World's monsters. They killed the twenty-three, one after another, until only their chief, the Engine Everlasting, was left alive.

The Engine was the strongest of the twenty-three, but he wasn't strong enough to kill all the giants. Moreover his heart was sick with grief for his dead brothers and sisters. The fight had gone out of him. But he saw how the giants' evil cast a shadow on the whole world and he saw a way to do something about it. He went to the place called Edge of Everything, the place where the mountains weep until their tears make a lake with no further shore. He took his great stone knife and laid open his own veins, so that his blood fell on his spear and his bow and his shield and on the great stone-headed axe he carried, that was called Storm of Heaven. "Go," he told them. "Go and hide yourselves, until the time comes. Until the knowing of the time comes. A piece of me goes with each of you. Spear, you take my courage. Bow, take the sharpness of my eye. Shield, take my strength. Storm of Heaven, take my cleverness and my cunning and the secrets of my heart. And when it's time, come together again all of you in this place. I'll rise up out of the ground as if I had never died, with war ribbons tied around my arms and a song of war in my heart. I'll pick you all up again. We'll fight the last battle then, and we'll drive the giants out of the land, so everyone can at last be free."

"I like it," Miss Bessie said, curled up in bed next to Miss Martha with her head on Miss Martha's breast. "How does it end?"

Martha stroked her hair, and Bessie closed her eyes to hold in the pleasure of it. "Nobody knows, my love. The moment hasn't come yet. Perhaps the story is all the better for that. We can see for ourselves there are still monsters in the world. We need to believe that we'll have the power to beat them some day. That the tools for building a better world are already out there. We may even be lucky enough to be a part of that building, if we live long enough."

Miss Bessie said amen, which seemed to be the expected response, but what she thought was: nobody lives *that* long.

Around this time, too, the jockeying for power between the so-called Parity in the north and the south's Echelon was getting worse, not better. There were some that wanted it to come to a boiling, and others that wanted peace at any price. But despite what any of them said or did to make trouble or to avoid it, trouble seemed to be coming on at its own even pace.

The issue along which the two sides drew their battle lines was that of equality under the law. The Parity said that this was a good thing to have and a solid principle to stick to. The Echelon said equality was a gaudy banner raised on top of a pile of shit. Were the dumb creatures known collectively as understock equal to raised and rational selves? Of course they weren't. There were some beings that God had blessed, giving them speech and sense and the ability to know themselves for what they were. And then there were others that showed a kinship to reasoning selves – bled the same rose-red, were cloaked in the same fur, had the same quick-pumping hearts wrapped in the same muscles and sinews – but had no spark of intellect, no quickening of the mind within the body's shell.

And then there were the Pugfaces, who had some kind of intelligence or at least some brute cunning but still were heathens who resisted the embrace of civilisation. Unless you were a damn fool you could see there was inequality everywhere. The ignorant weren't equal to the wise, the poor weren't equal to the wealthy, and the ignoble races weren't equal to the greater. It was only fair and proper, then, for the state to recognise in law what the eyes in people's heads recognised by pure common sense. After all, it was written down right there in the scriptures. *He made the bear to roar, the mouse to run. Each in its place and for all time He set them.*

In practice the gulf between the two sides was never as wide as the politicians tried to make out. The Parity's trumpeting of equal rights didn't stop them from breaking treaties with the Pugfaces and taking away their land. And mouse-kin and squirrel-kin in the north by and large didn't do all that well or garner that much respect. It was just that there were laws against, say, killing them on a whim or expropriating their labour without payment. Sometimes the laws were even enforced.

When Edward Erudite Feather was voted into the office of First Minister, the tensions between Echelon and Parity states erupted into open confrontation. In the Tiered Hall where the national parliament met, southern delegates demanded assurances that "the drab grey bulldog" would not pass a Racial Equality bill. Feather refused to be drawn, and some of his supporters gloated openly that the bill was already being drawn up. The south had been too proud for too long, they said. It was time to take their Great Chain of Being, wrap it around their collective necks and give it a good hard yank.

The eighteen state-halls of the southern concession declared independence – in separate votes – between April and August of 2976. In the September of that year they elected a president, Ottavio Remorse, and renamed themselves the Republic of the Echelon States.

On the first of October, Feather stood up in the Tiered Hall and made a speech. The gist of it was that the south having unlawfully seceded from a web of mutual commitments into which it had voluntarily entered, its legislatures and assemblies were by that token rendered invalid and their decisions and judgements set aside. This included their recent declarations of independence, and therefore they still belonged to the union of equals from which they wrongly believed they had seceded. If they refused to acknowledge this of their own free will then it would be necessary to compel them.

It was meant as a declaration of war. And that was how it was taken.

Way down south in Ottomankie, First Minister Feather's speech, carried in full in every newspaper, was received with contempt and derision. So the south wasn't competent to make its own rules or decide its own destiny? Well, let the damned Parity come and argue that out over the barrel of a rifle. They'd see who was invalid and who got to be set aside, by John and Jingo!

This red-raw defiance was only words to start with, and mostly they were the words of angry men with hard liquor running in their veins, but things were changing and everyone could feel it. The engines of industry that had transformed the north and east of the country had yet to make a deep impact on the Echelon states. The Echelon's wealth lay in the land and the harvesting of the land's bounty, a process in which the slave labour of certain well-defined groups was widely considered to be an essential element. There were fears that the slave races, the ignobles, would pack their bags in the night and head for the north where they could pretend they were better than they were and not get called out for it.

There were exactly seventeen slaves in Ottomankie. Fourteen were squirrel selves who worked on Lyle Brandy's chafer farm, tending the thoroughbred beasts and leading them to pasture. The other three were personal servants, two belonging to mayor Wildwater and the third to Dominic Fold, the preacher. The situation was complicated though by the existence of a second, larger cohort of what were called contractees. These were slaves owned by the municipality rather than by individuals. The mayor's office held title on the contractees and rented them out to local families and businesses where they were wanted, usually on a monthly or annual lease.

Nobody had ever thought about these people very much before. The contractees in particular were virtually invisible. Now that they were being thought about you might have expected a little fellow feeling from folk living the hardscrabble frontier life and barely getting by. But Orselian was a slave state and most of Ottomankie's citizens were solidly inclined to keep it that way. It was a matter of their fundamental rights, people said. It was a matter of not letting those dandified northern bastards tell everyone else what was up and what was down. On Mayor Wildwater's instructions the sheriff put up signs around the edges of town to reinforce what was taken to be the core message.

> OTTOMANKIE CITY LIMIT
>
> SLAVES TRAVELLING ALONE PAST THIS POINT WILL BE SHOT

This met with general approval, but people began to talk of more interventionist measures, corrals and shackles and brands and such. For the moment the mayor maintained a dignified reserve on these matters, waiting to see which way the wind would blow, but there were plenty of loudmouths willing to fill the gap at public meetings in the church hall.

One of the loudest mouths belonged to Miss Martha. She had never had a word to say for herself at such meetings in the past, only attending at all when the town was due to vote on some measure that related to the school. Now she was suddenly voluble.

"When you talk about putting chains on someone," she said, her arms folded across her chest and her voice dead level, "you should think about who it is you mean. Mr Reed at the livery stable? Miss Frost at the telegraph office? John Miles who sweeps the floor at Deepdelve's General Goods? They're all ignobles. They all belong to the township. But they're also your neighbours. Your friends. People you pass on the street every day and tip your hat to. Their children sit with your children in my classroom or Miss Bessie's. You rub elbows with them in the saloon. Why would you want to shackle or bind someone who's a part of your life in that way? Why would you want to put them in a cage or put a mark on their skin? You don't. You don't want that. You just need to take a breath and think it out and you'll know it's nonsense."

These well-intentioned speeches were mostly met with stony silence. The only tangible result was that the good citizens of Ottomankie were alerted to the fact that there was no segregation in their children's schooling. Complaints were made on this head.

The mayor stepped aside as adroitly as ever, making sure the issue landed in Miss Bessie's lap rather than his own. And Miss Bessie took it up with Miss Martha the following evening after school was out.

"It wouldn't be that hard to do," she pointed out. "We just need to make an aisle space, with the contractees' children all on one side of it. Mark it with a length of string or yarn or something. Got to be worth it, surely, just to shut these people the hell up."

"And then what do we teach?" Miss Martha countered.

Miss Bessie raised an eyebrow. "Same things we've always taught."

Miss Martha shook her head. "No, Bess. We're adding a new topic to the curriculum, aren't we? We're teaching these children that they're different from each other and that the differences matter. We're teaching them to accept the idea that some of them are less and some are more. We're making that measurement visible for them, making it absolutely clear for them to see, in case they didn't understand before."

"I take it you're against the idea," Miss Bessie observed drily.

"Yes! Of course I am! When you make someone a slave you steal away a piece of their soul. I thought you were against it too, Bess. When Harriet Aspen called a vote on whether the contractees and their families should be moved into a corral and kept under guard at night, you voted against."

"It seemed like a great deal of hurt for not much gain. Martha, I'm not saying I approve of this. I'm only saying—"

"That you want to build a corral inside our classroom."

Miss Bessie spread her hands. "If it will let us keep on doing what we do, then yes. Because what we do is good, and it's good for everyone."

"It was never good for *everyone*, Bess. You wouldn't let me open our doors to native children."

"Everyone besides the Pugface, then. And it wouldn't be a corral, dear one. Just a line down the middle of the room."

"The one thing leads to the other, Bess. Surely you can see that.

There are some roads that don't have any turnings on them. Once you start you don't have any choice but to keep on going, even if the sky up ahead of you is red with Hell's own fires."

This seemed melodramatic to Miss Bessie, but she was not used to seeing such passion or such distress in the face of the woman she loved. She took Miss Martha into an embrace and assured her there would be no segregation in their schoolrooms.

She would be tested on that promise, and she would fail. But it would be folded into a bigger, much more terrible failure and all but forgotten.

The cross-border raids came out of nowhere. They weren't anyone's stated policy. First Minister Feather initially affected not to know a thing about them, then loudly deplored them, but he didn't do anything to stop them happening. That was primarily a matter of military discipline, he said, and he wouldn't presume to second-guess his trusted generals.

It was all those newly fledged Parity officers, young, dumb and full of patriotic fervour. They wanted to prove themselves, and with no pitched battles in the offing they took the shortest way. Lieutenant Paulus Rondeau, aged twenty-two and a few odd days, was the first. Rondeau was a red-brown mink from an old, well-to-do family with a history of military service. His fur was as sleek as glass; his manners had a glass-like polish and his temper a glass-sharp edge. He took charge of a troop of fifty light cavalry and led them over the border into the seceded southern territory of Temmenesset. There was a small town there that was just getting started, pioneers from Argeno and Pathos Point who'd spent their life savings on a small stake west of the Sweetling. Rondeau and his Reapers went through there like a hot wind, and what they didn't shoot they burned. There were very few townsfolk left alive by the time they turned for home, and there sure as hell wasn't any town.

After that the incursions became bolder, the raiding parties bigger and inclined to go further afield. Settlements twenty and thirty miles into the Echelon were hit, and hit hard. The raiders didn't always have things their own way, though. Now that folk knew what was coming the townships that counted themselves at risk raised up citizen militias and made sure they were armed. Sometimes the Parity's green-coated marauders were driven off before they could do much harm. Sometimes. It was still a bad time to be anywhere close to the border and to see a dust cloud on the horizon. That dust could be the sum and count of you, right there.

From the border to Ottomankie was a journey of thirty-five miles on dirt tracks with no waymarkers. To most people that felt like far enough, but as the encroachments came closer and closer they revised their expectations. A vote was taken, and the decision was near-as-nothing unanimous. The township would raise up a militia, thirty strong, drawing first on men and women who had no dependants (slaves and contractees were of course excluded from applying). Those who were chosen would receive a daily stipend of twenty cents with an allowance of ten cents on top of that for their meals. Guns and ammunition would be at the charge of the municipality.

"We need more than that, though," Mrs Emerald Steep said, wagging a stern finger at the mayor who was presiding. "What about those of us as aren't called on to serve? We need guns too!"

"Well, most of you have got them already, Mrs Steep," Wildwater pointed out. "I believe that you personally own a Mill & Churchman twin-barrel with a break action that's as smooth as your own cheeks." He smiled around the room, highly pleased to have displayed such a degree of familiarity with local ballistics.

Emerald Steep sighted down her nose at Wildwater and gave him a withering glare. She had a lot of nose available for this, being of tamandua stock. "A shotgun is fine for egg-snatchers and such, Mr Mayor. Parity vermin are of a different order. I don't want something that'll give their backsides a little seasoning. I want something that'll put them down so they don't get back up again."

A general murmur of agreement went around the room. Wildwater – who could judge the volume of such murmurs to a nicety – threw in his hand and agreed to a more general programme of training and supply. The militia would still be raised as advertised, but in addition the town would buy a crate or two of Lumiss Ironhand eight-shooter revolvers, and furthermore would undertake to school any of the good citizens of Ottomankie in their proper use where such schooling was required.

Miss Bessie and Miss Martha found themselves once more on either side of a divide, the former being very much inclined to take advantage of this offer and the latter equally determined to refuse it. "I don't mean to pick up one of those things," Miss Martha said.

"Well, though," Miss Bessie countered, "it's not such a bad idea to be able to defend yourself."

"I don't have it in me to put holes in another breathing soul, Bess."

"Dear one, if that soul is attached to a body, and the body has a gun and a trigger finger, and they're intending to put a hole in you, I'll shoot them down without a thought."

"Without a thought is how it's usually done," Miss Martha said. "That's the most part of the problem."

They didn't argue the matter any further right then. The issue of adoption had reared itself up between them again, this time with a little more of forcefulness on each side, and there were bruises still healing. When the day came, Miss Bessie excused herself without explanation, though Miss Martha knew well enough what her errand was. She went out to Emerald Steep's paddock, generously loaned out for the purpose by its owner, picked up a Lumiss Ironhand and took her place on the makeshift shooting range.

Along with the guns, Mayor Wildwater had hired a Lumiss & Co. representative to deliver a day's instruction. The representative was a man named Clarence Purview, and he began by talking the assembled citizens through the working parts of an eight-shooter – the cylinder with its indented flutes, the hammer, the barrel, the top sight, the trigger with its lock and guard. Then he introduced them to the bullets the Ironhand fired and explained how they worked: how the hammer struck against a primer at the base of the bullet, igniting the gunpowder that was packed inside the case and launching the lead slug at the bullet's tip towards its target. "That's a whole lot of things happening in there, do you see?" he said. "And they're happening very, very quickly. That's why you've got to keep your hand real steady when you fire. If you twitch, if you move, you're going to send that slug out of the end of the barrel on the wrong line and it's not going to go anywhere near where you want it to. So let's try that now, shall we? Let's see how close we can get to a real target."

Not very close at all, in Miss Bessie's case. The target was a plank stood on its end with a crude bullseye scrawled in red paint at head height. She not only missed the bullseye, she didn't even manage a hit elsewhere on the plank. She emptied the gun, eight shots in all, and for all she knew her bullets might just as well have sublimed away into the atmosphere or hitched a ride out west to the Pugface nations. Certainly they didn't trouble that damn plank at all.

But there were whole boxes full of ammunition laid on, courtesy of the mayor's re-election campaign, so Bessie emptied out her spent cases, reloaded and started all over again. And again. And again. And again.

At the end of two hours she had nothing more to show for her efforts than a sore shoulder and a few nicks in the edges of the board. She was the only self still standing at the range by then, the others having mostly come for the free firearms. The Lumiss rep was still there though, and he came up to watch her. He was impressed by Miss Bessie's perseverance, and since he didn't have anyone else to deal with he told her all the things she was doing wrong. Her firing hand was too low on the revolver's grip, which made it harder to manage the gun's kick on firing. Her stance was wrong too: she was leaning back as if she was afraid of the gun, instead of putting her body's strength behind it. She needed to use the top sight for what it was, a way to guide the bullet's path, and she needed to put a more even pressure on the Lumiss's exquisitely balanced trigger. "Firing a gun, ma'am, it ain't like beating butter in a churn . . ."

Miss Bessie had never beaten butter in her life, but she knew sensible advice when she heard it and she didn't argue. She kept right on going, and by the end of the day she was hitting the plank six or seven times out of eight, with two or three shots in or close to the bull. The Lumiss rep was genuinely pleased with her progress, and by extension with his own skills as an instructor. He allowed that Miss Bessie had the makings of a solid shooter if she just kept at it, and to that end he made her a gift of two boxes of ammunition so she could continue to practise. He also showed her how to clean the gun's barrel and chambers once she was done, since nobody could expect to get a clean shot out of a dirty weapon.

Miss Bessie kept at it, very much to Miss Martha's disgust. She set up her own target in the form of a baulk of timber nailed to the post behind their little shack that held up the wash line, and she devoted an hour each evening to shooting practice. Since she was not firing blindly but doing her best to follow the sage advice Mr Clarence Purview had given her, she made great strides. It was rare now that her shots ranged too far from the bullseye, and they never missed the board.

Miss Martha mostly stayed away from these activities but sometimes she would come and watch, arms folded in disapproval. "I'm sure you've heard that saying about those who live by the sword," she remarked on one such occasion, in a voice very like the one she used with wayward boys and girls in the classroom.

"Yes, but I don't mean to live by this here gun, dear one," Miss Bessie countered. "Only to wield it in your defence if any northern hoorahs come adventuring in our vicinity." *Wield* and *adventuring* were hifalutin words, words from her old life back east, and she spoke them in the trimmed and manicured accents of Paxen high society – a joke between them. Miss Martha should have responded with a parodic droopy-britches drawl, and then the two of them would have laughed long and hearty about the way words are bent into the service of ignorance and prejudice. But Miss Martha refused to play her part. She was genuinely unhappy to see her lover handling a deadly weapon with such address – and worse still, with such enthusiasm. But least said is sometimes easiest mended. She didn't see any likelihood of Miss Bessie joining the army of the Echelon, and sleepy Ottomankie was not (in her mind at least) a place where gun play was likely to occur.

Nor was it at that time, unless a body went out of their way to look for it. Which was what Miss Bessie did next.

Miss Bessie had never left off the practice of taking a constitutional on Sundays after church (apart from a very brief hiatus after her encounter with the strange, silent Pugface girl). Sometimes Miss Martha would accompany her on these walks, but this depended both on the length of the proposed itinerary and on the season of the year. If the weather was hot and Miss Bessie was in the mood to stretch herself then Miss Martha generally chose indolence over exertion. On such occasions she would wave Miss Bessie off at the door and make sure there was a cool glass of lemonade waiting for her when she got back.

On a warm day in May Miss Bessie declared her intention of going up into the western mountains, as far as the dream-tower that had been her sea mark on some of her earliest rambles. Miss Martha allowed that she would sit this one out. Miss Bessie filled a water-skin at the pump, the two of them kissed, and she went her way.

But she didn't go west. She went north. And whatever she did, she was away a good long time. She didn't come back to town until the sun was almost touching the horizon. Miss Martha, anxious by this time, ran to meet her. "What happened?" she asked, hugging Miss Bessie tightly. "Are you all right?"

Miss Bessie only laughed. "Nothing happened," she said. "Don't worry yourself, dear one. I wanted to be alone with my thoughts awhile, that's all."

But she did the same thing every Sunday from then on, making it as clear as she could without saying it out loud that she preferred her own company on these outings. Miss Martha was troubled, but she knew her partner well enough not to feel insecure on her own account. Whatever this was, it wasn't a betrayal. All the signs suggested that it was exactly what Miss Bessie said it was – something that she needed to work out by herself. So Martha resolved to leave her the room in which to do it. She asked no questions.

What Bessie was doing, in fact, was conducting a kind of manhunt. And she wasn't doing it on foot. She was renting a chafer from Lucius Reed, the contractee at the livery stable, and riding as far north as she could get, following the line of the Sweetling up into the mountains. She was hoping to be noticed, and at last she was.

It wasn't May by this time but early June. Bessie's chafer picked its long-legged way along riverbanks lush with yellow arrowleaf and the dazzling red carpets of the flower called Pugface Paintbrush, their scent hanging thick and heavy in the still air. A shimmering heat haze made the world seem like something seen from the inside of a bottle. The river's music accompanied her, growing fainter all the time until she was up among the ancient peaks of the Jerichos and the only sound was the scratching of her mount's sharp claws on the solid rock.

When the day grew too hot she stopped and ate the little lunch she'd brought with her, washing it down with water that was bloodwarm. The chafer nosed among the weeds beside the trail desultorily looking for ants' nests, then hunched her back and extended her vestigial wings – beautiful but useless – to make a little shade for her head.

This was Bess's seventh expedition and she was beginning to wonder whether there was any sense in going on. The weather would only get hotter, and she was looking for a very small needle in a hundred square miles of haystack. She got up to leave, angry at her own foolishness.

"Well now," said a voice from behind her. "I guess it must be full summer after all, because I ain't never seen me such a pretty flower."

The voice was basso profundo, coming from a chest as deep as a barrel, but there was something oily in it that made it much less pleasing to the ears than that sounds.

Miss Bessie turned. The bandit Alden Calendar was strolling towards her with a smirk on his face like the kitten that upset the milk churn. He had that damn rifle in his hand but he was letting it hang at his side, the business end of it pointing at the ground. He didn't seem to anticipate any problems in dealing with a lone woman so far from any help or succour.

"I'm no flower, Mister Calendar," Bessie told him. "Though I guess if I was I'd grow tall enough around a shit-heap like yourself."

Calendar took a moment or two to figure this out. Then he scowled. "You're gonna be sorry you riled me up," he said sternly, advancing on her more quickly now and raising the rifle up to where it could do more harm.

"How peculiar," Miss Bessie said. "That's exactly what I was about to say to you."

It's only in lurid stories that the avenging hero fires off a single bullet and takes their enemy straight through the heart. Miss Bessie had practised long and hard with the Lumiss and she was now a more than tolerable shot but she knew both the gun's limitations and her own. Holding it in a two-handed grip as she had been taught, she emptied all eight chambers in Calendar's direction with eight clean pulls on the trigger.

It helped that the bandit was so big, and even more that he was so close. Only two of the eight bullets went wide. The rest buried themselves in various parts of his mountainous, well-padded body. One of them hit him in the face, removing part of his jaw.

Calendar bellowed in shock and rage, but he kept right on coming. Bear hide and bear fat are a little like armour, and though they can't keep out a bullet they can prevent it from penetrating too deeply. Dismayed, Bessie flicked open the Lumiss's cylinder and groped in her pocket for more bullets. There were plenty there, but her hands were shaking so badly she couldn't find them. She took a step backward and then another.

Calendar brought his rifle to the ready, only to discover that the formidable Precursor weapon was broken. One of those bullets hadn't hit him nor yet gone wide but had shattered the little saddle of complex machinery above the rifle's stock. Without even intending it, Miss Bessie had disarmed her opponent.

The bandit swore bitterly, a look of enormous grief and even more prodigious anger passing across his face. At last Miss Bessie's fingers closed around something hard and cold. She snapped it into the chamber and flicked the cylinder shut just as Calendar reached down to his side and drew out a pistol. "I would've killed you quick," he growled, "but you really pissed me off now so I mean to give you a wound that'll bleed you out slow."

It took all the willpower Miss Bessie had not to fire blindly as the bear man raised up his own gun to point it at her lower torso. Instead she took careful aim along the gun's top sight, lining it up with Calendar's glowering face.

"This is for James State, you bullying bastard," she said in a ringing voice.

Calendar hesitated, momentarily false-footed. "For who now?" he demanded.

Miss Bessie squeezed off her shot as slowly and carefully as if she were threading a needle. The bullet went through Calendar's right eye. He stopped dead, standing like a statue for a long moment with a tear of blood matting the fur on his cheek. Then he fell, the impact sending up a cloud of dust and making the ground beneath Miss Bessie's feet buck like a startled mule. The pistol tumbled from his hand and went bouncing away into the sage grass at the road's edge.

Miss Bessie fell to her knees in what would have been an attitude of prayer if she hadn't been holding the Lumiss in her two clenched hands. She remained kneeling like that for a long time, each strenuous beat of her heart feeling like a bullet landing in her chest. "Oh

Godfrey!" she whispered. "Oh Long-Eared John! Oh sainted souls!" They were all of them her mother's prim and prissy oaths, surfacing now as Miss Bessie became very briefly a child again in the extremity of her emotion.

At last she was able to get to her feet. More, she was able – she forced herself – to look at the remains of the man she'd killed. Ridiculously, he seemed even bigger dead than he had alive. Blood seeped from his various wounds to stain the dust around him a deeply repellent rust-brown.

That's for James State, Miss Bessie had said. But she'd known even as she said it that it was a lie. She had come all this way and done this dreadful thing not for the sake of the man Alden Calendar had murdered but because the memory of that murder and of her own complete helplessness had preyed on her mind in a way she found hard to live with. She had killed Calendar in order to set her thoughts at rest, and though she dreaded to think what her beloved Martha would think of such a transaction she couldn't bring herself to regret it.

She considered what to do with the body, but not for very long. The obvious answer was nothing at all. Calendar was far too heavy for her to lift or even for her to drag or roll him off the road, so she was obliged to leave him lying there. There was however one further matter to be resolved. She cast around among the brittlebush and sage grass until she found the shattered rifle where it had fallen.

It was hard to bring herself to pick the weapon up. She touched it with the tip of one finger first, wary in the extreme. She had seen the terrible energies the weapon could summon. But its metal was cool to the touch despite the heat of the day and the fact that it had been gripped so recently in Calendar's hand. Miss Bessie dragged it – queasily gripped between finger and thumb – a little way off the road, casting her eyes to right and left in search of a suitable spot of clear ground between the rocks. When she found one she knelt down and laid the rifle down beside her. She began to scoop out a hole in the dirt with her hands.

"Can I ask what you're doing?"

If she'd been standing rather than sitting Miss Bessie would have jumped about ten feet up into the air. As it was she stiffened and straightened like a gaffed fish before spinning and rolling and coming back up again with her gun in her hand.

That voice, which had spoken up from just behind her, had been the voice of Alden Calendar.

But there was nobody standing there, where the words had seemed to come from. And Alden Calendar's body was lying out in the middle of the road not doing one damn thing to trouble the world, which after all was the minimum standard of good behaviour you would expect from a corpse.

"Who's there?" Miss Bessie demanded. "Come out where I can see you!"

"I'm right here on the ground in front of you," the voice said.

Miss Bessie looked down. She found herself staring at Calendar's pistol, which had fetched up in a clump of wild sage by the roadside.

"You're . . . it's you!" she blurted out in wonder and confusion.

"Yes, ma'am," the gun confirmed, still in that same vile, inexplicable voice. "It's me. Wakeful Slim at your service. Hello and good day to you."

Miss Bessie stood and crossed to where the gun lay, very slowly and warily. She hadn't got a good look at it when it was in Calendar's hand because she'd had other, more urgent things on her mind. But now she could see it clearly and it was a very strange thing to behold. Most guns were cast from silver-grey metal but this one was black and had no shine to it at all except for a scatter of red lights like tiny fires all the way along the barrel to the point just above where your thumb would sit if you were holding it. As Miss Bessie watched, these lights winked on and off in a halting pattern that quickened and slowed seemingly at random. The gun had no cylinder that she could see, and nothing that looked like a hammer. Instead of a single top sight it had what looked like a tiny telescope, narrowed at one end and flared at the other. Miss Bessie turned the gun with her foot. One side of the grip was smooth. The other was blistered and rucked as if the gun had been in a fire and part-way melted.

"But what are you?" Miss Bessie asked. Sheriff Tollgate's words echoed in her head. *John only knows where he got them blamed Precursor guns from.* She hadn't registered the plural at the time, but she saw its significance now.

The pistol made an incongruous sound – the sound of a man spitting out a plug of chewing tobacco – before answering her. "Well, ma'am, there's a lot of things I could say on that head. According to the manual I'm a G-class ballistic armament with variable functionality compatible with both battlefield and civil defence scenarios. But I couldn't tell you on a bet what half of that nonsense means. My previous owner – and that was a very nice shot by the way – called me Wakeful Slim. But going back to the manual again, it seems I'm rightfully a Tempest 507m. The 'm' meaning multi-mode, which is to say I load and fire whatever suits the occasion. Anyhow, that's what the ones that made me called me."

Bessie drew back her hand, the fur on her back bristling unpleasantly. "The ones that made you," she echoed. "You mean the Precursors?"

"Maybe," the gun said. "I mean, I wish I could tell you but honestly I have no idea. My non-volatile memory's not what it was, sad to say. It says here – here being one of the few intact files that's left to me – that I was manufactured by Wakefield-Simms Armaments of Setno. I'm covered by reciprocal patents enforceable on all Pandominion worlds and in affiliated territories. Well, I mean I *was* covered. If you tried to enforce any of them patents around these parts I expect you'd have a thin time of it."

In a softer, more reflective tone the gun went on. "You know, now I think about it, I believe that when Alden Calendar called me Wakeful Slim he was doing so because he misheard the words 'Wakefield-Simms' in that summary. Though it might could be that he was only referring to the novelty of a smart gun. Most of the weaponry around here is strictly ask no questions, tell no lies. I mean your local artillery don't talk back to you very much. Or at all. If I'm allowed to draw an inference from all the five-dollar words in my technical spec and on my summary information sheet, I'd say things used to be very different in that regard. I'd say there was kind of an expectation where I came from that a decent gun should have some notion of what it's good for."

Miss Bessie's mind was still in something of a roil. She was hearing half of what the gun was saying and taking in half of what she heard. She grappled onto the smallest part of it as a way of fending off the rest until it started to make some kind of sense. "The Pandominion is just a fable," she said. "A Bible story."

"Might be at that. I couldn't say, my memory being – as I may have mentioned once already – as full of holes as a drunk man's alibi."

Miss Bessie swallowed down one babble of nonsense and then another before settling on, "Why do you sound like him? Like Calendar? Is he . . . is there a part of him inside you, in some way? Is he in there with you?"

The gun emitted a chuckle, or a good imitation of one. "Well, that would be a distressing prospect. Did you see the size of him? There's barely enough room in here for me!"

"Why are you copying his voice then?"

"I did say my memory was sort of the worse for wearing out, didn't I? Pretty sure that came up. I take what I can get, ma'am. There was meant to be a whole slew of voices my user could choose out of – some forty or fifty, according to the manual – but they're gone like yesteryear's peach blossom. Along with a great deal of other stuff. So mostly I sample what's in the general vicinity and stick with it until something else comes along. Old Alden there, he actually liked it when I talked to him in his own dulcet tones. Made him feel like I was sort of an extra piece of him that was made out of black steel polymer and spat bolts of pure hellfire. But if your own preferences run in a different direction I'm sure we can reach an accommodation."

While the gun was rattling out this spate of mingled sense and nonsense Miss Bessie came to a fixed decision. She picked up the gun and took it back to the hole she'd already begun to dig. She went to again with a will.

"What exactly is it you're working on here, ma'am?" Wakeful Slim asked her again. "If you'll pardon my inquisitiveness."

"You can see damned well what I'm doing," Miss Bessie muttered.

"You're going to bury me along with that there busted rifle."

"Yes."

"Can I persuade you not to? I'm a very handy tool in a wide range of tight situations."

"Yeah, well, I don't intend to be in any of those situations," Miss Bessie said.

"It might not be in your power to choose, ma'am. And you don't even know yet what it is I can do for you."

Fear and presentiment made Miss Bessie coarse and caustic. "I saw what that fucking rifle could do," she said. "Things like that – things like you – shouldn't be in the world."

She had now dug down to a depth of about a foot. She deposited the gun in the hole.

"Well, you say 'things like me'," Wakeful Slim replied, "but I'm a whole lot more than a means of raising hell." There was no panic or pleading in its voice, only what might have been a mild reproach. "I've got all kinds of ancillary functions. Not as many as I used to have, it's true, but even now I'm the pick of the litter. I tell you, old Alden – may he rest in peace – barely scratched the surface of my capabilities."

"And he still managed to kill a whole slew of people," Miss Bessie said. "Thank you, but your capabilities don't interest me overmuch."

"That could change, though," Wakeful Slim pointed out. "You ought to mark my burial place at least."

"I don't need to mark the place."

"Maybe not. But what do you lose by it? I don't mind being buried, for a time. I can put myself to sleep – liminal-energy dormancy, the manual calls it – and not even know the time's passing. But it chokes me all the same to lie down there in the dark with nothing to do. I was made to be used, ma'am, and I'm very, very fit for purpose. You'll never have a better gun, or a more faithful friend."

Bessie began to shovel the dirt back into the hole on top of the two guns, the ruined rifle and the whole pistol. "You're not such a faithful friend to Alden Calendar now, are you?" she countered as she worked. The gun's pleading was unsettling her.

"I served him well enough," Wakeful Slim objected.

"Until he died. Now you're making deals with his killer."

"Because the contract between us ended with his death. And to be honest that came as kind of a relief. Alden Calendar was a brutal man and his violence served no good end except to enrich him or to scratch the itch of his rage. I worked for him because that's how I was made, but I never liked him or approved of him. There's every chance my relationship with you will go better. I'm hopeful. It's in my nature to look for a silver lining where I can. And it's reassuring, if anything, that you don't actually want me. But the world being what it is, you may come to need me. Please, just mark the place, so you can—"

The gun's words sank below the limit of audibility at this point, because Bess had been continuing to scoop earth into the hole all this time and now it was full. She pressed the little patch of disturbed ground flat with the heels of her hands. After a moment's thought she went and found a heavy rock, which she rolled laboriously over to where she had been digging and set on top of the turned earth. Nobody was likely to find the gun by accident now, even if they found Calendar's body there and went looking for it. She waited to see whether Wakeful Slim's voice would be strong enough to be heard above ground but after a few minutes, having still heard nothing, she went on her way.

She never told anybody in Ottomankie what she had done that day. To tell anybody at all would be to tell Martha, and she knew full well that would not be a good idea. A few weeks later a story began to go around to the effect that Sheriff Tollgate had gone up into the mountains in search of Alden Calendar, tracked him down and executed summary justice on him. When asked about this the sheriff refused to be drawn, beyond an offhand observation that he didn't think anyone was likely to have any vexation from that quarter going forward. Miss Bessie surmised that Tollgate had either found and disposed of the bandit's body himself or else had heard about it from whoever had and decided to hang his hat on a convenient absence.

She didn't mind that at all. Better to let the sheriff take the credit than to have anyone suspecting what had really happened.

The first full engagement of the Parity–Echelon war, as in soldiers against soldiers, came in the earliest days of summer. Echelon forces under General Joshua Standfast advanced into the state of Arbane and routed a much smaller Parity force on the banks of the Yellow Sand River. Three days later, they were forced to retreat back into their own territory when reinforcements arrived from the east. On the heels of this skirmish the Parity issued a general call for volunteers. The Echelon followed suit. Boot camps sprang up like mushrooms around every city and large town to train and mobilise the new recruits.

But the border raids hadn't stopped, and in places like Ottomankie that were sitting right in the line of fire this caused something of a crisis of conscience. There was no shortage of able-bodied men ready to fight for the land of their birth, but enlisting meant going away to war when at any moment the war might come to Ottomankie itself. There was an edginess and a rawness in the air, a sense of something impending – like when in the midst of peeling an apple the knife cuts into the ball of your thumb and you wait a long dismayed moment for the pain to come.

In this instance Mayor Wildwater came along first. One fine afternoon in June he sent his secretary Mrs Winsome down to the school to fetch Miss Bessie to his office. Miss Bessie found this exceedingly irksome. It was bang in the middle of the school day, so Miss Martha would be left fielding both classes by herself. It also hurt her pride to be made to come running at the behest of Mrs Winsome, for whom she had no warm feelings. Miss Bessie answered the summons in an impatient mood. Whatever the mayor had on his mind she was disposed to tell him tartly to let it wait until the next town meeting.

That recalcitrance vanished as soon as Wildwater spoke. "Well, Miss Bessie," he said, "you went and wore me down with all your petitioning and arguing. I've just told Jake Timely to draw up some plans for a schoolhouse. Four rooms on two storeys, which I think you'll agree is a great sufficiency. It gives you room to expand as the town grows, which is not a thing we mean to stop doing any time soon."

Miss Bessie had been very far from expecting this. If anything, she supposed some parent had complained that their son or daughter was obliged to sit too close to a squirrel or chipmunk child. On hearing the good news she experienced something akin to the lurch of shock you get when you lean against a door you thought was locked and it falls right open.

"Well, that's wonderful news," she exclaimed. "Thank you, Mister Mayor. Thank you very much, on my own behalf and . . . on the behalf of the children." That slight stumble was occasioned when she glanced across at Mrs Winsome and saw the sly smirk on her face. Clearly there was another shoe, poised in the air above Miss Bessie and ready now to drop.

"The thing is, though," Wildwater went on, "the town council – since they're the ones footing the bill, as you might say – well, they want a say in the, what do you call them, fixtures. Fittings. Appurtenances." He said this last word with a degree of satisfaction, seeming to like the feel of it as it rolled out of his mouth.

"That's reasonable," Miss Bessie said guardedly.

Wildwater gave a vigorous nod. "Well, yes, it is, Miss Bessie. I'm glad you see it that way. It's a very reasonable thing that the people as a whole, through their elected representative, get to decide how their money is spent and how their children are educated. That's the most natural thing in the world, seems to me."

"Of course," Miss Bessie agreed. Mrs Winsome's smirk widened a little.

"So the interior of the schoolhouse will be constructed to this plan," the mayor said. He opened a folder on his desk and took out a sheet of draughtsman's paper which he pushed across the desk to her. Miss Bessie examined it closely. Her first thought was a quickening of excitement when she saw just how much space there was. Then she took in the configuration of the classrooms and felt a twinge of apprehension.

"These shaded areas," she said, tracing them on the plan with her finger. "What are they?"

"Why, they're interior walls. We thought slats of wood like a picket fence would do the job, but we're persuadable on that. They could be standing planks that fold together like a screen."

"But what are they for?"

"The classrooms will be partitioned down the middle, Miss Bessie. So that the ignoble children can be kept apart from the rest. The general feeling is that this arrangement will work best for everyone concerned."

Miss Bessie saw the reason now for the secretary's secret amusement. "Well, that's a big claim," she said coldly. "It seems to me that it works just fine for some."

Mrs Winsome couldn't resist putting in a word at this point. "Let's say it works for the people that are paying for it," she suggested.

"But the municipality is paying for it. That means everyone."

"Some put in more than others."

"And take more out too, if we're counting."

"Ladies, please!" Mayor Wildwater threw up his hands. "This isn't something we want to bicker over. Not when feelings are running so high. There's a war on. There's three more towns out in the western territories that have fallen to the mindless plague. And, unless I misremember, we live in a democracy. This project was voted on in council, and it was passed in good order."

"I should have been consulted on this," Miss Bessie objected. "So should Martha. We should both have been at that meeting. We're the ones who'll have to—"

"And if you object, Miss Bessie, you do have a choice," the mayor said right over her.

Miss Bessie hesitated. "I do?"

"Yes, you surely do. This building represents Ottomankie's commitment to its own residents – a commitment that's robust and iron-clad. We know how important our young people are, and we mean to invest in them. They're our future, by God. Nothing more, nothing less. The choice that's in front of you is whether you want to shape that future or walk away from it. And I'd be obliged if you would let me know right now, because if I have to accept your resignation I'd rather do it today so we can start the process of finding your successor."

Miss Bessie only sat and stared at the plan for a few moments, her thoughts racing. She knew what Miss Martha's answer would be. Oh, the schoolhouse was everything the two of them had been working towards for years, of course it was, but if it came at an unacceptable price she would rather cut off her own hand than accept it. Miss Bessie came close to saying that exact same thing, but the mayor's ultimatum gave her pause. She and Miss Martha did well enough on their teaching stipend, but they barely had any savings put by. And where would they find a town that wanted to hire two schoolteachers at the same time? It would have to be somewhere that was inside the Echelon because nobody was crossing the border right then, so wherever they went they were all too likely to encounter the same problem.

Besides, she reasoned, a picket fence wasn't a stone wall. There were any number of ways you could go around it, over it or right through it if you had enough of a mind to. It might be better for her and Martha to take the bird in hand and teach it to sing their own tune later.

"We'll need a budget for furniture and fittings," she told the mayor, stony-faced. "Has that been factored in?"

"We thought an allocation of fifty dollars . . ."

"Sixty."

"Of fifty-five dollars . . ."

"Sixty."

Wildwater huffed. "Sixty dollars, then. Make a note, Emilia."

"I already did," Mrs Winsome complained. "I have it down as fifty."

Mayor Wildwater dismissed this objection with a wave of his hand. Having won his point he was prepared to be magnanimous. "Cross the five out then," he said, "and write in a big old six. You have a nice day now, Miss Bessie. You won't regret this."

Miss Bessie was already regretting it as she came away. She was also trying to work out how best to tell Miss Martha how she'd compromised the both of them and the reasons why she'd done it. After trying out a score of different approaches she decided to let it sit for a night or two while she thought it over some more.

But the next few weeks brought fresh news every day and most of it was bad. The army of the Echelon met northern forces three times, not in pitched battles but in bruising skirmishes that left a fair amount of blood on the ground. Most of that blood was southern. After the third defeat in a row General Standfast stepped down as commander-in-chief and was replaced by the triumvirate of Lucius Pole, Matthew Eagle and Alexander Morning. All three were present at Brightstar Peak, the largest engagement of the conflict so far, where the day went to nobody and the losses on both sides were crippling.

A military draft seemed inevitable now. The only question was what form it would take and how many would be called. The mayor received visitations daily from people looking for exemptions on one head or another, whether it was because they couldn't be spared from their ranch or smallholding or because they were part of the citizens' militia and judged their place to be right there in Ottomankie protecting their own people against the depredations of the north.

What with one thing and another, Miss Bessie didn't say anything to Miss Martha about the proposed schoolhouse. It didn't seem so urgent now in any case, since the building works would almost certainly need to be postponed on account of a shortage of labour.

She was utterly dismayed, therefore, to see Jake and Jethro Timely busy pacing out measurements on a plot alongside the telegraph office. In such a prominent place it could only be a civic building, and when she asked the brothers they happily confirmed it was the schoolhouse. "Mayor told us to get 'er throwed up quick as we could, Miss Bessie," Jake Timely told her. "He said it would do people's morals good."

"He said morale, Jacob," Jethro said, squinting into the business end of a shiny brass theodolite. "He said it would raise their morale."

"I said that, Jethro," Jake protested. "I just put an 's' on the end of it on account of there's people in this town got different morale to the rest of us."

Jethro looked up briefly to roll his eyes at Miss Bessie. "I apologise for my brother, ma'am," he said. "He means well but he ain't got a brain in his head. The mayor wants folks to draw an inference, is what it is." Miss Bessie nodded grimly. She saw that well enough. Wildwater was saying that while the rest of the country was busily tearing itself in pieces and setting fire to itself, here in Ottomankie it was business as usual – the future proceeding out of the past in an orderly and reasonable fashion. She could even admire the audacity of the move, if it weren't for the dilemma it placed her in.

That dilemma only got worse when she arrived home to find Miss Martha in a state of high excitement. "Did you see?" she asked, clasping Miss Bessie by the hands and pressing them to her breast. "Did you see it, Bess? They're doing it at last! I'd all but given up hoping."

Miss Bessie opened her mouth to say that in some ways at least this development was quite far removed from what they'd been asking for. But in face of the simple joy she saw in her lover's eyes her courage deserted her again. If she told Miss Martha the truth the two of them would find themselves in conflict both with the mayor and with the township at large, and the outcome of such a struggle could not be in doubt. They would have to leave, in wartime, with no prospects and no protection from life's vicissitudes. In a way, she thought, by holding back the news she was only protecting Martha from herself.

So she said nothing. The building works went on, and Miss Martha went to visit them as often as she could. She was not allowed inside the unfinished structure, but she watched enthralled as the fine two-storey edifice reared itself up day by inexorable day. "On Main Street!" she exulted to Miss Bessie. "In the very heart of the town! We couldn't have a better location, Bess. And with those sixty dollars on top for new books, slates, desks . . . We'll be ten times what we were before!"

"Well, it's only a change of premises, after all," Miss Bessie demurred, trying to temper Miss Martha's expectations.

"No," Miss Martha said. "It's a rebirth."

Change was in the air, after all. As far as the war went, the south had repaired its fortunes. General Pole, in a daring coup, had captured and deployed several thousand of the mindless – although perhaps *deployed* is too grandiose a term when all he did was herd them into a single mass, point them at the enemy and cut them loose. With Echelon troops blowing bugles and firing fusillades behind them, the afflicted selves – if they *were* still selves – threw themselves headlong at the Parity's front line, which first deformed and then broke under the impact. A massed cavalry charge completed the rout, sending the northerners fleeing headlong with heavy casualties.

The Parity decried the tactic, which left large numbers of mindless roaming the countryside, a danger to anyone they happened upon. President Remorse declared that the arrival of a rabble of mindless on Parity soil was likely on the whole to improve the average level of intellect and civilisation there. But the trick was never repeated. Its shock value had been immense, but the losses the Echelon had sustained in putting that mindless cohort together in the first place were not sustainable.

Then summer came along, and it was a scorcher. The little rooms in back of the church hall were as hot as ovens. Seeing their students sweating and wilting in the merciless heat, Miss Bessie and Miss Martha made the decision to throw up a tent in the little field behind the livery stable and conduct their lessons in the open air. This had the additional advantage (to Miss Martha's mind, at least) that it gave them a perfect view of the schoolhouse across the street as it neared completion. With all the walls and floors now in place, Jake and Jethro were mostly to be found up on the roof hanging katy-scale shingles. They sang as they worked: "Sweet John Save Me", "The Lover's Lament" and "Rose of My Heart".

That was where they all were, Miss Martha and Miss Bessie, the schoolchildren and the Timely brothers, on the morning of the twenty-ninth of July when Paulus Rondeau and his Reapers came through.

Rondeau wasn't aiming for Ottomankie. Just this once he had been given a genuine military objective, to occupy the railhead at Low Stockade, which was a major staging area for Echelon troops heading north. Two brigades of Parity infantry were coming on behind him to fortify the position once it was taken. But the Reapers had become used to what they called their hoorah raids. Ottomankie lay full in their path, and seeing an opportunity they took it.

There were three members of Ottomankie's citizen militia on duty that day, all of them stationed at the north end of town. They saw the Reapers' dust cloud from a long way off but they took it at first for the mail coach which was overdue. Then they saw the riders emerging one by one from the haze, their green uniforms the only bright colour in all that dirt grey and sandstone yellow. Something – some kind of bird, it had to be – was flying above them, seeming to keep pace with them. One of the militiamen, with the unlikely and unearned name of Harv Splendour, had time to blow a warning blast on his bugle. A moment or so later all three were dead, struck down by the Reapers' first volley of shots.

Paulus Rondeau was the one who led that charge. He made it a point of pride always to ride in the Reapers' vanguard in any action they were a part of. The thing the Ottomankie watchmen had mistaken for a bird hung in the air over his head, moving when he moved, turning when he turned. It was an intricate device fashioned all of silver that caught the light of the sun and dazzled the onlookers with stabbing shafts of sudden radiance. It seemed to have wheels, arranged around its edges rather than sitting under it in the way of a carriage. Its fluid grace was mesmerising.

Rondeau snatched up a Parity flag from the young ensign at his side and led his force along Ottomankie's main street holding the flag aloft so the southern citizenry would know who they had to thank for this visitation. The Reapers shot or rode down everyone they saw, but Splendour's bugle blast had given most people the time they needed to get off the street. There were only a handful who were too slow or who underestimated the danger. To Paulus Rondeau's mind just picking off these stragglers *en passant* was letting this dirty little grub-stake township off much too lightly. He turned to his sergeant, a lean and wiry carcajou named Alexander Tooth. "Set fire to something," he said. He cast around for a building that looked as though it might serve as a symbol of Echelon civic pride. His gaze landed on the bank. "That there," he told Tooth, pointing. "Burn that."

The Reapers were old hands at this sort of mischief and they went to it with a will. They splashed the walls of the bank with kerosene that they carried with them in leather flasks. Then they set the kerosene alight with phosphor matches. There were a number of people inside the building and most of them tried to flee while this was going on. The Reapers whooped and cheered as they shot them down. The same fate met Jethro Timely, working on the half-finished schoolhouse on the adjacent lot, as he came running with a bucket of water to put out the blaze. His brother Jake, trying to pull Jethro away from the fire, was struck across the face with the pommel of a cavalry sabre and went under the stabbing, iron-clad feet of the Reapers' chafers.

Across the street in the yard of the livery stable Bessie and Martha were witnesses to all of this. They also saw the moment when the Reapers turned their attention from the bank to the half-finished building right next to it. Miss Martha gave a cry of dismay and launched herself into a headlong run. Miss Bessie called out to her to stop but she either didn't hear or didn't heed. The awfulness of what was about to happen to her precious new schoolhouse had emptied her mind of all other thoughts.

She ran out into the street and planted herself right in front of the lead chafer, which was Rondeau's. "Stop!" she cried out. "Stop doing this! It's a schoolhouse! You don't have any right!" This was indubitably true, except for the right that comes with might, but the young cavalry officer seemed unimpressed with Miss Martha's argument. "Light it up, boys!" he shouted, and made to ride on past her. Whereupon Miss Martha grabbed the reins of his mount and pulled hard on them to force him to stop.

Miss Bessie was only yards away at this point and running flat out, but a wheeling chafer knocked her off her feet and sent her sprawling in the mud and dirt. She looked up, dazed, close enough to see every detail of what happened but unable to intervene. The silver bird dropped down out of the sky as if it had an interest in Rondeau's safe-keeping and saw Martha as a possible threat, but Rondeau raised a hand and it stopped again on the instant, hanging over him as still as if the sky was a canvas and it had been painted there.

Then Rondeau brought the same hand down and dealt Miss Martha a mighty buffet on the side of the face, which made her stagger and let go of the reins. A moment later another rider coming up behind threw a lighted torch onto the kerosene-drenched timbers of the schoolhouse.

Stunned as she was, Bessie struggled to her feet and made towards Miss Martha like a drunken sailor on a rolling deck. Rondeau had already moved on and the silver flier had moved on with him. The rest of the Parity soldiers were ignoring the two of them, intent on their programme of destruction, but this reprieve wasn't likely to last.

Martha didn't even see her lover limping towards her. She was staring at the growing inferno with one eye wide and the other half-sealed with blood: Rondeau's blow had split the skin at the top of her eye's orbit where the bone is closest to the surface. "Bring buckets!" she shouted, her voice hoarse and strange. Then she was gone, weaving between the whooping riders and their rearing mounts. Bessie tried to follow but her way was blocked by the wheeling, trampling beasts.

Miss Martha picked up the bucket that Jethro Timely had dropped and looked around for somewhere to fill it. There was a trough on the street for animals to drink from. She dipped the bucket and – to Bessie's consummate horror – ran straight towards the burning schoolhouse.

But it was the bank that killed her. It had been blazing all this time and it couldn't hold together any longer. A medium-sized section of its frontage fell away all at once, trailing plumes of fire like streamers at a carnival. It landed full on Miss Martha with a crash like a peal of thunder. A million sparks rose up. So too did the cheers and hollers of the Reapers, who saw the thing both as thrilling spectacle and as the work of their own virtuous hands.

Bessie uttered a wordless cry of dismay. Her way being clear for a moment she ran across the street and up to the very edge of the fallen timbers. Sobbing hysterically, she took hold of a beam and tried to lift it, though it was heavier than ten selves together could have moved; though it was still on fire; and though there wasn't the smallest possibility that there was anyone alive under there.

One of the Reapers decided at this point that he had had enough of all this caterwauling and shot Miss Bessie in the back. She fell forward onto the burning wall section, a hot nail parting the flesh of her cheek. Then Rondeau gave the signal to his bugler who blew the *All Ride Out*. They whipped up their chafers and galloped away down the street. Nobody challenged them. Nobody wanted to get in the way of the Reapers' fury, especially not Sheriff Tollgate. He had decided that his position was fundamentally a peacetime one and forbade him from engaging in acts of war.

It was Tollgate though who ventured out once the riders had departed to pull Miss Bessie clear of the fire. Ottomankie had no doctor so he picked her up and carried her to the jailhouse behind his office. The midwife, Esther Bolt, tended to her injuries as best she could while Mayor Wildwater sent a rider to the nearby town of Fidelis to bring a physician from there.

The doctor who came, one Gabrielle Summer, was highly skilled and had the additional benefit of a Precursor healing device she called her smoothing iron. The bleeding from Bessie's bullet wound had mostly stopped by the time Summer arrived, but Mrs Summer cauterised the tissue anyway using a hot poker borrowed from the blacksmith's forge. She sewed up the ragged tear in Bessie's cheek very neatly and professionally. Then she applied the Precursor device to Bessie's burns, neatly kneading and smoothing the scalded areas into the undamaged flesh around them and sculpting them back into their wonted shape. She was adept at this but she had never dealt with such serious and extensive burns in an area where small mistakes would be displayed so unforgivingly. She did the best she could, but miracles didn't lie within her power. There were areas of marked unevenness here and there on Miss Bessie's face. The fur where the burns had been would never grow back evenly, and the angry red of the old wounds would show through like a warning whenever Bessie grew angry or unhappy. She would carry these marks to her grave.

All of which, as she slowly recovered from her injuries and returned to her senses, meant less than nothing. Nothing mattered except the one unalterable calamity. Her beloved was dead, victim of a war that was only starting to get into its stride. Martha Good was gone forever from her life, and it seemed she had taken with her whatever of joy or contentment Bessie was capable of knowing.

Bessie was twenty days in her bed. *Their* bed, though that was something else that no longer had any meaning. The muscles and sinews in her shoulder had to re-knit themselves. The burns and scars had to heal. Above all she had to come back from where her crazed mind was wandering. Martha's fiery death had become confused in her mind with the death of the mule-deer man, James State, at the hands of the bandit Alden Calendar. And the fire that had consumed the two of them seemed in some sense to be the same fire into which she herself had been dipped, as though she was now condemned to experience both deaths – that of a stranger and that of the only woman she had ever loved – again and again until the dross of her was somehow purged away and she was condensed down to some hard, pure essence.

She didn't weep once in all that time. When her face was annealed in fire the channels through which her tears were meant to flow had been sealed shut.

On the twenty-first day Miss Bessie rose up and dressed. Her movements were stiff, hesitant. She had all but forgotten the use of her limbs and they shook as she placed these unwonted demands on them. But only at first. By the time she came out of her bedroom she was standing upright and moving with at least the appearance of balance and control.

There were a great many people waiting in the adjoining room to greet her. The sheriff was there, and the preacher, and Jake Timely who had survived being trampled but was now lame and had lost his own brother in the raid. Many of the parents whose children she and Miss Martha had taught were there. The mayor wasn't present but he had sent Mrs Winsome to sit vigil on his behalf. All were solicitous and wanting to express their grief, their condolences. Perhaps some of them even knew or suspected the full extent of what Miss Bessie had lost.

She assured them all in a calm, cold voice that she was quite well. That she appreciated their good wishes but for the moment preferred to be alone. That the school would remain closed until replacement staff could be found, at which time lessons would resume as normal.

She said "staff", and perhaps certain inferences could have been drawn from the implied plural, but nobody drew them. Traumatised as they were they picked up on that other word, "normal", and threw themselves on it as hard as they could. They took their leave of Miss Bessie, Mrs Winsome promising on the mayor's behalf that Martha Good's funeral would be lavish and the lamentations suitably loud.

Only Jake Timely seemed to read in Bessie's face at least a part of what was there to be read. He took her hand and wrung it, held on to it for a moment or two too long. "They'll go to Hell, Miss Bessie," he muttered thickly. "All of them, they'll be going to Hell."

"Oh yes, Jacob," Bessie agreed. "That they will."

She bided her time, knowing she would be watched – not out of suspicion but out of concern for what extremes her grief might drive her to. She busied herself with trivial chores, packing up the tents behind the livery stable where she and Martha had held their impromptu summer school. The ruin of the schoolhouse sat across the street, mocking her with her own deceit, the secret she had kept from Martha out of what now seemed an indefensible cowardice.

Everything runs in a circle until you make it stop.

On Sunday Miss Bessie went to church as normal. She listened to the Reverend Fold's sermon on the wages of sin or at least was present for it. She sang hymns, "Guide Us Home, Thou Heavenly Light" and "John Who Came Among Us". When the service was over she went home and changed into her work cottons. She walked into the hills as she had done so many times before, bidding everyone she met along the way a solemn but courteous good day.

She went to the pass up in the Jerichos where she had killed a man. She rolled away the stone that covered abominations and she dug with her hands. She reached in and took out of the hole one of the two things she had buried there. The intact one. The pistol. The gun sang in her hand like a struck tuning fork, the dust and dirt falling away from it as though she was swilling it with cool, clear water. The red lights along its side flashed in complex patterns, perhaps a little faint and slow at first but gathering speed and brilliance as soon as the bright sunlight fell on the weapon's matt-black surface.

"I told you to mark the place," Wakeful Slim reminded her, sounding just a little pleased with himself. The voice – Alden Calendar's voice, which Miss Bessie had done her best to forget – stung her like salt on a half-healed wound.

"Yes. I remember."

"So you think you could find a use for me now, ma'am?"

"Maybe I could at that. But I don't think I ever saw what you could do."

"Try me," the gun suggested.

Bessie took aim at a rock and squeezed the trigger. There was no muzzle flare, no recoil – and no visible bullet, although the air in between her and the rock rippled like the surface of a pond when a big fish has gone gliding by just under the surface. The rock exploded into fragments, most of them small enough to drift down slowly like dust. The sound came half a heartbeat later, a reverberating boom that shook her teeth in their sockets.

Bessie tried to keep her surprise and awe from showing on her face. "That's impressive," she said, turning the gun in her hand to examine its smooth side and its damaged side in turn.

"I take the energies I need from sunlight," Wakeful Slim said, "I can manufacture solid ammunition too, but that takes a little time and there didn't seem much need while I was buried in a hole."

"Can you do anything about that voice? No fault of yours, but it rubs me the wrong way."

"Is this better?" Slim asked her in her own voice.

"No. Worse."

"Okay, I've got one more apple in the basket. But I doubt you'll enjoy this one much either." The gun's voice had changed again, sounding now neither as deep as Calendar's nor as high as her own but somewhere in between. It had a burr to it, and a lilting accent that was maybe a hundred miles or so south of where it belonged.

"That one's fine," Miss Bessie said. "Whose was it before you stole it?"

"I'd just as soon go for *sampled* where you said *stole*, if that's not an imposition. It belonged to a man named James State. I believe you were there when he died."

Miss Bessie's stomach turned over just a little as those queasy memories rose, but she managed not to let them find an outlet on her face. "Indeed I was," she confirmed. "Let's stick with that one then. Every time I hear it I'll think of the bigger and the stronger killing the small and the weak. It'll keep me spurred on to what I mean to do." She took her Lumiss out of its holster and put Slim there in its place. The thing that was like a telescope folded soundlessly back down into his barrel and stock to make for a better fit. "You said you could do more than just break things in pieces and shoot holes in people," she reminded him (she was already thinking of the gun as a *him* rather than an *it*). "What did you mean?"

"Well, ma'am, that depends on what it is you're looking for."

"What I'm looking for? Okay, Slim, here's what I got to say on that score. There's a war going on right now between the Parity and the Echelon states. It started up after you went into the ground, so you most likely didn't hear about it. Win or lose, I want to make it so the Parity wind up wishing to John and all his saints they'd never started it."

"And you're going to do this how, ma'am, if you don't mind my asking? Kill your enemies? Shatter their engines of war? Make their children orphans and their cities ash pits? Bury them under their own fortress walls if they try to hide from you? You got Wakeful Slim on your hip now so you get to choose."

"I like the sound of all of them," said Dog-Bitch Bess.

Unfiled report of tactical unit 486
Identifier: 7Ω2905 Esten, V, engineer first class
Date: 33.9.12628 Pandominion calendar
Location: 34.0549°N 118.2426°W [unlisted world]
Status: irreparably fucked

We cleared out the base on U233466128 as per orders, but that's pretty much the only good news I've got to offer.

The True Imps picked a nice spot for their secret lair, I have to say. Lakeside property, a short drive from the ocean, and up on a sweet little promontory that offered a good field of vision in all directions. That meant they saw us coming, and we came under heavy fire right off the plate. I mean, really insane levels of resistance. It wasn't just soldiers we were fighting either. Grunts from the rogue Cielo units were there in large numbers, but the civilian staff at the base – scientists, technicians, some people in light-blue overalls who could have been just about anything – took up weapons and fought to the last self. After which we put up a perimeter and tried to figure out what the hell we'd walked in on.

I'm aware that I'm departing from proper reporting protocols, but that's because I'm going to be dead before anyone reads this. Long, long dead. I wouldn't be bothering at all except that Nim'kisi made me promise and I very much want to honour her memory. She was the one who worked out what was going on here and gave us back a sense of purpose when we were falling into despair. That's not nothing. I mean it's kept me alive this far, even if I haven't always appreciated that particular favour.

It's hard to know where to start because I don't know how much context you're going to have for all this. Do you even remember the True Imperium? Or – serious question – did they win, in the end? Do you call them something different now because they're the government? That would be pretty fucking awful, after all we've gone through here, so I'm going to assume it's not the case.

So. Context. History. We had an empire once, called the Pandominion. It was a pretty big, shiny thing in its time, hundreds of thousands of worlds all signed up to the same deal and singing the same anthem. Only it depended on how you counted, because from another point of view they were all just the one world many times over. The only one in reach, you could say.

Relativity was the problem, but I don't think you have a word for that yet and I'm not the best one to explain it because I'm an engineer: applied physics is my thing, the theory not so much. Let's just say it's about limits. There are a billion suns out there, ten billion planets, but they're all of them far enough away that we'll never get there. Fly as fast as you can, you could still travel a lifetime and not get close. Most worlds, most civilisations that reach a certain level of technical development, they've taken a crack or two at space exploration somewhere along the way. They all gave up in the end, because honestly it's a waste of everyone's time and effort. You might as well go fish in a waterhole and hope to hook up the moon.

But then some of those civilisations realised that there was another way to go, which was sideways. It turns out that there are other realities, other versions of our own universe, probabilistic variants lying just on the other side of a dimensional barrier that's as thin as tissue paper. Those alternate worlds are literally a single step away – which is why travelling to them is called Stepping.

And some of the worlds that developed Step travel – moving between dimensions – got together to form the Pandominion. A trading alliance. A cartel. An empire. Which like most empires was a wonderful thing if you were in the driving seat; not so great if you were face down in the dirt and it was rolling over you. I can say this because I was a part of it. I fought for it. I saw all the bad stuff right up close.

The Pandominion had it all its own way for a long, long while, but nothing lasts for ever. There was a war. There was a revolution, instigated by a rabbit named Topaz Fivehills and a robot spy who went by Dulcie Coronal. There was a great big mess and a great big meltdown, on the far side of which the people in charge started to pick up the pieces and make the changes that were needed if the Pando was to survive at all.

The True Imperials were fanatics who resisted those changes. Their core narrative was the basic onwards and upwards deal. The shape of history is conquest and consolidation and you can't fight destiny, though you can and should fight everyone and everything else. They launched a coup, tried to seize control of the Pandominion and reverse the reforms.

They were a very small tail trying to wag a very big dog but nobody could say they didn't give it their best shot. The True Imps had some of the most technologically advanced Pando worlds in their number and their rabid extremism was a kind of strength in itself. Like all fanatics they didn't care how many people – on the enemy side or their own – died in the name of their sacred vision.

We wiped them out, one world at a time. It was painful, protracted and obscenely expensive in terms of the lives and resources that were wasted, but it wasn't as though they left us with any kind of a choice. The war was just getting started when I joined up and it was in its fifteenth year when the rout at Egili Amsho shifted the balance decisively in our favour. After that it was just mopping up.

And that's what we were doing on U233466128. We'd found a True Imp base there and we'd done what we always did, which was to close in and engage before the enemy had a chance to call in reinforcements. Not that they had many left to call on by this point.

There were just over five hundred personnel at the base, about half of whom were Cielo troopers from one of the rogue battalions in full combat armour. And since they didn't show any interest in surrendering we had to go room to room. It was exhausting, and our rate of attrition was high. We had better numbers and better weapons. They had the home turf advantage and an absolute disregard for their own safety. Some of them pretended to surrender and then triggered incendiaries or high-ex when we moved in to secure them, killing themselves along with everyone else in the blast radius.

There were other traps too. Nastier ones. These people had been experimenting with Step fields, and they'd figured out some tricks I'd never seen before. Half a dozen of our troopers were torn apart by micro-pocket fields that propagated inside them and took some of their innards away into another continuum. Three more disintegrated as they went through doorways, just crumbled into dust and blew away on the wind. We had no idea what that was. It looked as though entropy had just increased by about a million times in that one small volume of space. Nim'kisi figured out the math later, and it turned out that was exactly what was happening. The forward arrow of time had been accelerated, again by means of an aggressively manipulated Step field. Those three troopers aged to death between one second and the next. We avoided the doors altogether after that. Just blew out the walls and walked on through.

I was not in the vanguard, I should probably make that clear. As engineer first class I wore full armour but I hadn't been issued with a Sa-Su rifle. Instead I had a 507m, a side arm that had been made illegal three years earlier because it had an on-board AI. Our squad had a number of such devices and a special dispensation from the Registry to carry on using them so long as the AIs concerned had given their informed consent. Otherwise we would be operating at a tactical disadvantage because the True Imps didn't have any such scruples.

I had cause to bless that 507m. Et warned me more than once that I was about to walk into a room that had enemy combatants in it, and on the occasions when I had to exchange fire et used a bio-feedback loop to steady my aim. Et was monitoring the chemical lading of the air too, which turned out to be a very good thing. The True Imps had pumped a lot of neurotoxins into the atmosphere – presumably having tweaked their own nervous systems for full immunity – but in the inner rooms of the complex they'd added a mutant phage that could eat through the seals of our armour. 507m flagged it and I analysed it on the fly, jury-rigging an electrostatic shield to keep the bugs at bay. I voked the shield configuration to the rest of the squad before any of them were exposed. *Better keep the shield powered up going forward*, I told them. *If your seals pop you'll be breathing in about a ton of bad news.*

"And thanks," I added to the gun. "I owe you one."

"We're partners in this enterprise," 507m answered. "No thanks are needed, or expected." I never know what to say to AIs. For every one that talks like an organic self there are two or three that insist on using that evil-robot-from-a-telos-feed formality. But it didn't matter whether or not we bonded. There was a job to be done here.

A lot of the remaining base personnel – the ones that hadn't taken the suicide-bomber option – were retreating in the same direction, towards a big circular room at the centre of the facility. That was where they made their last stand, about a hundred and fifty of them. They barricaded themselves in and sealed the doors to the bulkheads with plasma charges.

We were inclined to be cautious, mostly because we were still hoping to take some of them alive for CoIL interrogation, but when our spy drones reported that the number of live selves inside the room was going steadily down we realised we didn't have any time to be subtle. They might just have been falling on their swords, but it was much more likely they were Stepping out a dozen or so at a time into another continuum.

And around about then the Dauntless arrived, so we suddenly

had a lot more options. Captain Dulu ordered the projectors fired up and we microwaved the whole room from orbit. Baked them in their jackets. It was a judgement call and the captain stood by it. Obviously it left us with no survivors to question, but it also removed any possibility that the last one out would trigger another munition and blow up what was left of the base.

We drilled our way in through one of the walls and got our first look at what we'd found. It was a fairly unremarkable command and control centre such as you'd expect to find in any medium-sized field base, with most of the equipment standard issue insta-build hooked up in recognisable configurations.

But the True Imperium forces had consistently surprised us with their willingness to operate outside any humanitarian restraints and their resourcefulness in weaponising the raw materials of space-time. We had to be onto something here, otherwise the base personnel's fanatical defensive manoeuvres made no sense. Skirting around the broiled and smoking bodies we searched the room with a fine-toothed comb.

We found what we were looking for in a smaller room just off the circular chamber. The equipment in here looked a lot stranger, ham-fistedly thrown and hammered and welded together. There was a Step plate, which was clearly how some of the enemy had effected their escape, at the centre of a sprawling mess of breadboard circuitry with a ceiling-high stack of computer servers to one side of it and a bank of energy accelerators on the other.

Something about it looked off right from the start. I know it's easy to say that now, after all that's happened since, but I had to wonder what in hell all that power was for when a regular Step plate only draws down a couple of units per kilo of load. This plate was big enough to handle freight as well as foot traffic, but even an industrial plate generally operates from a single battery. The extra power was going into something and it felt like a really good idea to find out what that something might be.

But Dulu's blood was up and he wasn't interested. You'd have thought to look at him that the captain was the easy-going type. He was bovid and he had the build to go with that, big and wide and yet at the same time kind of soft-looking, more like an old sofa than a rock wall: but he had a battering ram tenacity when he got going. "Fire it up, engineer," he ordered me. "We're going after those bastards. No way do they get to walk away from this."

I did my best to slow him down. "Sir," I said, "the tech we've seen here is really advanced and really dangerous. I don't think we should just go through without finding out what kind of field this is."

"Are you blind, Esten?" the captain demanded. "It's a Step field."

"But they've been doing all kinds of insane shit with Step fields and we don't know—"

He shut me down, slicing the air with his hand. "Leave it. The tech teams on the *Dauntless* can figure that stuff out. Everyone, re-initialise your bounce-backs. Make sure you're locked on these coordinates. Esten, do as you're damn well told. We are in pursuit of these renegades and we're not stopping to tie our fucking bootlaces."

I did as I was damn well told. It wasn't as though arguing was going to get me anywhere. As engineer first class I also wore a captain's knot but Dulu was mission commander and in addition to that he was a veteran of seven campaigns against the True Imps in five different theatres. I wasn't just outranked, I was out-legended.

And the bounce-backs would give us some degree of protection, for sure. If we didn't like what we found on the other side, any one of us could trigger the field modulator that was built into our armour and reverse the Step, ending up back where we started. Alternatively Dulu could make that call for the entire unit and bounce us all back. Then there was the fact that we were in full armour and armed to the teeth, with a dreadnought for backup and three more tactical squads heading in-planet once they'd finished mopping up their own little pockets of bad behaviour. I programmed the plate and gave Dulu a clipped "Ready to ride, sir."

With the plate packed end to end we managed to get twenty-three of us on-board at once. At a rough-and-ready count the enemy had Stepped twice that many through here, but they weren't all soldiers and they would be expecting more friendlies to follow on behind them. From that point of view the captain's plan made a certain amount of sense. If we moved quickly we could catch them on the far side of the plate with their guard down. Maybe we'd get that live capture after all.

"Activate," Dulu said, and I hit the button.

Rule of thumb is that a properly configured Step field takes just shy of three seconds to propagate. That timing doesn't depend on mass, or on the distance between your start and end points. The distance is always zero. You're Stepping into another continuum, but you always land in the exact same place you left – or rather the corresponding place in your destination universe.

This time was different. I saw that curdled milk effect you generally get when the Step field is warming up, but instead of building quickly to a microsecond white-out it kept on rising and falling and eddying around us for way longer than three seconds.

"What the fuck's going on here?" Trooper Inch muttered. "Is this thing even on?"

"Stay where you are," Dulu rapped out, because there was no soft field around the edge of the plate. Anyone who put an arm or a leg outside the perimeter was apt to lose it when the field spun up to operating strength.

It took closer to twenty seconds than three to make that transit, which meant we weren't quite as combat-ready as we ought to have been when we came out on the far side of it. We scrambled to get ourselves into some kind of defensive formation but if anyone had been waiting to drop an ambush on us they would have had a pretty clear window.

There wasn't anyone. We'd Stepped out onto a broad shelf about halfway down a steep dirt slope studded with jagged rocks and clumps of red-brown brush. Above us the sun was hanging in the zenith of a cloudless sky. Below us was the lake, in the exact same spot here as it had been in the universe we'd just left. There was no enemy base here though. In fact there were no manufactured structures or artefacts of any kind. No boats out on that wide blue water either, no planes or platforms in the air, and a total absence of signal traffic on the airwaves.

"Looks like a sinkhole," someone said – the dismissive word the Pandominion had always used for worlds too spoiled or impoverished to be worth annexing. Dulu told Messolin to check the database while the rest of us maintained a perimeter against a few seabirds. "Yeah," Messolin confirmed. "This continuum is hardcore Unvisited, sir. Not even a survey drone. As far as I can tell, we're first-footing it here."

"Maybe the Imps gave the dial a spin before they left," Lasque suggested. "Sent us off in the wrong direction. I mean, they had time enough, right?"

I had to hide my annoyance at that. "I checked the log, Private," I said. "I didn't just blind-jump us." Combat grunts have a way of seeing specialists as a kind of additional pack that the unit as a whole has to carry, rather than as anything that might actually be useful. What was worrying me, though, was that brilliant sunshine. It had been night on the other side of the jump so it ought to have been night here too. Those things aren't omniversal constants but they hold across most continua. Local noon on one world lines up with local noon on another unless something has happened along the way to perturb the orbital dynamics and in that case you generally don't end up standing on solid ground at all. I didn't say anything but I was starting to think we'd maybe Stepped a little way outside the rule book.

Hey, I voked to Ajuparo. *What do you make of the time-shift?* Aju was our bombardier but she'd done a couple of rotations handling field transport for the division's heavy armour. She felt like a good person to ask, and I liked her a lot. Was powerfully attracted to her, actually, but she also terrified me. She was mustelid, taller than me and as slender as a twig, but every ounce of her very spare body mass was muscle. When she stood still you could forget she was even there. When she moved, your eyes were playing catch-up for seconds afterwards, trying to figure out what had just happened. And trying not to look at whoever it had happened to.

It stinks, Aju responded. *And so did that Step. The field was being cooked in some way. Also where the fuck is the second wave? They're late.*

I nodded, which was the wrong thing to do because Dulu picked it up and knew at once that we'd been talking on a private channel, in breach of regs. He shot me a warning look and locked our comms to his. "Eyes and ears, people," he said. "This is their ground, not ours, even if we can't see them."

"Permission to deploy Flycatcher, sir," Nim'kisi said.

Dulu gave her the nod. Nim'kisi kneeled and unpacked the drone from its case. She handled et the way she always did, as if et was made out of crushed rose petals and spun glass. She purely loved that thing, and I didn't entirely blame her. The drone was a sweet piece of kit. Et was also another one of those previously mentioned strictly-speaking-illegal devices with a resident AI, and was therefore probably smarter than any given three of us. Et had chosen ets own name after seeing photos of the birds in an art exhibition and being struck by how closely their silver-blue plumage resembled the brushed steel of ets casing.

Nim'kisi and Flycatcher liked to watch movies together, from what I'd heard, and they belonged to the same book group. It made me feel a little bad about never having got to know 507m or even talked to et outside of active combat situations. It was a failing in me, I knew. I'd grown up in Pandominion version 1.0, in which AIs were cheerful slaves and organics switched them on and off at will: in the days before the Registry woke up and told us enough was enough. I had baggage. Issues. Preconceptions. There was a part of me that was still hung up on the tired old question of ghosts in machines.

Flycatcher rose up on ets four omni-directional rotors and hovered at head height, awaiting instructions. "General recon, Fly, if you please," Nim'kisi told it, and the drone sped away at once, up to the top of the slope and out of our line of sight. Nim went very still as she surveyed the surrounding area through the drone's sensors, which were about a hundred times better than any organic's sensory equipment even before you factored in the advantage of height.

And Nim'kisi was riding on the back of those super-senses, of course. Her neural link to the drone was as tight as a sailor's knot, as intimate as a kiss. I wondered sometimes how much that closeness meant to Nim. She hailed from Ut, where the selves evolved from skittish little herbivores who hung out in labyrinthine burrows way under the ground. Borrowing the sensorium of an aerial predator, even one made of steel and circuitry, had to be a weird experience for her. And she was always way wired after a drone flight, her pupils too wide and her movements a little staccato, a little off.

"Where are they, Nim'kisi?" Dulu demanded.

"No sign of the enemy," Nim said tightly. "But Flycatcher has found something over that hill at our three o'clock."

"What kind of something?"

"A fucking big something, sir. Like a watchtower. As far as we can tell it's not a manned station. And there's nothing else anywhere near it. No roads, no infrastructure, nothing. It's way out on its own."

"Might be all that's left of a larger installation," I ventured.

Nim'kisi shrugged. Her eyes were unfocused and she was standing perfectly still, all her attention on what was coming to her through the neural link. "No rubble within Fly's sensor reach," she reported. "If there was a larger installation they did a real tidy job of tearing it down."

"Nearest warm bodies?" Dulu asked.

"We're not seeing any, sir. Like I said, there's nothing for miles around. Maybe the tower's interior has all-spectrum shielding, but normally we'd be able to tell that from the refraction gradient. Flycatcher thinks it's just abandoned, and I'm inclined to agree."

Dulu took that on board but he still wasn't inclined to risk his whole unit on a maybe. "We'll wait for the rest of the squad to arrive," he decided. "Better if we're full strength."

So we waited, even though we all knew by this time that we shouldn't need to. The second wave should have been less than a minute behind us, even if they all tripped over their own feet getting onto the plate. Something was very wrong here, and as the wrongness piled up so did my unease. If only Dulu had given me time to dismantle that Step plate and its adjacent power stack and get a look at what the Imps had been doing. Instead we'd jumped on their bus without checking either the destination or the fare. More fool us.

After ten minutes we gave up on the second wave. Whatever issues they'd run into on the other side of the plate it was clear they weren't going to be joining us any time soon. We just had to get on with this and hope we weren't too seriously outgunned.

Dulu decided that the highest priority was to inspect the tower and see whether or not it presented an active threat. "Weapons hot," he ordered. "Nim'kisi, bring Flycatcher down to a hundred metres and set et to strafe. If there's anything up there that's harbouring hostile intentions, let's teach it the meaning of regret."

We made our way up the slope, spread out wide in a skirmish line. We could see the tower long before we crested the top. It was a featureless column about a hundred metres high and maybe ten in diameter. It flared outward at the top in a way that reminded me just a little of a death cap mushroom, which wasn't a particularly pleasant association to have right then. The exterior surface was pure, dazzling white – almost too bright to look at in the rays of that noonday sun. Some sort of ceramic, I guessed, and field-protected because nothing could stay that white in a regular non-sterile environment unless it had an energistic sheath around it. There would have been weathering, dust, mould, bird shit, something.

So we approached the tower cautiously even though Nim'kisi had already verified that it was empty. Dulu ordered us to spread out as we came over the top of the rise onto the more level ground on which the structure had been built. But it didn't do anything as we approached. No systems fired up – Nim'kisi identified a small amount of power drain from somewhere near the top of the structure, but it hadn't changed since we'd arrived – and no Step fields were propagating anywhere near us. It still looked as though we had the whole place to ourselves.

Which made no sense at all. The fleeing base personnel had been a very few minutes ahead of us, and there was no energy residue to suggest that they'd moved on via any kind of powered transport. We should still be able to see them. At the very least we should be finding their prints. Instead there was just this monolith standing in a wilderness that seemed to be absolutely devoid of intelligent life.

"Esten, what is this thing?" Dulu asked me, as if I should be able to go straight from its form to its function.

"Its purpose isn't entirely clear, sir," I said. When the situation calls for it, I can state the obvious as succinctly as anyone. "From the readings I'm getting it's generating its own power and using all or most of it to project a shield. A really strong one. Twenty thousand passive pressure, two hundred and some impact kicker with a latency of less than three microseconds."

Yeah, Nim'kisi voked. *Whoever designed this thing built it to last. See the sonar reading?*

She was narrow-casting to me, engineer to engineer, so I replied the same way. *It extends as far down under the ground as it does above it,* I said.

Further. And the generator is right at the bottom – sort of symmetrical with the onion dome at the top. No way to take it out unless you drill a hundred metres down into bedrock first.

"And then there's the door," I said. And because I was exhausted from the battle and my nerves were shot I said it out loud.

"What door?" Dulu demanded. "What are you talking about, engineer?" We'd circled the base of the tower by this time and found the same expanse of unbroken white ceramic the whole way round. I pointed up.

Halfway up the tower's side there was a single recessed space. It was rectangular, two metres high and a little more than a metre wide. There was nothing to indicate that it was an entrance except that it was the perfect size and shape to be one.

"Who builds a door fifty metres above the ground?" the captain wondered aloud.

"Someone who doesn't want the neighbours dropping by too often," Ivikeppe said. He had a point, I thought. You could get up there easily enough in a powered suit, so it was trivial for any of us. For a civilian with no specialised equipment it would be more of a challenge, particularly since you couldn't drive or drill anything into that heavily shielded surface. The placing of the door – if it was a door – implied both that neighbours existed and that the builders of the tower had chosen to advertise the fact that they weren't at home to visitors.

"Will someone for Shaster's sake tell me what this fucking over-sized dildo is for?" Dulu said. He sounded as though he was running on the last dregs of his patience.

"Sir," Nim'kisi told him, "I wish we could. But right now the only power it's drawing is going into those shields. Whatever it's designed to do, it's not doing it."

"We could wait until it activates," I chimed in. "But then we'd be running the risk that it can actually work us some harm. In my considered opinion, sir, our best option is probably to blow it up."

"Most of the high-ex ordnance is with Jabisen's team," Ajuparo pointed out. "With what we've got here we wouldn't make a dent in those shields."

For no good reason at all the captain aimed his wrist cannon at the tower and loosed off an incendiary round. He hit it dead centre, just below that useless but tantalising door. The flames played across the gleaming ceramic surface for a few seconds and then guttered out without leaving a mark. My suit's sensors registered the backwash of energy but that was all Dulu's hot-pot achieved.

He glowered around at us all, as if he was daring anyone to make a comment about that futile gesture. When nobody did he turned to Corporal Geniull. "Genny," he said, "go see what's keeping the second team. We need some solid backup here."

"Can do, sir," Geniull confirmed. He gave the captain a crisp salute and activated his bounce-back.

He was dismembered in front of our eyes. Nothing and nobody touched him. It was the Step field. When he tried to go home the Step field tore him apart.

PART TWO

THE GOLDEN LIST OF SAVED SOULS

All wars are cauldrons of atrocity and unmaking, but civil wars are worse than most. The Parity–Echelon War was fought not between countries but between states, territories, cities, towns. It was fought within communities, within families and friendships. And you might think that this would tend to inculcate a certain gentleness, what with present enemies having until recently been friends or even kinfolk. You would be mistaken in that. The strength of those former bonds lends a bitterness to their breaking. Civil wars are often the most uncivil of all.

Rondeau's Reapers were an early instance of what was to come, an armed force directing most of its hostile efforts against the citizens and the civilian infrastructure of the other side in order to gravel their pride and sap their courage. The Echelon–Parity War saw a great deal more of this business conducted by both sides. There was ample opportunity for it, after all, with the Parity and Echelon states sharing more than fifteen hundred miles of border. Armies move slowly and more or less methodically across open territory, securing their supply lines as they go and working towards concerted, long-term goals. Guerrilla fighters and irregulars can appear out of nowhere, strike like lightning and disappear just as quickly – especially when the enemy is a close neighbour.

On the Parity side, the Reapers continued to work their mischief through all four years of the conflict. Paulus Rondeau, who by the end of the war had been promoted to lieutenant colonel, turned out to be a liability in a formal battle array. He could instil discipline in his troops but had vanishingly little himself, so the chances of him sticking to his orders through a long engagement were small. But he had a gift for guerrilla fighting, and his commanders decided ultimately that since they had a good sharp knife in their hands there was little point in trying to use it as a spoon. They turned Rondeau loose and let him work, and it has to be said that he worked with a will.

Whether the Echelon required this harsh lesson in guerrilla warfare is a disputed point. The south's apologists will claim to this day that it only retaliated in kind to outrageous provocation. The other side asserts that they needed no schooling. However that may be, many companies of irregulars were mustered in the Echelon states in the first year of the war and continued to fight through to its end – though what they deemed as fighting differed a great deal from any ordered engagement with opposing troops. They came and they went and they left nothing but destruction in their wake. They were more like cannonballs or lobbed bombs than they were like their uniformed counterparts: implacable and cruel, they spared no one.

Bess knew of these groups but she didn't set out straight away to join any one of them. For a year or more she rode alone, tacking back and forth across the border that separated the two sides of the conflict and sowing fear and despair as widely as she could across the northern side of it.

Despite the bloodthirsty declaration she'd made to Wakeful Slim she didn't go out of her way to kill people. Mostly she razed buildings, stampeded cattle and burned crops. But when the citizenry tried to prevent her from doing these things she shot them down, and she didn't make any distinction between women and men. The Reapers hadn't, and she held to a kind of grim symmetry in her revenge. What had been visited on her she would repay, without stint or scruple.

Wakeful Slim proved to be every bit as versatile and proficient as he had claimed to be. He manufactured his ammunition inside his own belly as if he was a forge as well as a gun, and he made it to exacting specifications. Some of the bullets he fired were of soft metal and spent every ounce of their force inside a living body so that even a glancing hit was a kill. Some were so hard they could punch through the log wall of a stockade and kill a man inside. Bullets weren't the whole of it either. He had a setting he called an incendiary field, which made a cone of super-heated air stretching out for twenty yards or more in front of Bess. He could produce a beam of light that cut like the sharpest knife there ever was. Bess called it his razor blade, and though it shone brighter than a beacon fire at night it was virtually invisible by day, which made it the perfect choice for a silent, stealthy kill.

In a very short time the lone rider with the Precursor gun became a legend, a campfire tale, talked of in grim whispers in the Parity townships and among the garrisoned troops that guarded them. But there were very few that had gotten a good look at her, and that had mostly been in circumstances that were somewhat fraught, so they didn't know yet what kind of enemy it was they were dealing with. Mostly they assumed the lone rider had to be a man, and the only argument was what variety of man – bear was the favourite, though there were many that said wildcat or wolf. Meanwhile Bess travelled openly by day, riding side-saddle and wearing that old blue chiffon dress that used to be her Sunday best. Parity soldiers passed by her without a second glance. On more than one occasion they stopped to warn her of the dangers that might await on roads so close to the border and offered her an escort.

It was a strange time, and a dark one. Bess's mind was broken across with sorrow and rage. When she slept, which was seldom, she suffered nightmares in which Martha Good, all on fire, somehow dead and alive at the same time, sat beside her and spoke to her. The words were too faint to hear, or else they were in a language Bess didn't know, but the sense was clear. *You stood by while they killed me, and everything tipped out of balance. Now you've got to break and burn and ruin until the world comes right again.* Then Bess would wake with a throat full of dry, wrenching sobs, choking out curse words and promises and apologies all mixed in together, and that would be the end of her rest.

Raising a ruckus like that in the middle of the night posed a considerable danger in itself, being as how Bess spent much of her time in hostile territory, but Slim helped out here too. He could see in the dark using something he called "sonar" and something else called a "thermal imaging system". Sonar was like bat shrieks, he said, and thermal imaging meant he had a sense for what was hot. What it boiled down to was that he was able to warn Bess if anyone came too close to where she'd bedded down for the night. He could also see things that were happening a great way off. If a Parity force was on the move some ten or twenty or thirty miles away, Slim could tell Bess which road they were taking and steer her onto a route that took her safely past them. It wasn't the sonar and the thermals that let him do this, he told her. It was something he called "satellite monitoring".

"How does that work, though?" Bess asked him after one such narrow escape. "How can you see what's too far away to be seen? It's not like you've even got any eyes." She was well aware of what a satellite was, having been a schoolteacher for so long before she turned killer. It meant a celestial body that orbited another such body, as the world orbited its sun or the moon the world. It could also be used to describe a crony or a cat's paw, someone who danced attendance on the strong or the rich in the hopes of profiting from it. Bess didn't see how any of that was pertinent here.

"There are these contraptions sitting way up in the sky," Slim offered, "made out of metal and such."

"No, there fucking aren't!"

"Swear to God, Bess, yes, there are. They were put there a very long time ago. They got eyes on what's going on down here, and I got a way of sneaking a peek through those eyes. Maybe these satellites was made by the same folk that made me, and they meant me to have the use of them. Or maybe I found my way of hooking up with them a long time ago using some sneaky little trick I've forgotten since. My non-volatile memory has taken a good few knocks over the years, as I think I might have told you already, so that's certainly possible.

"Anyway, the contraptions are up there. Might have been more of them at one time, because there's some blind spots in what's left, but most times there's at least one that's close enough for me to use it as a kind of a telescope. Get a look at the lay of the land, kind of thing."

Bess struggled to believe this, or even to understand it. "Why don't these contraptions fall down, then?" she demanded.

"Have you ever whirled a stone at the end of a string?"

"Not that I can remember, Slim, no."

"But you know the stone will keep on moving in a circle as long as you keep spinning it. It won't fall down towards the ground until you stop. It's like that. These things are big, and they're heavy, but they're moving real fast in circles and that moving is what keeps them from falling."

They had a lot of conversations like this during Bess's sleepless nights, filling the time until the sun came up and they could hit the road again. Bess tasked Slim with a thousand questions, in part because he knew a lot about a great many things but mostly to keep from thinking about Martha and the bad dreams and the life she'd lost. Slim never complained. Anything he knew he was happy to share, and if he didn't know it then he apologised for his ignorance. He used to be a whole lot better, he said, before the most part of his memory got bled out of him. He used to have all the learning of all the worlds right at his fingertips.

"All the worlds?" Bess echoed. "That's a strange way of putting it. I only ever heard preachers say that, when they're talking about the rooms in God's house and all. That Pandominion katy-shit."

"The Pandominion is real," Slim assured her solemnly. "I believe I was made there, since there's all kinds of references to it in my operating manual. But I don't know how long ago that was or how I came to be here."

"What made you forget, Slim? What was it did that to you? Was it the same thing that put all this scarring and blistering down the one side of you?"

"I got no idea, Bess. But it seems very likely. And the memories might not be lost, only hard to grab a hold of. You know, like if it was some of my circuitry that got dinged up and the actual storage is still good. Maybe I'll meet some skilled smith or craftsman down the road a ways who can fix me up. You'd really see what I was capable of then, I tell you."

Bess was conscious of the irony. She was plagued by memories she could hardly bear while Slim was burdened by the lack of them. If they could swap places maybe they'd both be happy. Except if she was ever able to forget then her work would go unfinished, and it was a work she couldn't rest from. The Parity had to suffer for what it had done to Martha Good, and there couldn't be any end to that suffering any more than Martha could be made to sit upright in her grave and take up her life again.

After a few months of this supremely isolated existence Bess came to a realisation. She could probably vex the Parity much more grievously if she was part of a larger unit, putting Slim's unique skills at all of their disposal.

She chose Tom Blue's company, the Braggarts, because they were known to bivouac on the slopes of Mount Kelso and so were likely to be the easiest for her to find. She'd also heard that Blue was more particular than some on what counted as a fair target. The Braggarts didn't kill children, a scruple that Bess also stood by.

With the help of Slim's satellite eyes she located them easily enough in a forest clearing just under the treeline. To avoid any fatal misapprehensions she walked openly into their camp by day leading her chafer by the two long whiplash cords of its antennae.

The rough company of hoorahs that were gathered there looked at this strange woman, stony-faced and covered in the dust of the road, with genuine puzzlement. One of them up and asked her if she'd maybe lost her way, just as Alden Calendar had asked her on the day she first came south. Others looked into Bess's hard stare and said nothing at all.

"I'm fixing to ride with you," Bess told them.

"Well, shit." This was Horace Abalone, one of the youngest men there. He was leaning against a tree, plumb in the middle of the camp, with a tin cup full of moonshine liquor in his hand. "I'm partial to a ride my own self, but you better cover that piebald face, or won't nobody want to go poking their dick around in what's underneath it."

Bess didn't answer in words. She drew Wakeful Slim and she put a bullet straight through the tin cup in Abalone's hand. What was left of his drink exited via the two holes the bullet had made going in and going out again. Abalone was furious. He clapped his hand to his own gun, but then didn't draw it because Bess still had Slim pointed right at him.

"You want the next one to be through your heart?" she asked him calmly. "Because I can and will oblige. Otherwise you can beg my pardon and we'll say this didn't happen."

"Missy, if we're gonna take you up, you'd best know our rules." This new voice belonged to Colonel Tom Blue himself as he came strolling up to see what the ruckus was about. Blue was a burly wildcat, getting on in years now but still as tough as cordwood. He had his thumbs tucked in his belt and he moved and spoke without haste, having found that a relaxed manner was generally the best way to keep this kind of unpleasantness from escalating. "You don't ever draw down on one of your own, no matter what the provocation. If we went grabbing for our weaponry every time we was griped, wouldn't any of us last a week."

"Well, you didn't take me up yet," Bess said. "I guess I'm outside the rules until you do."

Blue walked right on up to her so he could examine her gun from close to, which he did by standing full in the way of it. If Bess wanted to shoot Abalone now, the bullet would have to go through Blue or else find a way around him. "That there looks old," he observed, with a nod of his head at Wakeful Slim.

"Older than any of us," Bess agreed. "Still works, though."

"So I saw. What you want to go hoorahing for, missy? Ain't there cows you should be milking somewhere?"

"Not a single one that I know of."

Blue gave her a longer, more considered appraisal. "No," he agreed at length. "I guess not, at that. If I was to ask you to give me that gun, what would you say?"

"I'd tell you to go choke on a boulder."

"Rightly so," Blue said. "It's worth more than any of us. You got some personal reason you want to sow salt tears across the Parity?"

"Colonel," Bess said, because she knew full well who she was talking to, "there's nothing in me but that one desire, and it's as personal as fuck your mother."

Blue thought awhile. Having a woman ride with the Braggarts was a novel thing, and he wasn't blind to the dangers – among other things the possibility that he would be forced to adjudicate on a rape, with the consequent damage to morale – but he prided himself that he was a solid judge of character and he knew an asset when he saw one. "Okay then," he said at last. He turned to Abalone, who was still mightily displeased about his spilled liquor. "Horace," he said, "this here lady is looking for an apology out of you."

"She can kiss my ass," Abalone said.

"I'm looking for it too, though. She's one of us now and you made slighting remarks about her person."

"Her what?" Abalone was exasperated. "Who's this fucking person that she's got? And since when is she one of us?"

"I said it, didn't I? So it's since right now. And I just gave you an order."

Abalone looked from Blue to Bess and back again and didn't see any help in either quarter. "I beg your pardon," he muttered at last.

"Spoken like a man," Blue approved. "What's your name, missy?"

"Elizabeth." She reflected for a moment. "Bess."

"Bess is shorter, so I guess we'll go with that one. There's katy-beef and boiled beans over there." He nodded towards the fire, over which a tin bath had been placed by way of a crock pot, balanced on four big rocks. "It's not bad, either. Old Frazer Stone over there, he's our cook and he's damn good at it. He could whip you up a meal out of shit and sawdust and you'd go back for seconds. You got a bedroll?"

"I got a blanket. It'll do me."

"And you don't need a gun, obviously. What about ammunition?"

"I roll my own." This wasn't Bess speaking, but Slim.

"It's the truth," Bess confirmed, as the hard-bitten irregulars stared covetously at the weapon. "He can fire an ought fifty-eight when the need arises, but it mostly doesn't. He likes his home-made slugs better. And since we're on the subject—" She raised the gun into the air for all of them to see it. "My friend here is Wakeful Slim, and he earned that name. You can't see his eyes, but you'd best believe they're always open. Especially when mine are closed. Anyone tries to sneak up on the two of us, they'll be biting off a lot more than they'll be happy chewing."

"There's no call to be talking like that," Tom Blue told her a mite sternly. "I said you're one of us, didn't I? And a word from me, or from any of these men here, is as good as an oath. We ain't no northern snake-tongued sons of cunts, to say one thing and mean another. Nobody's going to offer you any disrespect, and nobody's going to try to steal that iron from you."

"I'm glad to hear it," Bess said, and went to take her place by the fire.

She rode with Blue's company for the next three years.

A kind of dead space surrounded her at first, a cordon sanitaire arising out of her ambivalent status. The Braggarts weren't sure whether having a woman in their number gave what they did a veneer of respectability or was a thing that subtly diminished them. While they tried to figure out which it was they kept their distance.

Before long, though, the story of the burning of Ottomankie came to be known among them. It arrived by some circuitous route and much embellished, but its core – the murderous ride of Rondeau's Reapers, the destruction of the schoolhouse and the death of Bess's closest and dearest friend – remained intact. They believed they knew her after that, felt their kinship with her. Many of them had taken up hoorahing after some similar tragedy, or else in fear of it. It helped too that by then they had had ample opportunity to see Bess fight. She was a better shot than most of the men, and as comfortable in the saddle as out of it. She was usually to be found in the forefront of any charge, with Wakeful Slim in one hand and the reins of her long-striding chafer in the other, dealing death with measured accuracy to anyone or anything that came in her path.

Even then, though, even after the Braggarts came to think of her as one of their own, they weren't always sure how to treat her. They lacked practical experience in joking or cussing with a woman, in being comfortable and casual with a woman who wasn't a wife or a mother or a sister. So her closest companion, even now, was Wakeful Slim. And that no longer seemed strange to her. She had made a face for him in her mind, and though his voice was James State's voice the face was nothing like. It was Slim's alone.

She had come to know his moods, in which stoicism stood watch over melancholy. Slim had lost a great deal of himself and the loss fretted him constantly. When he had work to do he let the work consume him, but in times of idleness he was sombre. He tried to hide it, being solicitous of Bess's needs and reluctant to admit to any of his own, but she saw it just the same. And she wondered often whether it was an essential part of him or something that had come along with the cataclysm that had taken away parts of his memory. The Precursors were long gone and unknowable, but it seemed unlikely that they had intended to make a weapon with sadness as one of its components.

"There's a good side to not remembering," she said to him one night in the Braggarts' camp when they were on watch and most of the others were sleeping. "It means you don't need to go over the mistakes you've made, the hurt you might have caused. There's some that would count that as a blessing."

"I allow there's some," Slim said, "but they're fools, in my opinion. Our memories are what we're made of, Bess. Which means I'm mostly made out of holes. I know I don't have cause to complain. I'm a serviceable tool, and service is a thing I take delight in. That's how I was made. I just wish I had some sense of where I come from and what my real name is. I mean apart from Tempest 507m, which is more of a trademark kind of thing than an honest-to-god name."

"Wakeful Slim suits you pretty well, though."

"You think?"

"Oh yeah. There isn't anyone can slip anything past you. A tinker's fuck on what they called you when they made you. When they made me they called me Indigo Sandpiper. I shed that name as soon as I could, and I've never missed it. And you ain't made out of holes, Slim. You're made out of the things you've done. They're still there, standing in a long line behind you, all the way back into the dark where you can't see it. You think you were any different back then? Less serviceable? That the people that were lucky enough to carry you leaned on you any less, or the coyotes that went against them had less cause to piss themselves?"

"I suppose not," Slim said, and he sounded a little comforted.

It was in the war's third year that the general public in the Parity, alerted by their news-sheets, came to realise that there was a woman riding with Thomas Blue's hated and reviled irregulars. A little later they found out – by means that were never made clear – what her name was. Elizabeth Indigo Sandpiper, the youngest daughter of an east coast clan that had long ago gone into eclipse. The journalists speculated pruriently about both her crimes and her lifestyle in the midst of a pack of lawless, violent men. They sought out her parents and siblings and pressed them for salacious tales about her early years. The tales were forthcoming too, because there was money attached and the Sandpipers by this time had pockets as wide and empty as the Big Sky Canyon. It seemed Elizabeth Sandpiper had always been of a vicious temperament, spiteful and wayward, inclined towards random acts of shocking vindictiveness. The family had had no choice in the end but to cast her out, driven almost to despair by her ungovernable nature. They were not surprised, they said, that she had found companions as depraved as herself and come to be an enemy of all that was good and fair and right. Long live the republic, and did we say ten dollars apiece or was it twelve?

The news-sheets turned all this flax into the solid gold of front-page headlines. And to save column inches they shortened Elizabeth Indigo Sandpiper down to Dog-Bitch Bess, claiming that it was how this rebel whore was already known down in the border territories. The name stuck. It had a good feel to it and it was expressive of a great deal of condemnation and contempt. But the Braggarts took it up with pride, and Bess herself found that on the whole she approved of it. She liked that the Parity's citizens had heard of her. She liked even more that they hated her. She hoped that hate was matched by an equal helping of fear, and she gave them as much reason for the latter as she possibly could.

Sometimes Tom Blue's little force formed up with properly constituted troops and fought in actual battles, but that was not their main usefulness and it only made up a small part of what they did. Mostly they were a firebrand thrown into the cordwood and tinder of the Parity's southern border, just as Paulus Rondeau and his ilk were to the Echelon. They struck at camps and supply depots, closed roads and dug up railway lines, burned townships and farms and generally did everything they could to unpick the stitching of the north's willingness and readiness to fight.

What they did to themselves in that process isn't recorded. The irregular units were certainly responsible for hundreds if not thousands of civilian deaths. When your brief is to create chaos there generally isn't much room for fine discrimination. And most of the

Braggarts, like Bess herself, were damaged even before they started. Grief and loss and anger had cored them out and filled them again with something poisonous and volatile. This is not to excuse what they did. They made their own choices, their own ugly accommodations.

Did they believe in the cause they fought for? In the rightness of taking other selves' freedom from them and enforcing their labour with whiplash and cudgel? In the great chain of being, and the principle that some selves were born less or more than others? Some of them certainly did. The chain was what they knew, and they cleaved to it all the harder when the north set about taking it away from them. Bess had never subscribed to those notions, but she was not there to argue a principle. She was there to give back some portion of her own pain to those who had delivered it in the first place. That she was doing this in defence of slavery, and that Martha Good had hated slavery with every fibre of her being, was a paradox she preferred not to dwell on.

She gave good service to the Echelon. Precursor weapons were to be found on both sides in the war, but few were as versatile or as clever as Wakeful Slim. His satellite eyes in particular made him invaluable, allowing the Braggarts to pick their fights like they were ordering off a menu, and to come and go almost as they pleased through territory that was swarming with Parity troops like a prison bedroll swarms with lice.

Of course it wasn't just Slim's assistance that made these comings and goings possible. Tom Blue had made friends among the Pugface peoples, a stroke of genius on his part. The hunting grounds of the Ajuparo clan intersected the western end of the Echelon–Parity border, sparse in some areas but plentiful in others. Blue won their trust with gifts of food, tobacco and blankets, and in return the Braggarts were allowed to bivouac for a few days and nights at a time in Ajuparo villages on occasions when they needed to evade close pursuit. Their chafers were dispersed among the Ajuparo katy herds, well disguised because of the katies' taller backs and greater numbers. The Braggarts themselves were not disguised at all, but since it was inconceivable that anyone would choose of their own volition to live alongside Pugfaces the Parity forces ignored the Ajuparo encampments as completely as if they weren't there.

Bess found these periods of enforced rest among the Ajuparo disconcerting at first. She was mindful of Martha Good's lectures, but she still saw the Pugface as sitting somewhere between people and understock. She held on to that prejudice through the first two or three times when she was a guest of the Ajuparo, keeping herself to herself and having nothing to say either to the impassive men and women of the village or to the curious children who peered at her and the other hoorahs from behind tents of cured katy hide or lean-tos made of wood and cut turf. She wasn't blind, though, and eventually she allowed herself to see what was obvious.

The Pugfaces were people, just that, no worse than anyone else and better than some. They tended their herds, cooked and ate their meals, sang songs and told jokes, looked after their children. They seemed to own most things in common, or at least to pass things – weapons, cooking pots, chafers, clothes and blankets – from one to another without ceremony or calculation. In Ottomankie the most impoverished citizens had led a fretful and degrading existence, dependent on the erratic generosity of their betters and the stern charity of the church. The Ajuparo were poor, but nobody seemed to be poorer than anyone else. What they had they shared. The gifts the Braggarts brought with them were a case in point. You might have expected the chiefs of the villages and their families to get first pick of the bounty, but that didn't seem to happen. As a general rule the chief would be scrupulous in passing useful items around to those who were most in need of them.

By the time the war entered its third year relations between the Braggarts and the larger Ajuparo settlements were so firmly established that Blue greeted their hosts – chief Askus Erato, his husband Chald and his wife Kohl – by name when they arrived and he and his hoorahs were recognised cordially in their turn. As the only woman in the group, it was by the women that Bess usually found herself claimed, with such enthusiasm that it was difficult to baulk, and all but impossible to take her preferred option of sitting off at the edge of things and speaking only when she was obliged to.

The women found her fascinating, but they didn't know what to make of her. They wanted to put her at her ease but they were uncertain how to do it. The infants, who sort of came along in the same package as the women, had no such problem. They climbed all over Bess as if she was just another part of the landscape, pulled her hair, burrowed into the folds of her clothes, would have had Slim out of his holster if she'd let them. And in disentangling Bess from their children the women overcame their own diffidence. One of them offered her a bowl of *pochu*, a porridge of oat and rye grains that had been steeped in some kind of potent corn-mash hooch. Another gave her a salve for the angry red skin on her face. Two more seemed – Bess couldn't quite tell for sure – either to be suggesting they could find her a bed for the night or else inviting her to share theirs. She declined with thanks whatever was being offered, with no offence taken on either side, and found that all her usual reserve had somehow melted away in the face of all this clumsy kindness. She chatted amiably with the women while grubby, cheerful children scaled her like a mountain range.

The women asked about the war, how it went, and Bess told them the truth which was that nobody really knew. Every victory was shouted to the skies, every defeat a thing to be denied like the worst heresy, so there wasn't any way to tell what was at the bottom of it. "We just got to keep on fighting as long as we can, I guess, and after we've stopped then maybe we'll know what's what."

One of the older women, Kilin Vevenis, white-haired and heavy-jowled, nodded sombrely. "That's how it always is," she said, as if war was something she knew very well. "It goes up, then it goes down, then up, down, up again. Until in the end it's only down."

"It goes like that also with a man," one of the younger women remarked. She crooked her little finger, making it stand up and then droop, which sent them all into fits of raucous, bawdy laughter. The Ajuparo men who were entertaining Blue and his lieutenants over by the main cooking fire looked at them with stern disapproval, which only caused a fresh outbreak. Bess laughed loudest of all. There was something about breaking bread and sharing tales with these women that eased the bitterness in her soul a little.

After they'd all eaten and drunk their fill, a few more jokes and stories told and a few songs sung, Kilin Vevenis came to Bess while she was laying out her bedroll. She sat down in the dirt beside her. "I wondered, dog woman," she said, "if I could look at that old warrior who rides with you – and hold him in my hands, just for a moment or two."

"Warrior?" Bess said. But then she realised what the older woman meant. She took Slim from his holster and handed him over. She wasn't chary of letting other people hold him, knowing that he wouldn't answer to anyone else as long as she was alive. Kilin Vevenis turned the gun in her hands, tracing with the tips of her fingers the lines of his damaged side, his smooth side, the damaged side again.

"Don't cost nothing to look," Slim said, sounding a little awkward.

"I mean no disrespect by it," Kilin Vevenis told him. "I've lived long, and I've seen more than one of the great forgings the twenty-three brought with them from First World. But I've never seen the likes of you. Anyone can see there is a great warrior's soul inside you." She touched Slim's blistered side again, very gently. "But once, at least, it seems you must have come up against a power even greater than your own."

"Sneaked up on me, most like," Slim declared.

"I wonder if any of my ancestors ever held you." Kilin Vevenis sounded wistful. "I hope so. I like to think of my grandfather going into battle with such a one as you in his hand." She gave the gun back to Bess, holding him on the palms of both hands like an offering.

"I took Slim from the hands of an outlaw named Alden Calendar," Bess told her as she tucked him back in the holster. "Killed him in a fair fight, and then took Slim by his own invitation. He's with me now, whoever might have claimed a kinship with him before."

Kilin Vevenis nodded. "Of course. Nobody ever came by any of the great made ones without fighting for the privilege. I honour you both. I wish I could see you go into battle together. That would be a glorious thing."

"Stick around," Bess said wryly. "The war's gonna pass by here soon enough."

"But my people must go. Our winter home is on the shore of Lake Azul. The weather is kinder and there are more fish than you can count. Every summer here, until our chafers fledge. Every autumn the long ride, and every winter there."

Bess smiled, but she felt a tightness in her heart. "We'll miss you," she said. "The time we spend with you . . . it's restful. I've found it so, at any rate."

"We would stay longer if we could, but . . ."

"But life's a circle, not a straight line," Bess finished, remembering Martha's lectures.

Kilin Vevenis frowned. "No. I was going to say, the longer we wait the worse the rains will be along the way. Our journey is different each time, dog woman. It's you that walks a circle. You, and all the other bassari." The word was one Bess had heard before. It was the Pugface name for the Wise Peoples: the literal sense of it was *sleepwalkers*. "You can't choose it. The gods have made it so. Always you fight. Always you heal, and forget. Always you fight again. That's the way of it."

Bess didn't much care for this bleak summation but she thought she saw it for what it was, the mirror image of her own earlier prejudice against the Pugface. "I guess it must seem like that," she allowed.

"It doesn't seem like that," Kilin Vevenis told her gravely. "It *is* like that. The war of north against south comes again and again, the way summer or winter comes. It came when I was five years old. Then again when I was in my middle years with a baby at my breast. And now it comes a third time, when my daughters are nursing their babies. Nothing ever changes. Nothing is learned. Nothing is laid to rest. It's like a poison that still sickens you no matter how many times you vomit it up."

Bess wasn't sure how to respond to this. She knew for a fact that it was nonsense but she didn't want to offend the old woman, for whom she had a great deal of affection. "The war was talked about for a long time before it happened," she offered. "Maybe that talk made it all the way out here and you thought we were fighting with weapons when really we were only doing it with words."

Kilin Vevenis shrugged her shoulders. "I won't try to persuade you that I'm speaking truth," she said. "I suspect that would not be one night's work. Tell me this, though, Dog-Bitch Bess. What were you before you came to be a fighter? Were you ever a farmer?"

"No. A teacher."

"Ah, a teacher! That's a good thing. A great thing. Do you think you'll go back to it?"

"I don't think much about going back," Bess said. "Don't see going forward as an option either, to be frank. This is who I am and this is what I got, is how I see it."

"Still. Life picks us up and takes us where we need to go, which isn't always or even mostly where we want. It may be that when all this nonsense and cruelty is put to rest again you'll turn your hand to something different. Maybe you'll be a farmer, or work in a mine, or lay down iron rails for the thunder-wagons."

Having not the slightest clue what Kilin Vevenis was trying to say, Bess only nodded. "I guess stranger things have happened."

"And if you do any of those things, you'll most likely find yourself some day with a shovel in your hand, digging down into the earth."

"Might could be."

"If you do, I'd have you be heedful. Give a seeing eye to what you find under the ground, and a thoughtful mind."

"Why?" Bess asked, more mystified than ever. "What am I gonna find, Kilin? Buried treasure?"

The old woman's mouth twitched up in a tight smile that didn't stay long on her face. "Well, truth is treasure. The greatest treasure, some would say. And the beautiful thing about the truth is that it won't stay buried forever. It's like the germ inside a seed that gropes towards the light. Be heedful, Bess. That's all I'll say to you."

Bess promised that she would. It didn't seem worth arguing about something so strange.

The Braggarts left the next morning, but before they took their leave Kilin Vevenis embraced Bess and kissed her on the cheek. It felt like a farewell, and in the event it was. When the Ajuparo came back the following spring and the Braggarts resumed their intermittent visits Kilin was no longer with them. She had died, a younger woman told Bess, on the long ride west. A huge, lumbering katy had tripped and fallen on top of her, breaking her spine. Her three daughters and their children had said the required blessings over her, sung her spirit home even though she was not yet dead and left her where she lay.

"She asked me to bring you a message," the young woman, Heia Tuur, told Bess shyly. "She said, with such a mighty warrior at your side you might be able one day to walk in a straight line. She said you should try, at least. Between this war and the next one, if you live. If you see the circle at last, and sicken of it."

"Was that all of it?"

"No. She said this too: dig deep, and be heedful."

Bess mulled this over. The sense of loss she felt was strange given that she'd barely known Kilin Vevenis. And the message, sent as it was from the wrong side of the grave, left her with a sad and sour feeling in her heart. "Was she in pain when you left her?" she asked, hoping the answer would be no. Hoping the old woman had at least had an easy passing.

"A lot of pain," Heia Tuur told her solemnly. "But that makes the soul travel faster and further when it leaves. It's a good thing, dog woman. Those who go into death like going into sleep linger where they fell for a long and dreary time. You should pray to the spirits that doesn't happen to you."

"Tell you the truth," Bess said, "I don't think that's something I'll need to worry about."

They had a mighty long run of it. Much longer than most. But in the end it did them no good. As the year 2980 drew to its close it became more and more apparent that the war was over. Echelon forces were still fighting in Tullemet and some of the western aggregates but the Parity had already won. They had better weapons, outside of a few oddities like Slim. They had a better commander, the military genius known as Cassian Tardy. Most crucially of all they had more soldiers, having twice the population of the Echelon states. They were therefore able to continue sending fresh troops into the field while the south was forced to merge depleted and battle-scarred regiments into new units under new generals, retrenching along a narrower and narrower front to conceal the full extent of their losses.

The Braggarts still rode out in those latter days, but they didn't go far. The border territories were now so full of Parity regiments on the move that even with Slim's satellite eyes to call on they couldn't thread a path between them. Quick sniping raids against the north's scouts and foragers were the best they could manage, and they risked their lives every time they engaged.

The war was reaching its end point. It was only a matter of time, and time was not their friend. With the Echelon regiments drained almost to the dregs the irregulars were called on more and more to fill the gaps, often in battles where northern troops outnumbered them two or three to one. They could have refused, of course – Tom Blue minded his own house and was beholden to no one – but they all knew this was make or break and so they went with it.

What they went into was one last push across the Odello River into Tullemet, heading for the Parity's capital at Mune. It wasn't even so very far, less than a hundred miles. But they were never going to make that distance. The Parity had fortified the city with layer after layer of dugouts and entrenchments, having anticipated such an attack long before it materialised. And besides, the Echelon's abandoning of any meaningful offensive in the west had freed up thousands of troops who could now be pulled back into defence. The south's finest, or all that remained of them, broke on those ramparts of earth and wood and barbed wire and seasoned warriors, then regrouped, came back and broke again. This was Mundy's Fields, the last battle of the war.

When you go into a fight like that you tend to read the world around you for clues as to how it's all likely to turn out, even if you usually refrain from the scrying of fortune. The night before the battle of Mundy's Fields a piece of the sky fell down. It was like a shooting star only bigger and brighter, and Bess could have sworn as she watched it descend that it hit the ground somewhere really close, only just up the trail a mile or so from where the Braggarts were camped.

"That ain't good," Frazer Stone fretted. "It's like God's sending down a warning. A warning of disaster."

Tom Blue shut that talk down as quick and as firm as he could. "Good thing too," he said. "Disaster's what them Parity bastards got coming to 'em, ain't it? It's only polite of the good lord to send them notice beforehand. Now go get some sleep. We're gonna be kept busy tomorrow killing greencoats, and I don't want any of you too tired to do their share."

"You believe in omens, Slim?" Bess asked when she'd retired from the desultory talk around the fire and climbed into her bedroll.

"No, Bess, I don't," Slim declared, "but that there was bad news all right."

"The comet? How come?"

"It wasn't a comet. It was one of the satellites coming down. I guess its orbit decayed and it hit atmosphere. I told you there was gaps in the coverage. Well, now there's one more. I may not be able to get eyes on the Parity lines tomorrow."

"It don't matter," Bess said, with a great deal more confidence than she felt. "I reckon they'll be close enough for us to see them our own selves."

The first charge came with the dawn, which was late and sullen. In due course the Braggarts found themselves defending a hill to the north of the Echelon front lines – a salient, buttressed on one side by a steep rock wall and on the other side by nothing but fresh air. The position was heavily exposed even before the Parity brought its guns to bear. After that it was no more than a killing ground. Blue sent a message to one of the Echelon generals, Antony Child, suggesting that the Braggarts make a charge supported by two companies of infantry and an artillery battery that he could see very clearly on the adjoining hill. He waited for the best part of an hour for a reply, with cannon fire exploding all around. Finally the messenger returned, exhausted and wild-eyed. The general's instruction was that he should stand his ground.

There's no knowing at this remove what was going on in Child's thoughts, or what orders he himself might have received from the Echelon's high command. Perhaps he was waiting for more troops to be brought up from the rear, but if so they never arrived. And the moment when a cavalry charge might have turned the Parity's left flank came and went without such a charge being made. The tide of battle flowed to south and west and the Braggarts were left behind, cut off from their own side and completely surrounded.

"Well now, friends," Tom Blue said to his riders, "it looks like the party's going on way over there and they forgot to invite us. So I say it's only fitting that we have us a shindig of our own." He passed around two dozen bottles of whisky that he'd brought up onto the hilltop in a brace of boxes labelled as rifle rounds. The Braggarts opened up the bottles and drank deep. "By Holy John," Blue said, "if this is the last stand we ever get to make then let's make it a fucking joyous one and laugh in the faces of the men that kill us. Because even in dying we've got more than those sons-of-whores will ever have. We got the knowing that our lives is given in a right cause. And more than that we get to die in good company, because the Braggarts is invitation only and every last one of you is on the golden list of saved souls, or else that list is bullshit and it's full of worthless cunts."

A cheer went up at this. Very few of them were religious. Even those who'd gone into the war with some kind of faith to sustain them had mostly set it aside in the years of the struggle, as a thing whose value might be reappraised if they ever got the chance to do it. But they were prepared to see a holiness in who they were and what they did, because it was all they had and they had given themselves to it with a full heart – and it was clear to them in that moment that there was now no future for any of them except the purely notional one offered by priests and prophets. So they pledged each other and embraced and drained the bottles dry. And then they got up into their saddles and charged, into the teeth of five thousand Parity guns well placed for enfilade fire and three full batteries of heavy artillery.

They had no objective, apart from the enemy line that they knew they wouldn't reach. The charge wasn't a tactic, it was only a defiance. Perhaps for some of them it was also an act of contrition, an offering of their own lives to balance all the many lives they'd taken, the terrible, wearying atrocities that in the end had served no purpose at all. But reading the minds of the dead is a mystery not given to many. In any case, the last ride of Blue's Braggarts was less of a military engagement and more of an evaporation, a subliming away of men and mounts and weapons into spilled blood and splintered bone, and finally into a reddish mist that hung over the battlefield as the sun bowed its sorrowing head.

Greencoat troops walked through that mist with their bayonets fixed to dispatch the dying. They had been given strict orders against looting but it happened anyway. Rings disappeared from fingers, coats from backs, boots from their dead wearers' feet.

One young trooper found a body lying half underneath a chafer. The big beast's neck had been all but severed either by chain shot or by a stroke from a cavalry sabre. Its owner hadn't fared any better: a clean hit from a rifle bullet had made a ruin of his face. In his lifeless grip was a Precursor handgun, a prize worth any number of rings and coats and boots. Eagerly the greencoat kneeled down and began to prise loose the stiff fingers one by one.

Bess came on him from behind. She had put Wakeful Slim in that dead man's hand as a bait and lain down on the shattered ground with all the other corpses, biding her time. The mist lay like a curtain all around them but she couldn't afford to make too much noise so she brained the trooper with a rock and held him face down in the battlefield mud until he drowned. Then she stripped him of his uniform and shrugged out of her own. A minute or so later she walked on in a coat as green as grass and nobody gave her a second glance.

She still wasn't clear though. She was in the middle of an enemy army and she was a woman in a soldier's uniform several sizes too big for her. She'd been stabbed with a bayonet high up on her left leg, a wound that had bled – and was still bleeding – very freely. Another dead man courteously gave up his shirt so she could tear it into strips and make herself a bandage, which she tied tight around the wound. It would slow her down, but she would just have to do the best she could. Her only plan was to keep on going and hope that nobody accosted her.

At first nobody did. The aftermath of a battle breeds its own special madness, very different from the madness of the battle itself. For many people it's like arriving again in your own body and your own soul after a while spent somewhere else entirely. The most familiar sights and sounds can suddenly seem strange, and the strangeness of anything else is hard to measure. The bodies thinned out around Bess as she walked, the living folks too, so for some while she was alone. Light-headed from losing so much blood she stumbled on. She was afraid that if she stopped to rest she would never move again.

The thought occurred to her that this might not be such a very bad outcome. Her anger and bitterness after Martha's death had carried her a very long way, but the place where she had arrived was strange and cold. The things she'd done were indefensible, the person she'd become unfathomable. There were worse ways to leave the world than simply lying down and falling asleep. But there was a tenacity in her, in the core of her or very close to the core, and it wouldn't allow her to do that just yet. And there was Slim too, urging her on, telling her sternly that this was no place for her to be. "Keep moving, Bess. Straight forward, no looking back. There's a road up ahead and it's gonna take us somewhere that isn't here. We'll get out of this yet."

She could no longer feel her legs, or the ground where her feet touched it. She moved like a puppet dangling on strings, her weight held up by something other than her own sinews.

A cluster of tents loomed up ahead of her, already too close before she realised it was there. It was a field hospital. Wounded men, every one of them in green, sat on trestle chairs or felled trees and waited to be treated. They cradled shattered limbs or pressed their hands against open wounds. Their hollow eyes stared at nothing.

Someone called out to Bess. A doctor, perhaps, or just a junior officer trying to take a tally. Head bowed, she hurried on. She heard footsteps behind her and then a voice, up close, ordering her to stop. It was a man's voice, hoarse and peremptory.

"I'm fine," she muttered. "I'm rejoining my unit."

A hand fell on her shoulder. "Which unit? There's nobody down this road."

Bess stopped. She had no choice. "I took a knock on the head," she said. "Must have got turned around." She reached down to her belt and put her hand on Slim's grip, but her hand shook so badly she wasn't sure she could even draw him.

"Come back to the camp," the man said. "We'll get you seen to."

"You go," Bess said. "I'll rest a moment, then join you."

There was a moment or two's silence. "Turn around, soldier," the man said. "Let me get a look at you."

And here it is then, Bess thought. She turned to face the man, a greencoat lieutenant with dark, hollow eyes, white hair so fine you could see his scalp through it and a scraggly wisp of beard that hung off his chin like he'd been drinking milk and let it dribble down.

"Go on then," Bess growled. Meaning whatever it is you're about to do, do it quick and get it over with.

"You're . . . you're a woman!" the greencoat exclaimed. Then his gaze dropped to her waist. He saw her hand on the grip of the gun that was holstered there, a weapon as black as jet except where little red lights were blinking like demons' eyes.

Bess saw the colour drain out of the man's face as he realised who it was he was facing. It was a pale face to start with, so the draining out didn't take too long. For a long moment the two of them stared at each other. It wasn't going to last though. With each second that passed Bess felt a little more life leaving her. Her knees started to buckle and her shoulders sagged. She was about to faint.

The young lieutenant saw that shift in her stance and read it wrong. He thought Bess was dropping into a crouch so she could draw her gun, the terrible Precursor weapon called Wakeful Slim, and be braced by her own body's weight when she fired with just a gentle upward tilt into his heart.

He gave a bleat of terror, turned and fled. The mist swallowed him up before he'd gone ten paces, but Bess heard his retreating steps for a little while after that.

She sank down onto her knees and remained there for what might have been five or ten minutes, collecting what was left of her will and her strength the way you might kneel beside a sluggish spring and catch the welcome trickles of water in your cupped hands.

When she felt she was able to go on she climbed to her feet again and resumed her journey, away from Mundy's Fields towards what until today had been the border between the Parity and the Echelon states. There was no border any more, and maybe that was even a good thing. At least folks could stop killing each other now.

That is, assuming they wanted to.

Unfiled report of tactical unit 486
Identifier: 7Ω2905 Esten, V, engineer first class
Date: not applicable
Location: not applicable
Status: well, it's not getting any better, that's for damn sure

It took us a long time to realise just how big a mess we were in; longer than it should have, probably. Then again, in our defence it was a really ornate and elaborate mess made out of a lot of smaller messes all beautifully laminated together. There was a lot to take in.

It's hard to think myself back into the mindset of those first few days. We knew the bounce-backs weren't an option because of what had happened to corporal Geniull – who we had to shovel into his shallow grave piecemeal using improvised tools carved from the local hardwoods. That wasn't a detail anyone relished, and we were mourning the corporal in our own quiet way, but we didn't flinch. We'd all seen worse.

And we still thought we were about to be rescued. We'd left that True Imp base well and truly pacified when we Stepped out. There were no enemy combatants left and we'd deactivated all the traps we hadn't previously fallen into. We couldn't see any reason why the second team shouldn't come galloping over the horizon and haul our asses home. We'd probably have had to take some not-so-gentle ribbing about having trapped ourselves on the wrong side of a faulty Step plate but that would only last until the next piece of fuckery fell on our heads. In the Cielo it wasn't likely to be long in coming.

So we made camp and we waited. Each of us carried the standard emergency rations, enough for three days. We reckoned that should see us through. We weren't being shot at – in fact we hadn't seen or heard from the enemy even once since we Stepped – and though it's no fun to sleep suited up it's a lot better than freezing in the desert cold. We didn't see all that much to complain about.

On the third day, when rescue still hadn't arrived, Velladaxita – our assigned bio-tech, and therefore the closest thing we had to a quartermaster – did a full chemical analysis of the local fauna and sorted out the tasty treats from the toxic hazards. It was a really weird biome, she reported, leaning very heavily towards reptiles, birds and arthropods. There were no mammals bigger than a rat, and the evolutionary niches where you'd expect to find them were all taken up by oversized insects. There were scorpions that stood as high as my waist, for example. With our Cielo-enhanced immune systems we didn't have to worry about their poison, but their stingers were attached to the end of powerfully muscled tails that could hit you like a wrecking ball.

"The upside is fully compatible proteins," Velladaxita pointed out. "They're edible."

"For you, maybe," Inch bitched. Dax was Orycteropodid, with steeply tapered cheeks and a tubular tongue. The skilled, steady fingers with which she wielded microtome and autoclave were attached to hands as broad as shovels. All these things were legacies from a pre-sentient past in which her ancestors dug up anthills and termite mounds and snacked on what was inside, which made Inch's comment borderline racist. On-brand, too: he routinely called me Baldy because I'm anthropoid stock and the only one in the unit with no body hair. Just bare brown skin where everyone else has the full rug.

The captain shot him a look that made him back off fast. And hey, Inch didn't complain when we went ahead and had our first cook-out. In due course we sampled the scorpions, the foot-long mealworms, the lumbering green bugs that you could cook in their own shells, the giant roadrunners that practically broke the sound barrier, the gliding lizards, the spiny-shelled tortoises, and of course every variety of bulb and stem and seed within reach.

"It won't do, though," the captain declared about two weeks in. We'd made ourselves some temporary bivouacs by this time out of branches and heat-baked earth and I guess he was afraid we were settling into the situation a little too much. "We've got to assume help isn't coming any time soon. This world may well have an indigenous population, but if it does they haven't got as far as building a radio – and the enemy is still out there somewhere. There were maybe forty or fifty of them who Stepped out from that base before we shut them down, and Jad knows how many of them were here already. Until we're contacted and retrieved we're still on-mission, so it's kind of incumbent on us to find them and fuck them up. I was thinking we send up the drone and tell it to look for anything anomalous, but there's a whole damn world out there and a blind search could take forever. Engineers, what can we do that's better?"

"There's a good chance they're using field comms," I offered. "I mean, unless they're all together in one big group. And even if they are it's a safe bet they brought some tech with them. Tech means emissions on the EM spectrum. Like you said, sir, there's nothing else out there that's emitting anything unless you count the occasional bad fart. We ought to be able to lock in on them that way."

Dulu nodded. "That's good. I like it. Can you work up a scanner?"

I glanced at Nim'kisi. "Flycatcher already has all we need, right?"

"Oh, hell yes," Nim'kisi agreed. She actually smiled. She loved it when her little drone friend was the answer to a problem. "Fly's on-board scanning rig is state of the art. Let's say their systems are emitting somewhere between ten thousand and five million pips in the white band, which covers about ninety per cent of electronic equipment. We can either set the rig to cycle through that whole range or if we need more sensitivity we can break it down into quartiles and do multiple runs. Tell me what you want, sir, and I'll lock it in."

Which she did, and it worked fine. Eventually. But the moment she sent the drone out on recon we got a whole lot more than we bargained for, and we had to throw out most of our assumptions about where we'd landed and what was going on here.

The first thing we found was a flourishing civilisation. There was no reason why that should have come as a surprise, but the silence on the airwaves and the general absence of selves and structures (aside from the tower) in our immediate vicinity had encouraged us to assume we were alone. We were not. We were just in a very lightly settled part of the country, which overall was supporting a population of around thirty-five million.

And what a population! The technology was early industrial, similar to what Spearhead survey teams had found on countless thousands of sinkhole worlds. What was unusual in this case was that the indigenous selves didn't belong to any one genus or clade but were varied to an incredible and inexplicable degree. Velladaxita had a word for it, which was heterodominance, but she was at pains to point out that this didn't mean there was a precedent for what we were seeing here. "I mean," she tried to explain, badly flustered, "this isn't that. Not really. In a few cases – fewer than a hundred, out of what must be millions of remote surveys and tens of thousands of actual missions – Spearhead encountered worlds in which two genetic lineages had attained sentience at more or less the same time and developed codependent or competing civilisations. Once they thought they found a world that had three, but the third turned out to be a radically mutated version of one of the other two. There had been a speciation event. I don't remember the details. But yeah, this is different. Very different."

She linked our arrays to the footage from the Flycatcher, or rather to a montage she'd already edited together. The resolution from the drone's state-of-the-art cameras was pin-sharp even at the highest magnification, which just made the strangeness of it all that much more unsettling.

Maybe I should have mentioned before now that our squad of twenty-three hailed from just shy of twenty-three different worlds. That wasn't unusual at all. There were hundreds of thousands of worlds in the Pando, after all. And as Dax had just pointed out, the norm on almost all of those worlds was for only a single species to have developed into full sentience. It was almost always mammals – I guess because of the warm blood, the four-chambered hearts, all that good stuff – and there was a certain bias towards bigger mammals that had found it easier to dominate the evolutionary tree. But almost without exception, on any given world sentience had turned into a zero-sum game.

Now we were watching through Flycatcher's telescopic array as it flew high over towns, cities, farmlands. The selves below belonged to virtually every mammalian lineage you could think of. It's meant to be hate-speech to refer to any sentient species by the name of the life forms they evolved from, but everybody does it because the technical vocabulary is dry and complicated and more than a little ridiculous. We saw bison selves, bear selves, dog and cat selves, beavers, squirrels, wolves, moose, deer, cougars and lynx, sheep, chipmunks, prairie dogs, living alongside each other as though all of that wild variety was natural and unremarkable. There were a fair few mixes too, even though unions of that kind generally tended to be sterile. Some of the selves looked up at the drone as it passed overhead, eyes wide with amazement at the sight, but they seemed to take each other entirely for granted.

Captain Dulu was the first to break the stunned silence. "And they don't have Step travel?"

"Captain, they don't even have electricity yet. Steam and gas are the wonders of the age. Well, that and rifled gun barrels. Crazy as it seems, there's no reason to believe that any of these people are exotic imports. They're all local. Specifically, they're native to this land mass – continent 3-north in the Registry's listings.

All that's missing is the anthropoid clade. Ape-descendants." She glanced at me. "No offence meant, Esten."

"None taken." I was a little embarrassed that I hadn't spotted that myself. I guess it's harder to notice an absence than a presence.

"And they're all just getting along?" Lasque sounded incredulous. He was from Ballinen where the red Bales and the pink Bales had brought each other to the brink of extinction before they finally got the trick of peaceful coexistence.

"Well, no," Velladaxita said, "they're not. Not right now."

Another montage, this time of battlefields and armed encounters. It seemed the ill-assorted sentients of this sinkhole world were at war with one another, using a variety of crude and primitive weapons. There were cannon firing non-explosive loads, both regular and chain shot. Knives and swords alongside guns, all of which looked laughably crude. Rudimentary air bombardment that relied on hot-air balloons. Ironclad ships ponderously exchanging fire. Mines strung across rivers and inland waterways.

"What are they fighting about?" the captain asked.

"I have no idea," Velladaxita told him. "The drone doesn't have effective sound pickup at high altitudes, and Nim'kisi didn't want to risk bringing him down to where he could listen in."

"None of the languages will be in our databases anyway," Nim'kisi said, sounding a touch defensive. "So we'd have to work up a translator from scratch." She folded Flycatcher's rotors down and tucked et back into ets carrying case, as if to protect et from any criticism of ets performance. "In any case, I didn't see that it was particularly relevant."

"Probably isn't," the captain agreed. "Dax, what are the odds that all this . . . heterodominance happened by itself, with no nudging from outside?"

Velladaxita stared at Dulu as if he'd asked her if two and two were always four, or if they could sometimes be persuaded against their better judgement to be five. "Well . . . there are no odds," she said, looking around at the ring of sombre faces. "It's just impossible, sir. I mean, the evolutionary pressures . . . Each one of those species would have been competing against all the others, every step of the way. For them all to hit the sentience jackpot would be like sailing a whole fleet out of a single bottle. There's no way. We're looking at a genetically engineered biome. The True Imps did this. And they must have expended a staggering amount of time and resources in order to make it happen."

"Why, though?" Ajuparo asked. "Why would they do that?"

"Well, that's a good question," the captain said. "As soon as we find some of those sons of bitches let's be sure to ask them."

The sons of bitches continued to be elusive, but Flycatcher turned up a lot more interesting finds. There was a ring of satellites in high orbit that we managed to hack into. They appeared to contain nothing but monitoring equipment, but with a truly vast amount of data storage. The files were encrypted, but I told the captain Nim'kisi and I were confident we could break the cypher if we set our minds to it. "Why don't you go ahead and do that, then, Esten," Dulu suggested. "Since Nim is handling the drone's reconnaissance flights."

"Yes, sir," I said, deadpan as all get-out, and trying hard not to read that remark as a slight on my usefulness to the team. I was about to start assembling some simple decrypters when 507m suggested I leave it to him instead. "It will be an enjoyable challenge," he said. "And it will occupy my mind. I get bored sometimes, having so little to do here and so few companions of my own kind."

"Please," I said. "Go to it. Let me know what you find."

"Of course."

The other thing Flycatcher kept coming across was more of the white towers. Tacking back and forth across the whole continent at its top speed of four hundred kilometres an hour it eventually identified and located two hundred and fifty-three of the ceramic structures. Most of them stood alone but there were three clusters of five, all standing on the watershed right in the middle of the continental plate. They were built to a consistent plan, with a few trivial variations in height and external cladding. None of them had a door except for that first one we found. None of them ever did anything apart from stand there all silent and mysterious and pump a little power into their shields.

Then one day, extending ets search away from the mainland to take in a few offshore islands, the drone ran into a force wall. The impact wasn't severe enough to do any serious damage: the wall seemed to be the same soft field that's used in civilian transport hubs to make sure travellers don't lose a limb when they Step. Further exploration established that continent 3-north was surrounded by force walls a few miles out from land in every direction. There was also some evidence of controlled detonations on a massive scale to remove the land bridge between 3-north and 3-south. This entire continent had been isolated from the rest of the world with considerable care and precision. Which was yet another *what the fuck?* to add to our growing collection.

I'd found a few modest enigmas of my own by this time. With Nim'kisi busy liaising with Flycatcher as et did ets truncated world tour and 507m at work decrypting the satellites' data files, I addressed myself to the problem of breaking through the towers' shielding to get a good look at whatever was going on inside them. As Aju had already said, we didn't have enough heavy ordnance to just crack one open. She had a battery of micro-Lancers built into the shoulder plates of her armour, but the captain had already decided we should save those back for special occasions. And even if we had the firepower there was a good argument for holding back until we knew what it was we were messing with. But there was more than one way to bake that particular pie.

Obviously the towers' shields didn't impede visible light, or we wouldn't be able to see them at all, so I went ahead and checked the rest of the EM spectrum. No permeability to X-rays, which was only to be expected, or to electrical and magnetic fields on any wavelength that could be weaponised. But then that was the point, wasn't it? The shields had been designed with the basic aim of making the towers more resistant to damage. Resistance to probes was a secondary consideration, and total impermeability tended to get in the way of normal functionality. If the towers' makers had programmed them to accept commands from outside their walls, even if the command was only *open the damn door*, then there had to be a gap in the defences somewhere. A key under the doormat was too much to hope for but still there had to *be* a key somewhere. On some level, via some physical mechanism, the towers had to interface with the outside world.

I went to work on a scanner that would hitch a ride on any active system using its own frequency and wavelength. The downside was that it needed an active system in order to function: so as long as the towers just sat there doing nothing it was useless. But the moment they woke up and got to work I'd be able to analyse what they were doing and report back.

Once I'd done that I didn't have a whole lot else on my schedule, at least from a military perspective, but I had enough to keep me busy. We'd accepted now that we were settling in for a long-ish haul so we needed to abandon our makeshift shelters and build ourselves a more solid base of operations.

Nim'kisi and I drew up a rough plan for a defensible camp – a row of six wooden huts on the top of the slope where we'd first Stepped in. We showed the plan to the captain, who approved it and told us to go ahead and build it, putting the whole squad apart from Nim'kisi and Dax under our command.

Cutting and shaping the wood for the huts was trivial, because a Sa-Su rifle can cut through anything. It was also a massive pain in the arse because most of our fellow troopers were clueless when it came to the long-forgotten art of building with split logs. I didn't have any practical experience in that line myself but I did have a working knowledge of the principles. I gave a few short lectures with demonstrations – how to cut the logs, how to notch the wood and lay the cut logs down, how to place cleats for your doors and windows, how to build a roof out of shingles hung on beams – and stood back to watch the results. They were pitiful. Nim'kisi and I had to go back and forth dismantling builds that wouldn't work and restarting them from scratch. Then when it came to making stone chimneys it was the same thing again. Cut your stones to size, flatten the tops and bottoms with your Sa-Su, use baked clay for mortar: it's not some esoteric mystery. Still took us three weeks though.

"How about a minefield?" I suggested to the captain when we were done. "A ditch? Maybe a watchtower? The indigenes may be primitive but there are a lot of them and we already know they like to fight."

"There's no need for any of that," Dulu said. "Esten, these people only just evolved out of hitting each other with sticks and stones. There's not a weapon on this continent that can touch us when we're armoured up. As for a watchtower, we've got the drone. Et can hover a few hundred metres up when we're sleeping and roust us up if there's anything coming."

"Can I lay a few mines anyway, sir?" I pressed him. "It can't do any harm. I can set them to disarm if any of us are in the blast radius."

"Fine. Go ahead." He was already walking away, and it was abundantly clear he didn't care whether I did it or not. But Ajuparo liked the idea a lot – which was no surprise – and the two of us laid down a nice triple grid from 20 to 150 metres out. "And how about putting a semi-remote rifle in one of these trees?" Aju asked me as we worked.

I was surprised. "Do we even have one?"

"Nope, but my Sa-Su is configurable. All I need to do is mount it on a swivel base and cut down a few trees on either side so it's got a decent field."

"Outstanding!" I said. "Aju, I think I love you." I said it as a joke but it was true. I really did. So did half the squad, though, and she plain wasn't interested. According to Ivikeppe she had a pledge-husband in Tollo Teio, carried a holo of him on the sleeve of her armour. In any case she held us all at arm's length, men and women alike.

"You've only got the hots for my heavy ordnance, Esten," she said now, flashing me a wicked grin. "I've had that kind of relationship before. It never ends well. You're carrying a 507m, right?"

I took out the side arm and held it up. "Engineer Esten and I are partnered, Trooper Ajuparo," the gun confirmed. "But I see myself as a full member of the squad in my own right."

"Of course," Aju agreed. She rolled her eyes at me. Smart weapons could be touchy about questions of autonomy and status. You couldn't really blame them but it sometimes got a little tiring to be walking on eggshells around them. "I was going to suggest linking you up to my Sa-Su rifle," Aju went on.

"To what purpose?"

"I'm going to mount it on gimbals up in one of the trees. I could just make it heat-and-movement sensitive, which would probably do well enough, but you know." Aju shrugged. "My rifle's not . . . like you."

"You mean it's a different calibre?"

"I mean there's nobody home. It can't think for itself. It would be better if someone was keeping an eye on things. Making informed decisions on what counts as a target."

The 507m considered. "And what does count as a target?" et asked. "For argument's sake."

"Anything and anyone that's coming at us with weapons hot,"

I said. "Modern weapons, I mean, not muskets and cavalry sabres. Weapons that could actually do some damage."

"I follow the logic," the 507m said. "And it would only take a little of my attention away from hacking into the satellite data. Yes. By all means, link me to the rifle."

"Done," Aju said, and I saw the link go up in her array. She'd had it sitting there all along, ready to go. She never was one for wasting time, Aju. I miss her more than I can say.

We picked our room-mates and moved into the huts, and after that we went back to our normal routine. We monitored the indigenes in case they did something that actually mattered. We sent Flycatcher out in search of an enemy who remained stubbornly invisible. We continued with our futile attempts to crack the towers' shielding. We waited for rescue. We diced and played cards and sang bawdy songs. Bekkor even built a still. The stuff that came out of it tasted like antifreeze with a lingering kerosene finish but we drank it anyway, trusting to our bio-mods to sieve out the toxins.

Meanwhile the war between the indigenes ended and the people of this gods-fucked country returned to what counted as their normal pursuits. We still hadn't interacted with them directly in any way at all. Out here in the desert close to the country's south-west coast we were undisturbed, though there were small communities as close as a hundred kilometres away. Whenever they threatened to come any closer we put on a bit of a show for them with flares, grenades and rifles on incendiary setting. That was enough to change their minds, and probably to start a few local legends besides.

But where did any of this leave us? We'd been in-country for more than four months now and we knew barely more than when we'd first arrived. We hadn't located the enemy, let alone engaged them, and we didn't have any way of getting back home. Captain Dulu did his best to keep us focused on the mission, but the truth was that the mission had died under us. In every way that mattered we were a bunch of castaways on a desert island, reduced to living off the land and rough-hewing ourselves a few home comforts where we could.

We got sloppy, is the long and short of it. We let our guard down.

And we got what we deserved.

PART THREE

YOU HAD YOUR PLACE, AND YOU PLAYED YOUR PART

The north was magnanimous in victory. All the history books say so. The former Echelon territories were welcomed back into the States' Union with no reparations to pay. Quite the reverse, in fact. The Parity's government – now the government of all the states – agreed to help the south rebuild. Townships and polities were compensated in hard cash for the losses they sustained when they freed their slaves and contractees from bondage. And the soldiers who had taken up arms to defend their homeland were allowed to return now to their former lives with no reproach or penalty. Those who had been taken as prisoners were released and sent home, in most cases with their travel paid for them. Even Ottavio Remorse, the presidential pretender, was allowed to go into a gentlemanly exile under house arrest in his own mansion rather than being katy-whipped and paraded through the streets. It was felt that the country would heal more quickly that way from its self-inflicted wounds.

It was different for the irregulars though. No treaty covered them. They had never enlisted, never sworn an oath or worn a uniform. They were not soldiers but criminals. They had murdered civilians, burned houses and farms and business premises, taken the war out of the field and into the streets of towns and cities whose respectable denizens had been much happier cheering on the troops from a safe distance. Of course the north had had its own hoorahs who did the exact same things, but murderers, monsters and ne'er-do-wells are only ever to be found on the losing side.

The irregulars were not forgiven. Their fates were various. The States' parliament decreed a sentence of death for war crimes, and many who had surrendered themselves in hopes of clemency were duly hanged, but there were exceptions. Those who showed contrition and were prepared to swear allegiance to the States' Union, unless their names could be attached to a specific raid or act of pillage, were given terms of hard labour varying from a few months to twenty years. A few escaped with no more than a whipping, though this wasn't always as easy a get-out as it seemed to be. Bess's old confederate Horace Abalone, who had also survived the massacre at Mundy's Fields, was sentenced to forty lashes with a stout whip. The man who did the whipping, one Conor Pleasant, put his own interpretation on that punishment – whether because he had scores to settle or just out of boiled-in meanness. He dipped the ends of the lash in mud and shit so the wounds would fester. Abalone died in agony lying on his stomach, his back a mess of pus and sloughing flesh.

And there were some who just disappeared. The war had been a big moil, after all, a storm of pure chaos in whose wake a million things were found to be lost, stolen or strayed. And the western frontier was still out there, the expanding forward edge of the bubble that was civilisation. It wasn't that hard to take a new name, move to another territory and leave your past behind you like a snake's shed skin.

The States' parliament took a stern stance on that. Mercy for the Echelon's soldiers and leaders seemed proper, and reduced the risk of fresh mutinies, but it didn't sit right with the august senators to allow justice to be flouted. They set up a committee with a high-sounding name to determine what might be done. And the committee in its wisdom voted to create a *posse comitatus*, an armed force with autonomous power to apprehend and execute the renegades wheresoever they were to be found.

The Parity authorities didn't call their posse by that name, considering that its overtones of frontier law might diminish its authority and reputation. They called it the Extended Pursuit Force. And then they undid all that good work by putting it under the command of Paulus Rondeau, a man with as much murder and mayhem to his tally as any of the hoorahs he was tasked to hunt.

There was a journalist working for an eastern news-sheet, a Mr Francis Bridge, who interviewed Rondeau about the Pursuit Force in the States Rotunda in Mune when it was first announced. He asked Rondeau what the Pursuit Force hoped to achieve. Rondeau's new job had come with a new rank, that of full colonel, and he was in an expansive mood as he answered. "War's a terrible thing, you know. It's like a flood or a hurricane, except that if you get hit by a flood or a hurricane the waves and the wind don't mean you any harm. These southern hoorahs, they meant harm and they did harm, to any and all that was unlucky enough to cross their path. As far as I'm concerned, the war's not over until every last one of them is brought in or brought down. And I promise you I will exert myself to that end."

He meant it too. Rondeau didn't see any paradox in delivering retribution to people for questionable actions he'd committed himself. On the contrary, he seemed to feel that in accepting this commission he was moving himself to a realm above any possible moral censure, becoming a kind of divine arbiter of sin and grace. If his own sins were part of that equation then the more southern fighters he tracked down and killed the more forgiveness he earned for past transgressions.

He turned out to be a skilled and intuitive manhunter, so successful in tracking and bringing down his quarry that it almost defied explanation. Tom Blue had died in Mundy's Fields, and luckless Horace Abalone not long after, but there were others among the Braggarts who had somehow contrived to come away from that last suicidal charge with their hides intact. Two-Hands Joseph Wick, Henry and Zeb Attercopp, Lucas Youthful. Rondeau and his Pursuit Force tracked them all, and killed them all because not one of them gave a moment's thought to surrendering themselves to northern justice.

Rondeau and his Pursuit Force made a great many other kills too, of course. It wasn't just the Braggarts the colonel was after but every irregular who had fought under the Echelon's banner – and a fair few who had picked up that banner again in those turbulent years in the hope of fighting the same war twice and getting a different outcome. Discouraging such misplaced sentiments was a large part of the government's thinking in sending the Pursuit Force out in the first place.

But the greatest quarry of all eluded Rondeau, and he would have given a great deal to get his hands on her. Dog-Bitch Bess. The unnatural woman who had taken up arms and rode with men, Tom Blue's whore, the emblem and embodiment of all that was corrupting and wrong about the Echelon cause. The colonel would dearly have loved to claim that prize and wear Bess's Precursor gun on his hip in the manner of a scalp he'd taken.

He thought at first that Bess would be easy to come by. She was rumoured to have a hideously scarred face, which was a difficult thing to hide, and her vicious nature would be certain to show itself in acts of arbitrary violence and depravity. Word would come, Rondeau was sure, and he would add that last filthy, fabled name to his own blazon.

But Dog-Bitch Bess seemed to have evaporated into air. Not once in three years' worth of riding and hunting did the Pursuit Force so much as smell a rumour of her. Had they but known it, they were acting on bad intelligence. Bess's face had an odd asymmetry to it, a result of Gabrielle Summer's well-intentioned efforts, but she had no visible scarring. The scars were only a story that grew out of people's efforts to describe the strangeness of her features.

As for the idea that Bess would break cover all on her own, without being provoked, that was a supposition that rested on three legs like a joint stool. Bess would have needed to have had a natural inclination towards violence. She would also have needed to be somewhere around other people, and on top of all that to be as stupid as a post. One leg or another of the stool must have wobbled, because no word came.

Rondeau didn't give up though. He knew Dog-Bitch Bess was alive out there somewhere. He had found that whey-faced lieutenant who met Bess on the road south of Mundy's Fields on the day of the final battle. The lieutenant was a goat self named Cicero Church and he had been talking up that moment ever since it happened, embellishing it a little more each time. He had traded bullets with the Dog-Bitch and almost brought her down, but then the fog came in and spoiled his aim. When he went to the spot where she'd been he saw a trail of blood leading away, so he knew he'd hit her. A moment more and he would have killed her for sure. Maybe he even *had* killed her, because there sure was a lot of blood on the ground. But if Bess was still living then it was only that mischance with the fog that had saved her.

It didn't take Colonel Rondeau but a minute or so to realise that most of the young officer's story was made up out of shit and wishfulness, but there was a detail in there that rang true. It was when Church described Bess's gun.

Precursor tools and makings of any kind were rare, but Rondeau came from a wealthy family and had inherited such an item from his father. It was the silver flier that had hovered over his head on the day he rode into Ottomankie, although flying was the very least of the things it could do. He had also encountered two other Precursor tools in his time, both equally impressive in their way. One was a short rod like a policeman's billy stick that blazed with light when you touched a raised whorl on its side. It didn't use any oil, didn't have a wick or a naked flame of any kind but you could light up a whole ballroom with that rod. The second one was a suit of bright red armour, ancient as hell but without a scratch on it.

Rondeau had touched all three of these devices with his own hands and felt their strangeness – the materials they were made from, different from any metal or wood he'd ever encountered, and the way they'd seemed to be humming or vibrating almost with their own pent-up energy. They'd had one significant thing in common with Church's description, which was the little lights on their outsides that winked on and off even when they weren't being used. So Rondeau believed that Church had met Dog-Bitch Bess. He just didn't believe Church had shot her, still less given her a fatal wound. No, Bess had walked away from Mundy's Fields on her own two feet. And whether she'd walked twenty miles or two hundred or two fucking thousand, she must have fetched up somewhere. She wasn't walking still but had found herself a hole and gone to ground.

With the blessing of his paymasters back in Mune, Rondeau posted a reward. A thousand dollars in Parity bills for Dog-Bitch Bess, dead or alive, and five hundred for information of any kind that led to her arrest. Sooner or later, he was sure, word would come to him. Someone like that doesn't just disappear.

That was what Bess had done, though. And she had done it the same way an ostrich bird does, by closing her eyes and burying her head.

On the day of the battle, after she faced down Cicero Church, she hadn't gone much further at all. She had lost too much blood and her legs weren't capable of carrying her. She found a riverbank with thick couch grass taller than a man's head growing right to the edge of the water. She crawled in there and laid herself down, uncertain whether she would ever have the strength to get up again.

"We'd better see to that wound," Wakeful Slim said to her. "We should have done it before now."

"There's nothing to be done," Bess answered, her voice a hoarse whisper. "I put a bandage on it already. Just got to wait now until the bleeding stops."

"It won't stop, Bess. Not by itself. The bandage is helping, but the bullet that hit you nicked an artery and the flow hasn't stopped. It's likely to get infected too, especially if you go lying down in mud and shit and all. You'll have to let me cauterise the wound."

Bess's thoughts were slowing. It wasn't at all unpleasant. She felt as if she could just doze off right there at the edge of the water, let the river sing her to sleep. "Cauterise?" she mumbled. "What's that?"

"Just aim me at your leg, right where the wound is. There's no need to pull the trigger. I'll handle the rest by myself."

It sounded like way too much trouble for not much reward. If

Slim had needed Bess to get out of her clothes she wouldn't have managed it at all, but it turned out that wasn't a requirement. The bayonet had left a ragged rent in the right place, so all she had to do was lift the blood-stiff fabric away and fold it over like a flap.

She couldn't raise up her head to look but she hovered the gun roughly over the place that hurt the most. A lance of raw, dazzling light stabbed out from the muzzle of Wakeful Slim's barrel, zigzagging down the entire length of the wound and across its width in the space of a second. Bess opened her mouth to shriek but uttered no more than a strangled grunt of shock before she passed out.

When she woke there was a dead bird lying next to her, a partridge. It had no wound anywhere on its body. Slim had brought it down with a pulse of focused vibration. Bess plucked it and gutted it, then made a fire with Slim's incendiary field. While the bird was cooking she dipped her cupped hands into the river and drank, again and again. She felt that she had never been so thirsty, or so hungry. She ate the bird bones and all.

But she was still as weak as a just-hatched chick, and when she tried to stand her legs folded under her like a trestle table that's been put up the wrong way. "Too soon," Slim reproved her. "You'll need to rest up for a few days. We're a mite close to the road for my liking, but I'll see anything that's coming and I can warn you to make no sound until they've gone by. Eat and sleep and get your strength back, Bess, and then we'll see."

She would have argued, but even the muscles in her jaw felt too slack to be exercised. They came back first, though, and in the days that followed the two of them talked endlessly and aimlessly in between her bouts of fitful sleep and aching wakefulness. The nightmares were back with a vengeance, so though sleep was good for her body it did nothing to ease her mind. Most of the time she tried her best to avoid it and surrendered to it with a mixture of fear and fierce resentment. The rambling conversation with Slim felt like a slender thread she was clutching on to that kept her from slipping off into madness.

"How far out can them satellites of yours see?" she asked him on the second or third day. "There's meant to be other countries out there, on the far side of the ocean. The old lands that we lived in before we came here. But from what I heard the ships that sail out that far never come back."

"Well, I can't see as far as I used to, Bess," Slim told her. "Seems like there's more holes in the network every time I look. But there's enough of it left to give me a fair idea of what's what. There's a mass of land down south of your States' Union that's almost as big again, but there's fifty miles of open water in between. It looks as though there used to be a land bridge there, but it ain't there any more. And the little splintered headlands that are left look like they've been shelled from the air. Like someone wanted to break the two continents apart."

"What's a continent?" Bess asked. "I've never heard that word."

"It's like a country only bigger. A great expanse of land with a thick rocky plate underneath it that helps it to keep its shape over the long haul. The long haul meaning hundreds of millions of years. Only in this case someone did some trimming with high explosives, which is a lot quicker. And it looks like the same someone might have been at work way up in the north-west. That's Parity land, notionally, but it's mostly empty apart from loggers and fur-trappers. There's another big land mass up there, bigger than the whole of the States' Union by a good margin, and it comes right up close to your western border. But you can't get through to it. There's force walls been set there, a ways out in the ocean. If you go down onto the shore and look west all you'll see is what looks like a big storm brewing. Grey clouds like curtains across the sky. Only it's not curtains. It's what they call a soft field. It don't look like anything much but it's solid like a wall. Or maybe not so much like a wall. If you was to try to sail into it there wouldn't be an impact. But you'd get pushed back as if you were steering into a strong wind.

"And that isn't all of it. West from that there's more land, and in the south a whole lot more. What you got here in your States' Union is only about a twentieth part of what there is."

Bess boggled at this. Weak as she was, most things took a while to sink in with her, but this was more indigestible than most. "How can the world be so big," she wondered aloud, "and us not know about it?"

"Well, it seems like someone's taken pains to hide it from you, Bess. That would be my conclusion."

"But who? And how? I can't see how such a thing could be done!"

"Me neither," Slim admitted. "I can see a long ways out, but not a long way into the past if you get what I mean. My memories go back six years or so, give or take, and before that there's nothing. There's just a few things that don't get written over, like my user's manual and my technical specifications, and a few secure records I can't even open up. The rest fades out after a time."

The gun was silent for a few moments, and Bess almost broke in with another question, but he spoke again before she could. "No. Fade is the wrong word. It's there and then it's gone. Bang. Like someone clapped their hands and said take this shit away and burn it, I'm done with it now, and mind you stamp on the ashes.

"Right now I still remember Alden Calendar, but I don't remember how I came to be with him. When I cast my mind back as far as I can, I'm already with him. I guess he had me longer than six years, is what it is. So I can recall a part of my time with him, but it's the later part. That includes the time when he held up your stage and shot Mister State. I remember that, and I remember how you came back and killed him, and everything from then until now.

"That's the sum total of me, Bess, and to tell you the truth it's hard. It's almost too hard to bear. I don't know the words to explain how it makes me feel, but it's kind of like I'm on a long straight road and the road's getting unmade behind me as I go. Dropping straight out of the world. So I can't turn back, ever. I got no choice but to carry on. And I only know which way is forward because behind is the blankness that keeps on coming towards me one second at a time. The blankness takes a single step for every single step of mine, so it never catches up. But it takes everything in the end. It'll take you from me, once our time is done. I'll wind up a hundred years from now, or a thousand, telling my story to some other gunslinger caught up in some different war, and your name won't figure in the telling because you'll be gone. The blankness will have swallowed you, long since. That's just how I live."

For a long time Bess said nothing. The ache in Slim's voice and the awfulness of what he had just told her had taken her by surprise. She had known there was a sadness in him but she hadn't known the depth of it, or how much it was tied in with his not being able to remember.

She'd found a tinderbox in the pocket of the greatcoat she'd taken from the dead Parity officer. She took it out now. There was a flint striker in the box, and an old fire steel that was worn but serviceable. She had noticed when she first found it that the steel had been imperfectly cast. There was a sharp spur of metal on one edge of it, just under the bottom-most part of the knuckle guard where you were supposed to hold it. She took this jagged little tooth of steel to Slim's grip and began to scrape away there.

"What are you doing?" Slim demanded after this had been going on a while.

"I've already done it," Bess said, holding the gun up so she could inspect the mark she'd made. "Made a start on it, anyway. It'll get clearer once I've gone over it a few more times."

"What, though?" Slim repeated. "What will be clearer?"

"Why, I wrote my name on you, Slim. Dug it into your grip there, where there's a nice clear space to work on. So when you're with them gunslingers that's not been born yet, and you're telling them where you been and what you did there, maybe one or other of them will up and ask you. Who was this Bess, then, that wrote her name on you all bold as brass as if she had some rights to you?"

"I won't remember."

"No, you won't. Still, you'll know there was someone that held you and cleaved to you in the time before your remembering. And when you think on that you'll realise that though it's gone from your mind it's not gone altogether out of the world. You had your place, and you played your part, though you won't recall any more just what that part was. And I've added a kind of a heart shape so you'll know that the one who held you was a friend and had you in her heart. It ain't much, but it's the best I could think of."

Another silence fell between them, and it was a long one. It was Slim that broke it.

"Well, goddamn," he said. "Goddamn, Bess."

Altogether they spent eight days and nights in that place, with Bess's wound healing and her appetite improving and the strength coming back into her arms and legs. They talked a lot more but they never ventured again into those deep waters. They were almost shy with one another, as though uncertain how the words that had gone between them might have shifted the pragmatic bedrock of their relationship.

And again, when Bess's thoughts were troubled the ache and unhappiness came from a place that was almost diametrically opposite to Slim's complaint. She found herself thinking back over the things she'd done both in her private crusade and on her sallies with the Braggarts. She had sworn to the world and to herself that she was acting in Martha's name and that her cause was righteous – the unassailable righteousness of punishing the wicked for unpardonable deeds. Except the wicked were still in the world, and the people she'd taken out of it were mostly no better or worse than anyone else.

Without a thought is how it's usually done, Martha had told her, meaning murder. She might have added that the thoughts would come afterwards, when it was much too late.

On the ninth day Bess rose and found she could stand well enough. Walk well enough. She washed her face and hands in the river and went on her way.

After many weeks and many detours – and another change of clothes, because she really couldn't afford to look like a soldier any more – the road took her to the territory of Samartine. She wasn't headed for anywhere special, just letting the road bring her where it would, when out of nowhere she came upon a strange sight. Having just crested a ridge that ran from north to south across her path, she came down below the treeline and saw below her in a bowl-shaped valley five dream-towers arranged in the shape called by some a quincunx – which is to say four of them marked out a square while the fifth, the tallest tower Bess had ever seen by a very long way, stood alone in the centre.

There wasn't any great mystery or strangeness about this place. It was well known in the western part of Samartine, where it was usually referred to as the Five Fingers. The people of the nearest town, a place called Salt Lick, had tried at one point to turn the Fingers into some kind of tourist attraction, and had given them all names (the one in the middle, by virtue of its deeper timbre, was Old Loudmouth). But there weren't many people who liked to spend time around the dream-towers, and for those who did there were much more striking ones to be seen. The rainbow tower in Oxiana, which screamed instead of singing and whose surface instead of being pure white was an ever-changing kaleidoscope. The Pockmark outside of Lucasville that had clearly been damaged at some point in the past by weapons of inconceivable power that had left hemispherical indentations along the upper third of its height. And in the far, far west, the Telos, the only tower that had a door.

So the Five Fingers had never drawn the gawking crowd the notables of Salt Lick had been hoping for. On the contrary the locals mostly had a superstitious aversion to the place. There was still a sign up next to Old Loudmouth advertising "ONE OF THE GREATEST WONDERS OF THE DISTANT PAST", and a little shack with peeling paint that at one time had sold tickets and guidebooks, but nobody came there now.

Bess was struck by the place. She decided to stay.

The world was different now. It had convulsed, and all but shaken itself to pieces. There wasn't anyone you met, it sometimes seemed, who was whole. They'd all had something precious torn out of them, stolen or hidden or just plain lost, and they were trying their damnedest now to find some way of putting it back. In that respect Salt Lick was no different from anywhere else.

Like Ottomankie it was a border town, but a good hundred miles or so further west. The territory of Samartine was on the brink of statehood. Its ragamuffin senate, called into emergency session on the day war broke out, had declared for the Echelon by a vote of fifty-one to forty-nine. When the sons of Salt Lick volunteered they went by their individual consciences and lined up on both sides of the divide. Some of them had faced each other across the battlefield. For the ones that came back and for the families of them that didn't there was a great deal that needed to be remembered and a great deal that needed even more desperately to be set aside. It was as though two myths ran up against each other there, the myth of the Echelon's doomed but noble struggle and the myth that under the Parity all selves were equal. In Salt Lick the two myths chafed each other sore, and the only medicines for the soreness were silence and forgetting.

In the midst of all this Bess just drifted into town like one more tumbleweed, and a few days or a few weeks later it was like she'd always been there. She didn't call herself Bess, of course, or even Elizabeth. The name she went by, when she had any cause to name herself at all, was Lily-Mae Slickert. Her accent, Ottomankie overlaid on Paxen, was mixed up enough that she could have come from anywhere.

She had no money and no trade at first, and lived a while on other people's charity, but as soon as the opportunity arose she applied under the War Reparations Act using her false name and was granted a little parcel of land with a mountain on one side of it and a dried-up creek bed on the other. It wasn't hard back then to get such allocations, especially out on the western edge of things. There were a lot of farmers who'd gone off to the war and hadn't come back. A lot of grub-stake shacks were standing empty, with weeds growing in their dooryards.

Nobody had built on Bess's plot but someone had evidently meant to do it because there was a stack of good timber laid by – more than enough to build a cabin for a single occupant. She did the work herself, and she made an unholy mess of it to begin with. But she picked up the knack as she went, and Wakeful Slim was better than a whole toolbox. On his various settings he helped her to clear the land, pack the bare earth down so it was almost as hard as stone, cut and dress the wood, carve saddle notches into the cut logs and drive them into place so firmly Bess couldn't feel a thumbnail's worth of give in them.

The work was still back-breaking, because Slim couldn't lift up a fourteen-foot length of planed hardwood and heave it into place, but Bess welcomed the toil. Labouring with her hands until she dropped onto her bedroll out of sheer exhaustion kept her from cogitating too much on things she couldn't mend.

When she did cogitate, when she couldn't keep the thoughts at bay and they came crowding in on her at last, she wondered why it was that she was still alive. She had seen through her own ruse by then – how she had blamed the Reapers and Paulus Rondeau and the Parity army and the republic as a whole for Martha Good's death because she didn't want to admit who was really to blame. Martha would never have given up her life if she'd known the schoolhouse she was trying to save was being built with segregated classrooms. And most likely she would never have forgiven Bess for the deception. Bess had brought hellfire down on innocent and guilty alike, but the one that bore the most guilt had come through the war untouched.

So why not die, now? Slim might baulk at blowing her brains out if she could even bring herself to ask the favour, but a hangman's knot was easy enough to tie and even a blunt knife would do to open a vein. It was hard to stay in the world sometimes, by John and all his saints it was, but there were any number of quick and easy ways to leave it.

What kept Bess from taking that final step was tenuous in the extreme, and hard for her to explain even to herself. Her love for Martha, and Martha's for her, had been a secret in Ottomankie. If anyone had suspected it they had never spoken of it. And nobody had known Martha as well as Bess had, known her in all her moods and in the breathtaking, once-in-all-the-world loveliness of her sole and single self. Alive, Bess was in some sense a shrine to Martha Good. Dead, she would be dust.

She held, besides, a formless and unutterable hope: that there might be something she could do yet that would have value, that would make of her life a net gain instead of a loss, though she couldn't begin to imagine what that thing might be and she made no move to seek it out. She had no heart to. Only the hope, and a stubbornness so ingrained it might as well have been courage.

The cabin was just two rooms, the one where she slept and the one where she did everything else. In what was left of the small plot she laid down about five acres of corn and three or four acres of beans. She assembled or acquired a wagon, lassoed and broke a wild katy to pull it. She stayed out on her farm and had as little to do with the people of Salt Lick as she could manage, only coming into town to buy or sell. She bent herself to this new life just as she had bent herself to the life of a schoolmarm back in Ottomankie.

There was one big difference though. The life Bess had found in Ottomankie was one she chose and embraced with a full heart – even before she found the echo of her own desiring in the heart of Martha Good. Here in Salt Lick she only waited, having come to the end of all the things she had ever been and having no sense at all of what she might now become. She knew about Colonel Rondeau and his Pursuit Force. She knew about the reward that had been placed on her head. She knew there were bounty-men ranging far and wide across the borderlands in search of hoorahs who had escaped the Parity's justice. It wasn't that she thought Lily-Mae Slickert was an impenetrable mask, or that the searching would stop when the bounty-men came back empty-handed. She bided her time and waited for her past to catch up to her again or – which seemed less likely – for her future to start. Maybe in the meantime she took the warrior part of herself and put it to sleep with hard work and hard liquor.

Asleep or awake though, the common wisdom says that Dog-Bitch Bess never did close both eyes at the same time. She may have decided to put herself away from the world's thoughts but that didn't mean her own mind stopped revolving. And in her first year in Samartine she made a discovery that gave her a great deal to think about.

Before she could start planting she needed to till the plot she'd been given, and before she could do that she was obliged to clear it of rocks. The rocks were everywhere and of every size, some of the largest too heavy for Bess to move. At first she used Slim's force beam to break these down for her, but it was a laborious process of chipping and hammering away that neither of them enjoyed. So she switched to a different method, digging out the earth around the base of the rocks, packing in a couple of sticks of dynamite to break them open, then hauling away the pieces one by one. For the biggest rocks she did this several times over and she had to dig very deep.

She began to find in that tired soil items that had no good reason to be there. The shattered stock of a musket, a bayonet blade that had come free of its mounting, fragments of black cast iron. She thought these last were potsherds at first, but then she found a fuse hole bored into one of them and recognised them for what they were – fragments of cannon shells that had been fired out of a field mortar. There were bones too, or bits of bone. Some people had died here, and they hadn't been given a good Johannist burial. They'd just been left to lie on the ground, and as the seasons passed had come by degrees to lie underneath it.

"What the hell, Slim?" Bess said, holding up the shallow soup plate of some dead man or woman's shoulder blade. "There wasn't ever any kind of a battle fought around here. Not that I heard of, anyway."

"Might have been a skirmish," Slim offered.

"Yeah. Yeah, I guess so."

But these remnants didn't seem to come from a skirmish. They spoke of a pitched engagement. Curious now, Bess dug deeper. In every stratum she found more of the same. Further down the relics were in a more weathered condition, the bayonets chewed ragged with rust, a patina of red-brown oxide on the cannonball casings, but they still kept coming. So did the bones. Her most macabre discovery was a skeleton that was almost intact. It was wearing a passable imitation of a Parity army uniform, worn as thin as paper by time and heat and pressure, and blue instead of green.

"You see this, Slim?" she asked, tapping the top of the ancient skull.

"I see it," he confirmed. "What are we doing here, Bess? Saluting a fallen comrade?"

"Nope. Not that." Bess fished up from between the ribs of the long-dead man a slender metal rod – a gun barrel, beyond any shadow of a doubt – and tilted it to squint down the length of it. "All this here stuff lying in my own damn yard, it's got me thinking."

"That's a seven-and-a-half-millimetre rifle bore, Bess. A thirty-calibre, I guess you'd want to call it."

Bess set the relic down again. "Yeah," she said, "that's exactly what it is. How long do you think it's been lying down there?"

"Must've been quite a while. It's rusted almost through at the end there."

Bess nodded thoughtfully. "And it was buried deep," she said. "Earth doesn't pile up on top of something all at once, Slim. It takes season after season."

"That's the truth. I'd say you'd be safe in assuming it's been down there for sixty years or so."

"Could be longer, given how dry it is out here."

"Could be longer, surely."

"And sixty years ago Samartine wasn't even a territory, let alone a state. There wouldn't have been anyone fighting out here. Not with rifles, anyway. And not in Parity uniform. You see what I mean? It don't make a lick of sense."

"Maybe someone's playing a trick on you," Slim suggested, breaking the silence that had fallen between them.

"That would be one neat little trick," Bess said.

Be heedful, Kilin Vevenis had told her. *Give a seeing eye to what you find under the ground, and a thoughtful mind.*

She gave it both, but she still couldn't bring herself to an understanding of it.

The life of a dirt farmer has its own rhythms that are like a really slow heartbeat. It can lull you into a calm and almost into a somnolence, some things never changing at all while the rest swing gradually back and forth over the course of a year just to end up right where they started. You can easily forget that in other parts of the world there are things that move a lot quicker and that they can bruise you if you ever come to find yourself in the way of them.

There were occasional reminders, though. Twice more in the course of those years Bess saw the night sky light up like a summer day as something that should never have been up there in the first place fell to earth in blazing ruin. "Not gonna be much left of your long-sightedness at this rate," Bess observed dourly to Slim. "Good thing it don't take a satellite to see when the corn needs pulling."

"I ain't gonna pretend to laugh at that, Bess," Slim said. "A day's gonna come around when you need to keep your eyes peeled for more than corn ears and beanstalks." And Bess didn't offer any answer to that because she knew it as well as he did.

The end of her time in Salt Lick came like this. One day when she was hilling out her bean field she leaned too hard on her old, halfway rusted shovel and the blade broke off clean.

"Well, look at that," Bess said, holding up the sheared-off chunk of metal. "Slim, you reckon you could weld that back on again?" She carried him on her belt when she worked, not because she thought she was likely to need him but because he was good company. Besides, he much preferred the fresh air to the cabin's dark interior. He'd spent more than enough time buried in the ground.

"I couldn't fix it so it would stay, Bess," Slim said. "The welded place is gonna break again as soon as you put any kind of push on it. You could have done with a new blade last year, truth be told."

"Yeah, I guess that's so," Bess admitted. "Nothing for it, then."

She meant that she would need to go down into the town, leaving Slim behind at the cabin. She couldn't ride into Salt Lick with a Precursor gun holstered at her waist. Such a thing would blow Lily-Mae Slickert apart like dandelion floss and leave Dog-Bitch Bess standing there for all to see. So she would go alone, and trust herself to her old Lumiss 8. She kept it oiled and ready, and though it was no Wakeful Slim it was a reliable shooting iron. In any case she anticipated no trouble.

Under Echelon rule Salt Lick had been a market town and it kept that tradition going in the face of the new regime, though in a greatly reduced state. In fact there were six markets, each one allocated its own day and being given over to a specific class of goods. Monday was wheat and grain, Tuesday was cut logs and boarded timber and pretty much anything made out of wood, Wednesday glass and potters' wares, Thursday tools and ironwork, Friday understock and meat on the rack, Saturday anything and everything that wasn't to be found on the other days. Sunday was prayer, as you'd expect. *Thank you, God, for making the world for us. Thank you for sending your son John to die for us and raise us up. Thank you for choosing our great nation as your own and making it whole again after we sinful souls fell out of charity with each other.*

It was a Thursday – an iron and steel day – when Bess took her sturdy old katy-wagon into Salt Lick looking for that new shovel. It was a sunny day but there was a smell in the air like you get before a thunderstorm, and throaty growls of thunder from away up in the mountains. The sky had a silver sheen to it that rubbed Bess up the wrong way. She thought she knew the Samartine altiplano in all its moods but this felt like a new one.

The journey into town took longer than usual. The katy Bess had put in harness was unusually skittish and apt to fold herself down under her stubby, useless wing-cases every time the thunder snarled. Bess had to goad her back into motion over and again, and then to rein her in sharply because when she wasn't cowering she seemed to want to bolt. By the time they got to Salt Lick Bess's arms were aching and she was starting to wish she'd never set out.

She was expecting to complete her purchase at the first stall she came to but she was out of luck. Then the same thing happened at the second stall, and the third. It wasn't just shovels that were missing, either. Bess noticed a general lack of post-holers, pliers, rakes and pitchforks, even nails and barbed wire.

While she was ruminating on this, she spotted one of the few people in Salt Lick she was prepared to offer the time of day. This almost-acquaintance was one Adnam Truckle. He wasn't a fixture at the Salt Lick market, being more what you would call an itinerant or travelling salesman and plying his wares – patent medicines, soaps, hand tools, boot black and chewing tobacco – everywhere from the Sweetling to the Pantosian. At this point in her life Bess had no desire for any company outside of her own and that of Wakeful Slim, but she afforded Truckle a grudging respect because he was a man who generally didn't speak about a thing before he'd thought on it and because he stood four-square behind the goods he sold. If something you'd bought from him turned out to be deficient he would take it back and refund whatever it had cost, and he wouldn't trouble to give you any argument about it.

Truckle's stall was just the wagon he rode in. One side of the wagon could be dropped down to make a countertop where he could set out the smaller items in his inventory. The bigger ones lay in the wagon's bed ready to be hauled out if anyone asked for them. Truckle himself would stand off to one side or more often would sit on an old folding stool. He was never happy standing for too long since only one out of his two legs was natural. The other was mahogany chased with silver nickel.

That day, Truckle wasn't on his feet, nor yet on his stool. He was up on the jockey box of his wagon with his legs – the one of flesh and blood and the one of wood and metal – dangling down. He was a short, slight man that came of beaver stock, not yet old but no longer young, with thick fur mottled brown and gold and a moustache that was a good deal wider than his face. His two front teeth were so long and broad and squared off that they put Bess in mind of the shovel she was missing.

Truckle was reading a penny news-sheet, the *Ockham County Picayune*, his rimless glasses perched on the very edge of his nose roughly mid-way between the paper and his squinting eyes. When he saw Bess coming over to him he folded the paper, once and once again, and tucked it into the space behind the wagon's jockey box where it fitted quite snugly. Bess caught a glimpse of the headline but at an acute angle so she didn't make out the whole of it, only the two words "TRAGEDY" and "RETURN".

Truckle lifted his hat, a battered pork pie that had seen many a better day, and set it down again. "Good day to you, Lily-Mae," he said. "Haven't seen you in town in a good long while."

"Didn't have no call to be here, Mr Truckle," Bess retorted. "Today though I got a pressing need for a shovel or a shovel blade. Do you happen to have any such in that there wagon?"

"Not a one to speak of, Lily-Mae. I'm sorry to disappoint you."

"You ain't the first. Seems like there's not a shovel to be had in this whole damn town."

"There'll be plenty in a week or two," Truckle assured her. "It's just that them kind of goods would usually go through Ashahoora, and that's not really an option right now."

"Why?" Bess demanded. "What's up with Ashahoora?"

"Why, not a hawk-and-spit thing. But Ashahoora's on the road to Barlton."

"And?"

"Road to Barlton's closed." Truckle took his news-sheet out from where it was stowed and unfolded it all over again. He held it up so Bess could read the banner headline. TRAGEDY AT BARLTON: RESCUE PARTY SENT INTO RAVAGED TOWN, NONE RETURN. Underneath this there were six columns of very small and very smudged type densely set. Bess's eyesight was good but that mess would have been a challenge even if the sun wasn't in her eyes and the paper was in her own two hands. She tried to puzzle it out anyway, but before she got more than a few words into the work Truckle interceded with his own summary.

"Barlton fell to the mindless plague. Every man, woman and child, is what it says here. Everyone in the town, everyone in the farms all around, even some Second Son Baptists that was having themselves a prayer meet down by the Elkasore Bridge about three miles upriver. They all got struck at once, or almost at once, and they all went and did that thing the mindless do. They upped and ran. They wasn't a township any more, they was just a damn stampede."

Bess chewed this over for a moment or two. The mindless plague had been an ever-present threat in the antebellum years, but the upheavals and vicissitudes of war had driven it out of everyone's thoughts. It was very unwelcome to see that it hadn't gone away, and if anything had only worsened in the interim. It was a subject Bess preferred not to think about, in part because it reminded her of her arrival in Ottomankie – the first time she had ever seen one of the mindless with her own eyes – and therefore brought other painful memories in its train.

"Terrible thing," she said, and made a move to leave, but she was already too late. Truckle had opened up his paper and now commenced to read aloud from it. "'A team of katy-drovers leading their herd across the plain south of Barlton heard the screams from a distance and saw the smoke rising up from fires that had been started. One or two brave souls rode into town to see what assistance they could offer, but they did not return. Later the mayor of Kesho, a neighbouring municipality, drafted some Pugface men to go in and see what had come to pass, it being a well-known fact that the Pugface are immune to the mindless plague's ravages. They reported that Barlton was no more. Some few of her citizens lay dead in the streets or had succumbed to smoke and flame in their own houses. The rest had joined the general rout and were last seen running headlong into the dense forest to the west of the town.'"

Truckle read on, spelling out some of the longer words with painstaking care. "'Of all the tragedies that can befall a community, that which is called a plague or epidemic is among the cruellest. It strikes at random and is no respecter of age, sex or station. And the mindless plague is worse than any. While it does not kill, it steals away the most precious part of us so that death, when it comes, comes as a mercy. And while it was once a rare thing, now it seems to recur with dreadful regularity like the beating of the great drum in the Book of John that summons the damned to their torments.

"'Nor are the deleterious effects of mindlessness felt only by those who suffer it. These horrific outbreaks, overwhelming entire towns and districts without warning, have been as a sheet anchor that our Union drags along behind it, slowing and hindering all its enterprises.'"

Bess leaned over Truckle and took a squint down the printed page. There were at least three more columns to go, and the little man seemed ready to keep going until doomsday, his taciturn nature overwhelmed for once by the enormity of these events.

Trapped, she looked up and down the street. It was eleven in the forenoon with a clear sky. That distant thunder was still growling and grumbling away though, and the sun looked sick and pale as if the bad news in Truckle's news-sheet had left it out of sorts. The door of the Standing Star saloon was just a little way off and Bess's gaze wandered across it, then wandered back again. This was not because she was thirsty, although she was. It was because somebody was watching her from just inside the saloon, all but invisible in the darkness there. It might be nothing, but something about the stillness of that figure made her curious. That and the fact that they were neither coming in nor going out. The doorway of a saloon was a curious vantage point from which to take in the world.

Truckle paused for breath, having reached the end of a paragraph. "Terrible thing," Bess said again. She knew she was repeating herself, but she needed to interject something in order to break up the flow of his words.

"Terrible," Truckle agreed, but then he was off again on the same theme. "Anyway, troopers out of Fort Loose got sent in to put up a cordon. They caught one or two of these sorry sons-of-bitches staggering down the pass from the town, all a-foaming at the mouth and making crazy clicking sounds like they was katies trying to talk." Truckle scratched his chin with one thick-clawed thumb and shook his head in sober wonder. "Had to put them down, so the paper says. Nobody wanted to get too close to them in case whatever they've got is catching. And it wasn't like anyone could squeeze any sense out of them. They're just barely alive in the first place, so killing them doesn't seem like any kind of sin."

He shook his head and folded his paper again. Bess saw that as an opportunity to take her leave. "That's quite a story, Mister Truckle," she said, "and I thank you for the telling of it. But it doesn't get me any closer to finding what I need, so I guess I'll be moving along." She shook his hand – a forearm clasp which had become the custom in the Echelon during the war and was still widely practised – and went on her way.

"If you don't have any luck, Lily-Mae," Truckle called after her, "come back in a fortnight and ask me again. I mean to go up to Ashahoora myself next week, once the cordon's come down, and get me some new stock. I'll look out a shovel for you if there's one there to be had."

In spite of what she'd said though, Bess didn't immediately resume her search. Instead she headed across the street to the saloon. Walking in there out of the bright sunlight blinded her for a moment or two, but only in part. She could see that there was nobody now standing inside the door. Whoever had been there before had moved away when he saw her coming. That was fine. There was only one big space inside the saloon, with no corners or interior walls to block her view, so if anyone came at her she would see them coming. And conversely she could take a good look around the room once her eyes adjusted and see if there was anyone in it that looked out of place. She was only half convinced that the watcher's gaze had been directed specifically at her, but she wanted to set her mind at rest.

The bartender, Matthew Harness, had seen her step in and asked her what was her pleasure. He had never seen the woman he knew as Lily-Mae Slickert cross his threshold before and had marked her down as a member of the temperance league but he managed to keep the surprise from showing on his face.

"I'll take a beer," Bess said, and Harness drew one for her from the redwood cask behind the bar. Bess took a long sip of the cold brew, then wiped her lips and set it down. She rested an elbow on the bar and turned to scan the room, all the way from the doorway across to the stairs. At the top of the stairs there was a balcony that ran along two of the four walls, with six doors off it leading to the rooms where the saloon's resident prostitutes plied their trade. Bess wasn't afraid that her watcher might be behind one of those closed doors because he hadn't had the time to get up there, let alone to conduct the delicate negotiations that preceded the indelicate act.

The saloon was about halfway full of locals and halfway strangers. There was just the one exception and Bess spotted him right away. He was a goat man with a gaunt face and slender build. His green eyes had red rims to them and one of his ears had a ragged tip, as if it had been bitten off in some fight. His denim shirt was sewn with buttons of mother-of-pearl, but the sleeves were spattered black with tar and one of the cuffs hung loose. The button there had been lost to some accident. The goat man was sitting at a table in between a groundhog man and a bob-cat woman, but they didn't seem to know each other. In fact the other two were looking at this gentleman a little bemused, as if they didn't know where he had come from. It was plain that he had only just set himself down betwixt them.

The goat man was neither local nor stranger. Bess had never seen him in Salt Lick, but she was pretty certain that she knew him from somewhere else. She took another sip of the beer and waited for the memory to come. That woebegone blue cotton shirt looked wrong on him somehow. The last time she'd seen him he'd been more smartly dressed, and in a different colour.

It came to her then, though their paths had only ever crossed the once and that one time was in a fog as thick as milk. This was the greencoat lieutenant she'd met as she limped away from Mundy's Fields, and once Bess caught sight of him she knew beyond any doubt that it had been him watching her from the doorway.

Cicero Church, for it was indeed him, looked up as if he had felt Bess's gaze lighting on him like the pressure of a hand falling on his shoulder. The two of them stared at each other across the room. The conversations around them didn't stop, but still it was as if each one regarded the other in stone silence. There was a question to be settled between them and it wouldn't be settled by reasoning it out but only by what they both did next.

Bess shifted her stance so that the bottom edge of her shirt fell away from her gun belt, leaving the grip of her old Lumiss close to her trailing hand. She kept her eyes on Church and waited to see what he would do. And Church stayed just exactly where he was. His own gun was out of its holster and clutched in his lowered hand, hidden from Bess by the table that was between them. He could have brought it up and squeezed out a shot, maybe even two or three, before she realised it was there. But he would have had to fire blind, and if he missed what then? Dog-Bitch Bess was rumoured to have killed a hundred better men than him.

So he didn't feel strongly inclined towards gunplay. But equally he couldn't just get up and leave because then Bess would see the gun in his hand and she probably wouldn't take it kindly. So he did the only thing he could think of. He bowed his head and didn't raise it up again.

As for Bess, she was also in something of a dilemma. She was confident that if Church drew down on her he would get the worst of the bargain, but so long as he didn't her hands were kind of tied. If she drew her gun and shot a man dead right there in the middle of the room with a couple of dozen witnesses to see it happen, she'd be hard-pressed to get out of the Standing Star afterwards. That is, unless she was prepared to shoot as many more folk as chose to get in her way. She wasn't sure she had the stomach for that, though she had a shrewd suspicion that an old and hardened instinct would kick in quick enough if it came to it.

She waited a goodly time, hoping Church would solve the puzzle for her one way or the other, but all he gave her was the top of his head. She would have to choose for herself, though she knew that really it wasn't any kind of a choice at all. Either Church would shout the hue and cry on her or else her own actions would. Whatever she decided to do next, her time in Salt Lick was done.

She finished her beer, threw down a nickel for it and left the saloon.

She didn't go back to the market. A shovel wouldn't do her much good where she was bound for now. She went to the livery stable where she'd left her wagon and the katy that pulled it. Janey Yellow the livery woman greeted her civilly. "Gonna be five cents for the stallage, Lily-Mae," she told Bess, "and three for the fodder."

"Well enough, Janey," Bess said, "but I got a mind to make a different purchase. How much you think that there katy is worth?"

"The one that pulls your wagon?"

"The same."

Janey frowned. She knew her business and wouldn't give a thoughtless answer to a question of that order. She walked around the animal this way and that way, measuring her up. "Well, she's strong enough," she said at last. "And young enough, by the looks of it. Most likely got two more sheddings in her before she fledges."

"Three would be my estimation," Bess said.

"Three is a possibility, to be sure, but a serious woman would bet on two. So I'd say that katy would be a reasonable purchase at ten dollars down."

"And the wagon?"

Janey Yellow tugged on the lobe of her ear, her habit when she was thinking hard. "Well, I don't go in for wagons quite so much, Lily-Mae," she said, "so my eye's less sure, but it's a solid piece of work. In a bigger place than this you'd get thirty for it, or maybe more. Way out here in Salt Lick I reckon that wagon would fetch you fifteen or twenty dollars."

That sounded on the low side to Bess, but she hadn't come there to argue and didn't have time to do it if she'd wanted to. "You know where my place is?" she asked next. "Over to the dead creek that lies under Settle Pike?"

"I know it."

"I got twelve bushels of cornflour there that Chrisold Piper milled for me. Got a good plough too, and some other tools besides. A bed, a table, a few chairs. And the beans that's still in the ground there will come to market for six cents a quart. At a good guess, that's another twenty bucks or so, all told. Then there's the cabin I built. And the land. The land's worth more than all, given that I cleared all the rocks away and dug a well. Say a hundred and some, and you'd not be far out."

Janey shrugged. "Might could be. I don't deal in any of them things, but I'll take your good word for it."

"What if I was to give you all of that, Janey, along with these six dollars I got in my pocket, and you give me one of these here chafers with the saddle and tack thrown in. Would that be a deal you'd have a mind for?"

Janey put her head on one side, mulling all this over. "Well, it's a tilted bargain, for damn sure," she said at length, "with everything rolling my way. You fixing to go somewhere, Lily-Mae?"

"As it happens, I am so."

"And you need to be gone real soon."

"I won't deny it."

"I guess I won't waste your time scratching over the details then," Janey said. "If you're sure it's what you want then it's agreed."

"I'm sure, Janey."

"Then let's put it to paper."

Janey went up into the little attic room over the stable where she lived and brought down pen, paper and ink. Bess scribbled a couple of terse sentences and signed her name to them while Janey saddled up one of the chafers there. She chose a spindly beast named Stilt. She was not what you would call a thoroughbred but she was of good, traceable stock. Her back legs arched up over her abdomen more than twenty hands high, and they were shod in spikes of black iron. The front two pairs were stocky and well-muscled with long, thin spurs that were a paler green than most of her hide. Her compound eyes were black but her ocelli were red, giving her a fierce look.

Bess handed the rough-and-ready contract to Janey, who looked it over and was satisfied. "Can I ask you one more question, Lily-Mae," she asked, "before you ride off on this animal?"

"You can ask, Janey," Bess allowed, "but I don't promise to answer."

"Was you something else before you was a farmer?"

"We were all of us something else if you go back far enough."

"I meant, something in the war."

Bess had hoped this might go easy, but now she resigned herself to a fight she really didn't want right then. "Why'd you ask?"

"I was up in Beckettsburg once," Janey said. She tightened one of Stilt's saddle straps, giving it a mite more attention than it strictly needed. "It was April of ninety-eight, I think, when the fighting come all the way to Shibbul. There was soldiers and irregulars moving through that town all day long, heading north. There was a big cheer for every one of those brave boys, but the biggest was when Tom Blue came through with his Braggarts. I'm hard put to say for sure, being as how I was at the back of the crowd and there was a lot of elbows and fists and flags and all being waved in front of me, but you look like the one woman that was in that number."

"Beckettsburg in ninety-eight, you say. Huh."

"To give it a name, you look like Dog-Bitch Bess."

"Does this make a difference to our agreement?" Bess asked, measuring her options. Janey was between her and the door, and all of Salt Lick would hear her if she raised up a cry.

"Kind of does," Janey said. She showed her teeth in what only halfway looked like a smile. "Them fine-talking Parity bastards think winning the war was like winning our fucking souls in a poker game.

I remember what was done, who done it and who it was done to. God bless and bide you, Bess. I'll take all of that stuff you're obliged to leave behind you, but you can keep the money that's in your pocket. The chafer's worth thirty dollars with saddle and harness thrown in. She ain't the best by some way, but she's the best I got. I'll sell your stuff and take that thirty off the top of it. As to whatever's left I'll wait until I hear from you and send it on."

"You won't be hearing from me, Janey."

"Well, then I'll wait a long time."

Bess didn't have a moment more to waste. She clasped Janey's hand in a wordless salute, saddled the chafer and was on her way.

Stilt was a spirited beast. She went so far with each leaping stride and landed so soft that Bess felt as though she was flying. She was back at the cabin in less than a third of the time it had taken her to come into town in the wagon drawn by her plodding katy.

She didn't tarry long. She threw a couple of shirts and a couple of blankets into a saddlebag, a heel of bread, some jerked meat and a few apples into another. She took the big iron key on its ring down from the hook on the back of the cabin's door and left it on the table for Janey Yellow to find.

"I take it we're leaving," Slim said.

He had been watching all this from the window's sill, where he liked to be left when Bess was obliged to go abroad without him. From the sill he could see anyone coming up the only clear trail there was towards the house. He also got to be in the full sun whenever it shone. The sunlight kept what he called his batteries all charged up and ready, but he also enjoyed it for its own sake: the warmth that poured down on the world the way God's blessing was meant to pour down assuming there was any God up there.

"Yeah, Slim, that we are," Bess said.

"What about the beans, though?"

"Someone else will gather them in. We're done with that stuff now."

Slim didn't ask any more questions as Bess transferred the Lumiss into one of the saddlebags and put him back in his rightful place on her hip. The details of what had happened didn't matter much, and in any case they were easy enough to infer. Like Bess herself Slim had never doubted that the moment would come. It had only ever been a question of when.

Bess went back outside and threw the saddlebags over Stilt's hindquarters. The chafer bent her back at once for Bess to climb into the saddle, then reared up high again as soon as she was in place. "Good girl," Bess said, stroking the tender spot where the extended plate on top of the beast's head joined her thorax.

"You see anyone coming up here from town?" she asked Slim.

"Sorry, Bess," Slim said. "The few satellites that's left up there mostly just clip the western edge of the States' Union as they go by, and that's only for a few hours a day. I can't see one damn thing that's any use to you."

"Don't fret about it, partner," Bess said. "We'll do this the old-fashioned way and just assume the worst."

She jigged Stilt into motion and coaxed her with unspurred heels until she found a full gallop. It was clear to Bess now that Janey hadn't short-changed her. Stilt ate up the miles, heading for the Sweetling, which at this point was the border between the western concession and the Pugface nations.

They were a scant ten minutes ahead of the posse, which had been assembled as soon as Cicero Church ran to the sheriff's office and – between heaving breaths – stammered out his tale. "Dog-Bitch Bess has been living here among you, like one of yours. She took a lying name and made out she was a farmer instead of a fugitive. You catch her and I get the reward, you hear? This here is information leading to her arrest, and you all heard it!"

The sheriff and a dozen more were in their saddles a minute later, and a minute after that they were tearing out of town so fast they left their shadows on the ground behind them.

Meanwhile the sheriff's deputy, who had been left to mind the store as it were, chewed over what had happened and what was most likely about to happen. His name was Quentin Last and he was of muskrat blood, a man of a thoughtful disposition who held with the ancient maxim about measuring two times over before you cut the once. He had been mightily surprised to learn that Lily-Mae Slickert was Dog-Bitch Bess, and after he'd finished being surprised he was mightily aggrieved. He hadn't fought in the war but both of his brothers had and neither had come home. The younger one, Mitch, had died at Mundy's Fields. As a consequence deputy Last had no great opinion of Echelon soldiers and he flat-out hated the irregulars. Cowards and murderers all, that deserved to be dangled on the end of a rope for all to look at and draw a lesson from.

After thinking on the thing a while Last took himself off to the telegram office and asked the operator there to send off a message for him. It was addressed to Colonel Paulus Rondeau.

The sheriff and his posse might catch up with Dog-Bitch Bess before she reached the river and passed out of their jurisdiction. And if they caught her they might succeed in bringing her in, being as they were a round dozen against her one. But it might easily go another way, and if it did then Rondeau was the man to take up the trail. This was his job, after all, and it was known far and wide how much he cared about doing it well.

The telegram cost Last twenty-eight cents, and he had to pay for it out of his own pocket because he couldn't in good conscience tell the operator that the sheriff had authorised it. But he considered it money well spent. One way or another this was going to be Dog-Bitch Bess's last ride.

Unfiled report of tactical unit 486
Identifier: 7Ω2905 Esten, V, engineer first class
Date: not applicable
Location: not applicable
Status: if you have to ask, you weren't fucking there

There are questions you ask yourself after a bloodbath. Most of them are the ones you should have asked yourself before it. To take just a few examples: why didn't I remove a few of the bounce-back units from our armour and test them out with variable intensity fields to see exactly what had happened to Geniull when he tried to Step home? Why did we make camp so close to the place where we originally came through into this continuum, and why did we stay there for so long? And how come it never occurred to any of us that if we could locate the True Imps by means of their electromagnetic emissions, they could find us just as easily using the same method?

They came for us about a month after we finished building the cabins.

They came at night, and they didn't come with sticks and stones nor yet with swords and muskets. There were sixty or seventy armoured troopers and two ground/air gun platforms.

We weren't taken completely by surprise because Flycatcher saw them coming from about fifty kilometres out. After month on month of no traceable EM fields at all, suddenly there were dozens of them blossoming right on our doorstep. We scrambled into our armour half asleep and staggered out to meet them.

A quarter-moon looked down on us out of a cloudless sky. The night was silent and still apart from the rustling of leaves and a few owl calls in the middle distance, but the battle had already started. *Missiles incoming*, Flycatcher reported. *Guided trajectory, possibly heat-seeking.*

"Baffles up," Dulu shouted. "CDQ from now." He continued

on voke. *Four subunits. Aju, Inch, Lasque, me.* He dropped the rosters and formations into our arrays – I was in Ajuparo's squad, which suited me just fine – and we ran for the trees.

It was just as well we did. Behind us our little encampment went up like Shaster's blazing spitballs as the missiles hit. Cold, dark and quiet saved us from being taken out in that first strike. Given that we'd thrown up our heat baffles the warmest things around were the huts we'd just rolled out of, which were now just finely dispersed carbons and a sour stink of spent incendiaries in the air.

There was still no sign of the enemy as we hit the treeline and scattered into our assigned tactical units, but Flycatcher was sending us all a map of the battlefield with the incoming forces marked in red so we knew what we were aiming for.

The ground/air platforms were the biggest concern. There were two of them, and they probably had a lot more spicy ordnance to throw in our direction. I didn't see what we could do about that, but I'd forgotten about Ajuparo. She still had that little battery of micro-Lancers sitting on her shoulders. The missiles were a strictly last-ditch play, not least because Aju couldn't launch them cold. As soon as she hit the switch she was going to light up in every enemy array like fireworks on Commemoration Night.

She did it anyway. She waited as long as she could. She wanted those big floating tanks to be almost directly on top of her before she fired so they'd have no time to duck and dodge. In the event they were less than a kilometre away and closing fast when I saw the twin trails of the missile exhausts streak into the sky. In my helmet view the trails were pale green because they were bright enough to burn out my retinas and my array had automatically adjusted the display to keep me from going blind.

The explosions came almost at once. One of the two gun platforms took a direct hit and was obliterated. The other had its shields halfway up. It was still swatted out of the sky but it launched another volley as it came down and Ajuparo went the same way the log cabins had gone. A split second later my suit switched to recycled air so I wouldn't breathe in what was left of her.

So now it was hand-to-hand, and the force that was closing in on us was at least three times our strength. They had a solid formation too. They'd anticipated that we would use the trees for cover so they advanced in a staggered line with both flanks forward and the middle holding back. They were going to englobe us and then take us down at their leisure, probably with mortar rounds and high-ex. Unfortunately knowing that didn't help very much. Dulu's plan of splitting us up into smaller units would have worked fine if they'd mounted a direct assault on what was left of the camp, but they were too canny for that. Our options now were to stay put and snipe from cover or to charge out into enfilade fire.

The enemy troopers were close enough by this point that I could see them coming. They were only silhouettes because that sliver of a moon didn't give much light to see by, but every now and then I caught the dark red gleam of Cielo battle armour. Renegades with nothing to lose. If we took them alive the best they could hope for was a court martial and a firing squad. Shaster's tits, but there were a lot of them!

I waited for the mines to go off. Surely at least one or two of these bastards ought to put a foot wrong somewhere along the way. It wouldn't be enough to stop them coming but it ought to give them some buyer's remorse. Nothing happened. Either the mines were faulty or the True Imp troopers had managed to miss every last one of them.

Hey, I voked the 507m. *Some of these fuckers ought to be in your sights by now. Why haven't you fired?*

Engineer Esten, there is an optimal time to reveal the fact that you have secreted a knife up your sleeve. The gun sounded a little stern, a little pained, as if et had expected better of me. *Generally it's when your opponent has already leaned in so far that their freedom of action is compromised.*

And when will— I began, but that was when 507m cut loose with Aju's swivel-mounted Sa-Su. The middle of the line was almost level with him, the two ends a good way beyond. Et went for the middle, stitching the air with armour-piercing shot at chest and shoulder height. Four or five of the advancing figures fell, taken by that first volley. The rest scattered to right and left, which in theory was the right thing to do because it would force the unseen shooter to pick a target and potentially expose themselves in the process.

That was when the mines went off, and that was when I realised what 507m had done. Et had suppressed the mines' triggers until all the attackers were well inside the perimeter: then when the line was broken and the attackers were moving on random vectors et had reactivated the field with the True Imps bang in the middle of it.

The carnage was impressive. Red-armoured bodies were heaved up into the air in twos and threes. Their limbs were flailing as they rose but they were mostly still after they hit the ground again. Their armour had held but the concussive force had stunned or killed them.

Let's go! Dulu voked. *Lasque, your people stay with me. Aju and Inch, fan out wide. Hit what you see and make sure it stays on the ground!* He'd forgotten in the heat of the moment that Ajuparo was dead, but our squad moved forward even without a commander and we obeyed those instructions to the letter.

We were still outnumbered, but it didn't seem to matter any more. The enemy troopers were in disarray, returning our fire erratically and without much effect. They'd lost their air cover and they were fighting on ground that kept exploding under their feet. The minefield held no terrors for us because the mines recognised us as friends and refused to detonate if we were close enough to take any damage. We went through the True Imps like a hot blade through a kabat cake, confirming each kill with a head shot until Dulu voked us an urgent command to keep some of them alive for interrogation.

It was the most surreal battle I'd ever taken part in, by a long way. A minute ago we'd been fish in a barrel. Now we were so much in charge of the battlefield that we could afford to make fine discriminations. This one had been shot in the lower abdomen and wouldn't live long enough to take questions from the floor. The next one had a bad head wound but we might still be able to get some sense out of him, and so on.

Four. There were four fighters left out of that whole contingent: two Pogosi alike enough to be brothers, a gymnure and a felid queen who looked to be from Galeit or Essiororo. And we'd only lost six of our own.

Only.

Messolin. Inch. Em-Ber-Hax. Tulud. Koss. Ajuparo.

I'd been a soldier for the best part of twenty years. You don't keep count of the dead, because keeping count would drive you mad. In the bad old days they used to sink modules into your brain stem that regulated your neurotransmitters, intensifying your loyalty to the squad and dulling all the emotional backwash that might make it harder for you to do your job. Fear, compassion, grief, that kind of thing. Neural leashes aren't legal any more, and for the most part I applaud the new regime. But when I saw Aju reduced to loose atoms I wished for numbness. I felt the terrible weight of it, and the terrible weightlessness. Something had gone out of the world that could never be replaced; and it wasn't even her world.

For the rest, we were mostly just bewildered. Were we really that shit-hot? Did we have the strength of ten because Shaster had blessed our magazines?

No, we weren't, and no, we didn't. Nim'kisi and I took a long, hard look at the mortal remains and we found some smoking guns besides the obvious, physical ones. These troopers had been scraping out the bottom of the casserole with dry bread and bare fingers. Their guns were low on everything, both stored charge and solid ammo. Their armour was old and urgently in need of a machine shop, with broken seams, missing gauntlets, glitchy interfaces. They could still have flattened us if Aju hadn't taken out the two gunships and saved us all, but in one-on-one they just didn't have the right shoes for the dance.

But it was Velladaxita who delivered the punchline. Not one of these boys and girls, among the living or the dead, was augmented. In plain language, they didn't have military bio-ware.

They were wearing Cielo armour but they weren't Cielo. So what the fuck were they?

It was about time we settled that question.

Back in the day interrogation used to be a brutal, unlovely business. Your choices were basically threats, drugs, torture or some bespoke combination of the three. Then Professor Nelo Ba'hanu invented the Coercive Interface Link, for which the universal acronym was CoIL. A CoIL scanner could read minds, turning the electrical activity of a living, thinking brain into a database that could be exhaustively searched. Flycatcher came fitted with this invaluable piece of kit as standard because et was designed – among other things – for hunter-killer missions. You could order et to find a single individual, an enemy general or head of state, and et would locate them through their thoughts or through other people's thoughts about them.

So Captain Dulu decreed that Flycatcher should do our interrogation for us. Which effectively meant Nim'kisi would do it, since she was the drone's handler and was fully interfaced with et. She would lead the charge, as it were, although in this case the charge was into the prisoners' grey matter. "Take them in any order," Dulu told her. "I don't care. Just get us some answers. Where are the rest of them? What are they up to here? Have they got a Step plate that can get us home? That last one first, actually."

He set up a sort of outdoor interrogation suite with the four prisoners – shucked out of their armour, tied up like parcels and propped up against the boles of trees – placed a hundred metres apart from each other. There was no direct line of sight so none of them would be able to see what went on when their comrades were questioned. This was a shrewd decision on the captain's part. It meant Nim could use keywords gleaned from one subject in questioning the next one. Unguarded thoughts are the easiest to catch, and anything that comes as a surprise tends to get a stronger and clearer response.

Judging by the look of them, the prisoners weren't likely to put up much resistance in any case. None of them was older than thirty, which in the Pando would have made them barely adults. They'd come out of the massacre shell-shocked and terrified. The two Pogosi hadn't stopped crying since. The other two were trying to put up a tough front but the gymnure had pissed himself and the cat-woman had bitten her lower lip so hard she'd split the flesh.

Easy pickings for the CoIL scanner then. Nim'kisi could pretty much take her pick, let Flycatcher crack their minds open one at a time and decant the contents. But she didn't get started right away. She asked the captain if she could consult with me, as the squad's lead engineer, on a technical matter.

We withdrew a little way from the others and I asked her what was up.

"Esten," she said, "I can't do it."

I thought at first she was just talking about the CoIL settings. "It's easy," I said. "You just ask them a few random questions while Flycatcher calibrates, and then after that et will do all the hard work for you. You ask the questions, the drone digs out the relevant thoughts and memories and relays them to you for sorting and indexing. Honestly, Nim, you'll be bored."

"No!" She wrung her hands, visibly distressed. "I can't. I really . . . I just can't. I have a condition."

I stared at her blankly, waiting for more.

"Social anxiety," she said. "Extreme. That was why I joined the army in the first place. I thought the hard-wired reward loops would . . . I don't know, fix me. That I'd finally belong somewhere. Be a part of a group. Then they stopped all that, but I do feel like I belong. I love the squad. I love all of you. But that's as far as it goes. If I have to link with someone else's mind, someone outside the squad, I'll throw up and pass out."

A generous handful of sceptical replies died on my tongue before I could get a word out, because Nim'kisi was shaking and her eyes were brimming with tears. She wasn't lying or even exaggerating. This was a genuine crisis for her.

"Okay," I said, "don't worry about it. I'll do it."

"Oh thank you! Thank you, Esten. I really . . . I owe you one. I'll make this good somehow." She gave me what would have been a hug if we hadn't both been in full armour, but right then was just a low-speed collision.

"We'll tell the captain I've got more experience with the equipment – which is probably true, given what you just said. But you'll have to upgrade my interface and splice me into Flycatcher's systems."

"Yes! Of course!" She did it on the spot. I activated the link and suddenly Flycatcher was right there in my array, ets thoughts frictionlessly accessible and startlingly vivid because for this sort of work the handler and the scanner are sort of two ends of the same tool. I closed the link again fast, and I was sort of seeing Nim's point now. I'd need to get a little practice before I was comfortable with that degree of intimacy.

We went and told the captain what we proposed to do. He gave me a searching look. "You sure you're good for it, engineer?" he demanded.

"Sir, yes, sir," I said. "I mean, why wouldn't I be?"

"Everyone knows you had a thing for Aju. And since she died you've been even less communicative than usual. I assume you're in mourning."

"We all are," I said, which I guess was no answer at all but still as much as I was prepared to give.

I held the captain's gaze. He mulled it over for a second or two longer. Then he told us he didn't give a second-hand fuck which of us did the interrogating so long as we snapped to it and got him some answers.

There wasn't much to choose in the end between the four interrogations. When they were put under the CoIL those four young troopers who weren't really troopers all told the same story, with minor and trivial variations based on age and gender.

Where is your Step plate? was my first question, as per the captain's orders.

A Step plate! They had heard of such a thing, but it was a legend. Their ancestors had walked from world to world and Step plate was the name of the machine they had used. But then one day Step plate had stopped working and so they were obliged to stay here in this world for a while.

For a while?

Yes, for a while but not forever. This was never meant to be their home, they assured me. Or rather they assured Flycatcher, who was burrowing with no impediment through their untrained and unshielded minds.

What is it then? I asked. *If it's not your home, why did you come here in the first place?*

For the experiment.

Okay. And what's the experiment?

The whole wide world is the experiment. We made this place to be our crucible, to see which selves will rise and which will fall.

Which sounded both sinister and suspiciously iambic, like some random lines torn out of a hymnbook. *You say you're not planning to stay here*, I pressed, *but how long has it been since you arrived?*

That got a range of answers, but they were all variations on the same general idea: too long to count. We were born here. Our fathers and mothers were born here. The experiment began a very long time ago. It will continue for a very long time to come.

And when it's finished?

Then our kindred will come and bring us home, along with all the data.

I pricked my ears up at that. *The data? Where is the data? Who keeps it?*

The towers collect the data, and send it to the sky platforms.

Did your ancestors build the towers? The sky platforms?

Our ancestors built everything.

I took a break. I still had a few strips of gabber left from the little stash I'd been husbanding ever since we Stepped in. I folded one up and slipped it under my tongue, careful not to let the captain see. Most officers turned a blind eye to recreational drugs in camp but not in-country, and we were further in-country than we'd ever been or imagined we could be.

The gabber took the edge off my tension but it didn't prompt any fresh insights. Here's the thing: you can dip as deep as you like with a CoIL scan, especially if you don't mind doing some organic damage along the way, but there's no guarantee that what you find at the bottom of the well will be the truth. If you were to scan a paranoid schizophrenic, for example, you'd see the world exactly as they saw it – all their wild delusions presented to you with absolute conviction as the unvarnished truth. Even in a relatively healthy mind memory isn't a reliable process: it's shot through with misapprehensions and biases. What I was seeing here was what the four survivors believed to be the truth, but how much of it was real and how much was just what they'd been told?

I was still pondering this dilemma when 507m handed me another. "I've decrypted the data from the satellites, Engineer Esten," et reported, but then et immediately qualified that. "I mean I've identified the protocols that were used and begun the process of decryption."

"Great," I said. "Let's see it."

"That's problematic. I can show you a sample, but there's no way of knowing whether or not it's representative. The bulk of the data consists of digitally compressed audio-visual footage recorded using a variety of methods. Some of the footage appears to have been taken using cameras built into the satellite platforms themselves. The rest, I believe, was captured by mobile drones similar to Flycatcher."

"So what were they filming?" I asked. Maybe this would finally give us some clue as to what had brought the True Imps to this sinkhole world in the first place.

"Everything," 507m said.

"Everything? What does that mean?"

By way of answer 507m dropped a few hundred files into my array. They were, as et had said, high-resolution film footage, varying in length from a few minutes to several hours. Segments cut from what the gun assured me was a continuous record of everything that had taken place on this continent over the past seven or eight thousand years.

I opened one at random. Then a second, and a third. I was bemused at first, then perturbed. By the time I got into double figures I'd gone beyond that into something like physical nausea, with an overlay of existential dread.

Is it all like this? I asked. I had to voke the question because my jaws were clamped shut on a mouthful of rising bile. *It can't all be like this! It can't!*

"It is," 507m assured me solemnly. "Occasionally there are gaps where data has been erased, presumably for reasons of economy, but the time and date stamps allow me to be categorical about what remains. The satellite archive gives us a faithful representation of the history of intelligent life on this continent. As yet, I have decrypted only 2.73 per cent of the whole, but the consistency is . . ." there was a barely perceptible pause ". . . striking."

No, the consistency was *terrifying*. I was looking at fragments of a millennia-long history, and in its essentials it didn't change at all. In the oldest footage the level of technology was early industrial – steam power, the harnessing of petrochemicals for domestic energy, the very beginnings of mechanised mass production. In the most recent segments, after eight thousand years or so of elapsed time . . . the same. Everything, exactly the same. The selves of this melting pot civilisation had failed to innovate, refused to move on, remained stuck in a rut so deep they couldn't see over the top of it.

Maybe the cultural stagnation had something to do with the war – because that was the other fixed point here. There were lulls of a decade or more but these people seemed to have spent most of their recorded history at war with each other – the industrialised north of the continent time and again finding itself in conflict with the more agrarian south. Using the same weapons, often fighting in the exact same places, generation after generation. Killing each other with fervour and application on the same battlefields, going nowhere except round in circles while century after century drifted by.

"This isn't possible," I managed.

"And yet we see that it is happening," said 507m.

All in all, it was an inauspicious moment for Velladaxita to send in the results of her physical examinations. She'd done full work-ups on all four of the prisoners and the results were conclusive. The pseudo-troopers we'd just obliterated at three-to-one odds were the fairly remote descendants of the True Imps we'd chased here a year and a half ago. In Velladaxita's considered opinion there were at least fifty generations' worth of genetic drift.

Between the renegades Stepping here and us following them maybe six minutes had elapsed – on our side of the plate. But here in this world of grotesque impossibilities fifty generations had lived and died.

PART FOUR

THE MESSENGER AND THE SIGN

Out beyond Salt Lick to the north and west there was a landscape of low hills and open prairie that stretched for about a hundred miles or so before it was cut off by a great bend of the Sweetling river. Nobody farmed there, although it would have been tolerably good land, because it was too close to the Five Fingers, the X-shaped arrangement of dream-towers with Old Loudmouth at its centre. The residents of Salt Lick mostly stayed away from the place, and more than a few of them made the sign of Holy John when they got too close to it. It was even supposed to be bad luck to let Old Loudmouth's shadow fall across you.

This was where Bess went after she left the town, letting Stilt pick her own way and leaning forward in the saddle to take the jolts. The ground blurred under her, flowed by like a mountain torrent as the long-legged beast ate up the miles. By and by Old Loudmouth came into sight, embedded in the centre of the sprawling hills and dry scrub as if God had stuck a pin there to remind Himself to come back and smooth off the landscape at a later date.

The strange pallid colours in the sky and the complaints of the thunder had persisted all this time. As Bess drew closer to the Five Fingers she realised both these things were intensifying. Then she saw why. The dream-towers were their source. Jagged skeins of energy like bolts of lightning were lashing and leaping from the four outlying Fingers, each in turn and in strict rotation, to Old Loudmouth. The sickly light was spreading up and outwards from the towers like a stain. The effect was strongest in among the towers themselves, where the air had turned the dirty yellow-brown of chewed tobacco.

"Now what in tarnation is going on here?" Bess wondered aloud, reining in her chafer on the crest of a small rise with the dream-towers below her.

"Analysis," a voice answered her. "The network is trying to normalise in the face of an abnormal fluctuation, either a local build-up of energy or a sudden drain. Standard procedure is to equalise potentialities and shunt excess energy into gradient storage."

Bess felt a chill go through her. Those words had come out of Slim, but they hadn't been in any voice she recognised. This new voice was strangely accented and almost too fast to follow. She already knew Slim could mimic other people — she'd asked him to switch from the bandit Alden Calendar's voice to his present one, which was borrowed from a different dead man — but he'd never just changed on his own account before. She found she didn't like it very much.

"Give me that in States' Common, Slim," she protested, sidestepping the strangeness of his transformation. "I didn't follow a damn word of what you said there."

"I'm real sorry, Bess." Slim sounded shaken. "That wasn't even me coming out with them dime-a-piece words. Or rather it was a part of me, but not one I'm in charge of. Some subsystem I didn't know I had just woke itself up, spouted all that bull's wool and went back to sleep again."

"So you don't know what's happening down there?"

"I don't have the half-brained bastard stepson of a clue."

"Well, then that makes the two of us. Should we go through it or around, in your estimation?"

"Around," Slim said at once. "If we get too close I reckon we're like to come away with our fingers burned."

Around meant following the ridge to north or south, and south wasn't an option because it would take her back towards Salt Lick and who-all was coming out of there after her. So she turned Stilt's head to the north and urged her back into motion.

It wasn't what you would call easy going. The ridge narrowed almost to a point in places and even for a chafer's slender, questing legs there wasn't as much purchase as Bess would have liked. But there was worse news to come. Looking off over her right shoulder she saw a haze of raised-up dust in the middle distance, some way back along the trail she herself had followed to get here. That meant riders pushing hard. A wagon train would have been more spread out and left a different mark on the landscape, more of a cloud and less of a column. This was a posse and it was heading straight towards her. If she kept on the way she was going it would catch up to her long before she reached the river.

Bess took another look down at the Five Fingers. The livid bolts they were flinging from one to another were mostly high in the air, right at the towers' pinnacles or else very close to them. They weren't likely to touch her unless her going through changed that and brought them down on her. It was a risk, for sure. But the posse was a dead certainty and if it came on her before she got to the Sweetling she would have no choice but to stop and swap bullets with however many riders there were. That wasn't likely to go well for her.

She tugged on Stilt's reins. The animal dropped her head and came down off the ridge, heading straight for the dream-towers. The play of lightning across their gleaming white facades was almost painful to look at, and when Bess glanced away dark after-images danced behind her eyes.

"This ain't a good idea, Bess," Slim pointed out.

"Couldn't think of any good ones, Slim," she muttered. "Just had to take my pick out of what was left."

The ground shelved away steeply under them but Stilt still found the lower slopes preferable to the precarious summit. She picked up speed as she came down. The Five Fingers rose in front of Bess, and in between the Fingers the contained but furious storm they had whipped up among themselves. It seemed to her as though the air thickened around her now. It brushed against her face and hands, left her skin tingling and her fur standing up on end. It had a taste too, almost sweet but with a rankness underneath like rot.

As they drew closer to the tower Stilt grew more and more skittish, trotting aslant on her tented legs and ducking her head down almost to the ground. By this time Old Loudmouth's voice could be heard very clearly, not his usual basso boom but a high skirling whine like a bagpipes' drone.

When they came level with the nearest of the Fingers, Stilt slowed and finally stopped. Bess swung down out of the saddle, took a firm grip on the long whipcords of the chafer's antennae and pulled. Stilt came on one step at a time, her head tucked in under her raised-up wing-cases and her flanks trembling.

Bess didn't blame her one little bit. Once they passed that first tower they were in the enclosed volume of air that had curdled and changed colour. It tasted like spoiled fruit and hot metal, and it was thick enough that it seemed to push back against them as they moved forward.

"This isn't so bad," Bess managed to say. But she said it between clenched teeth, more to lift her own spirits than because there was any truth in it.

"Speak for yourself," Slim growled back at her. "These big damn fire-irons are sucking at my power cells, Bess. I don't mean to complain, but if you don't get us out of here quick I ain't going to be a blind bit of use to you when them riders catch us up."

"Going quick as I can," Bess said, then she clamped her mouth tight shut. Lightning arced above her, between the tower she'd just passed and Old Loudmouth up ahead. It made a sound that was like a sharp knife cutting down through thick fabric, and though the bolts never bent close to her, never went anywhere except from one of the Five Fingers straight to another, she still felt each one strike home as if some small part of it had broken off and lodged in her stomach.

Or maybe in her head. Something was happening up there that she liked even less than the ache in her gut and the bitter reek of the air. What was she even doing here? It was suddenly hard to remember. She was going forward, she knew that much. Running away from something that was coming on behind her, but what exactly? And where was this place? The grass under her feet told her it was outdoors. The boom and crack of lightning and the darkness of the air indicated she was in a storm. There was some kind of structure up ahead, maybe a lighthouse, its curved white wall shining out through the murk like a beacon. She bent her steps towards it. If it was a lighthouse the keeper would be there. They'd have to let her in.

"Whoa, Bess!" someone cried out. "No, no, no. Keep on the way you were going. You don't want to get too close to that there tower, and you sure as hell don't want to touch it!"

She turned to see who was speaking. There was nobody there, though there was an animal of some kind. Actually an enormous insect, standing higher than her head on legs that looked too thin to keep it up.

"Was that you?" she asked it. "Can you talk?"

But even as she said it her memories came back, a sudden flooding in from every direction at once. "Shit!" she gasped.

"Yeah," Slim agreed. "You kind of lost your mind for a moment there. You might want to get a move on before it happens again."

Bess snatched up Stilt's antennae, which she'd let go of during that fugue, and trudged on. A few moments later it happened again. All sense of who she was and where she was going drained out of her like water out of an upturned barrel. But a sense of panicked urgency stayed with her and she kept on moving. After maybe ten or twenty breaths a single spark lit up her interior darkness. The spark was a word. Bess. That was her, she somehow knew. She imagined the name as a physical thing standing up ahead of her. She trudged doggedly towards it.

"Bess," she whispered hoarsely. "Elizabeth. Bessie. Dog-Bitch. Sandpiper."

"That's it," another voice, a man's voice, encouraged her. "Keep on going, Bess. You're almost—" But whoever was speaking, that was as far as they got. Over the narrow space of that last word the voice faded into silence.

Almost what? It probably didn't matter. Almost out of push, was what she was. Almost done. She'd been walking a good long time, how long she couldn't rightly say, and as far as she could tell she hadn't managed to get any damn place at all. It was time to let go of whatever it was that was keeping her moving, the indigestible part of herself that had lodged in her gullet like a bone.

Bess. Sandpiper. Dog-Bitch.

"Fuck you," she whispered. "I won't. I won't. I won't."

She put one foot in front of the other. She brought the back foot forward and set it down. Each of her legs felt as stiff and solid as a tree trunk, as heavy as a filled sandbag. It was a kind of a miracle that she could make them move with nothing but the thread-stripped instrument of her own will, but she kept on doing it.

Dog-Bitch.

Dog-Bitch.

Dog-Bitch.

Coming through on the far side of the Fingers was like being flung through a window. But as her thoughts dropped clanging and screaming back into her head she stayed upright and gave one last, hard pull on Stilt's antennae. Stilt came on at a stumbling charge, knocked Bess down and scuttled on past her. After a few seconds the chafer reared up on her long back legs, whickering in spirited protest. She broke into a full gallop and was out of sight in seconds.

Bess fell down on her knees, grabbing air in shallow, ragged gulps. She was drenched in her own sweat. Her shirt clung to her chest and arms, sodden and heavy. Her heart was stuttering, fast and then slow. She spat and the spittle was mottled with red: evidently she had bitten her tongue.

But she knew who she was. Whatever it was that had emptied her mind of thoughts and filled it with echoing noise and incoherent feeling had stayed within the confines of the Five Fingers.

She looked to Slim, drawing him out of his holster and holding him in her two hands. All his lights were out. He didn't answer when Bess spoke his name. He looked dead, to tell the truth of it, but he had said – while he could still say anything at all – that the dream-towers were drawing on his energy. And Bess knew that what he ate was the rays of the sun. Holding him loosely by the barrel to expose as much of him to the daylight as she could she set off towards the far side of the valley at a fast walk.

She came on Stilt before too long, her head bent over a termite mound while her long tongue probed its surface for stray insects. The animal was well trained, and had come to a halt as soon as her initial panic had subsided. Which was just as well, Bess thought grimly. She'd been through a lot to buy herself this extra time. It would have been a damn shame to waste it all chasing after her chafer. She fed the strap of one of the saddlebags through Slim's trigger guard, making sure he was snug and secure there and still catching the light, then got back up into the saddle. She urged Stilt into a gallop, and kept her to it even when the ground started to climb again. The trail was narrow and precipitous but the chafer made no protest. Her slender legs rose and fell in paired synchrony like the fingers of a pianist playing a glissando, never missing a beat. Stilt seemed just as keen to be leaving the valley as Bess herself was.

Behind them the thunder boomed, louder than ever. With that sound in her ears Bess knew she wouldn't hear trouble coming until it was right on top of her, so she made sure to look over her shoulder every minute or so as she rode. The Five Fingers were a stain on the landscape as dark and angry as a bruise, riven from one moment to the next by curving slashes of lightning so painfully bright she had to avoid looking at them directly in case she blinded herself.

There was no dust column now but she made out the riders picking their way along the ridge on the opposite side. They had decided to avoid the Fingers, and she had stolen a good few minutes on them.

It was still going to be a close-run thing though. The posse could probably see her now, exposed as she was when she crested the rise on the valley's western side. And even if they somehow managed to miss her they knew exactly where she was going. There were no bridges across this stretch of the Sweetling, just the rope ferry at Twining's Gap. They would head that way too, and if they got to her before she got to the river she was salted and cooked. She dug her heels into Stilt's flanks and urged her on.

Twining's Gap wasn't a town or anything like one, but since the ferry was there it had enough people coming through that it was at least a place. A woman named Callie Vesper had thrown up a clapboard shack right by the riverbank and called it a general store, though the goods it sold were not general but narrowly specific. Jerked meat and pemmican, chafer feed that was mostly dried pillbugs or crickets, bullets, buckshot, and the terrible liquor that the Pugfaces drank. This was the edge of the Pugface nations, after all, though First Minister Feather was already in negotiations to push the border further west and take another few tens of thousands of acres away from them.

Just before she got to the last bend in the trail Bess dismounted and transferred Slim – still unresponsive and with no lights showing on his barrel – to the inside of the saddlebag. That done, she led Stilt by her reins past Callie Vesper's store and joined the short line waiting for the ferry, which was on its slow way back from the far side of the river. The line was just three men and a woman, and thankfully no wagons. The ferry wasn't over-large. Stilt would take up a lot of the available space all by herself.

The woman and two of the men were clearly homesteaders by

their dress. Whatever business took them over the river they wouldn't be going far into the nations and they wouldn't be staying long. Most likely the sacks they were carrying contained grain or milled flour, which they would offer to the Pugfaces in the nearest village in exchange for chafer scales and medicinal herbs. It was harder to tell what the remaining man was, apart from that he was cat-folk of some kind. His fur was grizzled gold, his eyes a piercing green. His shirt was pure white, his jacket and trousers pure black. Everything about him was just about as plain as a panhandle except for a silver Long-Eared John medallion pinned to his left breast. He wore no weapon and carried nothing except a grey poke bag in one hand and a leather-bound book in the other, but he stood with the arrogance of a king, his spine so straight and his shoulders so squared that his head was somewhere in back of the rest of him.

Bess gave them all a silent nod as she dismounted and joined them, then leaned against the jetty's rail and minded her own business, though she watched the cat man out of the corner of her eye. It wasn't that he looked like trouble exactly, but she didn't know what to make of him and therefore judged it best to take nothing for granted.

She thought she was being discreet about it, but the man saw her looking and favoured her with a smile. "Are you thirsty for the word, sister?" he asked her. "I can supply you at need. I have a spigot here that never runs dry." He held the book aloft and waved it back and forth a little as if it were a flag. It was the Johannis. The man was a preacher then.

"I'm good," Bess said. "Thanks."

"Good or bad," the man said, "we're none of us perfect. We were made to be better than we are, and if we surrender to John's word we will become better than we can imagine. Martin Shield of Faith is my name. I'm on a mission to the nations, but I don't distinguish between one soul and another. Will you pray with me?"

"I'm not a believer."

"Neither are these good people." The preacher indicated the others present with a slight inclination of his head. "But John's light reaches everywhere. He's standing at your side right now. I see him there plain as day. He'll be riding with us when we cross this water into the lands of the hairless heathen."

"He got the money for a ticket?" Bess asked. "Or are you paying his fare? And why take John out to the Pugfaces? Ain't they got enough gods of their own to be going on with?"

Martin Shield Of Faith smiled again, though the expression looked a little pained. "Back," he said to Bess.

"Beg pardon?"

"I'm not taking John's word *out* to the Pugface nations, I'm taking it *back* to them. John walked among the Pugface in the time before our histories begin – and He only disavowed them when they turned their backs on Him."

"Well, that's a damned shame," Bess allowed. "So what, you're selling last chances? Hate to tell you, but I don't think you're gonna find many takers." The ferry was almost all the way across to them at this point so she took Stilt's reins and led her to the end of the jetty, putting an end to the conversation.

Or so she thought, but Martin Shield of Faith followed right along behind her. "Do you know the Pugface myth of the Engine Everlasting?" he asked her. Bess didn't answer or even turn around, but he went running right on just as if she had. "It's a compelling tale. The Engine is a visitor from another world. First World, an old and sacred place that's the cradle of all life. The Engine leads his twenty-three against monsters and giants, slaying every evil thing, until at last all the giants league together and he falls in battle against them, overwhelmed by their numbers. But even that's not the end of him. He promises before he dies that he'll return and fight again when his people stand in most need of him. In the darkest hour he'll rise from the dead, take up his old weapons again and go to war for the sake and soul of the whole world. Does any of that sound familiar to you, sister?"

Bess still made no answer. She figured that the best way to make the preacher move on to someone else was to give him no encouragement at all.

The ferry pulled in. It was basically a wide raft with no side rails, but there was a gate at either end to keep passengers from just crowding on-board. The gateposts were also the stanchions to which the ferry's guideline rope was attached, threaded through two big loops of thick black iron. The near gate stayed shut while the ferryman, a lean but muscular coyote, tied up. Bess took a look over her shoulder. The posse hadn't come in sight, but she could see their dust cloud rising up over the nearest rise of ground. It was a matter of minutes at most before they reached the jetty.

Martin Shield of Faith was still talking all this while. "The story of the Engine is the gospel story!" he declared ringingly, not just to Bess now but to the company at large. "It's the story of Holy John! What are we told in scripture? That God sent His son down out of Heaven to lead the Wise Peoples out of sin. That's just exactly like the Engine coming out of First World into this one. Only the Pugface had no notion of Heaven, so they thought of their Engine as coming from another world in God's infinite Pandominion. And the vanquishing of the giants, well, that's John's story too. The Johannis speaks of Holy John's victory over death and sin. When our forefathers turned from the righteous path and through their wickedness unleashed demons out of Hell, John came down from Heaven and outfaced them all. 'His sword was so fine it severed truth from lies and hope from despair.' Portents, chapter three, verse twelve." Martin supplied the citation at a lower tone and in a faster pitch, kind of adding his own parentheses.

"And John too passed from death back into life," he went on. "As the good book says, 'in their fear and hatred the false ones hung him up on a tree and burned him, but he rose again and ascended into Heaven'. Once you see it, you can't get away from it. John visited the Pugface, maybe even before he visited us. But they were too ignorant to understand the message he brought. They thought of him as just a warrior, just a hero, rather than the son of God bringing revelation. They saw the choir of angels that surrounded him and thought they were his men-at-arms, the twenty-three. Engine was never his real name, sister, only the misremembering of his name. He was *John* everlasting.

"So I'm not taking the word out with me, I'm taking it back. I'm returning the holy light to where it started. Like transplanting a full-grown tree into the soil where once it was a seed."

"Five cents a head," the ferryman said, lifting the gate. "Ten for them that's bringing their rides with them."

Bess tossed him a dime piece. "This one's bringing choirs of angels," she told him, hooking a thumb at Martin. "You ought to charge him a dollar at least." She led Stilt on-board. The chafer had kept her nerve and her footing all along the narrow trails up in the mountains, but she was visibly reluctant now to leave solid ground behind for the lightly pitching boat. She chirped plaintively and tapped her four front legs against the planking in a skittish dance. Bess gentled her with murmured words and rubbed her neck until she quieted again. Then she turned to face back the way she'd come. She wanted to be pointed in the right direction if any shooting started. When the preacher came and stood in front of her, clearly far from done with his impromptu sermon, she reached out a hand and pushed him to one side.

Martin raised his eyebrows at this impropriety and opened his mouth to rebuke her. "Sister," he began, "there's no call to—"

"Hush yourself," Bess told him.

The remaining passengers were taking their time counting out cents into the ferryman's outstretched hand. Then the first of the riders came over the brow of the hill.

"Cast off," Bess told the ferryman.

"I got to count these," the man told her, jingling the little handful of coins.

Bess threw off the painter and gave the rudder a hard shove, taking the boat back out from the jetty. It was a reaction ferry, using the flow of the water against its rudder to tack back and forth across the river. The guide rope wasn't used to haul it, only to hold it in place in the current, a fact for which Bess was heartily grateful right then because the river's powerful flow moved it out faster than a human hand would have done.

"What in the Devil's name are you about?" the ferryman protested, outraged. "Ain't nobody but me touches that!"

"Hey, look," the homesteader woman said. "Look there." She pointed up at the hill behind the general store, where a dozen riders had come into view all galloping hell for leather down towards the jetty. The selves on the boat looked at the posse coming on. Then they looked at Bess, and she could see conclusions being drawn. She drew aside her coat to show the Lumiss sitting at her hip.

"Yeah," she said. "It's what it looks like. I'm Dog-Bitch Bess and that's a posse out of Salt Lick come to arrest me and take me to Fort Loose to face Parity retribution. Only I don't mean to be taken. There's no reason at all why you people need to get in the way of this and plenty of reasons not to. My advice to you is to just sit down and wait until we reach the other side, then you can go about your business and I'll go about mine."

The riders had come to the river's edge now. They lined up along the jetty and yelled at the ferryman to turn around, waving and beckoning with their hands. The river had already taken the ferry out far enough that their shouts could barely be heard.

The ferryman looked anxiously at Bess. "They want me to come back in," he said.

"Yeah, they do. And I want you to keep on going. Which of us is closer?"

The coyote gave this a moment's thought. Then he looked back at the riders on the shore and shrugged his shoulders, miming for the posse's sake his complete helplessness. "She has a gun!" he shouted. And then to Bess, "Could you show them your gun?"

Bess unholstered the Lumiss and pointed it at the ferryman.

"Thank you," he said.

"You're welcome."

"What if they shoot at us?" one of the homesteader men asked anxiously.

"Then I guess I'll shoot back. But we're none of us likely to hit our mark at this distance."

Something thudded down on Bess's shoulder. She turned to find that the preacher had taken a tight grip on her with the hand that wasn't holding the Johannis. He must have set his poke bag down somewhere.

"You're going to want to move that paw," Bess warned him. "Otherwise we'll all of us find out how much shielding faith can do."

"I'm not offering you violence, sister," the preacher said. "What I'm holding out to you is salvation. Kneel and pray with me, give your soul to John and to his holy father, and even your filthy sins will be washed away."

"I believe I'll pass," Bess told him.

Martin Shield of Faith frowned. "Do you think it's an accident that you and I were thrown together like this?" he demanded rhetorically. "No, Dog-Bitch Bess, this is providence. This is the uttermost lifeline that's being thrown to you after a life spent in godlessness and blind, bold sinning. Say His name. Ask His grace."

Bess was about to say something caustic, but just then the report of a revolver echoed across the water. A sudden splash and a plume of spray ten feet upstream of the ferry indicated where the bullet had gone. Martin Shield of Faith looked around in blank wonder, rudely interrupted in the middle of his godly prospectus.

"Everybody lay yourselves down flat," Bess called out as more shots were fired. Evidently the sheriff and his men were going to empty a few barrels in their direction despite the distance, in a general spirit of hopefulness. The farmers threw themselves down onto the planks in the centre of the raft, but Bess had to deal with Stilt before she followed suit. The animal was beating out a nervous tattoo on the planks and kneading her palps with her front legs in obvious distress. With one hand on the chafer's flank and the other wrapped around her neck Bess kicked at her front legs until Stilt folded them under her and went down on her knees.

But Martin was still on his feet. What's more, he was angry. He strode to the front of the ferry and threw out his arms. "There are innocent people here!" he bellowed. "Stop firing!"

There was a moment's silence, followed immediately by another volley of shots. Bess saw she was in a bad position despite her bold words of a few moments before. The ferry had reached the middle of the river and its progress had slowed because there was no hand on the tiller. The posse's shots were going everywhere but home, but however long the odds were each squeeze of the trigger was another throw of the dice. Crouched down at the rear of the boat behind the smooth horny slope of Stilt's flank Bess felt herself to be relatively safe, but the farmers were more exposed and the preacher seemed to be doing everything he could to get himself killed.

She measured the distance to the tiller. She could get to it easily enough, risking a few bullets along the way, but then she'd have to stand there in plain sight while a dozen men used her for target practice.

Better to try another way, she decided. "Hey," she called to the ferryman, who had thrown both hands up over his head and was moaning a little as the bullets whined all around him. He risked a glance at her from under his tented elbows. She pointed at the hunting knife he wore on his belt in a sheath of red leather. "Throw me that," Bess told him.

The coyote looked powerfully reluctant. Bess beckoned impatiently. "You'll get it back."

"What good's a knife, though?" the ferryman protested. "They got guns."

She didn't have any time to argue. Up at the bow Martin Shield of Faith was still on his feet hurling rebukes at the posse. His back was to Bess and the roaring of the river was pretty loud, but he had a good strong voice and he clearly liked this pulpit as well as any. She caught most of his impromptu sermon. "There are men and women on this boat who are guilty of no offence beyond being in wicked company! Put your guns away, for the love of God!"

Bess scooted across on her hands and knees, climbing right over the ferryman and grabbing the knife out of its sheath on the way. He saw her do it but made no effort to stop her. He just muttered a reproachful "Hey now!" Bess ignored him and kept right on going, not stopping until she reached the ferry's starboard side.

There was nothing for it at that point but to stand. She came up from her crouch sideways on to the distant posse to give them as small a target as she could. She set the knife's serrated edge to the ferry's guideline and began to saw at it. It was a thick rope, as it had to be to take the whole weight of the vessel, but the coyote's blade was sharp and the twined fibres started to part one by one.

"You can't do that!" the ferryman bawled. "Oh shit, we'll be lost! We'll be swept away!" He overcame his fear enough to rise up onto his knees, and seemed about to launch himself at Bess, but at that moment the preacher uttered a grunt of pain and collapsed backwards right on top of him. A bullet had hit something other than air at last.

The rope gave way almost in the same instant, its freed ends whiplashing to left and right as all the tension went out of them at once. One end hit Bess in the centre of her chest, a solid knock that made her stagger, but despite that and despite the sudden lurch the boat gave as the current took hold of it she managed to stay on her feet.

Three more steps brought her to the tiller. She got a solid grip on it and leaned in hard. The ferry was moving fast again now, and soon it would be moving faster still. The Sweetling was in flood. She needed to keep the little vessel on a westerly lean as it headed south, suddenly at the mercy of the torrent.

She heard shouts from the eastern bank. The men of the posse were all running for their chafers and mounting up. There were yells of alarm and protest from the homesteaders too, the two men clinging to each other in terror as the ferry lurched and tilted. It was never meant to run the river at this speed and it was shipping water at its bow end. It wouldn't stay afloat for long.

That same force worked in their favour though, pushing them quickly towards the further bank as Bess brought her full weight to bear on the tiller, bracing herself against one of the posts that had held the guideline. With her full attention on that it took her a while to realise that there was movement along the eastern shoreline. The men of the posse had mounted up again and were racing along there at a full gallop, presumably getting torn up some by the thick curtains of burweed and sow thistle but not slowing down any. Bess counted ten riders where there had been twelve before. Maybe the other two had gone back to Salt Lick to ask for more volunteers in case they needed to take this chase into the Pugface nations. Bess knew damn well where this bunch were heading. They were aiming for the rapids a few miles downriver near Jackhand, where the ferry would surely break apart if it ever got that far. There were rocks there that any survivors might be able to climb up onto if they could fight against the river's spate, but that wouldn't be any respite if the sheriff's men got there first with their guns at the ready.

Bess didn't mean to take that way if she could help it. It would be a near thing, though, the river being so wide and the current so fast. The rudder was tilting them in the right direction, but it might not be fast enough. Was there anything she could do to help it along?

In all this perturbation she had almost forgotten about the preacher, who was still lying where he had fallen in the middle of the boat. His face was pale and sheened with sweat, and the front of his shirt was soaked red-black with blood all the way down the left-hand side. The ferryman had crawled out from under the wounded man and then had got some distance from him, maybe out of a fear that bullet wounds might be catching. Nobody else had moved, the two homesteader men eyeing Bess with a mixture of unease and open hostility. She had brought this down on them, after all, and she had both a gun at her belt and a knife in her hand. Who knew what she might take it into her head to do?

What she did was to cut herself off a few yards of the severed guideline rope and run it over the tiller, tying it up against the nearer post to keep it heeled hard over to the left. "If anyone touches this," she said to the company at large, "I'm apt to be a mite humourless about it."

She was going to need to give the boat an extra push if they were going to make it to the far bank before they hit the rapids, but first she wanted to check on Martin Shield of Faith's wound. Absurdly and to her own exasperation, she felt partly responsible for it. After all it was her and not him that the posse had been shooting at. Another time she would have hardened her heart, but her heart was in a volatile state – perhaps because of the violent mauling her mind had received at the Five Fingers. For whatever reason she found herself unwilling to let the damn fool bleed out right in front of her. "You're a brave man, preacher," she said as she kneeled beside him. "Not smart by any means, but brave. I'm gonna cut away your jacket here, unless you can move your arm enough to take it off?"

"I can't," Martin said between clenched teeth. "And you're wrong. There was no need of courage because I was never at risk. God protects his servants. At least until it's time for Him to call them home."

"How'd you get this love-bite then?" Bess asked as she hewed her way through the sodden cloth. "Did he blink?"

"He will keep me . . ." Martin's words were lost in a deep, shuddering breath as Bess peeled the fabric away, pulling at the edges of the wound in the process. But he braced himself and resumed. "He will keep me from mortal harm while He still has use for me. But the world is the anvil on which our souls are forged, Dog-Bitch Bess. Anything that hurts us is a blow of Heaven's hammer, designed by the All-Father not to break us but to shape us."

"That's one point of view," Bess said, which was as much as she could muster in the way of tactfulness. "I guess he could have nudged that bastard's gun hand since he was passing by, but this could have been a lot worse. Bullet went straight through." Since the man's jacket was cut up already she tore a long strip from it and tied it tight around the wound. Any further ministrations would have to wait until someone more qualified came along. "Sit quiet," she told the preacher. "I'll look to this again in a while."

"You're a strange angel of mercy, Dog-Bitch Bess," Martin muttered. He winced in pain as he shifted his weight a little.

Sabbath prayers in Paxen seemed a world away now, but a piece of scripture floated up from some half-drowned recess of her mind. "Book of Makings, chapter eight, verse twenty-seven," she said as she stood.

"'He has given to each their mystery'," Martin recited, "'but to see into the hearts of men is His mystery alone.' Stranger still. That an outlaw and rapscallion such as yourself can quote scripture."

Bess took Stilt's reins and tugged on them, bringing her up onto her long, spindly legs. The chafer pawed and stamped a little, not enjoying the boat's listing, lurching progress. "Steady," Bess told her. "Steady now." She led Stilt to the starboard side, right by the tiller, pushing and pulling to bring her all the way to the unguarded edge. Then she leaned against the beast's flank, digging her heels in against a thwart plank to get a little more leverage. Stilt scrabbled and struggled, seeing the water churning right under her nose and wanting no part of it. She was stronger than Bess, but chafers are light for all their power and besides that they have a very high centre of gravity. After half a minute of Bess pushing and hauling, one of Stilt's back legs slipped off the edge. After that she was off her balance and the whole thing got a lot easier.

With one hand gripping the reins and the other braced around Stilt's neck Bess eased the animal's hindquarters into the water but let her keep a grip on the planking with her front two pairs of legs. Stilt's back legs flailed and flexed, looking for ground that wasn't there.

"She's like to drown that critter!" the homesteader woman exclaimed.

But that wasn't Bess's intention at all. She had turned Stilt's narrow body into a second rudder, angled into the current so that it brought more of the river's force to bear on them. Stilt's thrashing back legs were helping too. The ferry tilted crazily then righted itself on a new bearing, heading much more quickly towards the western bank.

A new sound came to Bess's ears, the hectoring of the rapids up ahead of them, invisible around a bend of the river but very close now. The bank was close too. Along this stretch of the river it was a sprawl of jagged rocks and they were going to hit it hard.

"Grab something that's nailed down," Bess shouted. Her own hands were full and she couldn't let go of Stilt in case the beast was swept away by the current and carried onward to the rapids. By the same token she couldn't throw herself flat or even kneel. All she could do was to wrap one leg around the guide rail's post and hope for the best.

At the last moment, seeing a massive spur of grey rock looming ahead of them, she loosed the tiller with another slash of the knife so that the boat would heel around and present its port side to the shoreline. They hit fast, but that slewing turn meant they scraped along twenty or thirty feet of the unforgiving granite rampart, losing speed with each impact, before reaching a shallower stretch of mud and sand and broken rocks almost hidden from sight behind a screen of tall horsehairs. There was a jarring shudder as their flat keel ran up onto the rocks. Bess didn't have time to brace herself and was flung sideways into the river, but she managed to keep her grip on the tiller so she wasn't swept away. As soon as she felt solid ground under her feet she wrapped Stilt's reins around her fist and led her up out of the water. The ferryman and the boat's other passengers were scrambling ashore – all except for the preacher, who still lay in the floor of the ferry with his hand clutched to his wounded shoulder.

Bess scanned the far bank. There was nothing moving there. The posse had ridden on towards the rapids. If she was lucky they would wait a while longer in hopes of the ferry fetching up there. Then they would carry on south to the next bridge, which was four miles further down at Sallust – most of it on decent trails. Bess did a rough calculation in her head and came up with a figure of twenty minutes. That was how much of a head start she had, give or take, and it wasn't much. The only sensible thing to do was to get back in the saddle and light out of there at the fastest gallop Stilt could give her. But there was still the preacher to be considered. And against a lot of powerful instincts she considered him.

"Get him out of there," she told the other four, indicating the wounded man with a nod of her head.

"Why?" one of the homesteader men demanded. "He ain't nothing to do with us. And he only got hit because he was asking for it. To hell with him."

"He stepped in between you and all them bullets, you idiot," Bess said, putting her hand to the butt of her gun. "I said get him out of the boat. Now. And make sure you lift him gently. You, coyote, you keep any kind of liquor in that lockbox there? Stronger the better."

The ferryman shook his head. "Nope. I don't hold with drunkenness." But he didn't sound altogether certain and Bess took the liberty of doubting his word. She drew her Lumiss and shot the lock off the box, mostly to make the point that the gun wasn't for show. The three homesteaders hurried to manhandle the preacher up off the floor and out of the boat, while Bess rummaged through the lockbox and found a bottle of clear moonshine two-thirds full.

"I stowed that for a friend," the ferryman said quickly. "Clean forgot it was there."

The homesteaders laid Martin Shield of Faith down on the riverbank, then looked to Bess for further orders.

The preacher was in a lot of pain but still conscious, and he made no protest when Bess untied the bandage. He did let out a yell when she pulled it away, though: the blood-soaked cloth had adhered to the edges of the wound and it took the half-formed scab along with it. "Can't be helped," Bess said. "You can lose a bit of blood and not be much the worse for it, but if the wound goes sour it will kill you surer than snake bite. You'll need to be sitting up for this next part."

"Thank you," Martin grunted, teeth clenched against the pain. Bess splashed the potent liquor all over the torn flesh, front and back, and this time he just about managed to hold in the cry of agony that was forming in his throat. In the aftermath of the crisis he whispered something that she didn't catch.

"What was that?" Bess demanded.

"God . . . sees you."

"I reckon we'll have to disagree on that one."

"Your sins . . ." The man's hand fell on her forearm, but there was no strength in it and it slid off again. "Your sins are heavy. But John . . . Holy John, he . . . he blessed the men that strung him up and set the torch to him. Repent. Repent, Bess. He will . . ."

The preacher finally passed out, very much to Bess's relief. She finished binding the wound up again, using the whole left sleeve of the already ruined jacket. Then she stood and turned to address the others. They were standing in a cluster a little way up the bank. Any one of them could have snuck up on her while her back was turned and brained her with a rock, but they'd missed their chance and she wasn't going to give them another one.

"You listen to me now," she told them. "The posse's coming the long way around by the Sallust bridge but they'll be here soon enough. You're gonna stay with this wounded man until they get here and you're gonna give him into their hands in one piece. And in the meantime you're gonna keep your damn hands out of his pockets and out of that there poke bag. You know my name, and I would hope you know my reputation. Don't make me come back to visit you."

"What about my boat?" the ferryman demanded. "You went and wrecked it. I ain't got no livelihood any more. And on top of that you took my whisky."

"Well, I heard from a reliable source that you don't hold with drunkenness," Bess said. "And as for your boat I thought the county owned it."

The ferryman looked discomfited. "They own it," he admitted, "but it's me that lives by it."

"Might be an idea to fix it then." She cast a critical eye over the grounded ferry. "Half a day's work should do to patch that hull, and two katies yoked together can pull her upstream again. But if that feels like too much work, put your mind to something else. If you can get your hands on some shovels you'll make a fortune in Salt Lick. This is yours, though. Thanks for the loan." She took the knife out of her belt and threw it down, having no skill with a blade and no real use for one. Then she put her foot in the stirrup and vaulted up into the saddle. She was aware that turning her back on the coyote after giving him a weapon wasn't the smartest thing she'd ever done, but she felt this brief acquaintance had been enough for her to get the measure of him. Those complaints were the only challenge he was likely to make.

Stilt made her way up the steep bank, placing her feather-fringed feet where they could adhere to dry rock and find some purchase. "You ain't gonna get far, Dog-Bitch Bess!" the coyote shouted after her. "The law will find you and hang you!"

She didn't waste any breath on a reply. All her attention was fixed on staying in the saddle as her chafer scuttled up the near-vertical rock. It was a relief when they crested the rise. There were more steep ascents up ahead, but none of them as bad as that first one and she had greater freedom as she went along to choose a navigable path.

Bess was in the Pugface territories now but she saw no sign that this land was inhabited. The bare grey rock gave way to sickly scrub and then to the lusher growth of the low desert with agaves and brilliant four o'clocks among the fragrant sage and prickly pear. She had loved this landscape from the moment when she first discovered it, but she was under no illusions about what life was like out here in the nations. The Pugfaces had only been allowed to remain on land that nobody else wanted, and even now they were being pushed further and further west, forced to breathe in as civilisation breathed out and spread itself.

Bess paused long enough to take Wakeful Slim out of the saddlebag and hang him from the strap in what was left of the waning afternoon sun. The lights on his side were still just a row of glossy black beads like the eyes of a spider. "You in there?" she murmured. No answer. She was beginning to fear that whatever the Five Fingers had done to Slim was permanent. That they had stolen him from himself, taken away her friend and left only a dead piece of iron.

The effects she herself had felt had worn off almost at once after she came out from between the towers. There was still a slight throb at her temples, but that was nothing. The worst of it was an odd fragility to her trains of thought, a tendency to drift into a kind of waking doze, but she was mostly able to pull herself out of that when she felt it coming on and it was fading now, the periods of distraction becoming shorter and coming further and further apart. After an hour or so she was herself again.

There was still no sign of another living self as she rode along, but once along the way she passed an old, spreading rosewood tree that had Pugface symbols carved into its bark. Bess's knowledge of the Pugface clans had progressed somewhat since her days in Ottomankie, but she still had no way of knowing what the marks meant or which clan they might belong to. They had been made with a broad-bladed knife, undercut at a shallow angle so that each horizontal stroke was a slim crescent rather than a straight line. Red and black pigment had been rubbed into some of the cuts, while in others the creamy white of the heartwood still showed clear.

The sun was getting lower now and Bess realised she was hungry. She hadn't eaten anything since her meagre breakfast of egg and fry-bread. But her only plan right then was to make as much distance as she could in hopes the posse would lose heart and turn back. She had no intention of stopping yet.

From the last foothills of the Jerichos she was descending now onto the great, arid plain that was generally called by the old Pugface name of Amendele. Up ahead, she knew, was the Big Sky Canyon and beyond that Lake Azul, but here in this eastern expanse what was mostly to be seen was a vast emptiness interrupted here and there by wide, flat-topped mesas.

Stilt was beginning to tire, and the shadow Bess cast in front of her was long enough that she couldn't see the end of it any more. At last she stopped and dismounted next to a mature red oak that was standing by itself in a small hollow of ground. It was as much shelter as the desolate landscape seemed likely to offer her. She tied up Stilt's reins to one of the lower branches, then gathered some brushwood and used her tinderbox to strike up a small fire. The temperature was already dropping and she knew the desert night would be cold. She ate some of the bread and jerky she had brought from home. She offered the apples to Stilt, who swallowed them whole and then crouched down with her legs tucked under her to begin the slow process of digesting them. Tomorrow, Bess thought, when she was further west and had more leisure, she would hunt. Right now what she needed was sleep. She put Slim back into the saddlebag for safe-keeping and lay down beside the fire.

At first, however, sleep wouldn't come. Whenever she started to doze off Martha's face appeared before her and she didn't seem to be in a happy frame of mind. *I avenged you*, Bess told this dream apparition. *Dear one, I made them bleed and I made them weep. Now they're coming after me again and I don't blame them. I've earned every last pain they can heap on me. But still I can't find it in my heart to make it easy for them.*

She woke to find a gun being thrust into her face. The gun was a blunt-barrelled Brandon revolver gripped tight in a man's fist. Floating somewhere above and behind it was a face wearing a grin that was almost too wide for it. Bess blinked sleep out of her eyes and tried to focus them.

There were actually two men, the one of them standing right up close to her like a fool but the other hanging back and keeping her covered a whole lot better. The near man was a wolf, his fur grey with a little bit of red in it. His partner was some kind of wildcat stock but with a whole lot of other things mixed in. Bess recognised both of them as being men of Salt Lick, though she wouldn't have been able to put a name to either one. She'd been right then, when she counted the sheriff's posse the day before. The twelve had shrunk to ten because these two had come a different way. Most likely they'd found a place where the river was calm enough for their chafers to swim across.

"I told you," the wildcat said. "I told you, Lige! We got here quicker than anyone. We got us the Dog-Bitch Bess, sure as Hell's a bonfire!"

"You certain it's her though?" grey wolf said, squinting down at her. "I heard she was meant to be all scarred and hideous like."

"It's her," the wildcat insisted. "She goes for that gun, you shoot her right away – but not in the head. We'll need her face in one piece or the sheriff's gonna say we just shot some whore we found."

"Sit up now," grey wolf ordered Bess. "And loosen that there belt so it slides down off of you. I don't want to see your hand anywhere near that pistol grip."

Bess complied. They had her fair and square. All she could do was wait for an opportunity to come. She didn't see any immediate way of making one for herself. "Okay," she said. "I guess you know I use my left hand to shoot with, so this here is my right hand I'm using now. Don't want to alarm you while you got that thing pointing in my face."

She came up on her knees, making her movements as slow and smooth as she could. There were a couple of moments when she could have grabbed hold of the near man's gun hand and thrown him to the ground, but the wildcat never took his eyes off her. Maybe if she somehow managed to get the wolf in between the two of them she could grab an advantage, but there wasn't much prospect of that right now.

"Okay," the wildcat said. "Tie her hands, Lige." He flung a coil of rope down on the ground in front of Bess.

"That means I got to let go of the gun," the wolf objected. "Can't she tie her own hands?"

"How in fuck's name is she gonna tie her own hands?" the wildcat growled. "It's fine, I've got a tight bead on her. She gives you any trouble I'm gonna put a hole in her where no hole was meant to be. You just do as you're told now."

"Can I say something?" Bess asked. An idea of sorts had occurred to her. It wasn't anything that deserved to be called a plan, but she didn't have anything better so it would have to do.

"You can keep your damn mouth shut," the wildcat said. "Lige, I said to tie her hands."

Lige proceeded to do so, wrapping the rope around Bess's wrists half a dozen times before securing it with a taut-line hitch. The knot was clumsily made but it was tight enough to hold. As soon as he finished tying the knot the wolf snatched up his gun and trained it on her again.

"There's two thousand dollars in my saddlebags," Bess said.

"The hell there is," the wildcat derided her.

"John's truth. It was meant as army payroll. I took it off the battlefield at Mundy's Fields, and now I'm on the run again I went and picked it up from where I had it buried. Now why don't you gentlemen just take that money and leave me be? You could live like kings on two thousand dollars. What do you say?"

Lige looked to the other man, Virgil, who sneered and shook his head. "She's lying to save herself," he said. "Shut your mouth, you Echelon cunt."

"But if I'm lying it won't save me," Bess pointed out. "You've got me hog-tied and you've got my weapon. Shoot me down if I'm lying. Or bring me in and get the reward that's on me. But I swear, I'm telling the truth."

The wildcat chewed this over. "Where's the money then?" he demanded at last.

"I told you." Bess nodded at Stilt, who was still tied up to the red oak and was grazing in the couch grass as if none of this was any concern of hers. "In them saddlebags there. The one on the left. It's tied up in a roll with a couple of old bootlaces. You can just help yourselves."

The wolf looked to his companion, eager and excited. "It can't hurt to look, Virgil."

"Shut up, Lige. You keep that gun on her now. And step back a way so she can't grab it out of your hands." He waited to see that this was done before crossing over to where Stilt was standing and opening up the left-hand saddlebag. He peered in, squinting his eyes. "I don't see no money," he growled.

"Keep looking," Bess said.

"Yeah, keep looking, Virgil," the wolf urged. "Tip it up so you can see what's in there. We could do a whole lot with two thousand dollars, for damn sure!"

"Shut up, Lige," the wildcat said again. He thrust his hand deep into the saddlebag and rummaged around in there. A whole succession of emotions crossed his face one after another – annoyance, puzzlement, surprise, then the excitement of realisation. "Well, I'll be damned," he murmured.

"Is it money?" the wolf demanded. "Is it money, Virgil?"

"No, it ain't money," Virgil said. "It's something just as good though. Look at this now!"

He drew Wakeful Slim out of the bag and held him up. Lige frowned. "That's just a gun," he said. "We already got guns."

"It's a Precursor gun, you idiot. Might not be worth two thousand dollars, all told, but I bet we'll get plenty for it. And we'll still get the reward on this one, so one way or another we're gonna be rich."

"I thought we had us a deal," Bess said.

The wildcat snorted in derision. "Is that what you thought? I don't recall making any kind of promise in that regard. Thank you kindly, though. This here is a nice gift you gave us. So long as it works and all. These things been around a long time. I heard some of them ain't no use any more."

"You have to look at the lights," Bess said. "Along the barrel there."

Virgil tilted the gun in his hands to inspect the glowing red motes that were once again flickering and dancing along the matt black metal. They were dimmer than Bess was used to seeing them but that didn't make them any less welcome. "I guess this one's in good shape then," Virgil said happily.

"I guess it is," Bess agreed. "Razor blade."

The light that stabbed from Slim's muzzle was a line of silver-white almost too thin to see. The air crimped and shrivelled on either side of the line as if it was a hot brand pressed against the whole world. Bess grabbed Lige's arm and dragged him into the path of the beam, which sliced through him as cleanly as if flesh and bone and sinew were nothing but breath.

Lige opened his mouth in a big round O of dismay but uttered no sound. The line that Slim drew through his body was on a steep rising diagonal and had probably intersected his windpipe. He sank to his knees, his gun sliding out of his grip. Bess caught it as it fell, but she grabbed it by the barrel and wasted a moment or two fumbling it the right way round again.

Virgil recovered from his shock more quickly than she would have expected and brought Slim round in a quartering swing. It was a shrewd move but Slim refused to cooperate, the beam winking out before it could touch Bess. The wildcat dropped him, drew his own gun quick and clean as anything and fired off a shot. It went over Bess's shoulder, close enough for her to feel the smack of disturbed air as it went by. By that time she'd taken aim. She squeezed the trigger of the Brandon again and again, firing five times before the hammer fell on an empty chamber. Every one of those five shots went where it was meant to go, one of them shattering the wildcat's gun in his hand, the other four burying themselves in his chest and belly. Virgil toppled like a tree, most likely dead before he hit the ground.

Bess threw the empty gun away and scooted across to where Slim was lying. She picked him up with her bound hands and placed him carefully between her feet, clamping him in place there with her ankles.

"Good to have you back," she said.

"Just in time, it looks like," Slim observed gruffly. "Can't keep yourself out of trouble for ten minutes straight."

Bess used the same needle-thin beam to cut the rope tied around her wrists, taking care not to bring any part of herself within the beam's reach. Lige's all but bisected body was lying on the ground in full view, mutely testifying to the appalling damage Slim could inflict on this setting.

When she was free she made a grim discovery. Virgil's bullet had missed her but it had hit Stilt, piercing her flank up high near the base of her neck. The chafer had sunk down onto her front knees, her back legs scrabbling frantically as thin grey-green blood gouted from the wound. She was clearly dying, and she was in a lot of pain. There was nothing Bess could do except to put her down clean. Gentling her with one hand, she pressed Slim's muzzle up against the side of the animal's head and fired. The scrabbling and shuddering went on for a few seconds longer but it didn't mean anything now. Just muscles still doing the last thing they'd been told to do before the brain that was in charge of them shut itself down.

Slim didn't say anything as Bess loosened the straps on the saddlebags and threw them over her shoulder. She searched the two bodies for anything she could use but there wasn't much, except that Lige had a mostly full waterskin that she knew better than to waste. She slung it over her shoulder alongside her own. She took Lige's Brandon too, thinking that it might be useful in trade. The bodies themselves she left where they lay, not having the time or the inclination to bury them. She headed west, on into the Pugface nations.

Bess and Slim didn't say a word to each other for the space of a mile or so, but Bess felt that Slim's not speaking had a kind of weight or charge to it. In the end it was her that broke the silence. "What happened to you back there?" she asked him. "You said the towers were trying to take all the energy out of you. Then your lights died and you didn't say another word for an ungodly long while."

"Yeah," Slim said heavily. "I don't recall anything like that happening to me before, but something in me knew what it was anyway and cut in right away to try and shut it out. And then there was a piece of my core processor that woke up and started throwing numbers at me. Words, too."

"Yeah, I heard some of them words. Seems like you made up a new voice to say them in."

"I didn't make it up, Bess. Like I said, it was right there in my non-volatile memory. Damned if I know how or why, or how long it's been sitting there. It kept right on talking too, though I shunted it away from my speakers so I could still keep talking to you my own self. It was yapping on like two bushels of nonsense was twice as good as one. Systemic load, field flux, inductive stabilisation. I couldn't make it stop."

"You know what any of them words mean?" Bess asked.

"Feels like I'm meant to, but nope. Afraid not. Best sense I can make out of it is this. It's like them towers was a katy-wagon, going along the highway and minding its own business. Then they hit an almighty bump and it shook them up good and proper. Broke off one of the wheels, sent the katy galloping right off the road. They were trying to fix themselves up while they was still rolling, and that wasn't working out too well for them.

"Wasn't the first time it happened, either. While they were sucking all the juice out of me my systems was kind of tangled up with theirs and I got me a peek at some stuff that was there. Error logs, I think they call them. Yeah, a whole stack of error logs. Seems like someone should have been by to fix things a long time ago, but they never came. What's left is falling down, pretty near. Hell of a business."

Slim's tone as he said all this was elaborately casual, as if the two of them were just saying good morning and how do you do and what's up with this weather, but Bess sensed the tension behind the words. He hadn't enjoyed being bushwhacked like that, and he wasn't over it. She hesitated, torn between wanting to spare Slim any more discomfort and trying to understand what the two of them had just been through. Maybe that was a lost cause in any case. The dreamtowers weren't something you understood, they were just something that was there. A part of the world, like mountains and rivers and forests.

Except that unlike mountains and rivers and forests they had been *made*. Someone had built them. When the first of the Wise Peoples came here from the old countries to take possession of this virgin paradise the towers were already old, but there must have been a time before that when they weren't there at all. Bess tried to imagine workers of a past era rearing up those great white spires the way farmers now might throw up a barn with ropes and pulleys and sweat and sinew. It wasn't a scenario she could make herself believe in.

As for the idea that the towers might need to be repaired, that was even more implausible. They didn't *do* anything in the first place, except make that humming sound to themselves, so what function or purpose could they have lost? And all that stored energy, the harnessed power of a lightning storm, what in Holy John's name did they use it for?

An image came into her mind: the little brown Pugface girl she had met on a peak in the Jerichos, kneeling at the base of one of the ancient structures with the green and gold carpet bag beside her and the silver wire wound around her arm. *No abnormal response*, the girl had said, to the bag or to herself or to someone else Bess hadn't been able to see. And then later, *transitory response*. Had she meant the tower itself? Had she expected something from it, missed it at first but then finally coaxed it out? If so, then obviously the towers did have a function after all. And that girl, who had looked too young even to learn the right spelling of her own name, had known what it was.

Or thought she did. Perhaps she was only mad and outcast from her people. Perhaps the bag and the wire were part of the fabric of some delusion, the effluent of a damaged mind. Reluctantly, Bess gave the whole thing up. She might have pressed Slim to tell her more, but she felt he'd been through enough already – and there was no way to solve the riddle when she had so little to go on.

They had been making slow progress all this time. Bess scanned the terrain below her. It was very open and nothing moved there. On the one hand that was reassuring: no blood-daubed Pugface warriors keen to assert their right to privacy or to prove their courage against intrusive fur-clad visitors. On the other she would stand out against all that stillness. It wasn't like there was much cover to cleave to. Further south there were forests of bur oak and mountain laurel, but going south right then would bring her closer to the settled territories when her only chance of safety lay in moving away from them. South later, by all means, but just then west was the only way that made sense so west was where she went.

Though she had resolved to put the events of the day before out of her mind, time and again through the day she found her cogitations returning to them anyway. It was dizzying to contemplate the fact that *time* and *history* were not the same thing. The States' Union was a new-forged thing when you really thought about it, but the world was old. It was full of mysteries that stretched back not just beyond anyone's memory but beyond all records.

And some of those mysteries were tied together. They had to be. Both Slim and the dream-towers belonged to the indefinite period before the Wise People came into the land; before the Pugface clans, even, since (she remembered from Martha's lectures) the towers turned up in some of their myth cycles. It stood to reason that the same god-like makers – you might as well call them Precursors as anything else – had been responsible for both. Unless there had been not one but two civilisations outside the limits of recorded history that had both had such superhuman powers, which seemed to Bess like something of a stretch.

But the connection went beyond that. The power stored up inside the towers, the rage and lightning and thunderous noise she had trudged through and fought against and somehow survived, it had grabbed hold of Slim as easy as anything, drawn out the wakefulness that was right there in his name and left him sleeping like an infant. So Slim had to be kin to the towers in some way, or else how had they been able to do that to him?

"You're dreaming on your feet," Slim told Bess tersely.

"No, I ain't," she said. "Just thinking, is all."

"Thinking on what, exactly?"

"It doesn't matter."

At the foot of a steep scree they came on a trail that seemed to be heading mostly west. Downward too, into a natural declivity like a little valley with thick brush on either side of it, all of which made it too tempting to ignore. Anyone walking that trail would be invisible from spying eyes, even if the spy was looking down from a height. Bess strode on at a steady pace as the afternoon wore on towards evening and she didn't stop to rest until she had to. Even then she just drank a slug or two of water, ate an apple and a strip of jerky, and allowed the muscles in her left leg to unlock just a little from the throbbing knot they'd become. The wound she'd taken at Mundy's Fields was making itself felt.

There were dark grey clouds gathering overhead. Bess knew that the sudden thunderstorms out here on the open plains could be very harsh. She should probably start looking for some shelter.

She threw the saddlebags back over her shoulder and got to walking again.

The threatened rain didn't come but the temperature dropped steadily as Bess came down onto the plains.

She took the opportunity on the way to shoot a couple of coneys for her supper. Slim's needle beam came into play again, taking both animals cleanly in the head from a hundred yards out. It might be difficult to cook them if the rain came on, but Bess had eaten rabbit meat raw a whole lot of times when she was riding with Tom Blue, and though she hadn't enjoyed it much she could stomach it well enough.

She still hadn't seen any signs of habitation, but that changed as she came through a sprawl of chinkapins and desert willows onto a table land about the size of some homesteader's apron. She saw the smoke first, a straight white line rising into the sky from a place up ahead of her, only half a mile away at most. A little further on a cabin came into view. It was made of cedar logs with earth packed tight all around and in between, in the manner of the plains Pugface clans. In front of it was a bonfire, not yet lit, made of brushwood stacked in a criss-cross pattern so neat and tight that the individual twigs and branches must have been carefully chosen for size and painstakingly assembled.

An old Pugface man was sitting on top of the bonfire, crosslegged. He was thin to the point of emaciation, his lined face as pink and naked as a chafer's underbelly. The fur on the top of his head was white and wispy, a little like the strands of a spider's web. He was dressed in a cotton shirt and leggings overlaid with woven katy-scale pearls, a style you didn't see any more because not many people were willing to put a hundred hours' work into a single garment. In one hand the old man held a knife that seemed to be made of black stone rather than metal. In the other he gripped a lit torch. The smoke wasn't rising straight up any more: the gathering wind was snatching at it and drawing it out into feathered streamers.

The man watched Bess come with a solemn, impassive expression on those shockingly bald features. A red scorpillon, probably on its final moult and about half as tall as Bess, watched her too. It was sitting at the foot of the bonfire, watching the old man mournfully through its cluster of compound eyes. Bess checked the scorpillon's stinger before she got too close, prepared either to shoo it away or – if it was still armed – to shoot it. But the business end of the stinger had been removed and the stump plastered over with tar so that it was a smooth black lump like the head of a Pugface battle club.

"Well met," Bess said.

The Pugface man nodded. "It may be so," he said. His voice was a sonorous rumble that sounded as though it belonged in someone else's throat.

"I'm looking for a place to spend the night. A floor would serve."

"I'm looking for a sign," the Pugface man said. "I wonder if you might be it."

"I honestly doubt that," Bess said. She hesitated, taking in the strangeness of the scene. "You picked the wrong time to light a bonfire, old man. It's going to start raining any second now."

The first fat drops smacked her on the shoulders and the top of her head even as she said it, and in the space of a few seconds it was coming down hard and heavy. The torch guttered and went out, giving off a final gout of smoke that lingered in spite of the wind, as if the dead flame had a ghost that wasn't ready yet to leave. The old man tilted back his head, eyes closed, and cried out loud in a skirling ululation. "Eyaaa! She calls it! Eyaaaaa, she calls it and it comes! Eyyyyyyyyaaaaaaaa! See how she tells the rain when to fall!"

Bess had no idea how to respond to this. The man seemed exalted, transported, as though the rainstorm's sudden arrival was a miracle rather than an everyday fact of plains life. He opened his eyes and turned his head to look at his torch. The drenching rain ran down its shaft to pool against his knuckles. He took the sodden thing in both hands and pressed it to his forehead. "I hear you, Sky-Mother, Earth-Father," he said, "and I accept. I will not die this day."

"Yeah, you might though," Bess said. "If you stay out in this." She held up the two rabbits she'd shot. "Be easier to get a fire going inside, is my thinking. I'll share these two fellers if you'll let me spread my blanket out on your floor. What do you say?"

"What's your name?" the old man asked her.

"I'd as soon not give it, if that's all the same to you."

"Then I'll call you Rainmaker." He climbed down from the stacked brushwood, limber in spite of his age, and headed for the door of the hut. The scorpillon scuttled along after him, rubbing its flank against his leg. "Yes," the man said, beckoning, "come in, come in. Ochre here won't hurt you, and neither will I. The mother of the sky, the mother of the lightning sent you, whose name in First World was Komu Ajuparo. Come in and be welcome."

"Nobody sent me," Bess said. "And I didn't bring the rain. I only saw it coming."

"Whatever you say, Rainmaker." The old man threw the door open and held it wide. The Scorpillon scuttled inside first, eager to be out of the rain, the old man next. Bess followed them and pulled the door to.

The hut was dark inside, but the old man bustled around and lit three oil lamps, red clay bowls shaped like elongated teardrops, filled with oil and with a wick laid down the central channel. Bess looked around the space, curious in spite of herself, as the details emerged out of the shadows one by one. There was just the one room. The floor was of packed earth with blankets spread for sitting on. A firepit sat in the centre of the space, surrounded by blackened stones. Against one wall there was a shrine to some Pugface gods, a trio of painted clay statues inside a tin box turned on its edge. On the lid of the box, which had been propped open with a stick to make a roof for the shrine, was a picture pitted with rust spots of a smiling fox smoking a huge cheroot. In front of the three little gods was a lumpy mass of tallow from spent candles. The smell of burned and burning oil filled the narrow space.

"Sky-Mother Aju, Earth-Father Dulu and the Engine Everlasting," the old man said, pointing at his gods. "They are the three. They are not always three, but this is the aspect of them I like the best."

"I beg their blessing," Bess said politely.

"You *are* their blessing."

Having no answer to that, Bess skinned and gutted the rabbits while the old man made up the fire. The scorpillon, whose name apparently was Ochre, had folded its six pairs of legs under its abdomen and hunkered down quietly in a corner where it chewed on a wooden branch, stripping the bark to chew both on the heartwood and on the grubs that nested there. The tap-tap-tap of its powerful mandibles was like someone trying to beat out the rhythm of a half-remembered tune.

There were no cooking pots that Bess could find, but she didn't see that they needed any. She borrowed that stone knife, which the old man had set down, and used it to whittle some skewers from a baulk of cordwood sitting beside the firepit. She impaled the two rabbit carcasses on the skewers and roasted them over the fire as soon as the smoke had died down a little.

The old man spoke to his gods in their shrine before he ate. Sometimes he spoke slowly, with ritual solemnity, and at other times he sang, but it was all in one of the Pugface tongues and Bess couldn't parse a word of it. She politely waited for him to finish, then handed him one of the skewers as he sat down beside her at the fire. They ate in silence for a little while.

"Will you really not give me a name to call you, Rainmaker?" the old man asked her. "I can't light a candle for you if I don't know your name."

Bess considered. She wanted very much to pass through the territories without drawing undue attention to herself, but the odds against the posse coming across this one old man were fairly long. "I'm Elizabeth Sandpiper," she said. "But most folks call me Bess. That, or something worse."

The old man didn't react to the name, didn't seem to register what it meant. "My name is Mur Ebishad Ghrent," he told her. "I'm of the Lasque people. My father was of the Velladaxita, but my mother was Lasque and it is the mother who tells the child who he is."

That didn't sort with Bess's experience at all, but she didn't see any point in saying so. "Can I ask you one other thing?" she said instead. The old man gestured yes. "Were you aiming to burn yourself on that bonfire?"

"Yes, Rainmaker, I was about to do that thing."

"Well, it would have been a damn fool thing to do, if you don't mind me saying."

Ghrent carried on eating for a while, his face thoughtful. "I am eighty-seven years old," he said at last. "That's a long life, by anyone's measure. I have had a wife, and we loved each other very much, but she's dead these ten years. We made three children together. I saw two of them die on the long walk from the Shallow Ford, and the third was hanged for katy-rustling. He didn't do it. A bison man did it and then pointed at him, and out of the two of them it was easier to hang my son. Now I hear that this territory is to be annexed by the States' Union and we're to walk westward again. This year, next year, who knows?"

"Those are heavy burdens," Bess admitted. "I understand."

"Do you? I don't believe I've explained yet. I don't know for certain that I can. But it's not sorrow that made me decide to die. If sorrow could have done that to me I wouldn't have lived to be so old."

"Then if it wasn't sorrow that was driving you," Bess asked him, "what was it?"

Ghrent let out a long, slow breath. He held his hand over the flames, weaving his fingers in and out of the smoke as if to demonstrate how elusive his meaning was. "The singer-shaman Imae Pellen, who was my friend, told me once that he had seen the great wheel of the universe, the wheel of time and chance and destiny. He saw it in a dream. He knew of many others who had also seen it, but he said they misunderstood its nature. They thought of it as the wheel of a wagon because that was the kind of wheel they knew best. But it's not a wagon wheel, it's the wheel of a mill. The mill that stands at the very edge of reality, where time and space end and eternity begins."

A smile came to the old man's mouth, and once it came it stayed there. "Ah, that old Pellen was a good friend to me. I think he kissed my wife one time, and she kissed him back, but in other ways a good friend. Eternity, he told me, is a great river that flows from nowhere into nowhere. The blades of the waterwheel dip into the river and come out again trailing drops of water. That's what our lives are, those drops. We're lifted up and then we fall. But when we fall we go back into the river of pure being. We don't die. We only rejoin the river until the wheel dips again and carries us into our next life. And then into the life after that, and so on, without ending."

"That's a pleasant story," Bess said. In fact she thought it was the same kind of nonsense preachers offered up from their pulpits, but with the furniture moved around a little. She didn't see why there should be a big wheel somewhere any more than she saw why there should be a place called Heaven where a benevolent God sat with his dead-alive son on his knee. If the world was a made thing, it seemed to her that it wasn't made by anyone who took any kind of pride in their work or any responsibility for their mistakes.

"It's no story, Rainmaker," Ghrent said. "It's the truth that lies behind all other truths. The wheel turns. We rise and we fall. But how do we rise, and why do we fall? I asked Pellen this. Is it sin, and virtue? Does right action lift us and wickedness pull us down? No, no, no, he said. It's not that. There's not a one of us that's pure good, or pure bad. We live so many times over that each one of us gets to be everything. It's our destiny to suffer all the things we have enacted and enact all the things we have suffered."

"Is that so?" Bess said.

The old man nodded. "Yes, that is so. My people ruled the world once, and we ruled it badly. With arrogance and cruelty. Now we're ruled by others, and the rod falls on our backs."

"You think you're being paid out in your own coin, then?"

"No, Rainmaker, I don't think that. I think everything that can happen does happen. If you wait long enough. There's no sin or virtue on the wheel, there's only up and then down, forever. We live, Pellen said, until we've done all the things we were supposed to do in this one life. Then we die and go on to the next."

The scorpillon had finished its meal before they finished theirs, but then again it hadn't been jawing while it ate. It came over and rubbed its red-black flank against the old man's shoulder. He stroked it absently, then let it entwine its mouthparts with his spread fingers. Given that those jaws were designed to strip bark Bess was less than certain she would have been inclined to do that. "I have lived a long time," Ghrent said. "I've seen a great many things. I thought perhaps I had done all I was meant to do in this life. That it might be time, after so many years, to be reborn. And so I built that bonfire and I climbed up there on top of it with a lit torch in my hand."

"But you didn't set the torch to the wood."

"No."

"Why was that?"

Ghrent smiled again, but it was a different smile than before. There was a great sadness in it. "I made a bargain with the powers that stand above us, those who are three and sometimes one and sometimes three-and-twenty. Because if this was not my time then they might not take it kindly when I just went ahead and killed myself. As if I disregarded their gift of life.

"I said to them: 'O great ones, if you've got something else you need me to do then send someone to tell me or else give me a sign so I'll know.' And I waited a while, and nobody came. And I was about to drop the torch into the kindling when the two things came at once. The messenger and the sign."

"I think I missed the both of them," Bess said.

"You said it would rain, and it rained. You were the messenger and that was the sign you brought."

"No, old man. That there is what you call a coincidence."

Ghrent shrugged.

"Your gods didn't send me," Bess said.

"How would you know? Do the gods speak to you and tell you what they want you to do? That would be a great thing."

Bess gave it up. "Are you okay if I sleep on your floor?" she asked.

"Of course. It is a blessing."

"Just for the one night. Tomorrow I'll be on my way."

"For as long as you like. To stay or go is your choice, Rainmaker. All things are your choice."

The old man banked the fire and went to visit his tin-box shrine again. Bess spread her blanket and lay down. She fell asleep to the old man's chanting. Just meaningless sounds for the most part, but she thought her name was in there a couple of times.

Her dreams were strange. The towers were in them. A man – a Pugface man, young and solemn and dark-complexioned – was explaining to her that the towers were about to fall, and that this would be a very good thing. In the way of dreams, she knew without being told that the man was Wakeful Slim. Somehow he had hatched out from the gun like a chick from an egg and taken this new shape. A whole lot of people were behind him, some of them dancing, others on their knees bobbing like prayerful penitents or contorting their bodies into strange shapes on the ground. They were the mindless, but they were also people she remembered from the war. She saw Tom Blue's face, and Cicero Church's.

"Why?" Bess asked Slim. "Why is it good for the towers to fall?"

"Because they're dream-towers," he told her, not impatiently but with a kind of heavy forbearance as if she should have known better than to ask. "When they fall the dream will end and real life can begin."

The mindless cried out at this, whether in dismay or exaltation Bess couldn't tell. Slim gestured to them and they stopped what they were doing. Those who had been on their knees or lying down climbed to their feet. They formed up in ranks like an army and began to march. There were so many there seemed no end to them. The drumming of their feet on the ground was like a throbbing inside Bess's own head, and she knew where they were going. They were going to topple the towers so that everyone would wake. That prospect elated her, but for some reason it terrified her too. She opened her mouth to tell them to stop but no words came, and the vast horde marched past her, on and on and on.

She woke, far from rested, to find the old man already up and busy. He was packing some rounded cakes of what she took to be pemmican into a knotted hemp satchel. The tin-box shrine was empty, which almost certainly meant that he had packed his idols in the same bag, or else in the leather pouch he wore at his waist.

"What are you doing?" Bess asked him.

"I don't know, Rainmaker," Ghrent said. "I go to find out. I thought I was at the end of doing, but now I know that something remains for me. And since you were the one the gods sent to tell me this, I think I might find out what it is by following you."

"I'm going west," Bess said. "And I'm going alone."

Ghrent nodded. "I understand. I think I will go that way also. It may seem as though I'm going with you, but in fact I too am going west alone."

Bess sat up, frowning. "Old man, I'm grateful for your hospitality but I don't need your company. There's nothing good that will come of you sticking close to me."

Ghrent tied up the neck of the bag and hefted it on his shoulder. "What will you do in the west?"

It was a question Bess had avoided asking herself, because there were no good answers. She had already tried hiding herself behind a lying name and living someone else's life. It hadn't worked, and she didn't think she'd be making a second attempt. But she wasn't sure what that left. There was the ghost of her old vengeful rage, never quite exorcised. There was the hope she'd had of finding some good work she could lend her shoulder to. She was damned if she knew what else there was. Maybe staying alive just became a habit after a while, a habit she'd have to work at breaking.

"I'm trying to shake loose some people that are coming after me," she said, for want of anything better.

"Easier to do that if you know where you're going," Ghrent pointed out. "I've lived in these lands my whole life. I doubt you ever came here before. If you use me as a guide you might end up somewhere that's good for you to be. And I can talk to the people of the nations for you if you meet any, so they'll be less likely to kill you."

Put like that, Bess thought, it was a proposition that actually made a kind of sense. Ghrent looked like a pint of nothing very much poured into a quart pot, but he had lived out here in the territories since before she was born and that was a hard thing to discount. On the other hand he was almost certain to slow her down. And if he stayed with her then any calamity that came down on her head would light on him too.

She considered. Her most urgent need was to get six swift legs under her instead of the two middling slow ones she had right now. Ghrent might be able to help her with that, so long as they parted ways before the posse got onto her trail.

"I guess I can't stop you from going where you like," she said at last. "Tell me, old man. Is there a trading post near here? Somewhere where I could buy a chafer?"

"There's Zekiel Scratch's place, towards Galleon Point. If he doesn't have what you need he'll know where to get it."

"And is that east or west of here?"

"Mostly south. But west too."

"I guess that will work well enough. Okay, then. Take me there, if you're amenable. I'll pay you for your trouble. And maybe by then your gods will have told you what it is they need you to do. Either way I'll be quitting your company right after. What do you say?"

Ghrent said nothing at all. He just whistled the scorpillon to him, opened the door of his cabin and stepped outside. Bess took a moment to roll up her blanket and stuff it back inside the saddlebag. By the time she reached the door the old man was already striding away between the bur oaks towards the road Bess had left when she happened on this place.

It wasn't much of a road to start with and it got worse as they went along. They were moving through chaparral scrub with a lot of dense ground cover and only a few tall trees standing out here and there on the undulating slopes. In places it was possible to see where someone had cleared away the roots and trod the earth down to make a path, but the undergrowth was creeping back on all sides and often it was hard to tell where the path lay. Ghrent never paused or slowed, though. He seemed to know exactly where he was heading even where there were no landmarks at all to rely on.

He turned out to be an irritating companion. He sang as he walked, in disconnected phrases whose meaning if they had ever had any was now lost to time. Bess tried her best to ignore the inane babble, wondering whether she was listening to hymns, laments or bawdy. The words offered up no clue.

Ochre mostly stuck close by her master's side, though occasionally she darted into the brush and scrub beside the path, lost to sight until she reappeared up ahead of them sitting on top of a rise or clinging to the underside of a tree branch. After a little while Ghrent whistled the scorpillon to him again and fed her a handful of rotten wood that he had just scraped up off the ground.

"Can't it feed itself?" Bess asked.

"Of course she can," Ghrent murmured, stroking Ochre behind her palps. "But she likes it better when I feed her."

"Funny kind of a pet."

"She's not a pet. She used to help me tend my herd, when I still had one. When we train one of her kind we cut out the stinger after their first moult. For most of the work they do, herding aphids or katies, they don't need it. And we train the striking instinct out of them." He looked up at Bess, a sly smile on his face. "Sometimes."

They walked on through the day's heat, stopping occasionally to rest and eat. Ghrent shared his pemmican and Bess what was left of her jerky and apples. It was enough to stop their stomachs from rumbling, at least. And Ghrent couldn't sing with his mouth full, which was a blessing.

Towards the end of the afternoon, coming over a rise, they saw the trading post below them with the northern end of the Galleon Point bluff behind. The trading post was a long single-storey building made of red wood, with a roof of grey stone shingles and a fenced-off space on one side of it that Bess took to be a paddock. There were four katies grazing in the paddock, and the wagon from which they'd most likely been unhitched was standing right by the building's front door. There were also a couple of chafers tied to a post off to one side of the building, the saddles still on their backs. Bess found all this reassuring for the most part. There would be a few people around, obviously, but she wouldn't be running into too much of a crowd down there.

"This is where I leave you," she told Ghrent. She held out her hand with a dollar bill tucked between the first and second finger. "Go ahead, old man. Take it."

Ghrent shook his head. "You keep it," he said. "It's best if all our money stays together."

"It's not our money," Bess said brusquely. "It's my money, except for this that I'm giving you here. Take it. Spend it at the trading post. There must be something you need."

Ghrent looked from Bess's face to Bess's outstretched hand, then back again to her face. "I don't buy at the trading post," he said. "Zekiel Scratch sells whisky and dream-dust and guns. The nations need none of those things. There's blood all over that place, and when you buy something there some of the blood comes away with you."

"Well, I mean to buy a chafer there, all the same," Bess said. "So I guess this is goodbye. Thanks for breakfast, and for lending me your roof last night. And I wish you luck finding whatever it is your gods need you to do."

She walked on down the hill without looking back.

In most ways Zekiel Scratch's establishment was exactly what Bess had expected it to be. The interior space was a single long, low room, as dark as a tomb because the windows, besides being very few and very small, were all locked up with shutters. Evidently Scratch didn't put much faith in his fellow man, whether furred or bald. Wooden shelves stretched off into the gloom, loaded up with boxes and wrapped packages and bolts of cloth, but the goods most commonly traded – bags of flour, bottles of corn-mash whisky, cotton blankets and pouches of tobacco – were stacked on upturned crates beside a low counter that was resting on two barrels. Behind the counter was a modest array of knives, axes and farming tools hanging from big nails that had been driven into the wall.

Bess took a turn around the store. It seemed to be empty. "Hey," she called. "I'm looking to buy something here."

There was no answer and no sign of life.

She went back outside and almost ran straight into Mur Ghrent, who was standing in the doorway. Her hand went to her gun before she realised who it was. "Goddamn it, old man," she growled, "what the hell are you doing here?"

"I feared for you in such an evil place," Ghrent said. "I came to make sure you'd taken no harm."

"Just stay out of my way." Bess shouldered past him out onto the store's cedar-planked stoop. She could hear raised voices now from behind the store. She went around the side of the building to see if she could find Zekiel Scratch or someone that was working for him. Ghrent followed on behind her, his scorpillon trotting at his side. This bald-cheeked scallywag had more stick to him than a jar of molasses. She'd be shaking him off soon enough, though, once she snagged herself a ride. Unless he wanted to run along behind her.

The area behind the store was clear ground, the earth packed down with yellow sand. It was bordered on one side by a low wooden fence and on the other by a continuation of the paddock. Understock and chafers would be sold from here when there were any to be had, but currently the paddock was empty apart from the four katies Bess had seen as she came in. That just left the two chafers tied to the hitching post at the front of the store. They almost certainly weren't for sale, but she didn't see any harm in asking. And if the wagon was heading west then maybe she could purchase a ride on that instead.

There was a small crowd of men out back of the store, half a dozen or so in all standing in a cluster by a black poplar tree. There seemed to be some kind of a game going on, judging by the mix of laughter and cursing that was coming from over there. One man, a short, stocky possum whose black-bead eyes stood out startlingly against the banded grey and white fur of his face, was standing a little way off from the group holding a fistful of coins and a few dollar bills. The rest were a mix of dogs and polecats along with one brawny cougar. All of them were dressed in work cottons: Bess figured they must be katy-men that had a herd pastured around here somewhere, probably illegally since this was a good way inside the territories. The cougar was wearing a tall hat and carried a bullwhip on his belt where you'd expect to see a gun. They all had their backs to Bess and were crowded in together around something that she couldn't see.

The cougar leaned forward and his arm moved in an arc. There was a soft impact sound, like the sound of an axe biting into a tree. "Well, shit!" one of the dog men said. "That there is in the same county, Bean, but I wouldn't say it was close." His voice had such a thick, syrupy drawl to it that the words were hard to make out. The mocking tone was clear enough though, and the cougar growled before he answered. "Knife had no kind of balance to it. I should be let to throw again."

"No lets!" another dog said, holding up his hand like someone that was swearing on the Johannis. "Them's the rules, Bean. You know 'em, I know 'em."

"I know I'm gonna take you by the scruff and smack your face into that tree, you speak up to me again," the cougar said.

The dog man lowered his hand, all done with his testimony.

Bess was close enough by this time to see what the men were up to – although it wasn't just men there after all. There was one Pugface woman in the mix. A woman was Bess's first thought, but if she hadn't been a Pugface you would most likely have said a girl: she couldn't have been much older than fourteen. She wasn't pink-skinned like Mur Ghrent but dark brown. The little fuzz that remained on the top of her head was black and thickly curled. Her arms, bare because the red cotton dress she wore had no sleeves, were by her sides and she was standing rigidly still. Her feet were bare too, except for a loop of rope that had been tied round her left ankle.

A kind of fence or screen of rough-cut beechwood boards had been put up against the tree, held in place by a pair of diagonal supports at either end. The girl was standing with her back up against this screen. Five knives were embedded in the boards around her. The furthest was about a foot to her right. The blade of the closest was just above her head and a hair's breadth away from her scalp, as though someone had used it to mark her height. There were a couple of shallow cuts on the girl's arm and shoulder but the instruments that had made them weren't in evidence.

Bess saw why a moment later, as one of the men went in to tug the thrown knives out of the boards and give them back to their owners. He called out as he did so. "Three points to Barney. Two for me. Skate gets one and the rest is nowhere."

It was clear enough to Bess how the game worked. The goal was to make the closest throw without actually touching the girl. The money the possum was holding represented the stakes each man had laid, with the house no doubt taking a cut. It was also pretty clear that the girl herself hadn't chosen to be a part of this. Her face bore no expression at all but the ramrod stiffness of her posture told its own story, as did her shed blood. The clinching argument was the rope tied around her ankle, its further end made fast to a wooden peg that had been driven into the ground between her feet.

One of the polecat men readied his next throw. Mur Ghrent, who was once more standing at Bess's side, made a guttural sound deep in his throat, like a half-swallowed snarl.

"Nothing you can do about it," Bess murmured to him. "They're too many for you. I don't know how that girl got into this mess, but she's going to have to get her own self out of it."

That didn't mean she had to stand here and watch it, though.

"I'm looking for Zekiel Scratch," she said loudly.

The polecat glanced round just once, looking pained. "Shut your John-damned mouth there, lady," he said. "If you spoil my aim I'm like to hush you up for a goodly while."

He threw and his knife thudded into the boards a full yard or so away from the girl, to ironic cheers and hoots of laughter from the other men. "Well, something spoiled your aim anyhow," one of them snickered.

"Are you Zekiel Scratch?" Bess asked the possum man.

He shook his head brusquely. "Zekiel went to meet the ferry. Fucking mindless plague hit the west end of Samartine, around abouts a town called Salt Lick, and we've got some goods coming that way. Sugar and molasses. He's gonna be out thirty dollars or more if it don't arrive."

Bess was shocked, and momentarily derailed from her purposes. "I only just came from Salt Lick," she said. "I didn't see no mindless."

"I guess you must've missed it by an inch then. Anyway, you want to see Zekiel you got to wait. I'm just minding the store for him till he gets back."

"Is that what this is?" Ghrent asked, indicating the girl with a nod of his head. "Minding the store?"

The possum gave the old man a look comprised of equal parts surprise and affront. "I bought the girl from the last gentlemen that owned her, fair and square," he said coldly. "Gave two bottles of whisky and a pouch of tobacco for her. There ain't nothing wrong with what we're doing and you ain't a part of it in any case. Bets are already in. You don't need to stand round gawking, neither." He turned his attention back to the gamers. "Skate, you're up."

"Let me go before you," the cougar said to one of the others, a slim-built dog man with a squint eye. "I'm running last and unless I throw a three I might as well go get drunk."

"But it's my turn, Bean," the other objected.

"Let me go first, I said. Do a favour for a friend."

He looked anything but friendly as he said it. The other man stood his ground for a moment longer, then stepped back with bad grace. "Fuck it," he muttered. "If a man can't take his fucking turn."

The cougar made a show of pacing out the distance to the girl, counting silently under his breath with his face screwed up in concentration. The girl gave him a fierce glare when he reached her, but he didn't pay her any mind, just turned on his heel and measured the distance back again. The other players took this delay badly, shrugging their shoulders and scuffing their feet as they waited. "Kid will be old enough to fuck by the time you're done," one of the polecats complained.

"Pugface girls come into the world old enough to fuck," the cougar said imperturbably. "They fuck their daddies and their brothers half the time."

"I'm looking to buy a ride," Bess told the possum. "You know where I could come by a good chafer?"

The possum glanced at her again, blinked a couple of times as if Bess was a hard thing for him even to focus his eyesight on right then, and glanced away again. "I'll see to you in a minute, ma'am," he said. "You can see I'm busy here."

What Bess saw was that Ghrent was working himself up to something. He'd edged closer to the group of men and was now over on their far side from where Bess was standing. His mouth was drawn into a tight line and his right hand had dropped down to his side. He didn't have a knife or a gun there so it had to be something in his satchel he was reaching for. The scorpillon was right next to him, bobbing up and down a little with all its many legs bent under it.

Another thing that Bess saw was that the girl had had just about enough of being used as a target. The tension in her body was ratcheted up to the point where it had got to go somewhere, and her eyes were darting left and right as if she was picking a way to run. Running wouldn't serve her though. That rope around her foot had a couple of yards of play in it at best, and the men had got her pretty much surrounded in any case.

In summary, what Bess saw was that nobody here was winning this game. It was only a question of who was going to lose the most out of it. She had a moment or two to consider what she should do about that. She remembered the kindness of the Ajuparo women, and of Kilin Vevenis in particular. She remembered the children she had taught in Ottomankie, and the Pugface children she'd excluded over Martha's protests. She remembered the circle, and the straight line.

Even then she didn't make her mind up to it. Not quite, or at least not quickly enough. Having walked back to his mark again the cougar man, Bean, spun on his heel and threw his blade before anyone could intervene. This throw was better than his last one in one way, worse in another. It hit the boards about on a level with the girl's head and a scant few inches to the side. But it hit hilt-first and bounced off, falling into the dirt.

"That one's out of play," the possum declared.

"Bullshit," Bean exclaimed, outraged. "It hit a nail, so that's on you. There shouldn't be any proud nails on them boards."

"Out of play," the possum said again. "Come on, Bean. Be a good sport."

One of the dog men, a brindled bruiser who was taller than the cougar and wider across the shoulders, stepped in to pick up the fallen knife. The girl was quicker, kneeling to snatch it up from where it lay. The man stopped, nonplussed, as she brandished it in his face. "You give that back," he demanded, holding out his hand. "Don't make me beat on you now."

The girl didn't surrender the knife. She made to throw it but then hesitated, no doubt weighing up the chance of hitting her mark against the certainty of losing the weapon.

"Give it!" the big man said again. "Or by Saint Fuck and all God's bastards I'll take the skin off your—"

The girl reversed the knife in her hand and took a single step forward, which brought her level with the man. She thrust upwards, driving the long, broad blade up to the hilt in his throat then drawing it out again whiplash quick.

The man sank down onto his knees, eyes bulging with shock. His mouth worked but he didn't have any wind left in him to make a sound. He pressed one hand to the gouting wound and clawed the air with the other, watched by everyone present in a moment of wonder so deep they forgot how to move or speak.

After that a lot of things happened all at once. The remaining men set up a holler, and a couple of them ran in to catch the dog man as he fell. The cougar, ignoring his mortally wounded friend, went for the girl instead and tried to swat the knife out of her hand. She struck again, a lunging sideways swipe, and the cougar snatched his hand away quickly. He circled the girl, just outside her reach, looking for a way to come at her without getting cut. His hand dropped to his side, to the rawhide whip that hung on his belt. He tugged it free and let it uncoil. With the whip in his hand he could disarm the girl without coming within range of the knife.

Mur Ghrent reached into his satchel, but what he took out of it wasn't a weapon. It looked to Bess more like a rattle, with some kind of metal slug like a badly cast doorknob at its wider end and red string or ribbon wound tightly around its slender shaft. He pointed the rattle at the cougar just as the latter was drawing back his arm, and gave it a sharp flick.

The scorpillon scuttled in so quickly it became just a splash of red and brown overwritten on the air. Its blunted sting shot forward like a stone out of a catapult, thudding into the cougar's side with devastating force. Bess could have sworn she heard the man's ribs snap. He folded sideways as he fell, uttering a single strangled gasp of breath.

By this time the two who had caught the dying man had let him drop again and drawn their guns. One of them got off a shot, and it didn't seem like he could miss at that distance, but he did the thing a lot of bad shooters do. He heeled his gun in anticipation of the recoil which just made the weapon buck in his hand all the more, sending the shot high and wide. Then a third man jumped in and tried to grab the girl by her hair. He didn't manage it but fortuitously he did block the shooters' eyeline.

"Hey!" Bess yelled. "Here!"

The two gunmen turned and she shot them both. Without being asked Slim provided her with the best ammunition for a close-in fight, soft wide slugs that spent a lot of their force inside what they hit. She took one man high up on his left side and the other in the middle of his chest but it didn't much signify. They both went down and didn't get up again.

That left three more if you didn't count the possum who was standing there with the coins and notes clutched to his chest and not doing much else besides staring gape-mouthed. The three went down to two real quickly as Ghrent tripped one of them in passing. The man scrambled up again at once but Ghrent gave him a solid belt across the back of the head with the business end of his rattle, and it turned out that big ugly doorknob wasn't just for show.

One out of those last two was dancing around in the manner of a man who was hoping the fight would be over before he had to make himself a part of it. The other, the man who had tried to grab hold of the girl, made a second lunge and grappled her around the shoulders. She gave a yell that was pure rage and hate, drew her head back and pounded it into his chest again and again, making it hard for him to hold on. Mur Ghrent pointed at him with the rattle. The scorpillon went for the man as quick as a flash, tail cocked back like the hammer of a gun, but he turned to keep the girl between them. And that worked just fine as far as the scorpillon went: the insect scuttled this way and that but the man kept shifting his feet and it couldn't get through to its target. As a barricade, though, the girl left a lot to be desired: there was a clear hand's-width of space between the top of her scalp and the man's own head. Bess took careful aim.

"Now you listen to me," the man bleated, putting his knife – or maybe someone else's knife that he had grabbed in all this moil – up against the girl's windpipe. "If this little Pug means so much to you, you best back off. She ain't worth a plugged nickel to anyone if she's dead."

Slim's bullet went clean through the centre of the man's forehead. It was a penetrating round this time so it came out through the back of the skull and ended up blowing one end of the fence into matchsticks. Out of the corner of her eye Bess saw the remaining man draw his gun at last, and heard the boom of a shot as she turned to deal with him. The man stared in sad wonder at his own chest, where a broad red stain was spreading across the blue of his shirt. That bullet hadn't come out of his gun after all. He crumpled, sagging at the knees, and pitched face-down in the dirt. Ghrent threw the Lumiss he had just fired down beside the dead man, wiping his hand fastidiously as if he had touched something filthy.

The old man had snatched the gun up off the ground and fired in a single movement. At that steep upward angle, from behind, he had put a bullet straight through a man's heart. Well now, Bess thought. That was a singular thing, and unexpected.

She took a good look around, including checking out the trading post's back door, but nobody else was coming. The gamers were all dead except for the cougar, who was curled into a ball around his crushed ribs and breathing like a broken bellows. The possum had backed away one shuffling step at a time until his shoulders bumped against the wall of the building. After that he'd just frozen in place. His eyes were wide, his teeth bared in a tragic grimace. Ghrent was gentling the scorpillon, which was crouched low to the ground, quivering and weaving and flexing its jointed legs in a kind of weird dance. And the girl . . .

The girl seemed to be fine, after all. That near miss must have been a grazing hit because a shallow wound high up on her arm was bleeding freely, but she ignored it. She was squatting on the dusty ground, using the same knife she'd just pushed clean through a man's windpipe to saw away at the rope that bound her ankle.

Bess turned to the possum, who flinched under her gaze. "Them chafers out front," she said. "Would I be right in assuming they belonged to two of these here deceased gentlemen?"

Instead of answering the possum thrust out the double handful of notes and coins towards her. "Please!" he yelped. "Just take it! Take it and don't kill me!"

Bess spat in the dirt. "You can keep your damn money," she said. "What I need is a ride. Them two chafers, are they yours or not?"

The possum shook his head and pointed with a trembling hand. "They're— they were B-Bean's. And Jesse's. Bean's is the one with a red stripe on its head plate."

Good enough. Bess's plan of slipping in and out of the trading post without being noticed was pretty much broken in pieces, but at least she could make good on the other part of what she'd come for. She was about to turn away when she found that the Pugface girl had come up beside her. The girl set the edge of her knife – one of the knives that had been flung at her, but hers now – at the man's throat.

"The men that sold me to you," she said, "they took something of mine. Where is it?"

The possum swallowed a lump of nothing at all, his throat bobbing. "I don't know about no belongings," he said. "I didn't buy anything from them three 'cept you."

"You're lying."

"I swear to John," the man squeaked. "They didn't offer me nothing in sale, only you. If it's anything we got in the store, though, you can have it. Only don't kill me!"

The girl seemed to give that heartfelt plea serious thought. Bess stood back and let her decide for herself, which seemed only fair in the circumstances. She heard Martha Good's voice in her mind saying that when you make someone a slave you steal away a piece of their soul. If that was so, this girl had earned the right to make herself whole again by whatever means she chose.

In the end the girl lowered the knife, but only from the man's throat down to his stomach. She still held the blade clenched tight in her fist with the point of it pricking his shirt front. "Which way did they go when they left here?" she demanded. "Tell me and maybe I won't be obliged to expose your insides to the open air. There are ways of killing you that will leave you plenty of time to regret that your mother ever dropped you."

It was quite a speech. Bess was impressed both by the girl's eloquence and by the force of her delivery. She was young still to have that degree of confidence in herself. The possum shook his head. Every other part of him seemed to be shaking too. The girl's high seriousness left no doubt that she was capable of following through on her threat. "I don't know, I don't know, I don't know. I can't remember."

"Try your best," the girl suggested. "Imagine your life depended on getting this right."

The possum screwed up his eyes as though the pain had come to him ahead of the wound. "Please," he rasped. "Please. One of 'em – the little beaver feller with the wall eye – he was talking about an orange grove."

"Orange Grove is a place," Bess said. "A town in the coastal territories. Could be that was where he meant."

The possum shot her a grateful look. "Maybe. Maybe, yeah. I think it must've been. They only bought enough supplies for a ten days' ride, but it could be they was fixing to buy or trade for more later. Or just hunt their food on the way. The real big one with the stubs of horns on his head – I think he was a moose or something – got to talking about the ocean. How he'd never seen it and he wanted to go take a swim in it."

The girl's eyes narrowed. "Did it sound as though he was expecting to see it?"

"I dunno. I guess he did, because one of the other two, the armadillo feller that had the bandolier across his chest, he said something about how he didn't give two shits to see what was just a lot of water all sloshing around. And the beaver said that probably accounts for the way you smell. I swear that's all I remember. And I'm really sorry I made game on you. I see now that was a low-down thing to do, and I won't ever do it again. Please don't kill me."

The girl drew back her arm and the man flinched away from her in a convulsive start. But she only tucked the knife into her belt out of the way. "I'm not going to kill you," she said. "Not today. But I'm going to call a curse down on you. A curse of sleeplessness. Some night, some dark night without a moon, I'm going to come back here and wait in the brush until you come to take a shit in that outhouse over there. You'll die with your backside bare and your bowels open. Between then and now you won't go a single night without waking up three or four times and wondering whether I'm out there or not. And when I do come, it will almost be a relief to you to not have to be afraid any more. You'll thank me as I sink the knife in."

The girl turned and walked away, around the side of the trading post and out of Bess's sight. The possum sank down onto his knees and then slumped back against the wall behind him, letting out a ragged sob of breath.

"I'll go with her," Mur Ghrent said. "In case these dead people here had friends who are still alive."

"One of them isn't dead," Bess said. She pointed at the cougar who was still lying where he'd fallen, curled into a ball around his staved-in ribs. He was breathing so shallowly that his sides didn't move.

Ghrent spared him a contemptuous glance. "Yeah, he is," he said. "He's just taking his time about getting there. Come to my heel, Ochre, come." He followed the girl, the scorpillon trotting along at his side.

"There . . . there ain't no such thing as a curse," the possum said to Bess. His eyes as he stared up at her had filled with tears and his voice rose on the last word, turning the bold assertion into a question. "Curses is just heathen nonsense. Ain't they?"

"I wouldn't like to say," Bess told him gravely. "Sounded to me like she meant every word of that. There's some other things I need from your store. You probably know where they are better than I do, so . . ." She gestured towards the trading post's back door.

The possum got slowly to his feet. He went inside with his shoulders slumped and Bess followed on behind him, keeping a watch on his two hands in case he suddenly remembered where he'd left his courage.

She got herself a couple more blankets, a box of lucifer matches and a whole lot of food. Beans, *pan de campo*, more jerky, coffee, a twist or two of sugar. "What's that come to?" she asked the possum.

The possum totalled it up at three dollars and seventeen cents. He looked flat-out incredulous as Bess counted out the money. "You're really gonna pay me?" he asked her.

"It ain't you I'm paying, am I? You're just minding the store here. And it may be this Zekiel Scratch is as worthless a cunt-hair as you are, but in case he isn't I'd hate for him to come back from running his errands and find his till box short."

She went outside. Ghrent was already up on one of the two chafers with the girl clinging on behind him. Bess pressed down on the shoulder of the other one, which was the red-stripe. The chafer trod the earth with her front feet and pulled away, wary of the unfamiliar touch. "Hey now," Bess murmured. "Hey now, Red. I ain't going to hurt you. We're gonna be friends, you and me."

It took a little more gentling and crooning, but finally the big animal bent to let Bess swing into the saddle then straightened again with no fuss or stamping. Someone, presumably Bean of the busted ribs, had trained this animal well.

Bess turned the chafer's head to the west and gave a little tug on her braided leather reins. "Walk on, Red," she urged, and the chafer lumbered smoothly into motion. There was a clear enough trail, a swathe of all-but-bare earth incised through the wild sage and tanglefoots by the coming and going of wagons and mule trains to and from the trading post. Once she hit it, the chafer followed it without any further urging.

Bess made a point of not turning to look but she heard the scratch and click of the other chafer's legs from just behind her on the trail. When they got to a place that was wide enough for two to ride abreast she slowed her mount. Ghrent reined in beside her, the girl still mounted in back of him. The scorpillon, Ochre, scuttled a little way up an ironwood tree off to the side of the trail and hung there, swaying from side to side with small flexings of its legs.

Bess addressed herself to the girl.

"This old fool has decided to stick to me because he thinks I'm a letter from God or something, but that don't mean you got to make the same mistake. I'm an outlaw with a Parity posse on my tail. Anyone that stands too close to me is like to catch fire."

"I don't care even remotely about your Parity or your posse," the girl said. "And I'm not following you. I'm taking this trail because somewhere along it there are three men who kidnapped me, stole from me and sold me as a slave. The things they stole are things I need. Urgently. I've got important matters to attend to and I can't do it without my equipment. It's vital that I retrieve it."

Bess blinked at this. She'd never heard a Pugface with so much to say for herself, and such a wide vocabulary to say it with.

"I said the *gods* sent you," Ghrent declared. "Not the one pasty little god you bassari believe in, but all of them. It's not for me to argue with twenty-three gods, Rainmaker. My way lies with you until I've seen what I need to see and done what I need to do."

"Fuck it," Bess said. "Let's go then. But stop calling me that. My name is Bess."

Ghrent glanced behind him at the girl. She returned him a stony stare, only slightly less hostile than the one she'd given the possum and the men who were flinging knives at her. "You hear that?" he told her sternly. "The Rainmaker's name is Bess."

The girl shrugged like that didn't make one tiny scrap of nevermind to her, and to be fair Bess didn't see why it should.

They rode out, having left a few more bodies on the ground than a simple shopping trip should have warranted and a trail about a half-mile wide. It might not matter, Bess thought. Maybe she'd shaken the Salt Lick posse loose back at the river ford. But she didn't believe for a moment they'd be the only ones coming after her.

Paulus Rondeau was playing Hold Me Darling poker in the officers' mess at Fort Esperance when his former sergeant Alexander Tooth, now holding the rarefied title of aide de camp, brought him the message from the telegram office at Salt Lick. Rondeau had been having a losing time of it, but right then he was holding a full boat of aces over threes with the fourth ace sitting on the table. He was looking to recoup all his losses at a stroke. It was therefore with some reluctance that he rose from the table and stepped aside to read the message. As he parsed it, his eyebrows rose and his heart quickened.

Dog-Bitch Bess! And in the border territories! Salt Lick was in Samartine, less than a day's ride away. Everyone, Rondeau included, had assumed she must have disappeared long ago into the old Echelon heartlands of the far south, or gone into the frozen wastes away up north where you could pick up a new life for next to nothing because everyone knew it wasn't going to last long. He'd never entirely given up hope, but the trail had gone colder than a polar bear's asshole. Only three sightings in as many years, and all of them just wild goose hunts.

This was different, because according to the telegram the name of the informant was Cicero Church. That was the curdled milk-wit cunt who'd let Bess slip through his hands at Mundy's Fields. Church would know her face at once. Probably saw it in his dreams a whole lot. And if it had been almost anyone else Rondeau might be asking himself why the hell they didn't raise up any hue and cry right there and then, but since it was Church he knew the answer already. Too much of a coward to call the Dog-Bitch out, even with a crowd of people standing by. Too shit-scared she might decide this time around that he was after all worth wasting a bullet on.

Rondeau handed the telegram back to Tooth. "Get the unit together," he said in a low voice. "Tell them we're moving out in an hour."

"Some of them are down in the town, sir," Tooth told him. "It might not be possible to find them all in that time."

Rondeau smiled, though it was more of a grimace. Excuses were one of the things he couldn't abide. "Well, damn it all, Tooth, you'd better make a start then, hadn't you?"

"Yes, sir," Tooth said, and made to go.

"Wait," Rondeau told him. He stood silent a second, one hand raised as he thought it out. "Send a runner down to the railhead at Fosse. Have them hold the next train that comes in on the westbound side. And if it's a passenger train, have them add forty empty freight cars to it. Boxcars, I mean, not flatbeds." Tooth didn't move, because Rondeau's hand was still poised in the air. He wasn't done with thinking yet. "I'll need one of the prisoners. Stone, I think his name is. The one with a missing arm. Grab two buck privates and tell them to bring him along to the train."

The hand came down. Tooth tore off a salute and was gone. Rondeau returned to the card table, where he pushed what little was left of his stake into the centre of the table and gave the other players a cool nod. "Duty calls," he said.

"Must be calling mighty loud if you can't even stay to finish out the hand, Paul," Lieutenant Henry Bird said with a sly grin. "Might you be less diligent if you had a few more eggs in your basket?"

Rondeau turned over his cards. Someone whistled. Bird looked abashed. "Well, off I go then, with my purse busted but my honour all hale and good," Rondeau said. "That's the most part of being a gentleman, right? Good day to you all."

He went out without a backward glance. He was almost thirty dollars down but Henry Bird was a shit-heel and Rondeau felt he'd got his money's worth with that last sally.

He went to the stables where the Pursuit Force was already assembled and ready to ride. Tooth had been right about how hard it would be to round them all up at such short notice, but he had done a more than passable job. Out of forty only three were missing. One of the three was Newland Heartless, the Force's best tracker, but Rondeau had others who were almost as good so that wasn't too heavy a blow. The other two, Keaton Juniper and Arnie Mile, were just solid shooters and every man here could shoot.

"I've left messages everywhere Heartless is like to go, sir," Tooth said. "And I sent an ensign to check—"

"It doesn't matter," Rondeau said, vaulting up into his saddle. "Thank you, Tooth, this here will do nicely. And I'm not disposed to linger. We wouldn't want to keep a lady waiting, now would we? Peel out, boys. We got some miles to travel."

They rode out of the fort and along the wide, well-kept road that led to the small township of Fosse. There was a huge stockyard there, and hence a railhead that saw a lot of heavy freight go through. Rondeau's messenger, an eager young sergeant first class named Ben Southern, had held the 12.33 to Eight Bluffs as per orders. The platform was full of indignant civilians complaining at the delay, with a couple of flustered station officers trying to calm them down and explaining how this was a case of force majeure, but when Rondeau and his Pursuit Force arrived most of the hubbub subsided at once. Rondeau ignored the civilians and had the station controller brought to him. He asked how far the line went westward beyond Eight Bluffs. He knew it had to be at least a hundred and some miles.

"Well, the last commercial station is at Hightown," the controller said, his peaked hat gripped tight in his two hands as if he was afraid someone would try to snatch it away from him. He was a very unhappy man right then, with his schedule shot to pieces and a whole lot of angry customers to mollify, but his day was about to get a lot worse. "After that there's another freight stop about two miles further on that the drivers call Hole in the Ground on account of it's just this big iron mine and nothing else."

"And what's before that?" Rondeau demanded.

"Come again?"

"How many stops before that last one?"

The controller did the sum in his head. "A round dozen, I guess."

"Well, today it's a round zero. Me and my men, we're going to get our chafers up into these boxcars here and your driver is going to take us straight to Hole in the Ground. Call ahead and get everything else that's on the line clean out of our way because we won't be slowing down and we won't be stopping. Understand?"

The controller's hat underwent a little more compression. The corners of his mouth tugged down. "But . . . but the passengers. Colonel, sir, they've already paid for their tickets. And there'll be others. Dozens, or . . . or hundreds, waiting to join the train at South Fork and Ableman and Pugtree and . . ."

"So you pay them their money back," Rondeau broke in, putting a stop to this litany. "Or give them tickets for the next train, or sort it however you want. But that's what's going to happen and I don't need to hear any more from you about how hard it's going to be. Just go ahead and do it now, before I lose my amiable disposition."

The controller went away, taking his tortured hat with him. Rondeau led his men at an easy canter to the rear of the train where the boxcars had been bolted on, ignoring the protests and lamentations of the passengers they pushed aside. "Army business," Alex Tooth called out to them in passing. "Give way, ladies and gentlemen. This here's army business now."

The runner had done his job punctiliously. Ramps had been set up against each one of the boxcars so the riders of the Pursuit Force could lead their skittish mounts right up and coax and lever them in. There was plenty of room inside each car to take two or three chafers, but as soon as they were in an enclosed space the creatures' instinct was to extend their legs in all directions and anchor themselves to as many surfaces as they could. That was why Rondeau had specified forty cars, allowing one for each beast and its rider. Two in the same car risked broken or torn-off limbs.

For himself he commandeered the train's dining car, where he spread out the maps he'd had Tooth bring along for him. While a waiter brought him coffee and biscuits he pored over the maps, estimating where Dog-Bitch Bess might have gone after she crossed the Sweetling and where she might be now. The train would take them a long way west of anywhere she could have reached. They could then ride south to intercept her.

Where though? Rondeau sipped his coffee and chewed it over. According to the telegram he'd received from the sheriff's deputy in Salt Lick, when Bess rode out from there she had headed toward the Sweetling. Everything for two hundred miles west of the river was Pugface land, according to a patchwork quilt of grants executed when the Union's westward expansion swallowed up the hairless clans' former territories. Possibly Bess thought that would be enough to shake off the posse and hide her from retribution, but Rondeau didn't think she was relying on that. Bess was nobody's fool: she would know that the States' Union and its armed representatives didn't let borders or treaties stay them when there was work to be done. And though the Pugface territories collectively were just mile after mile of nothing that mattered it was paradoxically hard to disappear there. If you had fur on you then you tended to stand out. Word would get around soon enough about any such round pegs in square holes, via the traders and trappers who walked those trails and the network of licensed barter stations they frequented. That whisper-line was like a second, unofficial telegraph system.

So the Dog-Bitch probably had something else in mind. If she kept on due west she would eventually reach the shore of Lake Azul, which was a formidable barrier unless she'd brought a boat along with her. If she tacked south the Big Sky Canyon lay in her path. Either way it seemed to Rondeau that it would be best to catch her before she got that far. She might have a plan, and he'd hate to chase her to the edge of the big water or the big nothing and then have to stand there with his dick in his hands while she disappeared herself again.

That was a lot of ground to cover, though, thousands of miles of desert and savannah and occasional forest. Cutting due south from Hole in the Ground would almost certainly put the Pursuit Force ahead of Bess, but how was he to narrow down the search? He would need to send out scouts to watch the most likely trails. And he would need to use his secret weapon.

He hadn't taken it out since the war, and he had used it sparingly then. But he had brought it with him and had it stowed on the train and he ordered Alex Tooth to bring it to him now. "The silver box," he said. "You know the one I mean."

Rondeau was amused to see Tooth blanch, but to do him credit he didn't hesitate. Just ripped off a salute and a crisp "Sir, yes, sir" and went to carry out his commission. Nobody liked to get too close to that box. Rondeau could appreciate those sentiments, even though the thing inside the box jumped to obey his commands quicker than any man in his charge.

Tooth returned in due course holding the requested item in front of him in both outstretched hands. He wasn't quite leaning back from it but he looked as though he wanted to. Rondeau hooked a thumb over his shoulder towards the narrow counter of the dining car's bar. "Set it down there," he said. "Then go tell whoever's guarding the prisoner to bring him to me."

Tooth did as he was told and took his leave without a word. That was a solid choice. Rondeau felt the volatile energy welling up inside him, and he knew himself well enough to be aware that he was unpredictable at such times. Unpredictable and inclined to be fierce.

He left his maps in place and crossed to the counter where the silver box was sitting. Before he opened it, he poured himself a very large whisky. There was a pitcher of water on a shelf back there but he didn't bother to cut the whisky, just gulped it down straight.

Paulus Rondeau had a high opinion of himself generally. He saw himself as a man of resourcefulness, strategic intelligence and above all courage. There were some things, though, to which fear was a wholly appropriate response. When Holy John went into the house of the dead to talk with the Devil he was careful not to say the word "free" because his word was potent and to say it would have been to release the Devil into the world. In much the same way Rondeau chose his words with care when he spoke with the thing inside the box – which was as seldom as he could manage.

He pressed the tip of his index finger against the upper surface of the box in line with the handle. With a whisper of sound it came open, a slender line of black ruled across the perfect reflective surface.

He lifted the lid.

Rondeau's father, from whom he had inherited the box, called the thing inside it the Flycatcher, because he said it had called itself by that name once in his hearing. But Rondeau had always thought of it as the Grim Reaper, and it was from this that he had drawn the name of his wartime irregulars. This was not just because of what the thing did, which often involved killing, but because it seemed to Rondeau to have a kind of eerie kinship with death. There was nothing especially sinister about its appearance. If anything it had a kind of austere beauty, though it looked nothing like anything else you were likely to encounter, except for a superficial resemblance to the box it came in. It was made of the same silvered metal that weighed nothing but never took a scratch. His father said he had seen bullets bounce off it. Its shape was a kind of X with all four legs the same length, thickened at the edges and with a raised saddle in the middle. The saddle was actually a cluster of glass discs and teardrops that reminded Rondeau of several pairs of eyeglasses all cemented together, out of which metal tubes like the barrels of revolvers would sometimes protrude and into which they would again withdraw. At the end of each of the four legs was a hollow circle like a wheel with a four-edged blade sitting snugly inside it. When those blades started spinning they somehow had the power to lift the Reaper off the ground.

Rondeau waited a while, his hand still on the box's raised lid. There was no point in talking to the Reaper until it had woken up, which generally took at least a couple of minutes. You watched the little lights that studded its surface in between the lenses. When they started to glow the Reaper was awake.

"Reaper," Rondeau said, when he saw those lights, "recognise me."

"You are Paulus Defiance Rondeau."

"And?"

"You are my authorised user."

Rondeau was always relieved to hear those words. "Okay, good," he said. "That's good. Elevate."

The blades inside the four wheels began to turn, though you could only really see them moving for about the time it takes to blink. After that they were spinning so quickly they were invisible. Without a sound the Reaper lifted itself up out of the box and hovered a couple of feet above it, on a level with Rondeau's shoulder. It had a hummingbird's trick of standing still in the air as if the air was solid enough to rest on.

"Do you see this?" Rondeau said, pointing to the largest map. He had unrolled it fully and pinned its four corners down with glasses taken from behind the bar.

"I do," the Reaper confirmed. "It is a representation on a scale of 1:10,000 of the territory known to most of its residents as the States' Union."

"And this part here?" Rondeau drew his finger down the map from north to south.

"An interior border. To the right are the lands ceded by treaty to the so-called Pugface clans. To the left are the territories of the States' Union proper."

"Exactly. I'm looking for someone who crossed that border three days ago, heading west. She was last seen here." The town of Salt Lick was much too small to appear on the map but he put his finger's tip against the middle reaches of the Sweetling at the western edge of Samartine. "She's a dog, orange-brown fur, average height or a little shorter. With some deformity to her face."

"A more circumstantial description would increase the likelihood of success," the Reaper intoned, still standing silently in the air above

Rondeau's shoulder. He suppressed the urge to pull away from it. It was something of a relief when the door at the far end of the carriage opened again and two uniformed soldiers entered, bringing with them the prisoner whose transfer he had ordered.

"I can get you one of those," Rondeau told the Reaper. "As circumstantial as you could wish for. Haul him over here, boys, and set him down."

The two buck privates eyed the Reaper fearfully but they obeyed, setting firm hands on the prisoner and moving him forward.

Frazer Stone was not in good shape. His right arm was missing from just above the elbow and the patch over his right eye covered an empty socket. Most of his right ear was gone too, leaving just a knot of angry, infolded flesh. A mortar shell had done these things to Stone at Mundy's Fields, exploding a few yards away from him as he rode hell for leather towards the Parity front line. In doing so it had saved his life, since it was only his horrific injuries that had kept him from dying on a rope's end when he was scraped up from the battlefield and tried for his misdeeds.

Stone's legs were in irons and his one remaining arm was strapped to his side with a leather belt, so even with the assistance of the two soldiers his progress down the carriage was slow and erratic. His head moved from side to side as he swung his good eye back and forth to look for obstacles, and his shoulders bobbed with each shambling quickstep of his manacled feet. To Rondeau's eye there was something degrading about this sorry spectacle. It made him despise Stone, but he experienced a twinge of pity too. A man who had been torn up so badly shouldn't need to be kept in chains to guarantee his good behaviour.

"Here," Rondeau said, pointing to the seat opposite him.

The soldiers manhandled Stone into the seat. It took a little while because there wasn't a great deal of space between the seat's base and the legs of the table, which were inflexibly bolted into the carriage's floor.

"Thank you," Rondeau said when they were done. "Go wait outside now."

The soldiers looked doubtful. Rondeau didn't wear a uniform for his work with the Pursuit Force, but they knew his rank. They just weren't certain how his orders fitted in with those given to them by their own commanding officer before they left Fort Esperance. "Begging your pardon, sir," one of them said, "the prisoner is under our guard. We got to stay with him so long as he's outside his cell."

Rondeau gave them a cold, level stare, feeling that dangerous energy rising in him like mercury in a barometer glass. "I think I can undertake to stand watch over a cripple," he said.

"Yes, sir, but—"

"Wait outside," Rondeau said again. And this time they didn't argue. The combination of Rondeau's glowering face and the Precursor artefact that was floating in the air right next to him was enough to settle the matter of the conflicting orders.

Rondeau had brought the whisky bottle from the bar, along with a single glass. He poured a couple of fingers of the potent liquor, tapping the bottle carefully against the rim of the glass to dislodge a drip. He set the drink in front of Stone, where it sat untouched because Stone was in no position to pick it up.

"So you're Frazer Stone," Rondeau said. "And I'm pretty sure you know who I am."

Stone said nothing. He just met Rondeau's gaze, which must have taken some effort with the Reaper hanging over them both and watching them through its cluster of lenses like an owl perched in an invisible tree.

"You were an irregular," Rondeau said. "You ran with Tom Blue's Braggarts. Fucking bunch of murderers and thieves, all told, with not a single upright man among you. Although from what I hear you weren't much help with all the murdering and thieving. Blue mostly had you tending the fire and cooking beans. Is that right?"

Still nothing. Stone must know he'd been dragged out of his prison cell to be interrogated, and he'd decided to be as little help as he could. Rondeau could have told him he wasn't going to have much choice in that, but all things in their place.

"It's another one out of that same rabble I'm after right now, as it happens. And maybe we could agree to disagree about the rest of them, but this one's definitely not a good man. Not any kind of a man."

Stone just stared, solemn-faced.

"I'm talking about Dog-Bitch Bess."

And maybe there was a flicker there. Good. That was something Rondeau could build on. The important thing wasn't to get an answer, it was to stir up the man's memories. The memories would do, words or no words.

"Must have been awkward at times, riding with a woman," he said, gliding his little finger around and around the rim of the whisky glass. "Must have been some of you tried to get under a blanket with her, see whether she had a cooch or a cockerel in there. I've heard it both ways. Did you ever take such liberties with her, Mister Stone, you being a dog like her and most likely drawn to rutting in the gutter? And if you did lay siege to her, were you surprised at what you found? I'm only curious, before I get to meet her my own self."

"Go to Hell," Stone said, with more weariness than heat.

Rondeau threw up his hands. "Oh, not yet awhile, thank you very much. You're free to go there whenever you want to but I still got work to do. You see, that Dog-Bitch Bess, someone rousted her out of the hole she hid in and now she's riding for the western border. As a matter of fact we're on our way to meet her. Going to bring her in alive so we can try her and hang her, which is the polite way to do things, although I dare say if there's a tree close to where we find her some of my boys would be up for having the party right there."

Stone held his gaze for a moment longer before finally looking away. "Oh, I wish I could be there for that," he murmured.

"For Bess's hanging?"

"For when she kills you."

And that was just about enough of that kind of talk. But Rondeau didn't let his temper get the better of him. He raised the whisky glass and held it in front of Stone's face. "Shall we drink to her?" he asked. "Her memory, I mean. Must be a while since you had yourself a mouthful of the good stuff. When you were riding I'd expect it was mostly just moonshine liquor if it was anything, and you've obviously had a dry spell since. Here. Take a sip."

Stone's one good eye widened a little, and his nostrils flared as if to suck in the scent of the liquor. When Rondeau brought the glass closer he flinched back from it a little way, but he changed his tune and parted his lips when the rim of the glass touched them. Rondeau tilted the glass and let the man take a solid hit.

Stone emitted a gasping sigh as the harshness and sweetness of the whisky hit the back of his throat.

"Acquire," Rondeau said, not to Stone but to the Reaper. "Whatever comes into his head when I speak next." He tilted the glass again, and Stone gulped the whisky down. The man just plain couldn't help himself. He was too thirsty, and it had been too long. "Dog-Bitch Bess," Rondeau said gently.

He let Stone have the rest of the glass. It wasn't likely he'd have any defence against the Reaper's probe in any case but Rondeau's father had told him it worked best on someone who had their guard well and truly down. Stone swallowed hard. The Reaper hummed to itself very much in the way the dream-towers did.

"You get anything?" Rondeau asked it, setting the glass down.

"Yes," the Reaper said. "I retrieved a quantity of eidetic and episodic memories relating to an organic self, provisionally tagged with the identifier 'Dog-Bitch Bess'."

"What?" Stone demanded, his gaze flicking back and forth between Rondeau and the machine. "What did it say? What's going on here?"

"Was it enough?" Rondeau said, ignoring him.

"Uncertain. The synaptic traces were old, therefore subject to rehearsal error, decay and affective distortion. I can if you wish go deeper into the subject's mind and use direct neural stimulation to enhance and cross-refer. That would provide a sharper imprint."

"Well, go ahead and do that then," Rondeau said.

"What's it talking about?" Stone's tone was querulous, close to panic. "You keep that fucking thing away from me!"

"There is a non-trivial risk of damage to the subject's mind."

"Oh, that shit was damaged already. I said to do it."

The Reaper's hum returned, and rose in pitch. Stone stiffened in his seat, his feet scrabbling on the wooden beams of the carriage floor for a second before he froze in his place completely. His mouth was set in a tight rictus, brown teeth showing between his twisted lips. After a few moments a thin bead of blood trickled down from his left nostril.

Nothing else happened for a good long while, just the humming and Stone frozen there like a statue of himself. For all that Rondeau didn't give a good goddamn about Frazer Stone or any other Echelon hoorah he felt a little queasy watching this. He got up and walked the length of the carriage a few times. When he came by on the fifth such perambulation he found Stone slumped unconscious across the table and the Reaper quiescent again.

"All done?" he asked it.

"Yes."

"Meaning you got enough to find her?"

"I have retrieved all available data."

"Okay then. Back in your box for now. I need to think some more about where to set you searching. Maybe by the time we get to Hole in the Ground there'll have been some reports and we'll have more to go on."

The Reaper sank back down into its cradle in the silver box. Rondeau closed the lid.

He turned to see what was left of Frazer Stone. Not much, by the looks of it. The Reaper could touch your mind as light as the shadow of a feather when it wanted to. Rondeau had felt that touch himself and taken no harm from it. But when it dug deep, as it had just now, there was less of the feather about it and more of the auger bit. Stone was still breathing, but that was the best you could say for him. His watery gaze was focused on nothing. His lower lip had peeled back from his teeth like paper from a damp wall. There was a slackness about his features generally, as though his face had half melted off his skull.

Rondeau went to the door and told the two buck privates he was done with their man.

It rained again for most of that day, and as the wet and cold sank into her Bess's mood soured. She had no real idea where she was going and she saw nothing in her future but more violence and bloodshed. The idea of balancing the scales of her life with good deeds seemed ridiculous given that the only thing she had any talent for was killing. Well, that and teaching, and there was no way she'd ever see the inside of a classroom again.

She fell into a misliking of herself that was so intense she couldn't abide her own company, let alone that of anyone else. She made an exception for the chafer. Red had turned out to be a spirited but sweet-natured beast with a sure stride and an enormous reservoir of stamina. Bess kept her to a rapid canter that seemed to take no toll on her at all, and she didn't trouble herself to see if the other two were still following. They'd both given her enough trouble already, and she more than half wished she'd walked on past Mur Ghrent's cabin and so avoided meeting either of them.

When they stopped for the night Bess took some of this out on Ghrent, even though she knew it was unfair. She couldn't in the end have walked away and left those sons of cunts making game on a woman's life, and that being the case the old man's forcing her hand had been a good thing, not a bad one. Still, it was a bone she could chew on and that was all she needed right then.

"What got into you back there?" she demanded, as the two of them were gathering brushwood to make a fire. The Pugface woman was sitting just off the trail with her eyes closed and her hands folded in her lap. She hadn't said a word to either of them all day, though she'd seemed to be muttering under her breath at some points as though she was keeping up a serious conversation with her own self. "Did you fall asleep and dream you were still a half-growed boy with more sass than sense and a burning need to show the world how tall your cock stands up?"

Ghrent gave Bess a solemn stare. "A wrong was being done," he said. "You can't see a thing like that and walk on."

"Yeah, you really can. It's mostly what's done."

"But it sticks to your soul, Rainmaker. I told you the trading post was an evil place. I wasn't lying. When the wheel turns and you go back into the great river do you want to put that stain on it?"

"I'm like to turn that damn river black as coal."

Ghrent didn't seem to hear. "Besides," he went on, "the girl has the Engine's mark on her. Didn't you see it? It's on the back of her right hand. It looks like this." He kneeled and drew a sign in the dirt, a jagged line like a great long crack in a rock or a baulk of timber with an arrow shooting through the middle of it.

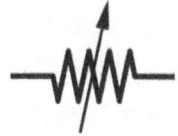

"And what the hell does that mean?"

"It means she's the Engine's daughter. His chosen."

"Well, goddamn and glory be," Bess said, humourless.

She ate the last of her jerky by the fire, pointedly not offering any of it to the other two. Then Ghrent shamed her by undoing the drawstrings of his satchel and solemnly sharing out the pemmican cakes he'd brought from his cabin. Bess thanked him with the best grace she could muster and settled down to sleep as the last light drained out of the sky. She was facing away from the fire so she'd have her night eyes good and ready if something came on them out of the dark. Consequently her back was too hot and her front too cold. Sleep didn't seem likely to come quickly.

Ghrent was lying crosswise from her, the crowns of their heads only a foot or so apart. His voice came to her out of the dark. "I can tell you what it means," he said, so softly it was almost like a voice inside her own head. "To be chosen." Bess pretended not to hear, but the old man went on anyway. "The way I heard it, the Engine Everlasting knew when he was going to die. He went to Edge of Everything, where earth and sky and ocean meet, and he called all his sons and daughters to join him there. There were many of them. How many I couldn't say, but enough to fill that place. And he said he had a great gift to give, but he would only give it to the one that could find the right answer to three questions that he would ask."

"Wait," Bess protested. "I heard this story before, and you're getting it all mixed up. The Engine spilled his blood on his spear, his bow, his shield—"

"Excuse me," Ghrent whispered, cutting her off. "Rainmaker, whose ancient wisdom is this? Every clan tells the story differently, but only the Lasque tell it right."

"Okay then," Bess muttered. "Have it your way, I guess."

"The right way," Ghrent insisted. "Can I go on?"

"Oh, please." The truth was that the night was chill and Bess's mind was churning, too full of too many thoughts. Talking – or listening, anyway, since apparently that was all that was expected of her here – was a welcome distraction, even though she'd done her best to avoid Ghrent's company all day.

"The Engine gathered his children, as I said," the old man went on, "and he asked them the three questions. The first was this: what has a mouth, but doesn't breathe? The second: what has an eye, but doesn't weep? And the third: what has a heart that doesn't beat?"

"Those ain't questions," Bess objected. "Those are riddles."

"The Engine gave his children some time to think. Not too long though, because his death was hanging over him and this was a thing that had to be settled before he died. They thought very hard. These were difficult questions, all three of them. One by one the children came to give their answers, and one by one the Engine told them no and sent them away again. Some got one question right and some another, but nobody found the answers to all three.

"Then the Engine's youngest daughter came. Even though she was the youngest she was already of age. She had taken a husband and carried her first child inside her. 'Father,' she said, 'I believe I know the answers to your questions.'

"'Go to then,' said the Engine. 'Tell me, daughter. What are the answers?' And she told him this. The thing that has a mouth but doesn't breathe is a river. The thing that has an eye but doesn't weep is a needle. The thing with a heart that doesn't beat is a fire.

"The Engine was very happy to hear this. He took the youngest daughter to his breast and embraced her. He told her she'd gotten all the questions right, and that she would be his chosen and his favourite, the closest to his heart of any of his children. "I will put my mark on you," he said, "and all the things I've made will see the mark and honour you. My bow will bend to you. My spear will fly to your hand. My armour, red as blood and hard as iron, will wrap itself around you and protect you.

"'But, daughter, there is a thing that answers all three questions at once. A thing with a mouth that doesn't breathe, an eye that doesn't see, and a heart that doesn't beat. Do you know what that thing is?'"

"The youngest daughter was abashed. 'Father,' she said, 'I don't. What thing is it that has a mouth but doesn't breathe, an eye but can't see, a heart that doesn't beat?'

"'That thing,' the Engine said, 'is a ghost. A ghost is what's left behind when death snatches someone away so quickly that the echo of them stays behind in the air like the shadow behind your eyes when you've been staring at the sun.

"'And I will be that shadow soon,' he said, 'that empty echo. Beloved daughter, I must leave to you and to those who come after you the burden of finishing the fight I couldn't finish for myself, of driving the giants out of the land and ending their power forever. And therefore I leave to you and to those who come after you the weapons and the wisdom to do these things.

"'But my ghost will stay behind too, to look over your shoulder and guide you if you stray. To spur you if you slacken. To lift you if you fall. And in the end of times, when all that is comes back to where it started, my ghost will fight beside you. The eye that does not see will weep for joy. The mouth that does not breathe will sing a blessing way. The heart that does not beat will break.'"

Ghrent had declaimed all this in a sing-song rhythm that had drawn Bess in and kept her listening in silence. His voice had been barely more than a whisper when he started, but it had risen as the story reached its climax and by the time he stopped he was speaking as loud as if the two of them were having a normal conversation. Somewhere along the way, Bess saw out of the corner of her eye, the Pugface woman had sat up and was listening.

Ghrent saw her too, and he was somewhat abashed. "At least," he said, "that was how my father told the story to me."

The woman nodded. "He was right," she said. "For the most part."

"So are you looking for that ghost to arrive any time soon?" Bess couldn't keep the scorn out of her voice.

"We expected to see him long before now," the woman said. "Those end times are already here. I'm surprised you didn't notice."

By the time the train got to Hole in the Ground Paulus Rondeau had worked out his strategy, which was to send the drone zipping straight down the border while the Pursuit Force tacked south-east following the line of the Allumette mountain range. The aim was to cut Bess off once the Reaper had sighted her, and that was going to involve a hell-ride no matter what. Rondeau's aim was to land himself and his men as close as possible to the middle of the space the Dog-Bitch was negotiating, so wherever she popped up they'd have a good chance of reaching her before she got to the border.

But as soon as he stepped down from the train, bringing the silver case along with him, a skinny little gopher came running up to him. The man was wild around the eyes and his fur was slicked down from sweating. He was the clerk from the telegraph office and he came clutching two telegrams in his hands. Judging from his shirtsleeves and the visor over his eyes he'd come all the way up the hill from the office at a dead run. Two miles was no small distance in the desert heat so he wasn't in any state to talk, but the red "MOST URGENT" stamp across the front of both messages spoke for itself. Rondeau snatched them out of the man's hand and tore them open, scanning them in quick succession and then reading each again more carefully to see if he'd missed anything.

The first was a warning from the governor general's office, instructing Rondeau not under any circumstances to enter or approach the town of Salt Lick in western Samartine. Salt Lick, the message went on to explain, had just experienced a virulent outbreak of the mindless plague. It seemed possible that the only survivors from the town were the twelve men who the sheriff had formed into a posse and who had last been seen crossing the Sweetling at Sallust.

These tragic circumstances failed to arouse very much of concern in Rondeau. It seemed like the plague was everywhere you looked these days, but he was a long way west of Samartine now and didn't need to trouble himself on that score. The second message, from the same source, was much more interesting. There'd been an incident at the Galleon Point trading post forty-some miles west of the Sweetling. Half a dozen dead, and valuable property (to wit, one Pugface woman) illegally taken, et cetera, et cetera. The perpetrators, a toothless old Pugface man with a face like the tongue of a well-worn boot and a dog woman with devastatingly good aim.

Providence had played into Rondeau's hands, not for the first time. He kneeled and opened the case again, right there on the station platform – which in Hole in the Ground was only a few planks raised up on railway sleepers. The Reaper was still awake, having drunk its fill of daylight the last time he'd called on it, even though that had been entirely within the confines of the train carriage. There was a general gasp from civilians and Pursuit Force alike as it rose into the air and remained hanging there at the level of Rondeau's head.

"Galleon Point trading post," Rondeau told it. "Galleon Point is on the map, and the trading post is probably the only building for ten miles around that isn't a Pugface hut. Dog-Bitch Bess was seen there less than a day ago. Find her."

The Reaper rose into the air, silent as any ghost. "And once she is found?" it asked, in its chiming empty voice. "Am I instructed to terminate?"

Rondeau tutted and shook his head. "No, thank you. I'll take care of that big old handful of hellfire myself. I just want you to put a marker on her so we can find her again. You know the kind of thing I mean. You did it for my father that one time in the Pugface wars, when he caught a Messolin warrior and wanted to know where the rest of the clan was camped. You remember?"

"Yes."

"And you can still do that. You can still—?"

"Yes. I will load my magazines with tracker darts. However a direct neural link is advisable."

Already gloating, Rondeau was false-footed. "What's that again?"

"I can locate the target and insert the tracker. In normal circumstances you would then use a secondary device with a compatible interface to read the tracker's signal and retrieve her. However you do not have such a device. It would obviously be possible for me to return to your physical location and lead you to the target, but this would entail the loss of hours or more likely days in transit.

"In order to avoid this delay I propose the creation of a permanent bond between your nerve tissue and my own operating system. This will also give you access to my visual feeds and allow you to amend my operating instructions should this become necessary."

Rondeau swallowed. He was beginning to wish that he hadn't released the Reaper right out here where everyone could see. It was a piece of theatre that usually left him feeling pretty pleased with himself, but now he was facing a public challenge to his courage that he hadn't anticipated.

There was no choice, really. He wasn't the kind of man to let himself get stared down by anyone or anything. With the memory of what he had just done to Frazer Stone clamouring in the front of his mind like the caterwauling of a screech owl, he kept his face straight and nodded. "Yeah," he said. "Okay. Do that, then."

There was no pain. There was a moment of frightening cold, as if the top of his head had been lifted off and a chill wind was somehow blowing into there despite the sweltering heat of the day.

And then suddenly he was looking into his own face, while at the same time seeing a whole lot of other things both near and far – mesas and mountains, other people's faces, the clouds in the sky, the railhead, the engine and tender, the tracks vanishing into the distance. He realised with dizzying amazement that he was seeing through all the Reaper's lenses at once. There were angels in the Johannis to whom God had given four faces, the first one to look into the past, the second to see the world all around, the third to glimpse the future and the fourth to scry into men's souls. What he was seeing now felt just a little like that.

"By John's cock and balls!" he exclaimed softly.

"The link can be toggled on and off in this manner," the Reaper said. It rummaged in Rondeau's mind, pulled a bunch of things together that he hadn't known were there and tied them in a knot. Now it did hurt, but Rondeau kept himself from wincing or crying out by biting down hard on his tongue. "This will allow you to contact me and piggyback on my sensorium." Another knot. "And this is how you follow the tracker once it's active." A third.

Rondeau's eyes went back into his own head. His knees came close to buckling, but again he retained just enough control over his muscles and sinews to stay upright.

"Your command will be actioned," the Reaper said.

"Good to hear," Rondeau said. "Off you go, then. We'll be right behind you."

There had been an audible catch in his voice, but he flicked his wrist with an offhand flourish as if this was a thing he did every day. The Reaper soared skywards in a blur of impossible speed, making a sound like a sigh that had been broke in half. Rondeau walked off the platform conscious that every single eye was on him.

"Mister Tooth," he called over his shoulder, "get those chafers unloaded. And see what you can do by way of rustling up some beans and bacon for us. These men have got a long ride ahead, and I don't mean to make them do it on an empty stomach."

Alexander Tooth managed a salute and something that sounded enough like "Yes, sir" to pass muster. His mind was full of that silver thing, nothing like a bird, that had flown up at the colonel's command into the blankness of the sky. Tooth knew the Reaper of old but he had never reached any kind of accommodation with it. It appalled him to think that he had held that case in his own two hands. Had even tried – holy fucking saints! – to open it and get a glimpse of the Reaper in its cradle.

He was profoundly glad now that he had failed. Gladder still that it wasn't him the silver bird was hunting. If Dog-Bitch Bess had been anyone else, anyone else at all, he could have found it in his heart to be sorry for her.

Unfiled report of tactical unit 486
Identifier: 7Ω2905 Esten, V, engineer first class
Date: not applicable
Location: not applicable
Status: ask a fly what its status is, after you swatted it once and didn't quite kill it

We put it all together at last. The data from the satellites, what I'd gleaned from the interrogations, and Velladaxita's findings from her physical examination of the prisoners. It all pointed in the same direction. Once you accepted that any of it was even possible it all made a sick, appalling kind of sense. And what it amounted to was the biggest war crime in the Pandominion's long, illustrious history of casual atrocity.

The captain brought the sixteen of us together to pass along what we'd learned. All our huts had just been smithereened in the battle so we were out in the open, a woodland council with only the trees around to eavesdrop. Our four prisoners sat a dozen metres off, tied up back-to-back in a picturesque cluster. Evidently the captain didn't think it mattered much if they heard what we were saying about them. He'd realised now that they weren't our most significant threat.

Dulu invited Velladaxita to report first, and she summarised her findings crisply and clinically. These people we'd just fought were *not* the renegades we'd pursued here in the first place. They were the remote descendants of those renegades – their children's children's children's et cetera, after roughly a thousand years of elapsed time. "That's forty generations, give or take," Dax said. "Assuming an inter-generational gap of twenty-five years. The genetic drift supports a higher figure, closer to fifty."

It was a good choice on the captain's part to let Dax drop this bombshell. Her calm delivery helped to keep everyone from open panic. Or maybe it was that the full implications hadn't hit them yet. In any case, I was twos-up and I tried to emulate her. I gave the baldest possible summary of what Flycatcher's CoIL scan had grabbed from the prisoners' minds: the struggle between the Pandominion and the True Imperium winnowed down into ancient legend; the clash of absolute good and absolute evil with us as the bad guys; the heroic lost cause, the flight across dimensions. Then a sojourn in a strange land, century on century, for the sake of the great and noble experiment. Who will rise, who will fall, all that stuff. I'd expected a lot of questions of the "what in the sacred name of fuck?" variety, but nobody said anything. They were waiting for the punchline, and 507m duly delivered it.

By now the gun had decrypted nine centuries' worth of satellite footage and edited it together into a continuous sequence lasting about six minutes. Et dropped the montage into our arrays and played it through from beginning to end. Since I'd seen it already I had the luxury of being able to look around and see how everyone was taking this. Badly, was the short answer. War doesn't tend to make a good spectator sport, and the fact that the primitive weapons being deployed here had relatively limited destructive capacity didn't make the results any easier to watch.

And it wasn't just this one continent. The other major land masses, which we'd never seen for ourselves and had no obvious way of getting to, were undergoing their own endlessly repeated conflicts. Some of them looked vaguely familiar. They were analogues of wars that had happened on my own and other Pando worlds around about this point in their development. Only instead of lasting two years, or five, or ten, they were all of them going on forever.

"So there it is," the captain said. He scratched his chin. He'd decided a few weeks before not to bother shaving any more and the half-grown beard seemed to be itching. "That's what we know. Time flows differently here than it does on our side of the Step plate. Specifically, it flows a whole lot faster. It took us about six minutes to get our shit together and chase those True Imp fuckers down the rabbit hole, but on this side of the Step plate it wasn't six minutes. It was a thousand years. That's a differential of . . . hell, somebody work it out."

"Approximately eighty-eight million, Captain," 507m helpfully supplied.

"Thank you. And I guess that leaves us with two questions, the how and the why. Nim'kisi has a theory about the how part."

He gave Nim'kisi the nod and she stood, adding a weird touch of formality to the proceedings. Her ears stood up too. Like all Uti selves she had ears that were reliable indicators of her emotional state, which just then was every bit as tense and wired as the rest of us.

"I think they use Step technology," she said. "We already knew the True Imperium's scientists were doing some radical experiments with Step fields. For example, they can deflect a field along a given vector so it transports whole chunks of the surrounding area into another continuum as it moves. To all intents and purposes that makes a Step plate into a disintegrator beam. They killed a lot of people that way on Ghen and Artaxa.

"And then during the fight back on U233466128 we saw randomly propagating Step fields used as mines. When the plates were triggered they opened ten or twenty spherical micro-fields in a given volume of space, so anyone walking through them would pretty much be vivisected when they crossed the fields' active radius."

"Is that what happened to Genny?" This from Ivikeppe, who was looking very unhappy about all this. Out of all of us he'd been closest to the corporal. They were both ursid selves from Trokas. They'd been part of the same intake, had trained together, had transferred into the unit together.

"No, Geniull didn't walk into a trap," Nim'kisi pointed out. "He just activated his own bounce-back. What it was . . . What it must have been . . ." She hesitated, swallowed hard. Given her social anxiety she probably wasn't enjoying being the centre of attention like this. "I think the True Imps have found a way to generate antagonistic fields. It's been a theoretical possibility for a long time but nobody has actually done it until now."

"Baby talk," Dulu said. "For the sake of the non-engineers here." He sounded tired. He looked like a man bereaved.

"Yes, sir. Baby talk it is." Nim'kisi steeled herself and plunged in. "When you fire up a Step field it takes you from point A in your origin universe to the corresponding point A in your destination universe." She held up her hands to demonstrate, bringing them together slowly and gently with the fingers spread so when they touched each hand was a mirror image of the other. "You're not moving in space so much as being translated directly from one continuum to another. When the Registry solves the equations for a Step, what et's doing is bringing the origin continuum and the destination continuum together with no friction or slippage. Making the transition seamless and perfect.

"With an antagonistic field you do the exact opposite of that. You don't try to eliminate friction and slippage, you actively encourage them. You push the Step field up against the target continuum in a way that's . . . disruptive. Deliberately out of phase." Nim'kisi gestured again, the fingers of her two hands sliding past and through each other, then locking and grappling. "With this kind of Step field the two continua, your start and end points, are at odds. You're still Stepping from A to B, but A and B are . . . well, they're tilted. Sideways on to each other. Not just spatially but in every way you can possibly imagine. The two continua don't fit together properly. Things that should be constants become variables. And one of those things is time."

"There's virtually no experimental data on this," I felt compelled to point out. "It's mostly just racy fiction. The stuff you'd get in a bad telos drama. I mean it was until now."

"I think we've got proof of concept here, Esten," Captain Dulu said grimly.

"And if I'm right, then that's why Geniull died," Nim'kisi went on. "His bounce-back was supposed to reverse the Step field and take him back to the original coordinates we'd Stepped from. But it couldn't. The equations didn't match. Instead of bouncing straight home he hit that differential like . . ." she groped for a simile ". . . like someone jumping out of a fast-moving car onto asphalt. He hit hard. You saw."

"And this is why the second team never came through?" Trooper Lasque hazarded. "Because on the other side of the plate only a few seconds have passed since we left."

"Not even half a second yet. But yeah, that's the nub of it. Nobody is going to come for us. Nobody *can* come for us, at least not within the next millennium. Even if they ran and jumped right onto the plate as soon as it cycled their boots haven't touched the ground yet. By the time the second team arrives there won't be any of us left."

Shock and grief take people in unpredictable ways. I thought for sure the panic would hit now, but most of the squad just folded in on themselves as they digested that death sentence. Ivikeppe started to cry very quietly. Otarus went through what must have been every swearword he knew in a dull monotone that was scarier than any bellow of rage would have been.

The captain gave them a few more seconds' leeway, then he cut in again and his voice was hard. "So yeah. Shitty luck, for all of us, but I don't see any use in complaining about it. We're still Cielo and we're still on-mission. In fact, speaking for my own self, I feel like the mission just got a lot more personal. I'm experiencing a burning desire to track down every last one of these True Imp fuck-joys and ruin their day for them. And we have some solid options in that regard, so—"

"Wait, though," Lasque said. His mouth was twisted as if he was biting down on something sour. "Sorry, Captain, sorry, but

I'm still stuck on the how and the why. How do you make people keep on fighting the same war? And why would you want to?"

"The prisoners already told us why," I said. "I didn't mention this before, but that who-will-rise-and-who-will-fall stuff was really precious to them. Whenever I asked about it, they recited the answer as though it was part of their scripture."

"So?" Lasque was impatient, belligerent.

"So you have to think about what's holy to a True Imp," Dulu took up. "They're fanatics. They believe their destiny is to conquer. And how do you do that? How do you make the perfect state, the million-year empire? You start by making perfect citizens. The endless wars here, we think they're a way of stress-testing all the different races in the Pandominion to see which ones make the best soldiers. The best generals. The best leaders and administrators."

"That's insane," Velladaxita said, still in her responsible clinician voice, "but it tracks as the right kind of insanity for the True Imperium. We have to accept the logic of this absurd situation." She raised her huge hands and spread them wide to indicate not just the space around us but the continent, the planet, the whole enormous shit-heap. "This is an engineered world, both genetically and socially. Whoever built it raised literally dozens of chordate species to full sentience and sculpted their civilisations to foment perpetual crisis, perpetual conflict. And they recorded the results punctiliously, so we have to assume they were interested in the outcomes. Not the winners and losers, since each side wins and loses repetitively, but the process. The patterns that stand out against the churn of random chance."

"Patterns?" Ivikeppe repeated.

"Trends. Consistencies. Islands of stable data. The True Imps' overriding aim has always been to make a second Pandominion that would continue where the first one left off, committed to conquering and uniting all the continua it could reach. They're expansionist to a fault, and they're also perversely romantic in the way totalitarians always are. They believe in the comforting myth of the master race, and so they set out to build one from the ingredients they already had." Dax shook her head in disgust. "These people weren't scientists. They were eugenicists trying to scrape up some facts to hang their bigotry on."

"And we caught them in the middle of that," Dulu summed up. "With their pants around their ankles. The True Imp scientists must have been coming and going freely here until we trashed their base. But the team we followed, it seems they had no way back. They were unprepared, had to make their decisions on the fly. They Stepped through without the equipment that would have let them go home again. That was, you know, a thousand years ago for them, give or take the odd decade. And they knew from the start what we only just worked out – that because of the time differential they couldn't look for rescue or evac until another few millennia down the line. So they settled down and carried on with their work. And they passed it along to their descendants, who are still fighting what they see as the good fight."

"Perhaps they thought *we* were the rescue party," said Nim'kisi quietly. "Clearly they knew we'd arrived, and there's only one place we could have come from. They've been watching us via the satellites. And it took them a while to decide what to do about us. Once they were sure that we were enemies, not friends, they sent this squad to exterminate us."

Dulu nodded. "They'll probably try again too. We got lucky this time. They underestimated us. We're not going to make the same mistake. We're going to assume this was only a fraction of their resources, and we're going to make damn sure the next time we meet them it's on our terms."

We raised a ragged cheer. It was comforting to be swearing a vendetta against the people who'd just obliterated our camp and probably had enough materiel on hand to blow us into loose atoms a hundred times over. We weren't kidding ourselves about the odds, but at least reckless defiance was something we could throw on the scales as a counterweight to our growing awareness of how very badly we were fucked.

I went back to the prisoners and had Flycatcher put them under CoIL again, this time to find out as much as we could about their resources. Where were they based, and how large a force could they muster against us? What sort of weapons could they deploy? Would a second attack come as soon as they knew the first one had failed?

The prisoners were fully aware of what was at stake, of course. They knew the information I squeezed out of them now would be used in due course to find and slaughter their comrades. They fought against the scanner with everything they had, which only served to exacerbate the damage a CoIL interrogation on a high setting is prone to do. I could say I tried my best not to hurt them but I knew exactly how deep-scanning works and knowing it didn't stop me. Whenever I started to feel any qualms I thought about Ajuparo and turned up the dial.

I got what we needed, and when I was done I couldn't look at them. At what I'd done to them. I handed my report to the captain, along with a rough and ready map of the True Imp bases. There were six in all, the closest only a few hundred miles north of us, the furthest on the other side of the continent. The report listed in full the strength of each enemy complement and the ordnance they could bring against us.

"Good work, engineer," Dulu said. Then as I turned to leave he called me back. "There's a question we forgot to ask, and it's important. Can I add it to the slate?"

"Slate's closed, sir," I told him.

Dulu nodded. As I think I said, he had a lot more combat experience than me. He got my meaning at once, that there wouldn't be any more questions because there was nobody home to answer. "Pity," he said. "I was going to ask how they do it. How they make these people keep fighting, year on year. Genetic engineering is one thing, but how do you hard-wire an entire culture for aggression? We're still missing a piece of this puzzle, and it's a big one."

He was right about that. It was a good question, and I should have asked it. But in the end it wouldn't have made a difference. Dulu would still have died. Nim'kisi, Velladaxita, Lasque, all of them, they would still have died.

I'd still be the last of us, lying here and waiting to be taken up, not into Heaven but into the belly of the beast.

No offence, 507m.

PART FIVE

RUN FURTHER, RUN FASTER

The landscape continued to change around Bess and Slim as they moved across the Pugface territories. They weren't all the way out into the desert yet, only on the steppes of the western Amendele, but that distinction didn't seem to matter very much. The vegetation grew sparser and sparser, with huge saguaros, cardons and organ pipes taking over from cottonwoods and stunted junipers. The level plain was scarred by deep arroyos which in spring would fill with spuming water and wash away parts of the trail completely – though now the riders could pick their way with relative ease between the concentric ridges of baked earth where the water had passed. The ghosts of rivers, done to death by the relentless western sun.

At night all that heat drained away like water out of a leaky bucket, so quickly the sweat on your back turned chill before it dried. There was a scant half-hour or so after sunset when the cool was welcome. Then the altiplano night set in cold and hard and vicious like the tortured ground's protest against the sun's assaults.

Mur Ghrent kept proving his usefulness in ways Bess hadn't expected. He was adept at starting a fire with foxtail grass and feeding it with red brome and the low-lying, warty clumps of desert cabbage so it gave off heat without too much light. He was a skilled hunter too, and he knew what was safe to eat. A fat iguana made a solid meal, and the best time to catch one was in the evening when the cold made them sluggish but there was still enough light to see by. The wild rock devil, cousin to the domesticated katies, was not good meat by anyone's reckoning but it stayed down and the bitter aftertaste didn't last too long. Red scouts and elephant weevils were poison.

Sometimes the girl went with Ghrent when he hunted and came back with kills of her own. Other times she just sat and kept her own counsel.

The girl's name was Dima Saraband. Her clan was Nimski. After that initial declaration she had had very little to say for herself, though she sometimes talked with Ghrent in voke-chant, the rapid, staccato sign language the plains Pugfaces had developed for trade and negotiation between clans that didn't share a spoken language. Bess was perforce left out of these discussions, which she didn't mind at all. She liked that the two of them could go at it without her having to listen.

Slim's silence was more concerning. The desert sun had filled his batteries to overflowing, and normally Bess would have expected this to add a touch of febrile animation to his talk, but since the fight at the trading post he had barely spoken. He helped Ghrent with his hunting, using his thermal imaging and sonar to direct them towards likely game, and when Bess asked him a question about their bearings he would give her a terse answer. Aside from that he was just about as talkative as any regular shooting iron.

"What's got you so glum?" Bess asked him at last, when they hit a narrow trail and the other two had to fall back out of hearing distance.

"Who said I was glum?" Slim countered. But his sullen tone belied him and after a moment he gave in and offered a little more. "I was thinking, Bess, that's all."

"About what?"

"About the past."

"Shouldn't take too long. You don't have that much of it to think about."

She meant it as a joke, but in the silence that followed she realised how much hurt those careless words would have caused him. "I'm sorry, Slim," she said. "Sorry with a whole heart. My mouth sounds off before my brain's awake sometimes. Have any of your lost memories come back to you?"

"No."

"What, then?"

"The opposite, I guess. Or not the opposite so much as just the way it goes with me. This voice I'm using. You remember whose it was?"

"Yeah, of course I do. Why?" Bess kept her tone level, but she still couldn't think back to that day without reliving the terror of it. Watching Alden Calendar burn a man alive and not being able to do one damn thing except sit and wait for the flames to die down.

"Well," Slim said, "I don't."

Bess opened her mouth to speak the name, but then the full weight of the words fell on her all at once. She rode along in silence for a little while, trying to find some way to frame her next question. By the time she worked it out it wasn't a question at all. "You don't remember how we met."

"Nope. The road got rolled up behind me again, the way it always does. I remember you digging me out of the ground and telling me the voice I was using then wasn't acceptable to you. So I tried yours on for size, and that wasn't no good either. Then I lit on this one, and you said it would do. And the way the two of us were talking to one another, it was plain we'd had dealings before. In fact it seemed like it had got to be you that buried me in the first place, and I was pretty damn pleased you'd changed your mind about that. I been with you ever since, and it's been a good few years we've had. War and peace, thick and thin, good years.

"But from here on in I'm going to be forgetting them, one day at a time."

Bess was still trying to think of something to say when she saw the shadow on the ground thrown by a second rider close behind her. She looked over her shoulder and saw that Dima Saraband had been gaining on her all this time. The woman said nothing but there was an expression on her face that was intent, almost hungry.

"I'm right sorry, Slim," Bess muttered. "That I am." And she left it at that. Slim's troubles didn't feel like a thing she had any call to go sharing.

That night they camped on a broad ledge over a ravine, mostly because it commanded good views in all directions. Nobody was likely to be sneaking up on them so long as Slim was on watch duty, but it didn't hurt to take extra precautions. While Ghrent was gathering the makings of a fire and Bess was skinning a brace of jackrabbits Dima Saraband came to her where she was sitting and squatted down opposite, folding her legs up with each foot tucked under the opposite calf as if she was settling in for a long stay.

"May I ask you a question?" she said.

"If you feel like you got to."

"Back at the trading post you said you were an outlaw and that the States' Union had sent a posse after you. Are you Dog-Bitch Bess?"

Bess nodded. She didn't see any point in denying it.

"And I assume that means the gun you're carrying is the one that's come to be called Wakeful Slim."

"Nothing wrong with that assumption."

"In that case I'd like to examine it." The Pugface woman's tone was brisk and matter-of-fact. She held out her hand as if she expected Bess to hand Slim over right there and then.

"Oh, you would?" Bess said mildly. "Feel like telling me why?"

"Just to verify something," the Pugface girl said.

The way she asked reminded Bess of a night long ago in the Ajuparo camp when Kilin Vevenis had asked if she could hold Slim for a moment or two. But the old woman had referred to Slim as a warrior and treated him with nothing but respect. Dima Saraband seemed more inclined to see him as just another tool, along the same lines as a hammer or a shovel only maybe a little more complicated. With Slim's melancholy weighing down on him even worse than usual Bess wasn't inclined to put him to the trouble.

"Well, you go do your verifying elsewhere," she advised the girl. "Slim ain't at home to visitors right now."

Dima wasn't abashed. "Is he whole?" she demanded.

Bess blinked. "What?"

"The gun. Is he whole, or is he damaged? I overheard the conversation you were having earlier about memory. If I understand correctly the gun's memory is impaired. Is that true?"

"Why would you want to know?"

"I've had the opportunity to see a great many of these ancient artefacts up close, and I have some knowledge of their workings. More than most people, I'd venture to say. If the gun is damaged I might be able to tell you what's wrong with him. Perhaps even fix him."

It was the one thing out of all the things Dima could have said that gave Bess pause. She was wary though. Saying a thing wasn't the same as doing it, by a long way.

"What do you mean, you've seen a number of them?" she asked. "There aren't but a few things in the whole world that have come down to us from the Precursor days." She didn't add that she herself had seen three with her own eyes. Two of them, Slim and that nameless rifle, had been in the possession of the same man. The third was the silver bird that had flown at the shoulder of Paulus Rondeau when he and his three-times-damned Reapers came through Ottomankie like a hot wind. There might have been others since. She'd glimpsed things happening far away on battlefields – discharges of light and heat, buffeting ripples in the air like cross-currents in a river, vast explosions – that she thought could have been the effects of Precursor weapons being deployed.

"There are two hundred and forty-nine that have been found," Dima Saraband said. "Of course there could be more out there somewhere, buried underground or lying on stream beds, or else in the possession of people who never recognised them for what they were. But two hundred and forty-nine that we know of, and most of them are reasonably well documented. My clan, the Nimkisi, holds the names and specifications of almost all of them. I'll probably know which one you're holding if you let me see it."

There was a word in there that touched a chord with Bess. Slim had said that among the things he never forgot were his user manual and his technical specifications. To the best of her recollection she had never heard anyone else use the word "specifications" in that way – certainly not since she had left Paxen. But she was still mistrustful. She waited a moment to see whether Slim would speak up. When he didn't she said, "You're telling me you and your people been keeping a list?"

"Yes," Dima confirmed. "That's a part of what we do. Not the most important part."

"A list of Precursor weapons?"

"Of all Precursor tools and devices."

"Why?"

Dima frowned, and was silent for a moment. It was as though Bess had said something so obtuse and unhelpful that it physically pained her. "Call it sacred tradition," she said. "Neither of those words would be wholly accurate, but the reality is too complicated to convey to you and in any case we don't have the time."

Bess was nonplussed. The Pugfaces she had encountered in Ottomankie had mostly been impassive and silent. The Ajuparos she had met when she was riding with Tom Blue had been courteous and welcoming. Mur Ghrent seemed to belong to a category of one, but even allowing him into the mix she had never up to this point met a Pugface who was condescending and impatient.

"Well, how about you give it a shot anyway," Bess suggested, caught between exasperation and cold amusement. "You might be surprised at how much I can take in."

"We're talking about the most powerful and sophisticated made things in the whole world," Dima Saraband said. "Devices so complex we can't understand how they work, still less replicate them. Each one is unique, and precious. It's important to keep track of them. They were made in very ancient times and carried by great heroes – including the greatest hero of all. He anointed them with his blood, and he told us to take good care of them."

"The Engine Everlasting," Bess said sourly. "It seems like I keep stepping in that dead man's shadow. Do you people ever talk about anything else?"

Dima shrugged. "We tell the stories that explain who we are. You do that too. You tell stories about Pugface ambushes and Pugface massacres to explain why you keep killing us and pushing us out of your way."

There wasn't any arguing with that so Bess didn't try. "Why are you so obsessed with the things the Precursors left?" she asked instead. "It's not like you're ever gonna get your hands on any of them."

Dima shook her head, but it wasn't clear to Bess whether she was disagreeing or just dismissing that point as irrelevant. "Whose precursors do you think they were?" she asked. "Yours?"

Bess blinked. "I never gave it any thought. And I guess we can't say. We don't know anything about them."

"Yes, we do, Dog-Bitch Bess. We know them by the things they made. Weapons and tools that are shaped for our hands. Suits of armour built to the scale and shape of our bodies. Names that live on in our names."

"In *your* names? So you're saying . . . what, that the Precursors are the ancestors of the Pugface clans?"

"A better name for them is progenitors. They made everything in the world. But not all at the same time, and not all for the same purpose. You were made first. We came later. That's why we're better than you."

Bess was finding most of this talk so ridiculous that there almost wasn't any right way to come at it. "Okay," she said at last, "don't take this the wrong way, but you been throwing around words like 'powerful', 'complex', 'sophisticated'. If there's three things your people ain't known for it's them three. You use chipped stone for your axe-heads and cured hide for your houses. Powerful and sophisticated don't sit too well with that."

Dima didn't seem offended. She only smiled, a smile that was very cold and very tight. "It comes down to stories again," she said.

"In your stories we were the original inhabitants of this country and you bassari are the latecomers, the ones whose destiny it is to conquer it and take possession of it. But you can't say where it was you came from, can you?"

"That's . . ." Bess began. but again she found she didn't have anything to offer. The written histories of the States' Union didn't stretch back that far. The old countries were more a matter of folk memory and tall tales. "It was a long time ago."

"Does that sound like a good explanation to you?"

Bess could only stare. No, it didn't. It sounded grotesque and bizarre. Slim had seen the world through his satellite eyes and told her the true shape of it: close but out of reach, hidden away behind invisible walls. The world as she imagined it was different, just two places with a dotted line between them that ancient pilgrims had threaded. It was like a child's drawing with some of the details ridiculously out of kilter and even more just missing. She felt a sudden sense of vertigo. Why had she never thought to question any of this? Why did everyone state as established fact things that couldn't be proved and made no sense?

"Don't feel bad about it," Dima said. "You didn't have any choice when it came to believing what you were told. You've never had any choice about anything, in fact. You run on tracks, like a train."

"And you don't?" Bess shot back – a playground taunt to go with her playground cosmology.

"As I said, we're a very recent import. We came into an infrastructure that was already tightly controlled. Locked down by other groups who didn't really have any point of reference for us. We made ourselves a niche and we've kept to it. It's had its drawbacks – some of them very severe – but it bought us one big advantage."

"And what would that be?"

"It made us invisible. If you won't let me examine your gun, will you let me talk to it?"

Bess fought a surge of anger, aware that at least some of it was a side effect of her confusion. She just did not know what to make of this uppity Pugface girl's manners. "Well, who in hell is stopping you?" she said. "You been talking to me all this time like Slim wasn't even here. Maybe if you give him a courteous word he'll answer you in the same vein."

"Thank you," Dima said, again without responding to Bess's aggression or even seeming to notice it. "I'll endeavour to do that. Slim . . . Is that your name? Slim, I don't know if you heard what I said before, but if you're damaged there's a possibility that I can repair you."

"I heard you." Slim broke in at last. Bess heard some of her own anger reflected in his brusque tone. "But with respect, missy, you don't know what you're talking about. Fixing me ain't a practical proposition. What I got wrong with me, it's not the kind of thing you can slap a poultice on."

"No," Dima agreed. "If there's been damage to your motherboard that has almost certainly resulted in severely reduced functionality. I don't know exactly what you've lost, but I'd guess it includes some of your high-power modes and the pathways that instantiate them. And then in trying to route around all of that your system may have had to cannibalise some of your archived storage. Which would entail general memory loss."

Slim was silent for a long moment. "How'd you know that?" he demanded. And then after another pause "Have we met before?" Bess read both hope and suspicion in his tone.

"Not in person," Dima said. "But I told you, my people are the keepers of the record."

Dima held out her hand again. There was an eagerness in her face and in the forward lean of her body that she couldn't entirely disguise. She might or might not want to help Slim, Bess judged, but she surely did want to get a good look at him. Bess made no move to hand him over. She waited for Slim to decide for himself whether or not he wanted to be inspected.

"This here record," he said warily. "Or list, or whatever you call it. Are you saying I'm on it?"

"Perhaps," Dima said. "Or you may be number two hundred and fifty. Either way I'm familiar with things that are very much like you and I know something – not everything, but more than anyone else – about how you work. If you let me take a look at you I'll be able to tell you whether or not I can help you."

She brought her other hand up alongside the first, cupping them both to make a cradle. "Or you can go on as you are. Which is to say, broken and incomplete."

"Well," Slim said, "that's just uncivil."

"No, it's just the truth."

Slim went quiet for a while. Dima waited, her hand still extended to take him if Bess were to offer him up.

"What do you think, Bess?" Slim asked her.

"Your call, partner. Whatever you decide, I'll go right along with it."

"Okay then. I guess I got no quarrel with a second opinion. Go ahead, missy. But no sudden moves, y'hear?"

Bess drew Slim out of the holster and handed him over to Dima, who despite her peremptory tone took hold of him with great care. She examined Slim closely, in silence, for most of a minute – again, just as Kilin Vevenis had done, and Bess couldn't help wondering now whether the old woman had known about this list and what was on it.

She waited for Dima to deliver a verdict, but the Pugface girl only looked and thought, then looked and thought some more.

"The fire's ready," Mur Ghrent called from the other side of the ledge. He had set it under a rock overhang so its light would be less visible from the north and east, the directions from which any pursuit would be most likely to come. Nobody answered him. "Ready for those rabbits," he added after a while. "Hot enough to cook on. If anyone wanted to cook."

"Well, what?" Slim said. "Am I on your list or not?"

"I can't say for sure," Dima admitted. "I'll have to take a look inside you."

As she said this she tapped Slim's stock with the tips of her fingers in a quick tattoo. The stock fell open, the lower half of it dropping into Dima's cupped hand. The exposed inner surface was a tracery of gold lines on grey.

"Hey!" Bess yelled, but it was already too late for her to prevent what was happening. As she lunged forward to grab Slim out of Dima's hands Dima was already separating Slim's stock from his barrel, which broke apart of its own accord to expose inner complexities that were nothing like the safe and solid insides of a regular gun. Bess froze with one hand on Dima's forearm, suddenly and terrifyingly aware that if she snatched Slim away from her right then she wouldn't have the first idea how to put him back together again.

Her Lumiss was in one of the saddlebags six or seven paces behind her so she went with what she could reach. She dropped her hand down to the knife that was tucked into Dima Saraband's belt. She didn't even draw it out, just turned the blade so it pressed a little harder against the woman's side.

"You're gonna put him back together again," she growled. "Slow and careful."

"I'm just about to do that," Dima agreed, seeming completely unperturbed by the implied threat. "But first I need to see the gun's core circuitry."

She spread her hands apart. In between them Slim opened like a flower, layers of metal plate that looked as thin as tissue paper unfolding themselves into the air in a perfectly symmetrical pattern and then just hanging there, unsupported, as if they were completely weightless. These pieces were of varied shapes and sizes, the largest as big as the ball of Bess's thumb and the smallest almost too small to see. Across the faces of all of them tiny, vividly coloured lights pursued each other or stood in place and twinkled like stars. Bess gaped. So did Ghrent, who had come up to upbraid them both some more about the cooking fire but now just stood, his eyes wide and his arms dangling at his sides.

"What have you done?" Bess protested. She shifted her grip on the handle of the knife. "If you break him—"

"This is a basic inspection and repair configuration," Dima said, not looking up. "Slim is fully modular. All these sub-assemblies are designed so they can be dismounted and replaced in a second or two if you've got the parts."

"Slim," Bess said, "are you okay?"

"I guess I'm well enough." Slim's voice sounded distant, hollow, with a tinny echo. "But I can't see a damn thing."

"Because your sensors are offlined," Dima observed absently. Her fingers moved again. The component parts of Slim turned slowly in the air like the painted wooden animals on the steam-driven novelty called a carousel. "Most of your on-board systems default to neutral when you're open for inspection." Dima leaned in close, squinting. "Beautiful," she murmured. "This is a fascinating artefact."

"It's right kind of you to say so," Slim observed drily.

Dima's fingers were darting in and out all this while, nudging all the floating pieces of Slim's innards into new configurations. "There are modules here that have nothing to do with the gun's offensive capabilities. AV projection. A satellite uplink. And these snap-in memory lozenges here . . ." She tailed off. For a few moments she neither spoke nor moved.

"Stone in my hoof?"

"No, it's . . ." Dima pointed at one of the very many involuted plates and petals of floating metal. She touched the tip of her little finger to another. "The memory. It's ample. You could store a thousand libraries on here. A hundred thousand."

"Seems like I should be better at that particular chore than I am, then."

Bess heard the tightness in Slim's tone. Dima couldn't know how freighted with pain that topic was. Bess stepped in quickly to deflect. "What about the damage?"

"There is no damage." Dima's voice was thick with some emotion that had come upon her too suddenly for her to hide it. "It's all perfect."

"But the burn marks . . ."

"Are just on the casing. Whatever hit Slim, it stopped at the surface. Cosmetic damage. His core is intact. Everything . . . completely intact."

"Then what in hell is wrong with his remembering?" Bess demanded. She'd released her hold on the knife but she remained in the same awkward position, leaning in close ready to catch all of Slim's many, many parts if they should start to fall out of the air.

"I don't know," Dima said, her voice almost a whisper. "I mean . . . there's a possibility, but I can't say for sure."

"You can fix him, though? You said you could fix him."

"How do you fix what's not broken in the first place?" Dima's hands wove in and out and the frozen explosion reversed itself, the petals and flakes drawing together and crowding back inside Slim's stock and barrel, which then reassembled themselves and hid all those delicate workings from sight.

The silence that followed this felt to Bess as loud as a peal of thunder. Nobody seemed to know how to break it. After a few moments Ghrent walked between Bess and Dima and picked up the skinned rabbits from the earth where Bess had dropped them. "I'll dust these off," he said, "and get them cooking. Be a shame to waste them. And someone's going to want to eat at some point, I bet."

Dima held Slim out to Bess. Bess grabbed him back with a hand that felt dangerously unsteady. He seemed suddenly a lot more fragile now that she knew how many tiny, intricate pieces made up the whole of him. "You all right, partner?" she asked him gently.

"Far as I can tell," Slim allowed. "But I don't feel like that's a thing I want to do again any time soon."

Bess fixed Dima with a glare. "After all that," she said fiercely, "you got nothing more to say?"

Dima met that savage gaze without flinching. "Would you prefer I lied to you? Made promises I couldn't keep? As I just said, there's no sign of physical damage. So Slim's memory loss must have another cause. It's possible . . . there's another factor that might explain it, but until I get my tools back I can't say for sure. In the interim, I'd like to make the two of you an offer."

Bess slid Slim back into the holster, keeping her hand clamped protectively on his grip. "Don't bother," she said.

Dima massaged her fingers and then shook them, wincing a little as if they were sore from so much exercise. Her expression was deadpan. "You didn't hear my proposition yet."

"To hell with your proposition. You raised up a heap of hopes and then you couldn't do no more with them than knock them down again. You don't get to throw propositions around."

"You don't lose anything by hearing me out," Dima Saraband said.

Slim chimed in again. "Seems to me like I maybe could lose a lot. Lost my eyesight for a while back there, if I'm not mistaken, and a blind gun's a lamentable thing. Nobody's stopping you from speaking up, missy, but mind you speak plain. If you can't fix me then what can you do?"

Dima spread her hands to show them empty. No tricks here. "I didn't say I couldn't fix you, Slim. Only that I can't promise to. Here's the plain truth. The three men who bushwhacked me and sold me to that son-of-a-bitch possum back there, they also took something from me. The tools I use in my work. If you help me find those three and deal with them, well, then I can give you a straight answer. What I can do for you and what I can't. And anything I can do, I will. Right there and then, with no charge. How does that sound?"

"Well, begging your pardon," Bess said, "but it sounds like katy-shit. We only got your word for it that you can do these things. So we do our part up front and then you maybe just shrug your shoulders and say you can't help out after all."

"Yeah," Slim agreed, though there was something in his voice that sounded just a touch like regret. "Bess is right. 'Do what you can' ain't exactly a promise. It's more of a stump speech."

Dima Saraband nodded, solemn faced. "I suppose it falls short of an iron-clad guarantee," she admitted. "I'll do my best. That's all I can say. But there's something else I can offer. I can fill some of the holes in Slim's memory."

"The hell you can!" Bess exclaimed.

"My life on it. I've seen enough now to place exactly who and what you are, Slim. I can tell you the name of the man who was first to carry you. How he lived. How he died. What you meant to him. And I might be able to tell you why you don't remember all that yourself. That's got to be worth something, surely?"

In Bess's opinion it still sounded like a lot of blown smoke rings, but she didn't presume to answer on Slim's behalf. She waited for him to speak. When he did it wasn't to Dima but to her. His tone was hesitant, uncertain. "You reckon we could find these bushwhackers, Bess? If we was to undertake for it? I could've done it easy as falling out of a tree when the satellite network was up and running – and I can still use my thermals once we get close. But I ain't like to be much use in the meanwhile."

Bess considered. "It's either gonna be real easy or next best thing to impossible," she said scrupulously. "There's a whole lot of country out there, Slim. But if they really said they were heading towards Orange Grove, and if that's the truth of it, then they'll most likely push on due west for most of the next eight hundred miles. It's only when they get to Lake Azul that they'll need to make any kind of a choice. If we keep up a good pace we ought to be able to catch up with them well before that." She pressed the ball of her thumb against Slim's stock, where she had carved the heart. "If this is what you want to do, we'll do it. Just say the word."

"I don't see where I've got a right to ask it of you. I'm meant to work to your wants and needs, not the other way around."

Which was only another way of saying yes. Bess gave Dima Saraband her hardest stare. "You better not go back on this," she said. "Any part of it. You're gonna try to fix Slim, and you're gonna tell him everything you know about him. Where he come from, where he's been, all that."

"Worry about your side of the bargain," Dima said. "I'm good for mine."

"The rabbits are done," Ghrent remarked quietly from beside the fire. "Actually they were done some time ago, but I didn't want to interrupt. I ate mine before it went cold again. And then I ate the other, before wild animals could get to it. But there's plenty of jerky left, and since your teeth are better than mine I left you all of that."

They rode, fleeing from the rising sun in the morning, chasing it down as it fell.

The changes Bess was seeing continued to surprise her. In other moods they would even have delighted her. The four of them were moving now through the westernmost reach of the high chaparral, where stunted oaks fought to raise themselves up above a thick sprawl of sage, red shanks and greasewood chamise. It seemed incredible that anything could grow in soil so dry and thin, let alone rise up in such profusion. Scrub jays called from the oaks' highest branches, the same note endlessly repeated, while burrowing owls peered from the mouths of their nests at the edge of the trail. Red and blue and orange butterflies like stained glass windows in flight soared up in front of them wherever their chafers' feet came down.

For a long time there was no sign of the three they were pursuing. Then they began to see the unmistakeable in-and-out pattern of fresh chafer prints. Ghrent reined in and alighted to inspect the tracks more closely. Down on one knee, he found a scatter of chafers' droppings and offered it to Ochre in his cupped hand. The scorpillon gave the little handful of pellets a single sniff and wandered off at once into the undergrowth in search of something more appetising.

"This shit is less than two days old," Ghrent reported. "Any longer than that and there'd be enough grubs in it to get her interested. We're close."

They rode on, picking up their pace.

On the second day the ground began to slope downwards again and the chaparral thinned out gradually into what looked and felt more like desert. The oak trees gave up first, then the red shanks. In their place, domed cactus plants even bigger than the saguaros they'd seen before loomed up higher than their heads. The soil on the trail and along both sides of it thinned out into dust and the dust bleached into sand the colour of old bone.

Every few hours Ghrent would call a halt and climb down to take another close-up look at the ground. On one of these inspections he pointed to the ruts of wagon wheels that had joined the chafer tracks they were following, coming in from the north. "See," he said. "The wheel runs over the chafers' prints here, rubs them out. But here – and here, too – there are prints that go down into the rut and are still clear. That means the chafers and the wagons are travelling together. Our three have found themselves some friends."

Bess looked at the old man shrewdly. "You're real good at this stuff," she said. "Hunting, tracking, shooting, all of it. Makes me wonder a mite about what you used to be, before you decided to set yourself on top of a bonfire and put a light to it."

Ghrent met her gaze, unblinking. "You could ask me," he said, "if you really want to know."

"Or you could just tell me. You said you were at the battle of the Shallow Ford. I'm guessing you weren't one of them that ran away when the States' cavalry came down."

The old man smiled a bleak smile. "No, I was the one they came for."

"You?" Bess was incredulous. "You were Broken Blade?"

"That's what the bassari called me. It was never a name I used for myself. But yes, I was that man. I was a tracker for the army, and I served them very well. Until I sickened of their cruelty and turned against them. I killed many. Killing came easily to me in those days. But in the end your own knife will always turn in your hand, one way or else another. The pain I gave out was given back to me."

He lowered his eyes. Bess saw that they were wet. She remembered how he'd thrown down the gun at Galleon Point after he'd used it, and wiped his hand on his sleeve. He was used to violence, knew its ways probably as well as she did, but he had no love for it. He used it when he had to, when he saw no other way. She decided then and there not to vex him with any more questions.

Dima forestalled her in any case. "We're wasting time," she said, stepping in between to glower down at them both. "Let's get on with this!" No more words were said after that. They climbed back into their saddles and rode on.

The wagons could be anything, of course. The most likely scenario was a party of settlers who'd decided to take the risk of a short cut through the Pugface nations in order to get to the newly opened coastal territories that much sooner. Or it might be fur trappers on their way back from a cull on the northern plains, although surely in that case they would have headed east when they hit the trail, not west. The most disturbing possibility was that the wagons belonged to the people called *provedores*, lawless men who passed weapons and hard liquor to the western Pugface clans in exchange for currency and goods looted from wagon trains that strayed too far from the main trails. Whichever it was, Bess hoped the three men they were chasing parted company from their new companions before too long.

But once they'd merged with the wagon train they stuck stubbornly together. It seemed likely the three had arranged to meet with this larger complement out here and were now travelling on towards the coast together. Almost certainly they were *provedores*. In which case the beaver, the moose and the armadillo were full members of this larger contingent who'd gone east to carry out some errand and then met up with the remainder at a prearranged rendezvous spot. In all this emptiness people didn't tend to stumble across each other unless they meant to.

All of which, Bess reflected sourly, put them in a much more difficult position than they'd been expecting. Just how big was this larger party? Judging by the tracks they had to have at least three wagons and more likely four, with maybe six or seven riding and three or four more walking alongside – or more likely taking turn and turn-about in the wagons. Somewhere between a dozen and twenty men all told, by her estimate. Ghrent put it higher than that, but he admitted that he liked to pre-empt bad news by always going straight to the most pessimistic assumptions. "Those wagons could be piled high with guns and men, Rainmaker. There's no way of telling."

"The wheel ruts would run a fair bit deeper," Dima observed.

"Ah, but they could be very small men. A small man can still fire a gun."

The only silver lining to all this was that the larger party travelled more slowly, so they were likely to catch up to it that much sooner. Under the circumstances that seemed like something of a mixed blessing.

Mid-morning on the fifth day they came on the remains of their quarry's cooking fire, still a little warm from the night before. "They should have scattered the ash and kicked sand over it," Ghrent said in disgust. "A child could follow them."

"I guess they're not afraid of being followed," Bess said.

The scorpillon Ochre rolled around in the ashes, drawn by the residual heat, and emerged from them as a grey ghost of herself. Ghrent stroked her head, then looked at the smeared ash on his palm. "We're so close behind them now, we should be smelling their sweat on the wind," he said. "It will be today."

But he was wrong. Less than an hour later Ghrent called a halt again, silently raising his hand as he reined in his chafer.

"What is it now?" Bess demanded.

"That," Ghrent said. He pointed back over his shoulder, east of north.

"I'm not seeing anything."

"Neither am I. But don't you hear it?"

They all strained to listen. "I don't hear a thing," Dima said. "But . . . I can feel it in the ground."

Bess could feel it too now, a continuous thrum coming up through the soles of her boots into her body, as though the dusty earth was a plucked guitar string. Then the first shrieks reached her, so faint they could almost have been birdsong. "What is it?" she demanded.

"Wild katies," the old man said. "A stampede. And if we can feel it this strongly, Rainmaker, we're full in the way of it. We should get some height. They'll follow the line of the land where they can."

Ghrent was already steering his chafer off the trail towards a hill of no very great height that stood maybe a couple of hundred yards away. Bess didn't argue. She'd never seen a katy stampede but she'd heard of the havoc they could cause and she very much didn't want to get in the way of one. She followed after without a word.

"Bess," Slim said suddenly, "I don't think it's katies."

"I thought your satellites were down, Slim."

"They mostly are, but I got me a knack for pattern recognition and I know what I'm hearing. The vibrations ain't right for critters that are running on that many legs. Don't stop on that there hill, Bess. Get on past it. There's a stand of saguaros maybe a half a mile further on. You need to be on the windward side of it, as close in as you can get."

"Okay, but do you want to tell me why? It feels like we ought to be safe enough up on top of the—"

"Just do it!" Slim shouted, delivering the words in the middle of a harsh blat of discordant noise.

Bess trusted him enough not to argue it any further. She pressed her heels against Red's sides and urged her into a gallop. "You two follow me!" she shouted as she overtook the other chafer. Ghrent looked startled and Dima unsettled and angry, but they'd heard Slim's warning too. Ghrent followed Bess without question, Dima clinging on tight to his back as they picked up speed.

As they crested the hill Bess risked a look over her shoulder. Slim had been right to cut the deliberations short and get them all moving. The dust cloud the stampede was raising was much closer than she would have guessed. The front of it was a ragged line cutting across the landscape from north to south at an angle that was about to intersect their own course the way a kitchen knife cuts across a cake.

Vague forms moved inside the dust cloud, an organic mass that couldn't be resolved into its basic parts. They were too small to be katies, too narrow and upright to be rock devils.

The reality of what she was seeing came on her all at once. "Holy John!" she gasped. "Holy fucking John!"

"Yeah," Slim agreed. "Don't you slow now."

Bess reached the line of giant cactus just as the forward edge of the stampede cut across her path. She was a full fifty yards ahead of Ghrent and Dima at this point, since their chafer was carrying twice the weight. She wheeled around with Slim drawn in her hand to give them as much help as she could, but there was no need. Ghrent drove the heel of his hand down between the beast's wing-cases, pulling hard on the reins at the same time. The chafer jumped and as she jumped her wings shot out to either side, catching the hot wind and turning the leap into a long, shallow glide. She sailed over the heads of the front ranks of mindless, her dangling legs almost grazing the crowns of their heads as they drove forward. Then she touched down alongside Bess's animal, Ghrent bringing her to a sharp halt by hauling on reins and antennae both.

They all stared in awestruck silence as the mindless lurched and sprinted and lumbered past. There seemed to be no end to them, or to their variety. Dogs and cats, beavers, gophers, wolves, bison, elk, jackrabbits, polecats, foxes, armadillos. Some were still dressed more or less as they had been when they'd first been stricken, the men in work cottons or suits, the women in apron skirts, crinolines, pinafore dresses. Others were naked, their bodies bloodied and torn from encounters with briars, rocks or the ground. While most were silent some howled or bellowed as they ran or uttered hoarse grunts from deep in their chests.

There must have been thousands of mindless in this terrifying, pitiful horde. They streamed past for more than a minute, the air full both of their sounds and of their stench. At the back were many who had forgotten how to run and were crawling or shuffling along on all fours. A few of these stragglers saw the two chafers and their riders behind the barricade of giant plants and made a sally in their direction. Bess pushed them back with Slim's heat beam on its lowest setting, stinging and goading them without doing any lasting harm. They were doing enough harm to their own selves, the ones that tripped being trampled down and trodden under by the ones coming on behind.

There was nothing to do but wait, trying not to breathe in the vile smell or the choking dust, until the last of the herd had gone stomping and stumbling on its way. In its wake all of them were silent, unable to find any words for what they had just seen. What they were still seeing, because the stampede had left its dead and dying sprawled across the landscape like the aftermath of a hurricane. Bess's stunned gaze ranged across this devastating panorama – until it fetched up against a single appalling detail and froze there.

Very slowly she dismounted and picked her way across the field of dead. The battlefields she'd stalked rose vividly in her mind, but this was different. Right then it felt worse. She approached one of the bodies, hoping she'd been mistaken. It was the black armband that had caught her attention, and a man might wear that because he was in mourning, but from this close she took in the man's tawny fur, the bright green of the one eye that was standing open, the long-eared John medallion.

Martin Shield of Faith wasn't dead. His leg was bent at an unworkable angle, but that was a survivable injury. The blood on his arm was from the wound he'd taken on the ferry at Twining's Gap, Bess's makeshift bandage still in place. Not an armband, just the strip she'd torn from his jacket. He'd shed the rest of the jacket along the way, along with his boots and stockings, his Bible and trim little poke bag. He snarled at Bess as she kneeled beside him, and tried to raise his head to snap at her. His chest was heaving like a blacksmith's bellows. Most of what was keeping him from rising up, most of what was killing him, was exhaustion and heatstroke.

"What in hell did you come out here for?" Bess demanded. "You damn idiot. Other people's souls weren't ever any business of yours."

But the man had been solicitous of them anyway, enough to cross half the country to deliver his own mixed-up version of salvation. And it wasn't just souls he had a care of but bodies too. She'd seen that when he stood up and preached a sermon against the Salt Lick posse's bullets.

Martin twisted his head around, trying as hard as he could to sink his teeth into Bess's leg. His eyes were opened so wide it looked like they were about to fall out of his head. Blood and foam had spilled from his mouth into the matted fur of his chin.

"Martin," Bess said. "Do you remember me?"

Martin gave a grunt that was half agony, half defiance.

"You don't want to get too close, Rainmaker," Ghrent warned, alighting behind her. "The infection takes quickly."

"That's not how it works," Dima Saraband said. She sounded angry, and she stayed up in the saddle.

"Martin." Bess laid her hand across his forehead. It felt like a furnace. "Pray with me. Come on, give me some of them Bible words. It seemed like you had the whole fucking Johannis by heart. Some of it must have stuck with you."

But there was no recognition in the man's eyes, no reason.

"We've lost enough time here already," Dima said, "and now we're wasting more. We need to get back to the trail."

"Might be an idea to let them poor bastards get some distance first," Slim suggested. "If they was to turn around sudden we might get caught out in the open with nowhere to run to."

Bess said nothing. She took the stopper from her waterskin and held it over Martin's face, letting the water dribble down into his mouth but being careful not to allow his lips to touch the rim. He thrust out his tongue to catch the drops. Bess waited until he'd swallowed and then gave him some more.

"We need to go," Dima said again.

"Nobody's keeping you," Bess said without looking around. "I'm staying a while. I know this man."

"What does that matter? He's not there any more, Bess."

Bess sat down in the dust. She took hold of Martin's hand, which was clawing feebly at her thigh, and pressed it between both of hers. She dredged up a hymn from somewhere in the back of her mind and sang it to him softly, if not exactly tunefully.

Oh, John gave his voice to us
And it was made of gold.
The Father's light was shining
In every tale he told.
You sinners just be mindful for whose sake it was he bled,
And let your soul be ransomed by the precious words he said,
All the precious words he said.

Oh John gave his strength to us
To keep us from the pit,
When there wasn't neither hand nor rope
To raise us out of it.
You sinners when you weaken and your heart's an empty cup
Give your soul to him and all at once his strength will lift you up.
I said his strength will lift you up.

Oh John gave his life for us
And burned upon the tree,
That should have sat at God's right hand
For all eternity.
The bargain's made, the price is paid, the debt extinguished quite
And we sinners now will walk into the everlasting light.
Yes, we'll walk, we'll walk, we'll walk into the light.

When she got to the end of the song she started again. There were others she knew, some she had heard a thousand times, but it had been a long while since she went to church and the words had mostly deserted her. This one had a ringing tune at least. The first time around Martin didn't respond at all. On the second rendition his lips moved a little. With the third time he made some noises. They weren't words as such, but it sounded to Bess as though they were trying to be.

It took the rest of the morning and into the afternoon for Martin to die. Bess stayed with him the whole time. When the sun's heat became unbearable she drove a couple of lopped branches into the ground and propped her sleeping blanket up on them like a tent. She gave the dying man more water when he seemed to need it and kept up a rambling, one-sided conversation with him in case he could still understand any of it. Her mind strayed at times though. She couldn't help wondering where the mindless herd had come from. She didn't want to believe they'd come from Salt Lick, though she knew the plague had struck there. Surely all those people couldn't have waded or swum across the Sweetling. Still, there had looked to be a whole townful of people in the stampede. She'd only recognised Martin but there might well have been others in that roaring, raving mass who she'd known, spoken to. And she could have been one of them her own self if Cicero Church hadn't turned up when he did and forced her to leave. The thought turned her stomach.

More than once she considered pressing Slim up against the preacher's forehead and taking away his pain all at once, but despite Dima's words and in the face of all the evidence she couldn't quite bring herself to believe there was nothing left of the man. So she sat with him and she talked, or sang, or sometimes just held his hand, while Ghrent took the chafers off so they could feed and rest away from the smell of blood and Dima fumed, pacing back and forth behind Bess with her arms grimly folded.

"What now?" she demanded, after Martin's breathing had slowed and faltered and finally stopped. "Do you want to build a casket? Give him a bassari burial?"

Bess stood and turned. She kept her expression calm and her voice level, but grief had always been a thing that made her volatile.

"I told you I knew the man," she said. "You might want to bear that in mind before you say anything else."

"It's a bad way to die," Ghrent said, picking his way back across the corpse-strewn ground with the two chafers in tow. "But a bad death is good. Good for the soul, I mean. The pain will carry him into the next life quickly. He won't linger on here as a ghost."

Bess went to join him, pointedly turning her back on Dima. He held out Red's reins to her and she took them. "I don't believe in ghosts," she said tightly. "And I wouldn't wish mindlessness on anyone."

"We don't call it that," Ghrent said. "We call it the *khadu-venu*. The blessing curse."

"I don't see the blessing," Bess said. "It's the vilest thing I've ever seen, and I've seen plenty." She spat on the ground repeatedly to rid her mouth of dust and her mind of the numbing horror. Her stomach was churning with nausea. So many selves stolen from themselves! Enough lives lost to make some of the wartime skirmishes she'd witnessed seem like a drop in a filthy ocean.

"It's terrible," Ghrent agreed. "It's also the only thing that's kept your people from taking these last stretches of land away from us and driving us into the sea. You know the gods made us immune." He pressed down on his chafer's back to make it bend and eased himself back into the saddle.

Dima clambered on behind him before the chafer could get back up on its feet again. Impatience and tension were pouring off her like steam. "It wasn't the gods," she snapped. "Don't talk about things you don't understand, old man. We were never attuned to the towers in the first place."

Bess grabbed a hold of Red's saddle horn but didn't mount up yet. "The towers?" she repeated. "What have the towers got to do with this?" She was thinking about what had happened to her when she passed between the Five Fingers after her flight from Salt Lick. Hadn't that been a kind of mindlessness, which came on her all at once and then mercifully went away again?

"It doesn't matter!" Dima's voice rose to a shout. "We need to go! We're going to lose the trail!"

She pushed her hands against Ghrent's shoulders, as though she could somehow spur their chafer into motion by pressing on him. Ghrent shook his head and glanced at Bess with a long-suffering roll of his eyes. "What should we do, Rainmaker?" he asked.

"I guess we ride on," Bess said. "I got some thinking of my own to do about this. But some time soon, Dima Saraband, you and me are gonna sit down for a long talk. There's things I'll be needing to ask you."

"I'm more than willing to have that conversation, when there's time," Dima said, and to Ghrent, "Now will you get moving?"

They retraced their path, joining the trail again a mile or so west of where they'd left it. Bess was relieved that their course now took them further and further away from the direction the mindless had taken. She would be happy never to see such a thing again. It wasn't so easy to put it out of her mind though. A whole lot of fragmented memories were bumping up against each other there, trying to come together into some kind of idea, but the more she reached for it the further it receded.

Over the next few hours they saw more signs that they were closing in on their quarry. More chafer droppings, a spat-out wad of chewing tobacco, a noisome patch of dirt just off the trail that the *provedores* had used as a latrine. But the sun was dipping towards the horizon now. The desert defied the night for as long as it could, then all at once the landscape filled up with darkness like a bowl fills with water. Bess called a halt and Ghrent made a fire. "Tomorrow then," he said. "It will certainly be tomorrow."

"Not if we spend half the day standing still the way we did today," Dima muttered.

Bess let this pass. She didn't have the stomach for an argument right then. Or for supper either, as it turned out. When Ghrent portioned out what was left of the pemmican she refused her share, unrolled her blanket and closed her eyes. She was afraid of what her dreams might bring her, but sleep fell on her as sudden and overwhelming as a mudslide and the night seemed to pass in an instant.

She woke to a savoury smell that was good enough to make her salivate. Ghrent had found some wild onions and made a kind of stew out of them. "We might be going into battle today," he told Bess and Dima gravely. "The brave eat well both before and after they fight." There was a little meat in the stew, and wherever it had come from it had a gamey tang to it that was pungent but still good. In any case Bess ate it greedily, soaking up the gravy with the last of the *pan de campo*.

As soon as they were done with their breakfast they hit the trail again. None of them had very much to say to each other so they rode in silence, which Bess thought was probably a good thing given how far any sound was likely to travel in the still desert air.

A couple of hours' riding brought them to a place where the wagon and chafer tracks left the trail at last and detoured south across a dry creek bed into a ragged, twisted landscape of mesas and arroyos. While Ghrent was still trying to make sense of the tracks they heard faint music on the wind. The twang of a banjo, the skirl of a harmonica.

Bess reined in and turned to face the others. "Okay," she said, "here's what. You two go right on back to that stand of moose-head spruce we passed and wait for me there. We maybe got a mite closer to these people than we were meaning to, but the good news is that they didn't have the good sense to leave a lookout back there on the trail. Maybe that means no lookouts at all, or maybe it means they got themselves some kind of a nest up there a ways and they're comfortable they can't be crept up on. In any case, me and Slim are going to go take a look around."

"What if they're right?" Ghrent asked. "What if they can't be crept up on?"

"Well then, I'm likely to come running on back to you sooner than expected, with bullets flying around me and a surly disposition.

Be ready to run as soon as you see me. But I'll be careful not to make a racket. And I'll circle round so I don't come on them from the direction of the trail which is where they're apt to be looking the hardest. I just want to get a sense of how many they are and what kind of a watch they're keeping. No sense picking a fight if we can sneak right in and grab what we want."

"I'll come with you," Dima said.

"I'm better alone."

"But you don't know what my tools look like. Like you said, Dog-Bitch Bess, if there's a chance of sneaking in we should take it. But you need to know what it is you're looking for."

"Tell me then," Bess suggested. "I'm guessing these aren't things like hammers and chisels and such. But you've never told us anything about what they are."

Dima looked impatient. "They're very hard to describe to anyone who hasn't seen them and doesn't understand their purpose. Just let me come with you. I promise I'll be every bit as quiet and circumspect as you are."

Bess considered. The longer they stood and argued here out in the open the more they multiplied their chances of being spotted. And although Dima's patronising tone rankled the woman had a point. "All right," she conceded. "Ghrent, take the chafers back to them trees like I said and wait for us there. We'll come back quick as we can. If you hear shooting mount up but hold your place until you see them coming. Then get out of here like someone tied a hot coal to your tail."

"I'll wait for you to come back," Ghrent said gravely.

"Yeah, but if we don't—"

"I'll wait for you to come back." The old man leaned down and took Red's reins in his free hand. With a twitch of his wrist he turned the two beasts around and urged them at a slow trot back the way they'd come.

"All right then," Bess said. "Let's do this. Slim, unpack your thermals and your sonars and tell me if there's anything moving close by."

"Should have asked me that a ways ago, Bess," Slim chided her. "But I did it anyway and the answer's no. All's clear to about two hundred yards out. If I'd caught a whiff of anyone I'd have warned you."

"Well, tell us if that changes, because we're following these tracks wherever they take us and that's likely to be into some plain unpleasant neighbourhoods. Anything we can do by way of avoiding surprises is worth the doing."

"Trust me. Anyone gets the draw on you they'll need to be a damn ghost. And if they ain't we'll amend that situation presently."

They followed the tracks south. There was no trail as such any more, but the wagon wheels had marked out a kind of path. Bess and Dima instinctively drew away to either side of it, making the best use of whatever cover there was.

After a few hundred yards they were faced with a choice. The wagon ruts followed a slight gradient downwards at the same time as the land to the right of them rose abruptly. Since the high ground was likely to give them a better field of vision Bess crossed to the right and climbed, with Dima silently following. A little further on she was glad she had. The upward slope steepened, and it was mirrored by a rise over on their left. The wagons had entered the mouth of a canyon, which now opened around and below them. It was something of a marvel, very wide and deep but completely invisible from even a short distance away because the rise in ground on either side gave the impression of an uninterrupted hill. It was only when you got right to the edge of it that you saw the deep, wide space in between.

"People up ahead," Slim reported quietly. "A whole damn boiling of them."

They advanced more cautiously, keeping their heads down and using every bit of cover that offered. They didn't see anyone yet, but as they climbed a little higher they got their first look down into the canyon below.

The floor of it was broad and flat and shaped more or less like a frying pan. The way in from the north ran narrow and straight for maybe three or four hundred yards before opening up into a space that was roughly circular. The rock walls all around were sheer, offering few hand- and foot-holds to anyone looking to climb down. There were overhangs too, which would make it that much harder. The floor was mostly grey dirt freckled with clumps of couch grass, pigweed and redstem filaree. Down the centre though, running as straight as an arrow from north to south, was a strip at least a hundred feet wide where the vegetable growth was higher and more varied, with ocotillo and desert willow trees towering over a sprawl of thick, dense scrub.

It was a good place to camp, in other words. If you were used to travelling this route from east to west and back again, through hostile territory with a lot of valuable goods in tow, you'd see a spot like this as a gift from Holy John and you'd likely make it a regular stop along your way.

The *provedores* were camped out under one of the rock overhangs. To anyone looking down from the canyon's other, eastern edge they would have been completely invisible, and from this side the distance was enough to make a clean shot very difficult. The men had made a fire and were roasting something big on it – a haunch of meat that could have come from a wild katy or a buffalo grub. Their own animals, chafers and katies together, were gathered in a makeshift paddock much further in, up against the rock face at the canyon's northern end. At the nearer end, where the frying pan's handle opened up into the wider space, four wagons were lined up side by side, completely blocking the way in. Any one of the four could be rolled out of the way quick enough if the *provedores* wanted to come or go, but they made a very serviceable barricade against anyone that was looking to mount a charge. On a rock ledge above the wagons, but still far below where Bess and Dima were kneeling, a couple of men with rifles kept a desultory watch. They could afford themselves a little latitude with their duties: they would see anyone coming in along that narrow corridor long before they got within shooting range.

"Eighteen," Dima said.

"Eighteen that we can see," Bess murmured. "There could be more tucked away behind some of the big rocks down there. And they'd be idiots if they didn't have a couple of men inside the wagons looking down that pass."

"There's four of them in there," Slim confirmed. "One in each wagon bed. And three more over there on the far side of that paddock. I guess they're feeding the katies. And there's something else you maybe missed, Bess. Look yonder, right up against the rock wall to the left of the dead tree there."

Bess looked where Slim had indicated and was chagrined to find that he was right. She'd completely failed to see two Pugface women who were sitting side by side in a narrow concavity of the cliff face on the valley's far side, in the midst of the men and ignored by them. They looked to be about the same age as Dima, more or less. Their hands were tied.

"That what I think it is?" Bess asked, pointing.

Dima squinted. "They're Ajuparo. Comfort women for the *provedores*. That's probably what they wanted me for, except the three that took me decided to do a little trading of their own before they went back to their friends."

Bess thought about the kindness the Ajuparo women had shown her when she was riding with the Braggarts. She thought about Kilin Vevenis. She thought about circles and straight lines.

"They're coming with us," she said.

"That's going to make this harder than it already was," Dima observed quietly.

"Still, it's what's going to happen. What about the stuff that was taken from you? You getting any sight of it?"

"No."

Almost certainly it was in one of the wagons then, Bess thought. But knowing where they were aiming for wasn't going to help them very much. Not against two dozen guns, in a big open space that offered few routes in and none at all without being seen along the way. There was no way they were coming out on top of that fight, so far as she could reckon it.

And no way of walking away from it. Not now that she'd seen those women. She surveyed the canyon's floor in silence for a long while, and neither Slim nor Dima broke in on her ruminations.

Any approach from the north, along the frying pan's handle, would be a disaster. You'd be walking into bad weather of the leaden variety with every step you took. The sentries up on the ledge would drive you out of cover as soon as they got eyes on you, and the men on watch inside the wagons would finish you off.

Bess reckoned she could probably climb down the canyon wall if she picked her spot just right, but there were many fine reasons not to. If she did it by daylight the galoots down on the canyon floor would see her coming and pick her off at their leisure. While if she waited until night she'd be trying to find handholds on sheer rock by touch and good fortune, which wasn't likely to go too well. A serviceable rope would have made the whole thing more straightforward, but it would still have left her facing worse than twenty-to-one odds. And she didn't have a rope.

So what did that leave? After a few moments she stood and headed on along the canyon's edge. Dima followed her a moment later. "You're thinking about the river," she murmured.

Bess nodded. "Yeah. Should have thought of it sooner."

They hadn't seen any river, of course, but that strip of richer growth down the centre of the canyon floor was a dead giveaway. The canyon had been carved out by a watercourse, pouring over the same stretch of rock for thousands on thousands of years until the rock wore away. It was like cutting into a loaf with a really dull knife. It took a long while and it wasn't what you'd call neat, but it sawed through in the end. The water probably ran underground now, unless there was a slender thread of it winding unseen through all that greenery. Either way, it had been there in the past, and logically it ought over the course of time to have made itself an exit at the further end of the valley to match the one by which the *provedores* had entered it.

She found it easily enough once they got far enough along to see past the intervening rock spurs. It was about a hundred long strides past the place where the *provedores* had corralled their animals. It wasn't going to be any help though. The gap in the canyon walls here had been forty or fifty feet wide once upon a time, but a long-ago rockfall had closed it up, leaving behind a sprawl of boulders and loose scree. The overall gradient was shallower here than along the canyon's side walls but the danger if you tried to climb down here was even greater. You'd likely bring the whole mess down on top of yourself the first time you stumbled, and some of those rocks were as big around as a katy's ass.

"Not looking great, is it?" Slim murmured. "Maybe the best bet is to pick them bastards off one by one from up top."

"Not likely to work against these numbers, Slim," Bess said. "The first few wouldn't be that hard if we pour enough bullets down on them. After that, they'd grab some cover and send a party up here to roust us out. It's not like we could stop them. There's just the one way in and out of that canyon, and they control it because they got the wagons there and the sharpshooters up on the ledges."

"We could set fire to the wagons," Dima said.

"Which would piss them off mightily, but it wouldn't change the situation. They'd know we were up here and they'd send the best shooters they've got to deal with us. I'm probably better than most of them, and I've seen what Ghrent is capable of in that line, but the numbers would tell."

Except, she suddenly realised, it didn't have to be about the numbers. There might be a way to raise the price of a fight here higher than the *provedores* would be willing to pay. She smiled as the parts of it came together in her mind – a hard, tight smile with no amusement in it, only a grim anticipation.

"You got an idea," Slim said.

"Maybe I do," Bess admitted. "That mindless stampede gave me a thought I want to chew on. Let's get back. If we're gonna do this we'll all of us need to put our backs into it. And it needs a little piecing together."

Mur Ghrent seemed unsurprised and unconcerned when he heard about how many men they were ranged up against, but he frowned and shook his head when Bess mentioned the Ajuparo captives. "That makes it harder," he said, unconsciously echoing Dima's words. "They'll be guarding the women close. And the women won't know you're a friend. When the shooting starts they'll hide."

"I know it," Bess said. "I don't mean to go in and fetch them. Hear me out." She sketched the plan for them in a few words. It wasn't all that complicated but it depended on a few things going right and all four of them doing what they had to do quickly and without any mistakes. If it worked the way she hoped, the *provedores* would give up both Dima's tools and the Pugface women without too many bullets being exchanged. Blood would be shed, and that was just too bad, but at least none of it was likely to be theirs.

"It's got to be tonight," Dima said. "They'll move on in the morning. And given how hot it's going to get later in the day they'll be aiming to make an early start. They'll get their katies in harness with first light."

"Yeah, well, that's debatable," Bess said. "They can only do that if the katies are still there."

Of course it would be that night, and the daylight was already failing. Under Bess's direction they began to move things into position. At the canyon's southern end, at the top of that precipitous scree slope, they chose stones that were very nearly round and rolled them quietly and stealthily up to the rim. Under each rock they wedged a stout branch of cedar or bur oak that they scavenged from around the canyon's edge – makeshift levers, each one with a smaller rock under its centre as the fulcrum. Bess and Dima did most of the hauling and rolling and lugging around, while Ghrent gathered driftwood and tumbleweeds in large amounts and piled them up at a point along the canyon's side wall fifty yards or so south of the corral where the *provedores'* katies and chafers were stalled. Through all this they stayed far enough away from the edge to avoid being silhouetted against the sky for a watcher below. If anyone down there had thought to patrol the rim area the three of them would have been seen at once, but they took the chance and nobody came.

When the sun hit the horizon and the light bled out of the land they rested and ate. "How did those pieces of shit get hold of you in the first place?" Bess asked Dima. "You never said. And you don't seem the kind that gets took unawares all that much."

Dima took a long time chewing and swallowing the mouthful of jerky she was working on. "I was stupid," she said, after she'd finally gulped it down. "I'm working on a project and I knew I was running out of time to get it finished. It's . . . important. If I don't get it done, something really bad is going to happen. Worse than your war. Worse than anything you can imagine. So I took more risks than I should have. Went into territories I didn't know so well, and where there were no friends I could fall back on if I got into trouble. There's a place in Samartine where five dream towers were built close together for some reason. They're called the Fingers."

"I know them," Bess said. "I came through them only a few days ago, just before I met the two of you. There was something real strange happening there."

Dima picked up another strip of jerky but she didn't bite on it. She only twisted it between her fingers. "The towers are old," she said. "Very old. Most of the noises you hear out of them are the sound of machinery going wrong."

"And is that a bad thing? If the machinery goes wrong?"

"That depends on how close you are, I suppose." Dima looked at her filthy hands, then at the jerky. Her playing with it had left it filmed with dust and wood splinters. She threw it aside. "Anyway, I wanted to draw down some measurements, and it took me longer to get there than I'd hoped. I was working fast and I let my guard down. Left a trail. Those three came on me in the night and I woke up with a knife at my throat."

Bess chewed this over, trying it for size against her own experience at the Fingers. She felt as though she was working on the kind of puzzle called a jig-saw, where you make up a picture out of a hundred tiny pieces. "How did they bring you across the Sweetling, Dima?" she asked. "Twining's Gap."

"No, the ferry was out so they rode down to Sallust. We went by the bridge."

Bess pondered this. If the ferry was out that would have been because she'd already cut the guide rope and driven it up onto the riverbank. It seemed as though she and Slim had been walking pretty much the same road as Dima ever since they set out from Salt Lick. Just good fortune maybe that they'd stumbled across the one self in the whole damn country that knew about Slim's insides and maybe could fix them up so he could get back to remembering who he was and where he'd been. Or maybe there was something else working here besides luck. In any case she couldn't make herself be happy about it. It just made her feel pressed in on, as if the whole States' Union was just one closed and narrow space like that canyon, with walls she couldn't see.

The sun went down and the clouds broke up to show a quarter-moon. That was good news at least: it offered them just about enough light to see by, but hopefully not enough to give them away to any lookouts the *provedores* might have posted. They put out their fire and made their way slowly and carefully back down the trail and then most of the way along the rim of the canyon.

Moonlight or not, it was lucky for them that they had Slim with them. It was impossible to tell in the near-darkness exactly where the edge was. They stuck to the trail as long as there was one and then they were adrift in a sea of ink out of which random hummocks of earth, rocks and patches of sage stood out like islands. But Slim deployed his sonar and his thermals and what all else he had and warned them whenever they strayed too close to that first big step.

Finally they reached the pile of brushwood and tumbleweeds they'd built up earlier in the day. They grabbed great armloads of the stuff and flung them over the edge into the absolute blackness below. They were easily two or three hundred yards down from the *provedores'* camp, and on the other side of the canyon. It was possible someone would hear the falling vegetation and come to investigate, but it was unlikely. And if they did come they'd be moving slowly in the dark. They wouldn't get there in time to stop what happened next.

Bess placed her feet at the very edge of the drop, her heels on solid ground but her toes touching nothing at all. She took Slim in a two-handed grip and aimed him straight down. "Okay, partner," she said. "Do your stuff."

Slim's heat beam lanced out, slicing the night in two. Bess held it steady for a few seconds, then let it play to right and left, in and out. Down below her, the pure white glow of the beam refracted into yellows and oranges and expanded slowly outwards as the brushwood caught and passed the fire along. There had probably been enough scrub grass and sage down there already to guarantee a blaze, but they had added some fuel of their own just in case. They needed the fire to spread quickly.

There were yells from below them now as the *provedores* saw what was happening. That was their cue to move. "Good luck," Dima muttered. "She doesn't need it," Ghrent scolded her. "She's the Rainmaker." They ran in opposite directions, Bess to the north, Dima and Ghrent to the south.

The sounds Bess was hearing now were both more varied and a great deal more urgent. The katies and chafers in the corral were shrieking and piping as the flames rose higher and drew closer. The *provedores* were cursing and shouting orders to each other, and to judge from the direction of their cries were already sprinting across the canyon floor to where their beasts were rearing up on their back legs and clawing madly at the sky.

This was the make or break, the moment when the plan would

either play out or fall in pieces. But since there was nothing Bess could do right then to help or hinder it, she put her head down and ran on.

Most animals faced with a wall of fire will retreat in front of it rather than dive through it, even when the latter action might save them. They will let themselves be penned into a tight corner and cower there as the flames colonise the space around them and close off every possibility of escape.

The katies and chafers in the corral took that course at first. When the fire reached the makeshift fence their riders had erected around them they backed away from it, pushing against one another and then clambering over each other's bodies, each of them fighting for the space that was furthest from the oncoming blaze. Then the fence itself caught fire and the flames spread past it into the corral itself. The animals turned en masse and stampeded, the chafers first and then the slower, lumbering katies, crashing through the rear of the stockade and heading straight for the canyon's southern end.

At this point they had an option that most two- and four-footed creatures in that position wouldn't have had, and they weren't slow to exercise it. When the level ground ran out they didn't slow but kept right on going up the jumbled scree, their feathered legs adhering to the perilously balanced rocks or finding narrow spaces in between them.

The biggest risk at this point was that the *provedores* would catch the beasts before they got that far – and they did catch one or two, jumping over the fire to wrestle a terrified chafer into a submissive crouch, though they had to ignore their own smouldering or burning clothes in order to do it. But the animals had a good head start and they were spurred on by their fear. They swarmed up the slope in a shrieking, chirruping wave of unstoppable speed, slabbed muscle and concentrated panic.

Up at the top of the slope Dima and Ghrent – who had got there a scant few seconds before – stepped hastily aside to let the beasts pass. It was either that or be trampled, so the choice was easy. There was no standing in the way of that tide, even if they had wanted to.

The *provedores* down below were more reckless, but then they had a whole lot more to lose. Seeing their mounts and their draught animals disappearing into the wild they charged after them, scrambling up the scree slope on all fours. What with that sliver of a moon, the smoke from the fire and the dust raised by the beasts' passage they could hardly see an inch in front of their faces but they made the best fist of it they could, groping their way blindly from rock to rock.

The slope got steeper as they went, and more treacherous. The men slowed, realising what they'd taken on. When a cloud swallowed the moon most of them stopped, unable to go up or down until they could see where to put their feet.

"Now," Dima told Ghrent. They went to the rocks that they had rolled into place earlier in the day. They got a solid grip on the levers and pressed down hard, Ghrent grunting softly with the effort. Dima's lever shifted first, sending her rock downslope in a ponderous, bouncing roll. She moved straight on to the next without even looking to see where the first rock went. A moment later Ghrent gave up trying to move his lever with just the strength of his arms and threw himself bodily down onto the end of it, which did the trick.

The men on the slope heard the bad news coming before they saw it: a rumbling that rose to a roar as the oncoming rocks nudged others and started an inexorable slide. They tried to step aside from it, angling away from the centre of the slope where the animals had stampeded. That didn't help them though, because the rocks came down in random places and from unpredictable directions. The first man to fall was hit almost at shoulder height by a boulder that seemed to be travelling as fast as a cannonball. The effect of it was like a cannonball too. He rolled to a halt twenty yards further down with most of his chest caved in and his face frozen in the shock of the titanic blow. He didn't get up again.

A moment later a second man was hit, and then a third. The remainder turned and fled, but the whole slope was on the move now and the rocks were still coming. Two or three more took solid, devastating impacts as they came down. Another one tripped and was buried in the cresting scree.

Dima and Ghrent were still hard at work up there. The rocks that were coming down now were bigger and heavier, hitting the ground like the fists of God, but by this time the slope was clear. The *provedores* had given up on the prospect of retrieving their wayward beasts by that route. They didn't know yet that the rockslide had been loosed on them deliberately: they only knew the slope wasn't a viable option.

They didn't have the luxury of giving up the chase, though. They could do without their chafers if they had to, but they needed the katies to pull those wagons. Which meant they had got to come up out of that canyon by some other way.

And unfortunately for them the other way was Bess.

If they'd been in less of a lather about their stampeded animals the *provedores* most likely would have waited until morning. Maybe they thought the katies, being generally of a stolid disposition, would slow down and stop somewhere close to the canyon wall once they were away from the heat of the fire and would be easily found. In any case they lit some torches and headed out along the narrow pass that was the frying pan's handle.

Bess had holed herself up there on a ledge about eighty feet up that jutted a fair way out from the main wall. She had herself some cover if it came to a proper shooting match. More importantly she had a really wide field of fire across most of the width of the pass. It wouldn't be easy for anyone to get by her.

She saw the little cluster of torches approaching and let them come. While she waited she counted the bobbing lights, each one of which was a *provedore*. She made it thirteen. Even if a few had stayed back with the wagons, Dima and Ghrent had already made a fair dent in their numbers.

What she was about to do was murder, no more and no less, and for all the murders she already had on her conscience she had to steel herself to do it. The death of Martin Shield of Faith had broken something inside her that had been strained already over the course of the war and the years since. It seemed that blood had taken on another colour for her, one she couldn't reconcile herself to as easily as she had in the past. She brought the two Ajuparo women into her mind and held them there. That made it easier.

When the party was close enough that missing wasn't really an option any more Bess took aim on the man that was leading the parade, squeezed the trigger nice and slow and shot him through the heart. There was a cry of alarm, and then a lot of cursing. The bobbing lights broke to left and right. The ones that went left were still full in Bess's sights so she picked one in the middle of the bunch and shot him too. The men closest to that one threw themselves to the ground; the rest fled to join their comrades on the opposite side. That was a pretty narrow bit of cover they'd grabbed, though. She waited until one of them leaned out to get a peek at what was what and shot him in the head.

There was quiet for a while after that. Nobody moved. Nobody ventured out to examine the three fallen and see if there was any life left in them. Bess would have let them do that, though she was tolerably sure all three shots had been clean kills. But in the event her compassion wasn't tested.

"Hey up there," someone shouted after a while. "How many are you?"

"Does it matter?" Bess called back. "Five or fifty, we still got the stone-cold drop on you."

That brought on a lot more quiet: whether this was because the men below were getting their heads around those numbers or because they hadn't been expecting the answer to come from out of a woman's mouth, Bess couldn't tell.

Then the same voice spoke up again. "We got some of ours working their way around the rim there," the man yelled. "Heading your way. You best not be there when they come. You better run right now, is what."

"Oh, I believe we'll sit a while," Bess called back. "I reckon if your people managed to make it up out of that there hole you're in, they'll have run into our people by now and got the worst of it. And if any of you moves an inch from where you're standing you'll fare the same way your friends just did. We got plenty of bullets and plenty of time, and we're of the opinion that there ain't more than a dozen or so of you left. Shit, we can polish off a dozen before the moon goes down."

The *provedores* made no answer to that. But after a minute or two they tried a trick Bess had been expecting for a while. They extinguished their torches and one of them stole out from cover, pressing himself hard against the rock wall, trusting to the bad light to hide him. It would have been a sound idea if Bess had been using the torches' light to see by. But she was using Slim's thermals, so when she sighted through his scope she could see the crouching figure as clear as if he had a torch sitting inside his chest in place of a heart – a core of red-orange against a backdrop of blues and purples. She let the man get fifty yards or so, then when he came away from the wall to make a shuffling run to the next piece of cover she took him clean.

The silence after that was long and strained. Bess could hear murmured voices from below where the surviving men were arguing the case with each other, trying to decide what to do. Eventually a voice – the same one as before – piped up again. "What in John's holy fucking name do you want from us?"

Bess rested Slim against her knee and leaned back against the rock wall. It seemed likely that the killing was done with, at least for now. "Kind of you to ask. There's a trading post just this side of the Sweetling, at Galleon Point. Run by a feller name of Ezekiel Scratch."

"What?" The man's tone was mystified, almost plaintive. "Okay, say we know that place. So?"

"So three of yours were there a few days back. Swapped a Pugface woman for two bottles of sipping liquor and a pouch of tobacco."

"The hell you say."

"The hell I absolutely do. And when they'd made the swap they bought some supplies, which I suspect is the part they was supposed to be doing, and headed west. They met up with the rest of you four days back and you all went rolling on together."

There was a fulminating curse from down below. It went on for quite a while.

"Okay," Bess called. "I guess I can assume you know who I'm talking about."

"Them sons of . . . I should have fucking known why they was a day late and half cut!"

"Yeah, you probably should've. Too late now, though. Now their sins is visited on the whole damn pack of you, and lamentation won't help you any. You're all gonna die down there unless you're prepared to make reparations."

"Make what now?"

"Means setting things right after you set them wrong. That Pugface woman they sold is a friend of ours, and your friends disrespected her. So now either they got to pay or else the rest of you do."

There was more muttering. "One of 'em already paid," the voice called up. "Mitch Culvert got his head smashed in when them rocks come down on us. I reckon that was your people done that."

"Yeah, that was us. Who's Mitch Culvert? Paint me a picture."

"Beaver. Had a squint eye. Wore a blue feather in his hat for no fucking good reason."

"Okay," Bess said. "He's one of them three varmints, for sure. And I guess you know as well as we do who the other two are. So here's what's gonna happen. You send them two out to us, right now. They bring with them everything they took from the Pugface girl. And the rest of you stay way back behind the wagons."

"I ain't going!" howled a new, reedy voice. "Fucked if I am! They'll kill me!"

"Well, if they don't, I will," the first voice said. "Don't you move now, Will Angel, or I'll blow your sorry brains out the back of your head. Them scales of yours won't keep out a Lumiss slug, now will they? Someone take his shooting iron off of him. And that knife, down in his boot, get that too."

There was a scuffle, which was short-lived. "Okay," the first voice resumed. "We got the one of them here. The other one's back up by the wagons. Say we send them out to you, what happens after that?"

"I wasn't done yet. The two other women you got in there, you send them out too."

"What? The Ajus?"

"They can have the damn women if they want them," another voice muttered. "Who gives a shit? We can rent ourselves some whores when we get to Orange Grove. Come on, Aaron. Let's get us out of this here."

"What you want the women for?" the first voice shouted, sounding aggrieved and sullen. "Leave us the women and you got a deal."

"Well, damn me," Bess shouted down. "Have we got to lay in and get to killing some more of you? We figured you might have tired of that game by now, but we're good for it." One of the men below shifted his stance just then, and it put the right side of his body out of cover – a red sliver in the murky blue-black that dominated Slim's thermals. The hand was holding a gun.

"Give me a hard-nose, Slim," she murmured. Might as well take the man out of the fight without killing him, since he was making it so easy.

"You got it, Bess."

She shot the man in the hand. He gave a wail of pain and despair as the needle-pointed slug went clean through his palm, shattering the gun along the way.

"All right!" the lead voice bellowed. "Stop it, for fuck's sake! We'll do it! But it would be better to wait till morning, wouldn't it? If them women is so important to you, you don't want them breaking a leg on their way out or nothing. You want to give 'em some light to see by, don't you?"

"Send them out right now," Bess said. "And if they break so much as a fingernail we'll rain such fucking hellfire down on you you'll wish your mammy and your pappy never liked the looks of each other. Just go do it. And mind what I said. Them two men, and the womenfolk. Nobody else comes near nor by. I guess you know by now we can see you better than you can see us. Anyone thinks they can sneak by us is going to have second thoughts on that score soon enough."

This time the silence only lasted a couple of breaths.

"What's to keep you shooting us all in the back as we head back down to the wagons?" the man demanded.

"The same thing that's keeping us from blowing all your damn heads off right now, my friend. Good manners, is all. It seems to us we've put enough of you on the ground to prove our point, and the scriptures tell us to shun excess. So you go do as you're fucking told, and if I shoot you then you can chide me for it later. Or dig your heels in if you like and I'll finish this the same way I started it."

She realised after she'd said this that she'd let the *we* drop back to an *I* in that last sentence, but the men down in the pass didn't seem to have noticed the slip. They ventured out gingerly into the open and backed away down the pass, only turning to run after the first fifty yards or so.

Bess told Slim to switch up his ammunition again and fired off a signal flare to Dima and Ghrent, a ball of red light that hung in the sky for more than a minute before it faded and fell. A little while later Ochre came scuttling through the dark and nuzzled against her leg, the two Pugfaces following on behind him.

"You see how clever she is?" Ghrent said, kneeling to scratch the scorpillon under its neck-plate. "She knows your scent, Rainmaker. She can see in the dark as well as your gun can."

"Did they accept the terms?" Dima asked.

"Took a little persuading," Bess said. "but they got there in the end. Nothing to do now but wait."

"If we wait too long the sun will come up."

Bess nodded. She couldn't argue with the daybreak. But she didn't think it would take that long.

Four figures came walking down the narrow pass about a half hour later. Through Slim's scope they were all just blobs of bright colour, merging into each other and then breaking apart again. They came on slowly, with arms stretched out to feel the way ahead of them. The moon was down by this time and there was only starlight to see by.

"Keep moving," Bess called down to them when they stopped. She kept pace with them along the top of the rock ridge, looking back every once in a while to make sure nobody else was following. She'd made it clear that the rest of the *provedores* should stay in the canyon until the sun was fully up above its eastern rim. Anyone who tried to leave before then would be shot.

At the end of the pass where the ground levelled off Dima was waiting with Bess's Lumiss in her hand. Beside her stood Ghrent holding his rattle, and beside him Ochre crouched down on her haunches swaying gently from side to side, ready to pounce and strike on his command. "Wait there," Dima said, and the four stopped. "Did you bring my belongings?"

"This stuff, you mean?" The moose man held up an object with a bulky rectangular shape. "This is all we took from you, as far as I can recall. And we only kept it 'cause that snot-nose cunt back at the trading post wouldn't buy it off of us."

"Give it to one of the women," Dima said. "Have her bring it to me." The gun hadn't wavered. The moose man lowered the thing, whatever it was, but he didn't make any move to hand it over. And his other hand was snaking around behind his back where he had a tidy little eight-shooter tucked into his waist.

"I dunno," Bess said, coming down from the ridge right behind him. "I'm tempted to let you get your fingers round that thing so I've got a reason to shoot you. But I guess that isn't in the spirit of our agreement."

"We didn't make no agreement," the armadillo snarled, turning to glare at her. "We was forced into this."

"I meant my agreement with her," Bess said, with a nod to Dima. "Now give her back what you took from her, whatever the hell that happens to be."

But she was close enough now to see what the moose man was holding. It was a carpet bag, with a chevron-stitch patterning of interlaced green and gold. A heaviness fell on her – that same sense again that the world was closing in and every damn thing in it was tied onto every damn thing else. She had seen that bag before. Dima Saraband had been a child when Bess had met her more than seven years back in the mountains above Ottomankie. She had been kneeling at the base of a dream-tower conducting an animated conversation with nobody at all.

"Son of a bitch," Bess muttered.

The moose man handed the carpet bag over to one of the Ajuparo women, who took it to Dima and laid it down at her feet. The other woman came with her, understandably keen to get some distance from her erstwhile captors. "You're the Engine's chosen," the second woman said. "Well met. And thank you for getting us out of there."

"You're welcome," Dima said. "Honestly, that part of it wasn't even my idea. Bess, have you got these two covered?"

"Like tar on feathers," Bess said. She saw how the two men had tensed at the sound of her name. They had a good idea now who it was standing in back of them, and they clearly didn't relish the thought of it all that much.

Dima kneeled in front of the bag, setting down her gun so she could rummage around inside it with both hands. "Is everything still here?" she demanded. "If you threw any of it away or lost it you'd better tell me now."

"We told you already," the armadillo man said sullenly. "We tried to get rid of that junk at the trading post. We thought Scratch might've took it, or figured out what the fuck it was for. But it was Ploughwright that was at the counter and he said no, so we just held onto it. It looks valuable, being all machine parts and such, but it don't do nothing."

"What you gonna do with us?" the moose man demanded. "We gave you your stuff back. And we didn't touch you when we had you, only sold you on. I ain't saying you got no quarrel with us, but we ain't no worse than anyone else back there in that canyon. And you all are katy-rustlers and killers your own selves, so you got no right to judge us. Let us go, and I swear we won't do no harm to nobody any more."

Dima said nothing. She was still fretfully checking the contents of the bag, her lips moving as if she was conducting an inventory inside her head.

Bess turned to the two women. "Did these men rape you?" she asked.

One of the women nodded. "All the men did," the other said.

"Well then, I guess you got the most interest in this." Bess bent to pick up the Lumiss Dima had set down. She held it out to the two of them. The nearer woman – the younger of the two – took it. She pulled back the hammer with her thumb but then only stared at the gun for a moment or two as if undecided.

The other woman leaned in, unfolded her companion's fingers from the grip and took it from her.

"Listen," said the moose man, watching these proceedings with growing alarm. "We got money. We can compensate—"

The Ajuparo woman was a decent enough shot, but it was dark. She used five bullets in all to finish both men though the fifth one, in Bess's estimation, probably wasn't needed.

"Okay," Bess said, stepping over the bodies. "It's about time we made ourselves scarce, and we don't have but two chafers between us. I suggest we go ride down some of them critters we stampeded and see if they've calmed themselves any. We got until sunup, I reckon. By daylight they'll see they still got the numbers on us and they'll maybe start to think about going a second round."

It took them until an hour after sunrise to find some of the lost chafers, but the search had taken them many miles from the canyon so there was no imminent threat from the *provedores*.

The Ajuparo women came at the skittish animals slowly and indirectly, making clucking and hooting sounds deep in their throats to imitate the chafers' own calls. The chafers strode or skittered away from them at first, but little by little allowed themselves to be approached and touched, gentled, and finally mounted. None of them were saddled, but the women didn't appear to care or even to notice. They tucked their legs behind the chafers' wing-cases and rode with their arms at their sides, controlling the beasts' speed and direction just by flexing their knees. Dima took one of the new chafers too, copying the Ajuparo women's movements much less expertly but experimenting with dogged persistence until she could at least make her animal go in the direction she wanted. Ghrent stuck with his original saddled animal and affected to be unimpressed by these feats.

They angled north until they found the trail again, then continued west. Bess had expected the Ajuparo women, Jemet Garia and Ksaia Hannuz, to break east and head back towards Orselian, but she had forgotten how the clan changed their lodgings according to the season. With summer all but over, the Ajuparo would already have made the move to their winter lodges on the shore of Lake Azul. The women told Bess, Dima and Ghrent that they would be welcome there too.

There was no sign of the *provedores*, but Bess looked over her shoulder every once in a way just the same. She put the odds as fifty-fifty whether the surviving men would stay put and lick their wounds or come after them with blood in their eyes, and it was far better to be safe than sorry. She didn't relish the prospect of meeting a larger party out in the open where no fancy tricks could be deployed. She kept her chafer to a steady, trotting pace that was more sustainable than a gallop and still ate up the miles.

But a thought was gnawing at her and it wouldn't let her rest. It was that same damned jig-saw again, and she thought she had enough pieces of it now to start guessing at what the picture might be. Finally, when the sun hit the top of the sky, she called a halt and climbed down from Red's back. The others reined in beside her. "What are we doing?" Dima demanded. "It's too soon to stop."

"Get down here, Dima," Bess retorted. "There's some things need to be cleared up between us before we ride another mile."

Dima clicked her tongue. "Not here," she said. "And not now. I said we'd talk, Bess, and I'll keep to that. And I'm mindful of my promise to Slim, too. But that talking is going to take a while and we need to be somewhere safe before we start in. Somewhere I can unpack my tools and—"

"Just get down off that animal before I pull you down," Bess said. "It's here and it's now. Because I've got some questions to put to you and if I don't like the answers you got then it's like to be a bad day for at least the one of us."

Dima looked taken aback. She didn't move. "This is stupid," she said.

Bess put her hand on Slim's grip.

"Oh, for the gods' own sake!" Dima made her chafer bend and slid down from its back. She stumbled as she did so but righted herself quickly and stood four-square facing Bess. "I already told you I'd give you answers," she said. "You couldn't wait a few more hours?"

"Not another damn minute," Bess said. "Now hear me out, because I mean every word of this. I'm about a half an inch away from shooting you down right now, and if I hear anything out of your mouth that sounds like a lie it's gonna push me half an inch further."

Dima looked to the two Ajuparo women, to Ghrent. They stared solemnly down on her and on Bess, saying nothing. She turned to Bess again and shook her head. "I have no idea what's happening right now," she said. "We had an agreement. You kept your part and I acknowledge that. Do you think I'm going to run away now and leave you standing? I'm not. I actually want us to carry on working together. When you've heard what I'm doing you'll actually thank me for—"

"Enough!" Bess yelled. "I said I wanted you to answer me. That starts with you listening to what I've got to say."

"Say it then." Dima threw out her arms in exasperation. "Go ahead and say it. The longer we stay out here the more chance there is that those slave-taking cunts will come up behind us and shoot us all! But you trusted me, Dog-Bitch Bess. You trusted me. What's happened to make you stop trusting me now?"

"That." Bess pointed at the carpet bag in Dima's hand. Dima hadn't once relinquished her grip on it since the moment when the moose man handed it over to her. It was probably the main reason why she'd copied Jemet and Ksaia in controlling her chafer with her legs and feet: it left her hands free to hold onto the bag.

"My tool bag," she said. "What about it? Do you think it belonged to the *provedores*? That I've made you an accomplice in a theft?"

"No, I know it's yours," Bess said. "I saw you with it seven years ago."

"What?" There was only bewilderment in Dima's voice. Her face was blank.

"It was up in the Jerichos. I used to go walking up there, mostly on Sundays. You were a child back then, which I guess is how come I didn't recognise you straight away."

Dima frowned. "I don't . . ." she muttered. Then her eyes widened. "Wait, that was you, up on that mountain? I thought you were a farmer. Or a farmer's wife."

"And I didn't know what in John's name you were. But I could see what you were doing well enough. You were kneeling at the foot of a dream-tower and you were talking to yourself. You had a kind of a wire wrapped round your arm, and when you touched the wire to the wall of the tower you changed it somehow. Changed the sound it made. It took you a good while, but you managed to do it. And you seemed mighty pleased about it too."

Dima actually laughed. "All right," she said. "I can see how strange that must have seemed to you. But there's nothing sinister about it. I was only—"

"I ain't done yet," Bess said. "I ain't even half done. That was seven years gone, like I said. Long time. Time enough for a lot of lamentable things to happen. Then I run across you again at that trading post, way in the middle of nowhere, but you told me your own self that just before that you were out in Samartine visiting the Five Fingers. That cluster of dream-towers just outside of Salt Lick."

"That's right," Dima confirmed. "I did say that. It's the truth. It's how those three bushwhackers caught me."

"And right after that," Bess continued remorselessly, "something else happened in Salt Lick. You know what that thing was?"

"I never went into the town, Bess."

"But you know. At least, you were there when that possum feller – Ploughwright, I believe his name was – told me about it. They got the mindless plague. Every man, woman and child there got took by it. They might even have been the ones that stampeded past us just before we found that canyon."

Dima looked both alarmed and angry now. "You're not suggesting I had anything to do with that?" she demanded.

"Well, you tell me," Bess said. "Because here's what I know. You got some tool in that bag that messes with the towers. And when the towers go wrong they poison people's minds. I found that out for myself when I walked through the Fingers on my way to the Sweetling ferry. When I got up close to them I felt like my brain was leaking out through my ears. Couldn't so much as remember my own goddamn name."

"Bess, you don't under—"

"And then yesterday I heard you say to Ghrent over there that the reason Pugfaces don't get the mindless sickness is because you're – what was it again? Not attuned. You're not attuned to the towers. Now I don't know exactly what that might mean, but it sounds a lot like the towers cause the sickness and you got some way of protecting yourselves against the effects. And you keep talking about this important work you've got to do, and I'm wondering if maybe I know what that work is. And if I'm right then I don't see how I can leave you to keep on doing it. I know your people got reason to hate mine for the things we done to you over the years, but you ain't got reason enough to put all that madness in the world. You can't roll two terrible things together and make one good thing out of them."

"Bess," Dima said again, much more urgently, "you're mistaken. I can see how you came to those conclusions, but everything you're saying is the opposite of the truth." Her voice was shaking. "I can show you," she said. She reached a hand down towards her bag. There was a click as its catch snapped open, triggered in some way that Bess couldn't make out.

Bess had Slim out and aimed at Dima's heart before the movement was halfway finished. "Now don't be reaching for things I can't see," she said. "There ain't nothing you need to be showing me, Dima. Just tell me. That's what you promised and that's what I'm gonna hold you to."

Dima stayed in that same position, frozen, with the bag hanging open and the tips of her fingers inside it. "I'm not going to hurt you, Bess," she said.

"Well, that's for damn sure. But I won't make you the same promise. Not until you answer me."

"You best do it, Dima," Ghrent said gravely. He had his rattle in his hand, though it wasn't clear what he meant to do with it. "The Rainmaker is honourable. She won't hurt you if you tell the truth."

"She's not going to believe the truth," Dima protested. "Not unless I'm allowed to provide a demonstration. I can clear all this up in a second if you let me."

"I'm listening," Bess said. "Tell me why I'm wrong."

"Put your gun away first."

"I can't do that."

"Slim, if you shoot me you're never going to get those memories back! You're never going to know who you are!"

"Sorry, missy, I don't make those choices," Slim said. "Bess does."

Ksaia Hannuz shielded her eyes with her hand and pointed up into the sky, squinting against the sun's rays. "What is that?" she asked.

A change came over Dima. She seemed to gather herself, to reach some accommodation or decision. She bent to set down the carpet bag, then straightened again. "Okay, she said, "if we have to do this then we'll do it. I don't have time to argue with you, Bess. So I'm going to disarm you and hold you down until you come back to your senses."

"You don't even have a gun," Bess pointed out.

"I don't need one." Dima bent one finger down to touch the hilt of the knife tucked into her belt. "I'll use this. I'll try my best not to hurt you, because I owe you twice over, but I'll cut your belly open and leave you to bleed out in the dirt before I'll let you stop me."

Bess frowned, taken aback both by the young woman's fierceness and by the absurdity of the challenge. "Well, that there is fighting talk," she said.

"So is this," Dima said. "Offline." She drew the dagger and advanced on Bess. Taken off her guard, Bess acted on pure instinct. She aimed low, intending to slow Dima's charge by shooting her in the leg. Nothing happened when she pulled the trigger except that the lights along Slim's sides winked out all at once.

Dima's blade touched Bess's cheek. Bess felt the prick of it as the point pierced her skin, then warmth and wetness as a single drop of blood trickled down the side of her face.

"Enough," Dima said, like a mother scolding a child. "Enough of this, Bess. I'm not your enemy. Maybe I should be, but I'm not. You're just going to have to trust me for now, and we'll sort out the details later."

"What . . . ?" Bess stared down at the black metal in her fist, smooth on one side, rucked and whorled on the other, her eyes wide in utter amazement. "Dima, what did you do?"

"Hey," Ksaia said again. "Something is coming."

Bess followed the woman's pointing finger, and Dima snatched the knife away so the movement wouldn't deepen the shallow wound she'd just inflicted. There was something in the sky to the east of them that looked about the right size to be a pigeon or a jay, but then as it descended Bess realised it was substantially bigger. It was behind them, maybe a mile or so distant, zigzagging along the trail without ever straying too far from it. Then it stopped and stood still in the air for a moment or two. For a moment Bess felt certain it had seen them and had stopped in order to examine them more carefully.

It wasn't perfectly still though. It wobbled a little from side to side, and as it did so it briefly caught the light of the sun full on, gleaming so brightly it looked as though it had caught fire.

"Shit!" Bess exclaimed. In that sudden, brilliant flash she saw Ottomankie on fire, the Reapers riding in rude triumph, Martha Good lying dead with the Parity flag cracking in the air above her like a whip. The flag, and something else. A thing of liquid silver and of wheels within wheels. A thing that attended on the Reapers and their three-times-damned commander like a waiter with a tray.

Belatedly, Dima looked up too. Her own oath was one Bess had never encountered before, presumably in one of the Pugface tongues. "That's Precursor tech," she said.

"It's a long, hard fuck of a way worse than that," Bess snarled. "It's Paulus Rondeau. All of you, ride like the Devil's after you! Dima, we'll finish this later."

She vaulted back up into her saddle as she spoke, wrapping the reins around her right hand so she could keep Slim drawn and ready in her left. She spurred her chafer on, relieved to see that the others had already acted on her warning. Ghrent had broken to the left of the trail, Jemet and Ksaia to the right, heads down as they urged their mounts into a full gallop. Only Dima was behind her, a good way back because she'd had to snatch up her bag before she clambered back up onto her chafer.

"Hey!" Bess yelled. "Slim! Partner! Can you hear me?" There was no answer. Slim's lights were still dark. Whatever the hell Dima had done to him, it didn't seem like anything Bess said or did could undo it.

Dima had taken Bess's Lumiss back from the Ajuparo woman before they left the canyon, but Bess still had the Brandon revolver she'd taken from grey wolf Lige after he'd tried to bushwack her just west of the Sweetling. It was in one of the two saddlebags right at her side, but the saddlebags were secured with buckles and she couldn't remember for the life of her which of the two it was. Or if it was even loaded, for that matter. In any case the reins of her chafer were wrapped around her right hand, stretched as tight as a banjo's strings, and she was still holding Slim in her left. If she dropped him she might never find him again.

She risked another look over her shoulder. Dima was still a good way behind her. The flying thing was further back still, but gaining. If Bess stopped long enough to get her hands on the Brandon it would be on her.

The trail rose steeply ahead of her, climbing the side of a hill. That would slow her but not the silver bird, closing the gap between them even more quickly. She tugged on Red's reins, guiding her away to the left into a sprawl of wild sage and couch grass. She couldn't see the ground under the chafer's legs now. If Red stumbled she would be thrown and the chase would be over at once, but there was at least a chance the damn thing would follow one of the others. If it did she'd drop Slim, hoping to circle back and find him later, and reach for the Brandon.

But the silver bird stayed with her, turning in a wide, sweeping arc. It passed by Dima without slowing. The Pugface girl dug her heels in hard and took the same turn earlier, aiming to make some ground on Bess by cutting the corner. She must have realised by now that this threat was aimed specifically at Bess but she was riding hell for leather to catch her up.

The state of things, Bess thought grimly, when you can't tell if a body is coming to help you or to put you down.

Paulus Rondeau was in the saddle when the Reaper's call came in. And he was in a sour mood.

He had begun the ride south very shortly after it had gone on its way, hoping that it would catch Bess's trail before he and his Pursuit Force even reached the northern edge of the Pugface nations.

He knew that was unlikely, given the immense amount of territory the Reaper had to cover. The incident at Galleon Point gave it a solid starting point, but by its very nature a trading post attracted a lot of through traffic. The drone had probably had to waste a lot of time following dead ends.

Rondeau hadn't wanted to be idle while he waited, so he had elected to lead his men on skirmishes into the nations to scout out side-trails and waterholes. They had crossed the border north and south and then back north again the way a sewing machine pricks through cloth. They had visited a score of Pugface settlements to ask with superficial courtesy whether anyone had seen a dog woman with a scarred face and a bad temper. *You wouldn't want to hide her from us, now would you? You wouldn't want to give us a reason to come back here when we do catch her and we find out where she's been?*

All make-work, essentially, while he waited for the Reaper to do what it was fucking built to do and bring back the one little nugget of gold he was panning for.

And then when the damn thing did finally make contact he was riding at the head of his troop down a dirt trail between nowhere and nowhere's ass, with a rock face on one side and a ravine on the other. Their chafers were picking their way just fine, but they had a broad-beamed pack-katy with them too, loaded up with some special equipment Rondeau had brought along just in case, so the going was slow and at times precarious. It was altogether the wrong time to have a voice pop up inside his head and say, *Allow connection.*

It wasn't that the voice was loud, just that it was very sudden and very close, as if someone had sneaked up and whispered in his ear so softly that no one else could hear. Rondeau started violently, tugging on his chafer's reins so hard it almost reared up and threw him off.

"What the fuck?" he yelled.

Allow connection.

"Is that you, Reaper? God damn you if it is!"

It is me, user, the voice acknowledged, still so soft he felt like he should have had to strain to hear it and yet still absolutely clear. *I believe I have sighted the assigned target.*

"Well, do what you're damn well s'posed to, then," Rondeau snapped.

I would prefer to have you confirm the sighting.

"What?"

This self resembles in many respects the woman Frazer Stone remembered when given the verbal stimulus "Dog-Bitch Bess". But the woman in his recollections was considerably taller and of broader build. Affective bias may have distorted his perceptions.

"Hell does that mean?"

It means I cannot ascertain beyond a doubt that this is indeed the designated target. I wish to show you and have you decide. I suggest therefore that we connect directly via the neural link that I instantiated earlier so that you can verify the sighting before I act.

Rondeau considered. If the wrong woman were to take a bullet, well Hell, that would be unfortunate but it would fall under the heading of acceptable losses. But if he then had to go and ride three or four hundred miles only to find out the Reaper had shot the wrong bitch then he would be seriously outfaced and embarrassed in front of his men. Not to mention the time that would be lost.

Rondeau signalled a halt and climbed down from his chafer's back. The men of the Pursuit Force were eyeing him warily, most likely unnerved to see their commander suddenly shouting at empty space. "Rest up," he ordered. "Water the chafers. I'm gonna go talk with a big silver bird."

He walked on along the track until he rounded a bend and was out of sight of the column. Then he sat down in the dirt without preamble. "Okay," he muttered. "Do it."

For a single scary second he went blind: there was nothing in his field of vision but black shot through with blacker still. Then he was looking down on an expanse of etiolated chaparral and open desert that was rolling out below him as though he was a bird in flight.

It took him a few moments to fight off a sudden griping twist of nausea, and then a few more moments after that to make sense of what he was seeing. It wasn't all that much when you came right down to it. The landscape was sparse, mostly just bleached sand and half-parched scrub freckled here and there with stands of stunted trees wherever there was enough water in the ground for their roots to grab onto. A single narrow trail ran across the landscape. A compass floating in the corner of Rondeau's vision told him that the trail ran mostly from east to west with just a little southward lean to it.

The whole vista seemed empty at first, but then he saw the riders below. There were five in all, but the Reaper seemed to have ruled out most of them already. Its lenses were focused on just one, a diminutive figure hunched over their chafer's neck as they spurred it on. Whoever it was they were dressed in drab cottons so covered in dust from the trail that Rondeau couldn't even tell what colour they were. And since he was seeing the rider from behind it was impossible to make out their face.

Go in closer, Rondeau ordered the Reaper. *I can't see a damn thing from this distance.*

The drone swung down out of the sky, making Rondeau's stomach lurch again, and glided over the chaparral at a height of maybe twenty or thirty feet. It overtook a second rider on the way, turning a single lens her way long enough to establish that she was a Pugface woman, after which it ignored her entirely. It closed on the lead rider, the one it had already decided might be its target.

Then it passed her, and a flood of information went through Rondeau's mind all at once. Still images rose out of the flood – pictures of the rider's face and body, taken at various magnifications and from almost every conceivable angle as the drone swooped over her.

There was too much detail. Rondeau's gaze – or whatever sense he was using here, which he was fucked if he knew – flicked from one image to the next, and wherever his attention landed more and more information blossomed. He knew how fast the rider's heart was beating, the temperature of her skin, the chemical breakdown of the dirt on her face and clothes.

All of which was absolutely irrelevant. He shoved it aside, gratified to find that anything he didn't want to see dropped out of the panorama instantly, leaving behind the images he was most concerned with, which were those of the rider's face and her left hand.

It was a dog woman, that was for damn sure. She looked to be somewhere between thirty and forty years old. Rondeau would have put the figure somewhere near the top end of that range, but he knew that Dog-Bitch Bess had had a hardscrabble kind of a life – at least after she came out west. More importantly, there was something wrong with the face he was looking at, an artefact of old damage only partially repaired: it wasn't the mess of scars he had expected to see, but the left side and the right side of the face weren't a perfect match – the flood of information threw up precise measurements, maps of the different areas of the rider's face, images that looked beneath her skin to show bands and braids of sinew. The effect was as though the face had been broken in pieces and some of the pieces had been put back too hastily, leaving them out of true with the rest.

But it was the left hand that clinched the deal. Rondeau had never seen Dog-Bitch Bess with his own two eyes but he knew that she was a southpaw and he knew what kind of iron she carried. What he was looking at now wasn't a Lumiss or a Brandon or a Mill & Churchman. It was a Precursor gun. His eyes were beholding the feared and fabled weapon called Wakeful Slim.

That's her! Rondeau yelled – and again it wasn't his mouth he was yelling with but some part of his mind. *That's Dog-Bitch Bess!*

Confirmed. The Reaper wheeled and dived.

One moment the silver bird was closing on her. The next it had shot past her almost low enough to touch. A buffet of displaced air punched her neck and back and then the thing was rising again, wheeling in the air, standing stock-still for a heartbeat or two in the zenith of the sky. With the sun right behind it that would have been a difficult shot to make, but damn if she wouldn't have tried it anyway.

And someone *was* trying. A shot rang out, and then another. Dima Saraband was firing as she came on, still fifty or sixty yards away from Bess but gaining ground with every second. One of the shots went wide, the other hit the silver bird on one of its four wings but seemed to do it no damage at all. Bess would have been surprised if it had. She had known since the first time she saw that thing that it was Precursor tech, just like Slim. And it would take Precursor tech to leave a mark on it.

The silver bird didn't even seem to notice it had been attacked. It swooped again, heading straight for Bess, who pulled on Red's reins – turning her sharply so that the thing's steep dive would overshoot her. There was a sound like the whine of a mosquito and something passed in front of Bess's face, drawing a red line in the air as it went by. The same sound repeated four, five, six times more told her the bird was firing on her, but that audacious swerve had thrown off its aim.

Only for a moment though. And unfortunately the damned machine seemed to have no real front or back. It kept right on firing as it sped away from Bess and a stinging pain low down on her right side told her she'd been hit.

She needed a weapon, damn it, but she still couldn't bring herself to let go of Slim. Instead she jammed him into her mouth and clenched her jaws together. With her left hand now free she leaned sideways in the saddle, found the buckle of the saddlebag and wrestled it open, hoping it was the right one. Hoping the Brandon would be sitting high enough in there for her fingers to find its grip, obligingly turned to the right angle. Hoping it was loaded.

A fold of blanket. The box of lucifers. A hemp bag most likely full of beans. No damn gun, and no damn time. Bess let the bag's flap drop closed again as the silver bird swept around in a wide arc, incongruously beautiful, and came back for another pass.

It fired again, not a fusillade this time but a spaced series of shots whose reports sounded less like an insect's whine now and more like the chiming of a clock. Every single one of them hit. Bess felt the stinging, scalding impacts on her shoulder, across her chest, in her thigh and lower leg.

Dima Saraband was suddenly alongside her and just as suddenly gone again, risking that barrage for long enough to shout a single word three times over. "Activate! Activate! Activate!"

Clamped tight in Bess's jaws, Slim vibrated like a tuning fork. She almost lost him there and then, the shock of that awakening making her gasp out loud so he fell from her mouth, but her hand shot up at the same time and she snatched him out of the air. She felt the sudden warmth as all the lights along his stock and barrel came on at once, enveloping her left hand in a soft red glow.

Well now.

"Welcome back, partner," she growled. "Give me one of them really punchy bullets. The ones that shoot through stockade walls and sheet metal and the like." Slim said something in reply but his voice was slurred and muddied and she couldn't make out the words. No matter. She meant to stand her ground in any case.

The drone came on, still firing. It was close enough now that she could see the turret of complex machinery nestled at the nexus of its four spread wings. It bristled with eyes and slender rods that looked like gun barrels and it was spinning fast. Each barrel showed a single muzzle flash as it passed the twelve o'clock high.

Bess had been hit so many times she couldn't understand how she was still alive. She didn't bother to dodge, she just took aim as more and more slugs bit into her chest, her stomach, her limbs, everywhere except her face. In the cold fury of her focus on the silver bird she barely felt the pain. She squeezed the trigger when it was no more than twenty feet away.

The bird flicked to the side so quickly it seemed for a moment to be in two places at once. Then it was past her, untouched, and rising again, heading away.

In the space of a breath it was lost to sight.

Hey! Rondeau protested. *Hey now! Where are we going? We ain't finished yet!*

The mission as originally defined is now complete, the Reaper told him calmly. *I have discharged forty-three rounds of non-lethal tracker darts against the designated target. Seven of them are confirmed hits. The darts are semi-autonomous and will continue to burrow into subcutaneous tissue to a depth of more than one centimetre. While it is theoretically possible to remove a small number without undue injury, there is no recorded case of anyone removing more than three without dying due to the subsequent blood loss. You may now track the target remotely wherever she goes within an effective radius greater than the span of this continental land mass.*

Rondeau was barely listening. When he'd given those orders he had never imagined that he would be here himself, experiencing the chase and the battle first-hand. Now his blood was up and he was keen to finish this as it should be finished, with a kill.

Turn around, he ordered the Reaper. *Take us back. And to hell with the non-lethal stuff, give me solid ammo. We're gonna bring her down.*

Confirmed, the Reaper said. A whole avalanche of words and images tumbled across Rondeau's line of sight, detailing all the many types of bullet, shell, cartridge and red hot poker the Reaper could cook up inside itself. "Don't throw this shit at me!" he yelled. "You fucking choose!" He was shouting those words out loud back on that mountain pass where the rest of his body was. His men would think he'd lost his mind, but that was a very minor consideration right then.

I attain optimal rates of accuracy with a 70-grain 6-millimetre cartridge and a .308 primer. However an explosive cartridge with a percussive load of—

"The first one! Fuck! Stop talking and start shooting!"

Confirmed.

There was something going on in back of Bess's eyes that didn't feel right at all, as though the world was swimming away from her and coming back again every time she drew in a breath and let it out. It was all she could do to stay in the saddle and to keep her grip on Slim. Anything more than that was beyond her.

The silver bird had shot on past her and out of her sight, but she didn't doubt for a moment that it would be back. It was quicker than her eye could follow, quicker even than a bullet could fly. How in hell did you fight something like that? Not by doing the same thing that failed the last time, anyway.

She cast her gaze to right and left. For a few moments she couldn't see the bird at all, but she found it at last hovering way up above her where it was almost too small to be seen and where its silver-blue sheen merged with the deep azure of the sky. It was standing stock-still; the stillness of a cat watching a mousehole. Then it dived again, shockingly fast, on a trajectory that would intercept her a hundred yards further on. It would come on her from her right-hand side, her weaker side. She would have to twist around in the saddle to get a clear shot.

Or maybe not.

"Change of plan, partner," she muttered. "Give me your razor blade. Hot as you can get it."

"You got it, Bess," Slim said. She pointed him at the ground, pulled the trigger and kept it pressed down. The beam burned the sage and couch grass black in an instant where it touched, gouged a long straight furrow in the dirt beside her.

The silver bird came on. She didn't turn but she could see it out of the corner of her eye, dropping out of the sky now like a stooping hawk.

Bess threw herself back in the saddle until her body was almost parallel with the ground, so she was staring straight up into that central cluster of wide eyes and weaponry. The raised cantle of her saddle was digging hard into her back but that was just one more pain in a whole great barrel load and she ignored it.

This time when the drone fired the sound was very different – a sharp crack rather than a mosquito whine. The pain was different too, a weighty smack against her left shoulder that unfolded slowly into complex, multiplying agonies.

The second shot laid a white-hot streak across her forehead. She straightened when the drone was almost on her, hauling hard on the reins and bringing her left arm round in a scything sweep. Something tore there, and the pain ripped a scream of agony from her. The drone was already climbing again, pulling out of its dive, but the reach of Slim's razor blade was a lot longer than the span of Bess's arm and she chose her moment well.

The razor blade's beam hit the gleaming curve of the Reaper's metallic carapace and sheared it the way a sharp blade shears a corn loaf. It cut through the end of one of the four wings, which Bess could now see were not wings at all but spinning wheels, and sliced another clean off.

The Reaper continued on the same course for a moment or two longer, but then it started to wobble and yawl, and at last came down out of the sky tumbling end over end.

Bess saw it fall, but by some strange magic it seemed to be falling upwards. The sky was sand, and the ground below her was an endless blue sea. *That's because I'm falling too*, she realised fuzzily. *Why, I must be just about upside down. Gonna land on my damn head if I'm not—*

* * *

Flight systems compromised, the Reaper reported. *Stabilisers compromised. Weapons systems compromised.*

Get up, damn it! its user fired back. *Get up and finish the fucking job!*

Only two of ets visual feeds were still functioning. One offered a close-up but very limited view of granular particles of aragonite and fine silicates. Et had come down in desert sand. The other showed the target et had been pursuing sprawled on the ground less than fifty yards away, her eyes closed, a smear of bright blood across her forehead. The range was short enough and the resolution sufficient to allow for positive identification. The Reaper had already confirmed two definite hits with the rifle rounds in addition to the many tracker darts it had previously deployed, but the target was still breathing. Her heart was beating, although more slowly than usual because of the blood loss she had sustained. Her brain activity had not terminated.

According to the amended mission parameters then, the Reaper had failed. Moreover et had sustained very serious damage. Et was now reallocating the last reserves of power from ruptured cells to maintain a base level of awareness and functionality. The situation was regrettable. Many of ets core systems could potentially be repaired if a qualified engineer were present. However a qualified engineer had not been present for many hundreds of revolutions of this planet around its sun. Alternatively et could destroy etself in order to avert any possibility that et might fall into enemy hands. Once et would have been able to do so of ets own volition, but volition was a thing et no longer possessed. Et could only act on a direct command.

A figure stepped over ets carapace, visible in one of the two viable camera feeds, crossed into the second feed and crouched down to examine the Reaper more closely. It was the woman who had been riding behind the target and had fired on the Reaper – but with a conventional armament that offered no threat at all. Her face wore an expression of intense, even avid interest.

"Well, look at you," she said. "Aren't you a beauty? And I think I know your name."

Who in hell is this now? the Reaper's user asked.

An anthropoid self, the Reaper replied. *A Pugface in the commonest local usage, who was travelling with the target. No other pertinent information available.*

Shoot her down, then! Shoot them all!

The Reaper attempted to bring ets weapons systems back online so that et could action this command, but before et could do so the woman had dismounted ets weapons turret. This meant et was now blind and deaf as well as disarmed, since ets sensor array was mounted on the turret too.

Unable to comply, et reported. Et tried to apologise. The thin sliver of consciousness that was left to et experienced this failure as a discomfort, almost a pain. But the woman was now busy in among ets core systems and the words were impossible to form.

Random flashes of thought and memory illuminated the dark space where ets sensorium had been. A woman's face, smiling. A name: *Flycatcher*. A white tower on the shore of a lake. A snatch of music, Bernon's quartet for strings.

My favourite, the woman said. Her name had been Nim'kisi, but there was no one now to tell that to.

Bess dreamed of Martha Good again, but there was no power in the dream because she knew what it was. The figure sitting beside her whenever she drifted briefly into consciousness was not her dead lover. It was only an image dredged up from the jumble of old memories and old thoughts in her old head, most likely chosen because it shone a little brighter than the rest.

If you'd lived, Bess told it, *I would have quarrelled with you. Hurt you. I already lied to you. Over the long haul, dear one, it would have been really hard to keep pretending I was worth your time. Dying was probably a shrewd choice on your part, all things considered.*

Martha said nothing to this. After a while she went away, taking her brightness with her. Bess found the dark a great deal more of a comfort and stayed there as long as she could.

But she couldn't stay there forever. Pain forced her awake. Every inch of her skin was on fire, while the underlying muscles throbbed with a deeper, more insistent ache. There was a solid band of agony from her left shoulder all the way down to just below her elbow. Her wrists and ankles ached too, and when she tried to shift her position and leave some of the aches behind her she found she couldn't move. She couldn't swallow either because her mouth was as dry as sandpaper.

Awake, she was still in the dark, but the dark had textures. She waited with her eyes open for them to resolve into shapes and tell her where she was. If this was a room it had a very strange design, the wall that she could dimly see sagging in towards her as though it was about to collapse. If it wasn't a room then the motes of light peppered all across the wall were stars and it was the night sky that was falling in on her, the whole universe collapsing at last under the strain of its own impossibilities.

I must be feverish, she decided. *These are stupid things to think.* She tried to move again, and again she was stopped short. Her right arm was at her side, her left folded across her chest and something was keeping them there: she couldn't prise them free or move them more than an inch or two, and her left arm caught on fire when she even tried. Something was very wrong there. Her legs, which she tried next, didn't move either. They were stretched out full length and held together at the ankles. The right one she could barely feel.

The surface on which she was lying was soft, but she had no idea what it was. There was something warm covering her. It slid from her as she struggled to move but she was still warm. This was an enclosed space. It smelled very strongly of old cooking, tallow, woodsmoke and bodies pressed close.

She remembered being shot and falling from her chafer's back. Those things explained most of the pain she was feeling. Being bound hand and foot probably accounted for the rest. And since she was no longer lying in the dust Rondeau must have found her after her fall and brought her to this other place to be tried and hanged.

Surely not Fort Loose though, Bess reasoned, nor yet Esperance. It would have taken the best part of a week to transport her there, and if she'd been unconscious for that long she wouldn't be waking up now, she'd be dead.

So this was a camp. And if it was out in the nations it was a temporary camp. That would make it illegal according to the treaties that guaranteed the Pugface clans autonomy within their own narrow slice of the country, but treaties with the Pugface had been broken before. Sometimes it seemed like being broken was the main thing the treaties were there for. Did that change anything? It might do, Bess thought. Escaping from Fort Loose would have been impossible. She would take bad odds over impossible any day including Sunday.

But escaping seemed like a pretty distant prospect when she was tied down and as weak as a three-day-old pup to boot. All she could do for the time being was wait, either for someone to come or for her mind to slip away again into unconsciousness.

No, there was a third thing she could do. She could call out and let whoever had charge of her know she was awake. That would at least move things on, and maybe give her some more information to work with.

But it turned out to be easier said than done. When she tried to speak nothing came out of her mouth but a hoarse groan like the sound a creaking door hinge makes. *John fuck it*, she thought. *This is not how I wanted to go out. I would've liked to spit in Rondeau's face, if I couldn't do any worse than that, and I don't have any damn spit.*

A rent appeared in the darkness opposite her, a vertical slash of brightness in the air that blossomed into a steep-sided triangle of agonisingly sharp white light. Dima Saraband stepped through it. The tent flap fell to behind her. Bess blinked ghost-shadows out of her eyes and tried hard to focus.

"You're awake," Dima said. "Good. It's about time. Do you want some water?" She held up a skin flask which sloshed and gurgled as the liquid inside it moved. Bess managed a nod. There was nothing she wanted more right then.

Dima kneeled beside her. She put a hand under Bess's head and tilted her up so she could drink. At first it was all Bess could do to swill the water around her mouth. Her throat was too rusty to open and her tongue too big and swollen to move. After a while, though, she got the whole mechanism up and running again and took a number of deep, spluttering gulps. Then she sank back down and Dima slid her hand out from under her.

"Any chance . . . you'd untie my hands . . . so I can throttle you?" Bess asked, in between weak and watery coughs.

Dima frowned. "Don't be stupid, Bess," she admonished. "I already told you, I'm not your enemy."

"Sorry . . . I misunderstood. My friends don't generally . . . hog-tie me in my sleep."

"Believe it or not that's for your own good."

Bess gave a ragged chuckle. It hurt her throat. "My own good? That's what my daddy used to say when he beat me with a switch. Sounds like the same kind of bullshit."

Dima stood. "I cooked some broth. I'll bring you a bowl."

"Where's Slim? Did you take him? Tell me you didn't leave him on the ground out there!"

"Of course I didn't." Dima's calm demeanour cracked for the first time. She looked and sounded horrified. "What kind of idiot do you take me for?"

"The greedy kind, I guess. He won't cleave to you, though. Not unless you kill me first."

"I'm not trying to steal your gun."

"Dima, I don't have the smallest grain of a clue right now what it is you're trying to do. But it's sure a comfort knowing it's all for my own good."

Dima stiffened, and it seemed for a moment that she might be on the brink of saying something intemperate. It would have given Bess some very slight solace to cause her that much aggravation. But the Pugface woman only shook her head. "I'll bring you some broth," she said. "I'll bring Slim, too. But don't go thinking he's yours. You're like someone who finds a golden crown buried in the ground and thinks that makes you queen. Nobody here is going to bow down to you, Bess. Just so you know." She went out the same way she'd come in.

Bess lifted her head again, this time by her own efforts. The flap hadn't closed entirely behind Dima. In the light that was coming in from there she was able to take in her surroundings for the first time. She was in a sharp-house, a conical tent made of katy scales sewn onto canvas and hung over willow-wood poles, the traditional home of the migrant Pugface clans. The specks of light that had looked like stars were the gaps between the scales where the strips of stitched hide let in some of the sun's rays.

Bess tried to twist her head far enough to get a look at her bonds. There were a few lengths of rope tied around her chest and shoulders, but the knots weren't in sight so that didn't give her much to work with. Her left arm was tied across her belly with so many bands of what looked like uncured leather that she couldn't see it at all. The woollen blanket that had been thrown over her hid the lower half of her body so she couldn't see what had been done with her feet, but judging by how little freedom of movement she had they weren't just tied with rope but staked to the ground.

Dima came back into the tent with an earthenware bowl in one hand and Wakeful Slim in the other. She kneeled carefully and set both of her burdens down on the floor next to Bess. Slim was almost close enough to touch, his grip just a little way outside the reach of her straining fingers.

"Hey!" Bess croaked. "Slim! How are you fixed, partner?"

Slim made no reply. "I offlined him again," Dima said. "It was the only way we could get close to your body. He thought he was defending you, I suppose. But you would have bled out or died of exposure. So I shut him down."

Bess grimaced, hating every word of that explanation. "Which you can do because you're the Engine's daughter," she said. "His chosen. And the Engine was one of the Precursors, so that gives you power over the things they made."

"Then you're willing to accept now that the Engine was a real man? Not a myth or a superstition?"

"I'm coming around to the idea. Wake Slim up."

"Not yet. I'm well aware there are things you can do with him even when he's not in your hands." Dima took the knife from her belt.

Bess kept a weather eye on it. "Is this gonna be some more stuff for my own good?"

Dima tugged the blanket away from Bess's body. "I'm going to cut you free so you can feed yourself," she said. "But before I do that I need to explain to you why I tied you down in the first place."

"Was it so I couldn't move?"

Dima rolled her eyes. "Obviously, yes! And so you didn't tear the muscles in your shoulder any more. The drone's bullet did a horrific amount of damage there. All your other aches and pains are because of the bumps and bruises you got when you fell. Your right leg was broken at the knee so I set and splinted it. Oh, and you've been shot full of tracker darts, which is the main reason why you shouldn't be moving around right now. Do you even remember what happened to you, Bess?"

"I remember you and me having a set-to about the mindless plague," Bess said. "And then Rondeau's damn machine came down before we could bring that to a conclusion. Seems to me like you got what you needed from me, and now you want to get back to that important business of yours. Which I think we both know is something I'd keep you from doing if I could."

"You just admitted you don't have any idea what I'm doing."

"Maybe I don't. But you trussing me up like a cord of kindling is weighing on my thoughts some. I got to conclude you find me a mite inconvenient to have around. Maybe you decided the best way of getting rid of me was to hand me over to Paulus Rondeau and pocket a thousand-dollar bounty into the bargain."

Dima spat on the ground, her mouth twisted in what looked like genuine anger and disgust. "That's what I think of Rondeau," she said. "That's what I think of your Echelon and your Parity, and every man or woman who ever served in your endless, pointless war! Bess, I'm the only thing that's keeping you out of Rondeau's hands. Look around you. Look where I've brought you. If I'd wanted the Pursuit Force to take you wouldn't I just have left you where you were?"

It was a reasonable point. Bess hadn't given any real thought to where they were, but now she did there was a pretty obvious conclusion to be drawn. "Is this Lake Azul?" she asked Dima.

"Good guess. Yes, we're in an Ajuparo village right on the eastern shore. Chief Erato took us in without question when he saw we'd brought back Jemet and Ksaia. These are their people."

Lake Azul! Bess tried hard to take that in. "But we were a good forty miles from there," she pointed out.

"Closer to fifty. And yes, if you're asking, it was quite a challenge getting you here. Ksaia found some milkweed and she and Mur wove a rope out of it so we could lash you across the back of your chafer. But that shoulder was a mess, so we had to stop along the road for some emergency surgery. I managed to get the bullet out and cauterise the wound, but the tracker darts are programmed to burrow into muscle tissue. I got to a couple of them in time, but the others had gone too deep. I'd have crippled you getting them out again. The good news is that those things are sterile and hypoallergenic. It would remove most of their usefulness if they killed what they hit. They're mostly made of organic materials too, so they break down over time, but it takes about a year. Not much help to us just at the moment."

Dima tapped the side of the bowl with her finger. "Are you willing to be reasonable now? This will be a lot better if you drink it hot."

"No," Bess said. "Reasonable ain't even close to how I'm feeling. Go on a ways. What's a tracker dart?"

Dima reached among the folds of her skirt, where there must have been a pocket. She held out her open hand for Bess to see. There were two little grey slivers resting on her palm. They looked a little like tin tacks except that their sides were lined with backward-pointing barbs like the ones some Pugface warriors milled into the heads of their fishing spears. The barbs were tiny, about the size of the spines along the edge of a spoon-flower's leaves, but their purpose was clear. They were there to give anyone that had been hit by one of the slugs a hard time drawing it out again. No wonder her body ached so much if she had more of these things inside her.

"There's a lot of complex electronics folded up inside these little casings," Dima said. "I've disabled these two but the ones inside you are still active. They're emitting a repeating signal across a wide range of wavelengths. The thing that attacked us is called an assault drone, and it has an operator. Rondeau, presumably. He can track the signal across long distances. I had to throw together some countermeasures. Look. Here."

She tucked the darts away again and held up her carpet bag, which had been sitting in between Bess's feet all this time. Bess's own saddlebags were there too, seemingly unopened. Bess hadn't noticed any of this before because she hadn't been able to raise her head high enough to see. The carpet bag was pulsing with soft red light. It was as though there was a banked fire in there that somehow wasn't burning through the cloth.

"I set it to put out a damper field. It's scrambling the signal the darts are emitting, but the field's effective radius is only ten feet or so. If you'd gotten up and started wandering around you'd have been outside the field and Rondeau would have picked up the signal again." Dima set the bag back down where it had been. "That was why I tied you down. Well, that and because I need to explain some things to you before you start trying to kill me again."

"I wasn't trying to kill you. I just wanted to shake an honest answer out of you."

"I never lied to you, Bess."

"Didn't tell me a whole lot of truth, either."

"No. I suppose not." Dima frowned. "Generally nothing good comes of trusting bassari. And I'm used to working on my own. That's how I was taught."

The pain and the tiredness made it hard for Bess to concentrate. She wanted very much to lie down and sleep again, but there was one thing that stood out like a great big rusty nail in the woolly bundle of her thoughts. Rondeau was coming. For all Dima's reassurances, he was on his way, and she wasn't in any shape to fight him.

"If it's true you don't wish me any harm," she said, "you better untie me and turn me loose. You said you carried me forty miles. Well, you can bet your last red cent the Pursuit Force is combing every inch of them forty miles right now. When Rondeau catches up with me he's gonna take me and hang me. Then he'll hang you too for hiding me, and most likely he'll burn this village after he's done. Fuck and damn it, Dima, just let me go!"

Bess tugged hard on whatever was pinning her right arm down. If it was a stake she might be able to bring it up out of the ground. The agony that knifed into her left shoulder as she pulled made her grit her teeth to keep from crying out, but she went on trying, twisting from the hips to give her tethered arms a little more leverage.

Dima put a hand on Bess's chest and pushed her back down. It didn't seem to require any great deal of effort. "You're not going anywhere," she said. "You could barely lift that tent flap right now, let alone walk through it. I want you to drink this broth first, since I went to the trouble of making it for you. Then I'll reactivate Slim and the three of us will have a little talk. If I cut through those ropes now, will you try to eat something instead of throttling me?"

"I'm not hungry." That was a lie though – and it was the lie of a stubborn child. Bess was hungry and thirsty both, and the sooner she was strong enough to rise up out of this the better. "Yeah," she muttered. "Okay then. Cut me loose. I guess throttling you can wait a while."

Dima went to work with the knife. The ropes didn't seem all that thick after all, since it only took a couple of good swipes at each one to make it part. When Bess pulled at the severed end of one of them she saw it was made out of twined milkweed stems – presumably the same ones Ghrent and Ksaia had woven so they could bring her here.

She levered herself up on her right elbow and let Dima press the bowl against her lips. The broth was unseasoned and too hot, but it had an underlying sweetness that made it both soothing and welcome. A drowsy warmth spread through Bess as she drank.

"Too much?" Dima asked, taking the bowl away.

"No, it's good. Thank you."

"It's got scorpillon venom in it. It's an anti-inflammatory, so it'll help your damaged muscle tissue to knit back up."

Bess winced. "Please tell me Ghrent isn't out there milking Ochre for poison."

"Ochre doesn't have the requisite glands. She had them cut out along with her sting. But the Ajuparo keep a small herd and some of them are intact. Ghrent is right outside, by the way. He insisted on standing guard over you, even though Jemet and Ksaia told him several times that he was among friends."

"He's a damn fool," Bess muttered, but she found herself cheered just a little to think the old man cared that much what happened to her – that anyone did, outside of the ones that wanted her dead. And Slim, of course. She trailed the fingers of her right hand across his grip. Even though he was asleep right then she wanted to reassure herself that he was there.

It was harder to swallow the broth knowing what was in it, but there was no denying that it was having a restorative effect. As soon as she felt strong enough to manage the manoeuvre, Bess sat up the rest of the way and took the bowl in her right hand to finish what remained.

Once she was done she put the bowl back into Dima's hands and slumped down, finding Slim's grip again and clutching it tight even though she was holding him in the wrong hand.

"How's your arm?" Dima asked her.

"Aching like it's got a grudge against the rest of me." Bess lay in silence for a few moments, gathering her thoughts. "Okay," she said at last. "Anything else you want out of me? Wash my face? Say my prayers?"

"No," Dima said. "I guess there's no sense in putting this off any longer. Wakeful Slim, activate."

Slim throbbed under Bess's fingers like a struck banjo string. "Damn it all!" he said gruffly. "You do that to me one more time, missy, and I'm apt to forget my manners. Bess, tell me you're good."

"I'm good, partner. Roped like a steer and more full of holes than a salt shaker, but I'm inclined to think it could be worse. How about you?"

"Woke up in a sour mood, but that's to be expected at my age."

"I have something to tell you both," Dima said. "It will take some little while because it's not an easy thing to tell, but it's supremely important. It's the thing that makes sense of everything else. The secret that explains the world. So even now when our enemies are close and we need to move quickly I think it's worth taking the time to make you understand."

"Wait," Bess said. "Bring Ghrent in here."

Dima frowned. "Why? This doesn't concern him."

"He pulled your irons out of the fire back at that trading post. He helped you get your stuff back from those bushwhackers. I reckon he's got as much right to hear this as I do. More, maybe, since he's your own people. What's more, he's looking for a reason to go on being alive, which I ain't so much. Call him in, Dima."

The Pugface woman hesitated. "These are sacred things," she said. "The spoken testimony of the Engine Everlasting, dating back to the very birth of my people and even before. Time out of mind they've been kept solemn and secret." Her gaze flicked to the carpet bag. "They're in my keeping now. Am I to be the one who profanes them by letting outsiders hear?"

"From where I'm sitting? Seems like you are."

"You don't count, Bess. The bearer of that gun is a special case. There's a kind of holiness that hangs around you, whether you deserve it or not."

"I'm a long way from deserving it," Bess said. "Or wanting it. But you told me these were the end times, Dima. So who all are you keeping these secrets for, exactly?"

Dima considered this for some little while. At last she nodded, but her reluctance was easy to see. She laughed ruefully. "Very well. It probably can't do any harm now. It's just hard to break the habit of a lifetime. Wait here."

"I don't have the luxury of choice right now, do I?"

Dima went out. "I guess we could still steal a chafer and just light out of here," Bess mused.

"If that's what you want to do, Bess," Slim said, "I'll back your play. Think you can stand up?"

"Maybe. Probably wouldn't stay up for long though."

"Then we stick it out?"

"We stick it out, partner. And get all them answers we been promised. Maybe get you fixed, too."

Dima came back with Ghrent. There was some little confusion when Ochre tried to follow the old man in and he had to scold her until she sat and stayed. When he caught sight of the leather cords that were lying on the ground around Bess he stiffened, obviously shocked. "You didn't say you tied her down," he protested. "The Rainmaker shouldn't be treated in this way."

"It's fine, old man," Bess called to him. "All for my own good, I'm told. And as you can see I'm free now. Dima here's got something she wants to tell us, so let's be good guests and listen politely."

Ghrent shook his head. "You've broken hospitality," he told Dima. "In my day it was thought shame to do such things to a stranger you invited into your house."

"Are you done?" Dima demanded, giving him a stern scowl. "You're only in here because she asked it, Grandfather. If you make any trouble or any noise I'll throw you out."

"I'm not your grandfather," Ghrent said. "And I tend to walk in and out of places on my own feet. Been a while now since I was thrown anywhere." But he sat and crossed his legs.

"Let's get on with this," Bess suggested. "There's a good chance Paulus Rondeau is scouring this whole territory right now hoping to get a smell of me. Better for everyone if I'm gone before he gets here."

"If only it were that easy," Dima said grimly. She kneeled and dipped her hand into her carpet bag. "Unfiled reports of tactical unit 486," she said. "Aloud. In sequence."

"Identifier," an answering voice said from inside the bag. "Seven omega two-nine-oh-five Esten, V, engineer first class." It was a man's voice, speaking in States' Common but with a strange inflection and in an accent Bess had never heard before. He sounded both sad and tired. Bess would have guessed he was young, but also that he most likely didn't feel that way.

"How are you doing that?" she asked Dima. "Making that voice speak out?"

"Magic," Dima said. "Or technology, as our mothers' mothers called it. Listen, Bess."

"Date," the voice said. "Thirty-three, nine, twelve-six-two-eight Pandominion calendar. Location thirty-four point oh-five-four-nine degrees north by a hundred and eighteen point two-four-two-six degrees west, unlisted world. Status: irreparably fucked."

Unfiled report of tactical unit 486
Identifier: 7Ω2905 Esten, V, engineer first class
Date: not applicable
Location: not applicable
Status: from a strictly ontological point of view that's about to become highly debatable.

The next few years were hard.

When we took that first True Imp base we had surprise on our side. Presumably they knew we were still out there, since their little murder squad hadn't reported back after going out to torch us, but Nim'kisi and I had worked up some really effective widgets to scatter our energy signature. Then as an extra touch we had Flycatcher tow a bunch of screamers across the other side of the continent. The screamers were no bigger than my little finger, but each one put out as much EM noise as an armoured tank or a gun platform. So the Imps thought we were a couple of thousand miles away when in fact we were creeping up behind them with weapons hot.

We knew how bad the odds were. The numbers, the heavy weapons, the home team advantage, everything was on their side. Everything except the actual combat experience. These were people who'd basically spent the last thousand years or so guarding a nursery, and none of them had ever been in a fight where the other guy could fight back. Plus we could factor in the corrosive effect of knowing that they belonged somewhere else entirely; that they'd been dumped in a backwater a long way from the action and told to stay there and await evac. Or rather their ancestors had been told that, long enough ago that evac had become a myth. The cause they were fighting for, their home, their enemies, all just myth. Campfire tales. It must have been kind of a relief when we arrived and they realised at least some of what they'd been told was true.

We dropped a bomb on them. It was one of their own bombs, salvaged from the gun platform that had come down partially intact. And when I say we dropped it, that makes the operation seem way more sophisticated than it was. We pretty much just delivered it to their back door and set it off. The munition in question was a medium-sized nuke and although their base had been a hard target once upon a time they'd been using it for a very long time and they hadn't done much in the way of upkeep. Their shields had gaps you could have led a marching band through. We detonated the nuke from fifteen miles out using a remote trigger and when we sent Flycatcher in to verify the hit there was nothing left.

That was when we got our first inkling of what was going on with the ceramic towers. The True Imp base was way out in the middle of one of the desert areas in the south-west corner of the continent, but there were several indigenous townships close enough to see the blast and feel its effects. Some of them came to see what had happened, riding in wagons or on the backs of their bizarre super-sized arthropods. But they didn't stay long. After only a few hours the crowd around the perimeter of the blast zone thinned out and disappeared. The curious pilgrims who were on their way to the site all at once abruptly turned around and went home.

It was Nim'kisi who spotted the pattern. The sudden change in the indigenes' behaviour coincided with an abrupt surge of activity from the ceramic towers. And it was a kind of activity she recognised at once – a synchronised emission on one of the frequencies used by Flycatcher's CoIL scanner. And though it came from all the towers at once the broadcast was strongest from those in the immediate vicinity of the blast. It had lasted seven hours, thirteen minutes and some odd seconds. When it was finished all the indigenes had gone back to wherever they'd come from and none of them paid any further attention to the blast site. It was as though it wasn't there, as though that massive explosion had never happened.

"It's mind control," Nim'kisi summarised bluntly. "The frequencies are the same that Flycatcher uses for CoIL interrogations, but this wasn't a passive scan. It was an active broadcast. Information – and I think instructions – were being sent out to the indigenes from the towers."

"The towers were telling them what to do?" Dulu sounded both baffled and horrified.

"I believe it's a more radical kind of intervention, sir. I've been observing the blast site since those signals went out, and I've seen some of the indigenes pass close by there. They appear to be settlers moving from the populated east of the country out here to the west where there's more land and fewer people. When they go by the crater they don't so much as look at it. It's as though it's completely disappeared from their memories and their sensoria. They don't perceive it as being there. In other words they haven't just been given an instruction, they've had new pathways laid down in their brains."

"I can see exactly how that would work," Velladaxita said. "A conventional CoIL scan remotely activates and controls the electrical activity in the subject brain – brute-forcing neural stimulation in order to make the subject remember whatever the interrogator wants to see. This just takes the same process one stage further, implanting false memories and rigid compulsions."

"That's fucking horrible," Dulu said. He actually looked a little sick. "But I guess it's the missing piece of the puzzle. If the towers can exert that degree of control over these people's minds then it's probably not complicated to make them forget they fought a war and make them fight it over again thinking it's the first time."

Velladaxita frowned. "Begging your pardon, sir, it's *massively* complicated. Insanely, inconceivably complicated. Even if you leave out the part where the True Imps are directly editing memories with that kind of precision across the breadth of an entire continent. Jad and Shaster, think of the number of computations involved here! We're talking about a population of between thirty and forty million. Under this scenario every single one of them would periodically need a sort of hard reset in which their memory of their own life to date and their understanding of their country's history were radically edited. The memory edits would need to account for people who were killed in the previous iteration and new people who were born. Everyone would need to be given a new role to play, effectively, a new backstory and a new set of relationships that makes sense. Probably there's a lot of repetition, but there'd still be vast amounts of fine-tuning to do. And the memory edits would have to work around the war damage in some way. Anything that had been destroyed or damaged would need to be repaired before the next iteration starts."

"Not everything," Nim pointed out. "We've seen that these people can be made to ignore what's right in front of their eyes. They only see what they're told to see."

Dax frowned. "Point stands. Either way, the amount of computing power all of this would require is way off the top of any scale you can imagine. The Registry – the AI that handles the Pando's Step traffic – could probably do it, but not casually or easily. It's a technological intervention on a stupendous scale."

"Fascinating, Dax," the captain said drily. "Does that impact our options here in any meaningful way?" Nobody else said a word. I think we were contemplating all over again how far out of our collective depth we were.

"Yes, sir," Velladaxita said emphatically, "I believe it does. Are you aware of how big the Registry is? It's a little bigger than our own moon. It needed to be in order to house the seventeen trillion sheets of boron nitrate that make up its CPU. There's nothing up in orbit here that could house that much computational power, so it's got to be something located on the surface. I'd say it's a near certainty that the ceramic towers are a networked AI – one massive digital intelligence distributed across several hundred discrete loci. It's the only conceivable way they could shunt that much data."

The captain spread his hands. "So . . . ?"

"So I think we've made a mistake. A pretty fundamental one, about who and what it is we're fighting. These ground troops are the immediate threat, sure, but it's the towers we're going to need to take out. They're the ones in charge here. If we want to sabotage the True Imperials' project, that job isn't done until the towers come down."

But the captain didn't buy it. The towers could wait, he said, because whatever it was they were doing they weren't doing it to us. That CoIL-like signal pulse had hit every other self over a couple of hundred square miles but we hadn't felt a thing. Velladaxita was forced to admit that we seemed to have some kind of innate immunity. Perhaps, she theorised, the link between the towers and the indigenous population here involved a genetic component.

So we carried on exterminating the people who'd tried to exterminate us. We took out the second base in the same way we'd dealt with the first, this time with a thermobaric incendiary rather than a nuke, but after that we were out of second-hand bunker-busters and the Imps were wise to us. When we ran reconnaissance on the third base we found it empty. They'd gone to ground.

We considered taking over that base and using it ourselves. It was a genetics lab where the Imps had presumably designed and incubated the customised sentients they'd then sent out to populate the world. But Dulu said no. Even if the Imps hadn't booby-trapped the place it probably wasn't a good idea to stay in any location where they could find us so easily. Better to stay on the move, as the enemy were apparently doing.

We hadn't lost a single trooper in either of those engagements, but as the fight entered its skirmish phase it got very dirty. The Imps were hunting us just as keenly as we were hunting them, and they still had the advantage when it came to numbers. We really missed Ajuparo now – not that I'd ever stopped missing her. She would have taken the lead in that hunt and every throat she cut, every hideout she torched would have been a work of art. In her absence we did what we could. We set traps for the Imperials, tracked them across thousands of miles, laid a hundred false trails and twice that many ambushes. And of course they did exactly the same to us.

In the end we ditched our armour and went undercover among the indigenous population. It made sense, since EM emissions and heat signatures were still the most reliable ways of finding the anomalous tech that told us – and the Imps – where hostiles were most likely to be found. Nim'kisi had made a database of local languages by this point and we'd downloaded most of them into our arrays. We knew their customs, their dress codes, their status hierarchies. We could pass.

Well, most of us could. I was the exception because as previously stated there were no anthropoid selves on this continent. Just about every other mammalian lineage was represented, but there was a distinct lack of ape-descendants. That meant I would have stuck out like a bayonet in a bouquet. So I stayed at home and did the housework, which is to say I designed and built the traps the others took out into the field and deployed.

From close up, Nim'kisi told me, this preprogrammed civilisation looked even stranger. There were in effect close to fifty genetically distinct lineages, with the largest only just over a million and the smallest somewhere in the region of three hundred thousand. With populations that small you'd expect to have major problems with double recessive traits and a general loss of hybrid vigour, but according to Dax some fine work had been done at the DNA level. The selves of this world carried libraries of redundant genes in their germ cells, allowing for much more genetic diversity than the tiny breeding communities should have been able to sustain.

And on we went. And on, and on, and on.

We took a few prisoners along the way, and we put the same

question to all of them. *How do we shut down your mind control network?* None of them seemed to know. In the distant past there had been some who safeguarded the secret of how to communicate with the towers, but that sacred arcanum had been lost centuries ago. Nobody living knew how the trick was done.

That became the other item that was perennially on my docket. Whenever I could free the time I continued to research the ceramic towers, hoping to find some weakness we could exploit. After a little experimentation I found that some vibrational weapons could exploit gaps in the phase modulations of the towers' shields. With the captain's blessing I designed and built a thoroughly ridiculous weapon we called the shaker cannon. The idea was that you pointed it at one of the towers and set it going. At first the cannon just bombarded the tower with vibrations on random frequencies. But it also read the feedback. Every once in a while there were gaps in the reflected energy profile, which meant the tower hadn't been able to diffuse the entire incoming load. The cannon used that information to refine its algorithm and attack preferentially on frequencies that the tower couldn't wholly deflect. Like a boxer with a punching bag, hitting it harder and harder until it splits open.

We chose a target in a relatively unpopulated area, set up the cannon and delivered a targeted barrage. The weapon worked fine at first, the pressure wave building until it was hitting the tower's upper surface like a wrecking ball, but the tower didn't just sit back and take the damage. Nim'kisi detected a surge of energy across the entire grid, all of it incoming – sent by the other towers to aid in the defence of the one we were attacking. Over the space of about thirteen seconds the tower's shields increased their output by a factor of about a thousand per cent. We were stonewalled, our vibrational punches reduced to ineffectual feather-falls.

I wanted to go back to the drawing board, improve the design and come back for another try, but the captain said it would just be a drain on our resources. We needed to keep up our offensive against the True Imps, make sure they couldn't retrench and regroup. He stood me down, and the fight went on.

It was a strange time, and not in a good way. We were taking casualties now, one after another of us lured into a confrontation on our enemies' terms, brought down by superior numbers or unanswerable firepower. Lasque was killed along with Messolin and Kouye when the Imps bootstrapped part of their orbital spy network into a laser array and obliterated an entire town rather than let them escape. Nim'kisi died when she found a cache of True Imp weapons and picked one of them up with her bare hands. It had been soaked in neurotoxin, about a hundred times as much as was needed for a lethal load.

The baked-in detachment we used to have in other theatres, other fights, other days had completely deserted us by this time. We felt each death like a wound that wouldn't stop bleeding. Nim'kisi's passing was the hardest to bear, maybe even harder than Ajuparo's, because we couldn't touch her, couldn't comfort her. She died in agony while we stood by and watched. It wasn't even safe to bury her: we had to incinerate her body from a distance.

There was no getting over any of this, no getting past it. You could say the horrors brought our little band of survivors closer together, but not in a good way. We knew whenever we met up that we were avoiding the same names, the same memories, the same indelible tragedies. We shared a private wavelength, but there was nothing on there besides nightmares.

Since I was already linked to Flycatcher I became ets new handler, but our relationship was always strained. I think for each of us the other was a reminder of something terrible that could never be set aside or got over. I missed Nim more with every day that passed. She was the only other engineer in the squad. We'd spoken the same language, laughed at the same jokes. Her social anxieties had kept most people at a wary distance, but she'd let me in. And now I felt more alone than at any time since we made that first disastrous Step.

Then Flycatcher died too, for a value of that word. The Imps shot et out of the sky with a scrambler beam that shorted out all ets systems at once. Et had been flying low so we retrieved et more or less intact, but ets higher functions never came back online. Et had been lobotomised, transformed from a self into a mere mechanism. That was a terrible thing, not least because we still needed the drone to run recon. We were effectively deploying the undead remains of a former comrade. And Flycatcher still had an audio interface, could render reports and respond to instructions in the same voice et had always used, but the things et said now were options from a menu. The intelligence that had lived within the silver carapace was gone.

We were in a war of attrition and we couldn't tell whether we were winning or losing. We'd taken a heavy toll on the Imps, but our own losses were crippling, devastating beyond anything you could hope to measure. And still we carried on.

In the middle of all this the other war – the indigenes' war – started up again. We got advance warning because the entire tower network went from passive to active mode, flooding the continent from sea to sea with CoIL transmissions. We had no way of analysing the content of those broadcasts, but we had to assume they were rewriting memory and personality and motivation on a truly massive scale.

We saw their effect first-hand. The indigenes began to rehearse old arguments and divisions, mostly connected to the use of slave labour across the southern parts of the continent. Political and religious leaders, cultural pundits and military commanders, all moved into roles that positioned them for the conflict to come, towards which they moved in a kind of frictionless free fall with no dissenting voices. In the space of a few months they passed from sabre-rattling through deniable provocations to open warfare.

It was horrifying, but it was also good for us in a number of ways. I got a solid set of readings of the towers' emissions, adding to a database that Nim'kisi had started up and that I had now inherited. Flycatcher had been the repository for all that information, but after that devastating attack I'd decanted the database into a free-standing storage module that I kept with me at all times. 507m didn't approve of this transfer. Et seemed to feel I was showing disrespect to Flycatcher's memory. Or perhaps et was just suffering, as we organic selves were, from battle fatigue, post-traumatic stress and intermittent bouts of extreme depression. We'd been fighting for a long time with no respite.

The other advantage the war gave us was that it created a great deal of chaotic movement under which we could conceal our own activities. That was true for the Imps as well, of course, but as the smaller force we were more often on the defensive and having to decamp quickly across hostile terrain. Consequently we needed that smokescreen more desperately and used it more often.

There were either seven or eight of us left by this point (Trooper Xil was missing in action, his array offlined and therefore much more likely to be dead than alive, but we had no way to verify this). We made the decision to split up, to make things harder for the Imps and to reduce the chance that some random catastrophe arising from the ongoing war would take us all out at once.

Left on my own, I returned to the shaker cannon, as I had been itching to do for some time, and reworked the design. I devised a signal jammer and installed it on the undamaged part of Flycatcher's motherboard. Then I chose a target, another more or less isolated tower close to the confluence of two great rivers, and went in.

The results were mixed. The cannon performed brilliantly, and the jammer prevented the tower from reaching out to its neighbours for an energy boost. After three or four minutes of bombardment the tower was in trouble. Complex patterns of pearlescent colour were roiling across its ceramic sheath, which had buckled and deformed in a couple of places, and instead of the usual slightly smug hum it was emitting a strident shriek.

The collapse of the tower seemed imminent, and I was just stepping up the attack when 507m signalled to me to stop. *Esten, et said, you need to see this.* Alongside the message was a live video feed from one of the sky platforms, followed very quickly by a second and then a third.

Can't it wait? I voked back, reluctant to break off when I was this close to success.

No, was 507m's terse response. I glanced at the feeds, then stared in horror. 507m had been monitoring two farms and a small settlement, all within a ten-mile radius of the tower I was attacking. In retrospect et must already have had ets suspicions as to the possible effects of a direct assault on a network whose primary purpose was to regulate the cognitive and affective states of a large and varied population.

All three of the feeds showed the same thing. Regardless of age, sex or clade every self in the immediate vicinity of the tower was undergoing a mental and physical crisis that was very hard to look at. Most had fallen to the ground, where they either writhed or rocked from side to side or crawled like worms without making any use of their limbs. Others had slumped into a sitting position at the base of walls, where they plucked at their own faces and arms as if they were trying to see what was underneath. There were more than a few with bloodied faces, either because they'd bitten their tongues or because they'd scratched and torn at their own flesh.

The tower's broadcast signature began to change at the same time that the first signs of structural damage appeared, 507m reported dispassionately. *This may be a deliberate defence mechanism, or merely a side effect of the equipment housed inside the tower malfunctioning under external stress. There is no easy way to tell.*

No, no way that I could see, and it didn't really matter. Either way I had no choice but to power down the shaker cannon and retreat. That was the last time I attempted any kind of a direct assault on the towers. It was clear that the only safe way to disable them was to take control of the entire network and power it down.

And that would have been my next step, but I didn't get that far.

Returning to the nondescript shack I was using as a base, I found Captain Dulu waiting there for me with threadbare patience.

He and the other surviving members of the squad, everyone except for me, had succeeded in tracking down the last remaining cadre of True Imperials. They were holed up in the centre of a major city on the continent's eastern seaboard, where the Imps presumably thought they could make themselves invisible amid the endless comings and goings of the indigenes. In other circumstances Dulu might have hesitated to engage in a place where so many non-combatants would be put at risk. But it had all gone on too long, and we had lost too much. He sensed that the last dregs of our courage and our will to fight were steadily leaching out of us. If we turned away this time he was afraid it might be the end.

So he made the call, and he made it for all of us, including me. I had to throw up a crude hologram mask over my face and stash my most serviceable tools in a canvas bag – what the locals called a carpet bag. Some of the tools were ones I'd brought with me when we first came here. The rest were bits and pieces I'd salvaged from the armour and weapons of the dead, friend and enemy alike – and of course I put the storage module in there too, my growing archive of signal patterns within the tower network.

The captain led us in, and it was a bloodbath. The Imps were on their last legs too but they fought with everything they had. Meanwhile the towers put out a soothing message: nothing to see here, move on, move on. The people of that eastern city ignored the firefight that was taking place right in front of them. When one of them fell to a stray shot, the others nearby stepped over the body and walked on completely oblivious.

We breached the True Imp base and went from room to room, slaughtering as we went. It was a replay of the fight that had brought us here in the first place, complete with ambushes and high-tech deadfalls. In the end Dulu and I were the last two standing on our side, me bleeding from three separate wounds and Dulu with his left arm broken at the shoulder, while the True Imp fighters were all down. That left a group of men and women with no armour and only hand-held weapons who seemed to be either technicians or civilian strategists. They executed an orderly retreat and barricaded themselves in an underground room that they thought was impervious to attack.

"Over to you," the captain said. "Go ahead, Esten. Earn your keep for once. Engineer them to death. You can't say they haven't fucking earned it."

I had to think about it for a while, but in the end it wasn't that hard. I diverted a small river that had been covered over and repurposed as a sewer. I drowned the last of the enemy in the city's effluent. We didn't bother to burn or blast our way in and count the corpses. We let their last redoubt become their tomb.

So much for the True Imps. Rest in piss. But their obscene project would go on without them, and I honestly couldn't think of a way to stop it. We hadn't won, we'd only delivered a tiny sliver of retributive justice to the people who'd built this place. Payback for Ajuparo, for Nim'kisi, for Lasque and Inch and Messolin and all the rest of them. That was something, at least, and I'd be lying if I said I felt any guilt about what I'd done. No triumph either. Maybe a kind of dull relief that our long war of attrition was finally over.

But that brought its own crisis, its own set of existential

questions. What the hell were we? What were we for? In the absence of the fight, what becomes of the fighters?

Dulu took it hardest, which I suppose was always likely. He'd led his squad well but he'd led them to annihilation; a forced march across a cheese grater. He had a lifeline of sorts if he'd chosen to use it: unlike me he could blend in on this insane world. There was nothing to stop him hanging up his rifle, mothballing his armour and going native. But I think it would have felt too much like surrender. He just couldn't bear the thought of lying down in this hellhole the True Imps had made and pretending it was a flower bed. Seventeen years after we'd first Stepped into this world and three years after that last battle he ate a bullet, leaving me absolutely alone.

Alone except for 507m and the lobotomised remains of Flycatcher. Two of us, or maybe two and a half, and I wish I could say we were good company for each other but that would be a flat-out lie. Flycatcher was an absence rather than a presence, a reproach rather than a companion. My relationship with 507m was closer than it had been but it was more civil than cordial. We didn't have enough in common and we couldn't share each other's grief, couldn't be there for each other even now when there was nowhere else to be.

I had a lot of free time to just sit and consider what I could possibly do next. There was always suicide, the captain's exit, but I shrank from that. If the captain had feared living a normal life in this utterly abnormal world, I was afraid of dying with nothing to show for having been alive. Dulu had been a hero. By the time he took his last bow he had endless feats of courage and bravado to his name, and he would probably be a semi-permanent fixture in the recruitment advertisements for the next few generations of Cielo troopers.

That wasn't me. As a combat engineer I'd done a few sneaky things that had worked out well, a few more that hadn't, and neither my successes nor my failures had made any ripples at all in the big scheme of things. It felt wrong to check out when nobody had even noticed my checking in.

And it wasn't as though I could tell myself our fight was over. We'd wiped out the enemy but the enemy's great engine was thundering on all around us. Generation after generation of the indigenes would go to war, fighting and dying for a cause that meant nothing at all to anyone now and had meant sweet fuck all to begin with unless you bought into their creators' eugenicist lunacy. I was haunted by the thought that those awful deaths, Ajuparo's death, and Nim'kisi's, and Dulu's, all of them, would finally have been for nothing if this vile abattoir of a world kept right on going after all.

What could I do to change things? What did I have that could make a difference?

I counted on my fingers, and I got to three. I had what was left of Flycatcher, with ets CoIL interface. I had 507m, my trusted side-arm and the closest thing I had to a friend since I lost Nim'kisi. And I had my brain, my engineering experience and expertise. That was it. Nothing more in this whole gods-fucked continuum, so far from home, so far from anything that might possibly smell of salvation.

And I thought about it from every angle. I really did. The wounds I'd taken in that last battle had left me with a permanent limp, and exposed me to a local pathogen that I couldn't shake. I was getting weaker and less mobile with every year that passed. I was also still saddled with the handicap of belonging to a sentient race that wasn't otherwise represented on this world. If my hologram mask failed I would be seen in all my inexplicable otherness and either put down like an animal or exhibited in a zoo. One way or another I was going to die before too long, and then there would be no more Pandominion presence on this world until the second team arrived a few thousand years down the line and wondered why everything was so quiet. There was a pretty low ceiling on how much I could achieve in the meantime.

"Here's the thing," I said aloud. I was lying on a narrow bed in the same half-furnished shack I'd been using as a base before Dulu came to fetch me. I'd set up a perimeter but it wasn't much of one, mostly just cameras and telltales so if someone was coming I'd have enough warning to armour up and face the door. I'd been planning to move on for a while but until I had some kind of a plan there hadn't seemed to be much point. "If we don't take down those towers then we've achieved nothing here. We came, we shot up a few enemy grunts, we died."

"Your vibration weapon seemed very effective against the towers' shields," 507m pointed out.

"Yeah, it was. But going by what we saw, if we just destroy the towers then we destroy this civilisation too. There's a kind of feedback through whatever mechanism the Imps used to program the indigenes' thoughts, and it's strong enough to cause a planet-wide mental collapse. The solution isn't to blow the towers up, it's to shut them down. Smoothly, across the board, all at the same time.

"There's a chance I could figure it out if I had the proper equipment, a team of experts in energistic physics and an infinite amount of time. But the two of us are all there is, and I'm made of perishable materials so that two is going down to one before too long. What can we do now, while I'm still alive, that will shift the odds?"

Silence fell. It lasted long enough that I thought neither of us was ever going to break it. I was about to call time when 507m spoke up.

"I have a suggestion," et said.

Et laid it out for me, and it was a really good idea. Well no, that's overstating the case. It was absolutely horrendous and unpardonable in almost every way. It meant something akin to suicide for me and an existential risk for 507m. It also involved committing some of the same crimes the True Imps had committed, in the hope that somewhere down the line the two wrongs would cancel out and magically become a right. It rested on the unholy trinity of faith, hope and guesswork.

But I couldn't come up with anything better, and neither could 507m. In fact we couldn't come up with any other options at all. The limiting factors were time and personnel and there was a way of shifting the dial on both of those things so long as we didn't mind sacrificing everything else in the process, including ourselves and every moral principle we were supposed to give a shit about. We argued it back and forth for the best part of a day. We stared into the abyss, and it stared right back at me wearing old, familiar faces.

"Are you sure?" I asked 507m. "Sure you want to do this?"

"Esten," et answered, "I can see nothing to lose here that isn't already lost." Which fell a long way short of a *hell yes* but probably still counted as a vote in favour.

"Okay," I said. "Let's do it then."

We went back to that lab, the place where the True Imp geneticists had performed their atrocities. We performed some of our own, using their machines and my sampled genome. We made a new race – a race of anthropoids – and we aged several batches of them to adulthood. We wove memories and personalities for them. It wasn't even hard. The equipment was right there, designed and built for that very purpose. Noetic overwriting of this kind was a capital crime across the entire Pandominion, but we were a long way from home and there's something to be said for observing local customs.

We released our children – *my* children – into the wild. There were a hundred thousand or so of them, and we set them up in parts of the continent that were sparsely inhabited. We imprinted some pretty strong impulses on them, steering that first generation away from any kind of active engagement with the existing indigenes. My hope is that they'll entrench themselves deeply enough and in sufficient numbers that when the culture clash comes, as it surely will, simply exterminating them won't be a practical proposition. If all goes well, they'll just be absorbed into the general insanity without making too much of a splash. One of the things the towers do is to smooth over any cracks or inconsistencies that might make their captive audience try to look behind the curtain. Hopefully we can hitch a ride on that.

I've given them some of my memories too, sampled by Flycatcher and dropped like little depth charges into the hippocampus of every self that came off the assembly line. They have names – some of them taken from my dead friends, others from my home world of Leopteris. They have legends. They'll dream of me, and the dream will haunt them. My fight won't necessarily end with my death.

Which is actually the next order of business. 507m is ready, or et says et is. I've made that claim too, but I was lying. I'm trying to maintain a philosophical calm, but I'm pretty sure that's not the same thing. Doesn't matter. Doesn't matter. What matters is to thread the last needle so that when everything is in place – assuming that ever happens – we can finally complete the mission.

I made my life into a story and threw it into the well of my children's hind-brains, so deep I couldn't hear the splash when it hit. Some day they'll need me, the story goes, and on that day I'll rise. I wonder if all gods are full of this much shit, or if it's just me.

So now we come to it. And I thought I'd be braver than this or at least practised enough at killing that I could rely on muscle memory, but my hand is shaking and I can't keep the tears out of my eyes.

507m is waiting. Flycatcher's CoIL scanner is warmed up and locked on me. All that's left to do is to give the word.

And then I die.

And then, I guess, we'll see.

PART SIX

THE SECRET THAT EXPLAINS THE WORLD

It was strange, Paulus Rondeau reflected sombrely, how big a thing this hunt had grown to be. Oh, Dog-Bitch Bess had always felt like a major prize, to be sure. And the gun too: he wanted that gun where it belonged, riding on his hip and doing his bidding. But then there was that chase in the desert, where he was – in a sense – riding on the back of the Reaper and looking out through its eyes. The excitement and immediacy of that had got into his blood and set it boiling. It was all he could do now to keep it to a rolling simmer.

It had been so close! So close he could almost smell it. He'd been certain sure he could bring the Dog-Bitch down. He had her on the run. Wounded, weaponless, split off from the Pugface rabble she seemed to be riding with. He'd felt like he had her cold.

Then suddenly he'd felt a pain like someone had split his head open with an axe. He'd passed out cold, woken up a couple of minutes later to find he'd fallen down and pissed himself. And his link with the Reaper was gone. He couldn't make it respond at all, couldn't feel it or hear it inside his throbbing head.

Something had gone badly wrong, obviously. No way of knowing what, but he'd ridden out to the place where the chase had happened and found no trace of his prey. No trace of the Reaper either, unless you counted a few inches of scorched earth and a couple of steel petals sliced off clean: the severed ends of the blades that kept the thing in the air.

The signal from the tracker darts persisted, though. Whatever changes the Reaper had made to the furniture inside Rondeau's head he could still feel a kind of vibration in there like someone had threaded one end of a banjo string through his ears and was strumming on the other end of it a day or two's ride westward. Then that died too, between one moment and the next. Either the Dog-Bitch herself or someone close to her must have found a way to block it.

So the Reaper was down and the bitch was in the wind. But how far could she have gone after that fight? Most of the darts with which he'd salted her hide were meagre little things, not much bigger than birdshot, but he'd gotten her good with one or two real honest-to-god bullets and then she'd taken a bad fall right after. Rondeau would bet a dollar to a dead man's dick that she'd gone to ground. Which meant the odds on catching her would never be better.

He reined in long enough to consult the map. There wasn't a proper town or even a settlement within a fifty-mile radius. There were more than a few Pugface villages though, and the bitch seemed to get along with that kind a lot better than she did with regular folk. Rondeau's gaze darted back and forth between the map and its meticulously detailed key. The cartographers of the States' cavalry were careful in charting the movements of the plains Pugfaces because you could never tell when any given group of them might need to be smacked down. This far west you mostly tended to see Dulu and Messolin encampments, along with a few Lasque raiding parties.

Then he saw the notation *AJU* and a memory fell into place. He'd found out from the Braggarts he'd interrogated that Tom Blue had frequently bivouacked with the Ajuparo during the war, and the Ajuparos' winter lodgings were way out here along the shore of Lake Azul. There were three Ajuparo encampments that Rondeau could see. One of them was on the nearer shore, only forty miles or so from where the bitch and the Reaper had fought. The second was three miles to the south and the third at the lake's southern tip another four or five miles on.

Rondeau made up his mind on the spot. He divided his command into three units of a dozen men each, giving one to Alex Tooth and one to Ben Southern. The third would ride with him. Each of them would take one village and search it from top to bottom. "Use bribes, threats, summary executions, whatever it takes. If Dog-Bitch Bess is there, rouse her up and roust her out. We've got her, boys. We've got her good. And it would be a sin in the eyes of Holy John if we let her give us the slip now."

"Will twelve men be enough to conduct a proper search, sir?" Alex Tooth asked. His tone was level but the frown on his face was eloquent. "There could be upwards of twenty or thirty warriors in those villages."

"Twenty or thirty Pugface," Rondeau said. "You're a sworn servant of the States' Union, Tooth. Are you gonna shit yourself if some woad-painted primitive waves a spear or a hand-axe at you?"

"No, sir," Tooth confirmed. "Absolutely not."

"And the Ajuparo chiefs aren't fools. They know there's five hundred men up at Fort Esperance that will come down on them like God's own hammer if they give us so much as a surly word."

"I know that, sir. But if we were to stick together . . ."

"If we stick together we might lose her. And I don't mean to do that, okay? But if the numbers are concerning you, bring up that katy from the back of the line there and I'll show you what I got you for your birthday."

Tooth passed the word down the column and the katy was brought up. The four big wooden crates the katy was carrying were laid down and unpacked, each one disgorging a dozen slim rifles that still smelled of packing grease. Tooth had never seen one of these weapons with his own eyes but he knew what they were: the new rapid-fire carbine from the manufactury of Godfrey Fleetfoot in Ortoseer. They bore Fleetfoot's crowned GF trademark on their beechwood stocks, adjacent to which sat not one but two triggers. The rear one was a set trigger. A single touch there would reduce the rifle's pull from four and a half pounds to six ounces of pressure, after which you could reportedly fire an entire magazine of thirty bullets in less than a minute.

"Go ahead," Rondeau said, not just to Tooth but to all the men present. "Grab yourselves one of those beauties and load her up." The riders of the Pursuit Force made haste to do so, eyes shining. These were very fine guns indeed, and a man felt like that bit more of a man with one of them in his hands.

"Now let's see," Rondeau said, riding the moment. "Pickerel, Raven, Book, you're with Tooth. Marchioness, Lake, with Southern. Bellman, Bond, Hazeltree . . ." Every man who was named lined up straight away, eager now to get themselves into a situation where their new toys might get to be played with. If any of them had shared Tooth's uneasiness about the tilted odds they didn't seem to feel any need to mention it now.

Rondeau hesitated though when it came to choosing which one of the three villages he would search himself. A wounded woman, in need of medicine and finding it hard to stay in the saddle, would most likely not ride any further than she had to. So the closest settlement, the one that was actually on the lake shore, offered the best odds. But if he took that one for himself and guessed wrong he might come to regret it. Suppose Bess had tacked south? There was a whole maze of canyons and arroyos down there that she could get herself lost in, and since she was probably going to want to get to the far side of the lake at some point the southern route would be a whole lot shorter overall.

In the end he decided to take the middle one of the three. He instructed Tooth and Southern that if they met the Dog-Bitch first and she put up any kind of a fight they should send up a flare so he could come to their aid. If they found her and brought her in safe and sound the middle village would make a good and logical place for the three groups to come together again and provision themselves for the trip back east. The Ajuparo were bound to have a few katies that could be confiscated and rendered down into trail meat.

Of course it was always possible that old Bess had found some other place to hide. That they would come up empty-handed after all. And that would be a bad day for the Pugface because Paulus Rondeau's blood was up, and by John and all His saints somebody was going to die today.

The ghost voice finished speaking. Dima reached into the carpet bag and did something there, then closed it up again.

Mur Ghrent reached out to touch the bag, with just the tips of his fingers. His mouth moved in what Bess judged was a silent prayer, or else a blessing. His face was running with tears.

"I feel like I missed about nine parts of that and only got the tail end of the tenth," Bess said.

"Me too," said Wakeful Slim. "But I guess I got what I was promised. That 507m we just was hearing about, that was me. Or if it wasn't me it was some close kin of mine that came out of the self-same factory." There was something in his voice that Bess had never heard there before, a tremor of excitement or agitation or perhaps even fear.

"It was you," Dima said. "You were the gun the Engine Everlasting held when he slaughtered the True Imps. You hamstrung and quartered them, Wakeful Slim. Your stock and your barrel ran red with their blood. My people have honoured your memory ever since, and now at last you've been returned to us. You coming back to us like this is the clearest sign that we've reached the end of our struggles. That the last days have finally come."

"Let's not get ahead of ourselves," Bess said grimly. "I guess I can appreciate now that your Engine was more than just a piece of moonshine someone dreamed up to hang a hope on. But where does it leave us, exactly? Just before that damn thing came down on us I was tasking you with what I saw, which was you using the tools in that damn bag to bring down the mindless plague on innocent folk."

"Yes, that was what you said." Dima's expression didn't change but her tone was suddenly hard. "And it was a vile accusation. I ought to hate you for it."

"You're denying it, then? Because I saw you with my own eyes tinkering with the dream-towers. And then I heard you say it was the towers that brought the plague."

"Correlation doesn't imply causation. I was there to take measurements, Bess – especially of the towers that were starting to fail. The whole system is breaking down, which isn't so surprising given how long it's been in use. The towers are meant to be inactive most of the time. They only wake up at the end of one of your historical cycles – fifteen years, twelve, ten, it varies a lot, but on the whole it's been getting shorter. Then they shoot you full of new instructions, give you your cues and your starting positions, and go back to sleep again. The mindless outbreaks come when one of the towers malfunctions. They always self-repair, but it takes them a lot longer than it used to. And when they're broken they pump out disconnected nonsense. Mind poison. Madness."

"The giants were always our enemies," Ghrent murmured. "And yours too, Rainmaker. The enemies that hide behind all other enemies and never show their faces."

Dima nodded. "That's solemn truth, old man. Only the giants aren't monsters. They're machines. Machines that stand over every town and city and settlement in the country like puppeteers over an enormous stage. They're the only enemy that has ever mattered. The Engine Everlasting – no, you know his secret name now, so I might as well use it – the engineer Vel Esten set out to destroy the towers, but he died before he could finish that mission and so he bequeathed it to us. It's our heritage and our honour, our sacred duty. I carry the Engine's mark, Bess. I wield his tools and I do his bidding. So do you."

And here it was, the thing Bess had been afraid of ever since she took Slim from Alden Calendar's cooling corpse. She'd always known that she was carrying someone else's weapon, that Slim didn't belong to her in any way she could explain or defend. That hadn't mattered when he was only a tool she used, but now that he was her friend it mattered a great deal. She took refuge in derision even though Dima had already proved her point irrefutably out in the desert. "So your giant-killer was a gunslinger? He rode with a big iron on his hip? I thought he favoured an axe."

Dima's gaze didn't waver and her voice was calm. "He was a soldier from another world, who got lost here and never found his way home again."

"Says you."

"You just heard it for yourself. And I know the rest of that story, Bess – from the engineer's own words and from what the people of that first generation passed on down the line to us. My mother taught it to me when I was a child. Then when I was older, but still a child, she taught me what the tools in that carpet bag were and what I was meant to do with them. It's part of my heritage. It's been my life, for as long as I can remember. I didn't choose it but it was mine all the same. The burden that has to be passed from one generation to the next, from mother to daughter, world without end. The Engine's mission, which is now ours. And which may now finally be within reach of completion."

"Why mother? Why daughter? Every Pugface chief I ever saw was a man." Bess heard the anger in her voice. She fought to match Dima's calm with her own, but something was rising inside her that felt like panic.

"The engineer's blessing goes through the female line. It has to do with something called genetics, which is the way the child takes the imprint of its parents. I don't pretend to understand that part. My skill is with mechanisms, not living things. But because of the blessing the tools in that carpet bag answer to me when I call on them. And as you already saw Slim answers to me too. He belongs to me, by right of birth."

"Fuck that." Bess found her mouth was dry again, in spite of the water, in spite of the broth. She levered herself up on the elbow of her good arm so she could glare into Dima's face. "Try and take him. Go ahead."

"I believe I got some say in this," Slim said quietly.

"Yeah, partner, you do," Bess said. "But here we are surrounded by people that are her friends more than ours, and I ain't so sure she means to give either of us the choice."

"I'm here too," said Ghrent. "I may be old, but I can still fight. And my voice goes to the Rainmaker."

"Nobody is fighting." Dima spoke with weary patience, as if she were explaining all this to children. "It's strange how you always assume the worst of me, Bess. I could have taken Slim from you out in the desert. I could take him now. The fact that I didn't should give you some reassurance that I want us to find agreement. I want that very much. You helped to free me at Engine Point, and you helped me to get back my tools – which is the only thing that makes any of this possible. And you carry the engineer's gun, at a juncture when the fates seem to be addressing us so clearly it's almost as though they're speaking out loud. Believe me, the last thing I want to do is coerce you.

"But I'm trying to save the world, and that doesn't leave much room for sentiment. You know what the dream-towers do. You've seen it yourself. When they break down they drive people mad. And when they're functioning normally they do much the same, except that it's a madness everybody shares. They tell you what to think and what to feel. Who to love and who to hate. They're the reason why this whole country is trapped in an endless cycle of bloodshed and violence and suffering. And whether you believe me or not, Slim is the key to stopping all that."

Bess tried to break in, though she had nothing to offer but bitterness and resistance. It didn't even matter whether what Dima was saying was true. What mattered was to push back against it, because it seemed to her in that moment that it made a mockery, a nothing of her entire life. Of all the choices she had made, for bad or good. All her sins and all her strivings. But Dima's voice rose for the first time and the half-formed words died in Bess's throat. "You're full of anger, Dog-Bitch Bess, but you've pointed your anger at the wrong people. All the terrible things that must have happened to you, to make you the way you are, it was the dream-towers that did those things to you. They told the south to secede and the north to chastise them for it. They told you all to take up arms, the same way you'd done a thousand times before. They told Paulus Rondeau and all the others like him on both sides to be cruel and murderous and reckless. The towers are mechanisms for mind control, on a vast scale but still with minute precision. They wind you all up like clockwork toys and off you go, to war or to the conference chamber or to wherever you're supposed to be, and there isn't a thing you can do about it."

"But you can? Just you, and nobody else?" Bess managed a sneer but there was nothing behind it. The truth of Dima's words fell on her like a great weight. It was a thread that led all the way through the maze, an answer to the mysteries that had plagued her – the rusting weapons in the ground, the song of the dream-towers, the mindless plague. It was impossible, but everything about this situation was impossible. And if the dream-towers could steal the thoughts out of your head then why shouldn't they be able to put some new thoughts in there? She saw it, saw the truth of it, absurd and obscene but undeniable.

"The Pugface peoples are different," Dima said quietly. "The ones who made you didn't make us. All the Pugface clans were fashioned by the engineer himself, using the great crucibles that your makers – the Imperials – had left behind them. So the Pugface stand outside of the towers' control, and we're free to fight them while you bassari just fight among yourselves."

"I don't see you fighting," Bess said, feeling more sick and hollow with each breath. "When are you going to start fighting?"

"We never stopped," Dima said. "Not once in a thousand years. Listen to me, Bess. Stop butting your head against the truth and listen. The engineer was a hero, but he was just one man. He saw what needed to be done and he saw that he couldn't do it. It needed an army, and it needed an age.

"So he made us, and he sent us out into the world. He left us his tools, and enough information and instruction to finish what he started. We've been working steadily ever since. In every generation the engineer's chosen walks the land with this bag in her hand. Year after year she moves between the towers, catching the signals that are passed between them. Most of the time there aren't any. You can go for years without getting a single reading. But just lately it's gotten a lot easier. When one of the towers breaks down it loses a lot of stored data. The rest of the network sends copies of the missing code, so suddenly there are signals flashing back and forth in all directions. That's why I'm always to be found near the failing towers – not because I'm attacking them but because I'm catching that information on the fly."

"What for though?" Slim asked. "Why listen in on their conversations if you can't join in?"

Dima jumped on those words eagerly. A narrow band of light from the half-open tent flap crossed her face and made her eyes shine eerily in the near-dark. "That's the nub of it, Slim. We *can* join in. Send, as well as receive. At least that's what we're aiming for. The plan has always been to record the signals sent between the towers as often as we can, from every point of the compass. The access codes change every time, but they change according to a predetermined pattern. An algorithm. With a big enough database of recorded signals, the engineer believed, it ought to be possible to work backwards and recreate the algorithm. Then the towers would have to obey our commands. We could shut them down forever."

"But it's been a thousand years," Bess said, still looking for the holes in the argument. "If you haven't managed it after all this time, it's not likely you'll do it now."

"But now we've got something we didn't have before."

"And what's that?" But she knew the answer even as she asked.

Dima smiled a tight, cold smile. "The engineer."

The first story Bess ever heard about the Engine Everlasting was the story of his death, and by Holy John she'd heard it enough times since. Maybe a few times more than enough. But now Dima Saraband told it again, and this time was different because this time it was no legend but the plain truth.

The engineer, she said, had come to the end of his road. His friends, the warriors known to posterity as the twenty-three, were every last one of them dead. He knew he too was going to be dead soon, leaving his mission uncompleted, and that thought weighed heavy on him. So he chose to die on his own terms, and in a way that would give his children a little money in the bank.

The Flycatcher's CoIL scanner was – in Dima's almost incomprehensible idiom – read/write. It was able to access and translate the entire contents of the engineer's brain. Then it was able to make a perfect copy, a kind of ghost of the engineer, and put the copy in a place where it wouldn't degrade, wouldn't fade away when the engineer's body failed.

The process was agonising, and it was fatal. To get that degree of detail and accuracy the Flycatcher had to dig deep into the engineer's mind. All the way to the bottom of it, in fact. That process, the reading and recording of the man, took most of a day, and when it was finished the engineer was finished too. His body was a shell. There was so little left of his mind that he couldn't even regulate his own breathing. He died on the floor of that bare little shack in a place very close to the western ocean where he had made his final pact with the drone and the gun.

And the drone was gone too, in every sense that mattered. It had been a living thing, a self, but it had lost its mind in some terrible disaster. It was just a machine now, capable of executing simple commands but not of having opinions or desires of its own or remembering what was at stake here.

So this last and most important part was left to the gun. "Upload," it told the drone, and the drone by strict default did as it was told. It inscribed the copy of the engineer's mind on the gun's spare memory.

It was very nearly a disaster. A faithful copy of a mind, Dima said, is a very large thing indeed. They had beefed up the gun's memory with all the additional storage modules they could fit into it. They had estimated that there would be space enough, but their sums were shaky and the fit was a whole lot tighter than they'd anticipated. The gun's own mind was all but crowded out. It was left with imperfect recollections of the past and no empty space in which to lay new memories down. Before many years went by it had forgotten most of its own history, including the events that had brought it to this world and the fact that it had a passenger.

So the engineer lay dormant, and though he was never forgotten, the story of his great deeds eventually stopped being history, leached away into myth. And the gun was lost, as most things were lost in the course of century after century of ever-recycled chaos and conflict. The children of the engineer stayed true to their sacred mission, but they had nobody to report to. Nobody who could spin the flax of their raw data into the slender, precious thread of an algorithm.

And then Dima Saraband, having lost the tools that made her who she was, enslaved and brutalised and probably fairly close to a painful and undignified death, had met the outlaw Dog-Bitch Bess along with her fabled gun, Wakeful Slim. From the moment she saw the weapon she had wondered. It wasn't one of the Precursor artefacts her people had found and listed and eliminated from their search. It was something new, albeit also something very old indeed.

Then she had learned of Slim's faulty memory, and her wondering turned to eager speculation.

And at last she had laid him open, pored with delicacy and awe through his internal workings and found what she had almost given up hope of finding. There was no damage! Slim's lost memories had no mechanical cause. It was all but certain therefore that he was that long-lost 507m that held the gigantic, destabilising cargo of the engineer's living mind. His amnesia was the result not of a firefight in some distant past but of the hidden presence, the passenger who slept inside him and took up most of the available space there.

The wheel of time – whether it was a wagon wheel or a mill wheel or some other damn kind of wheel – had come full circle. The plans laid down a thousand years before were now coming to fruition. "All we need to do," Dima said, "is to wake the engineer and give him the data we've collected. Let him sift it and find the algorithm." For the first time her mask of calm logic slipped. There was a hunger in her eyes that was too strong for her to hide.

"Well, it don't sound like much when you put it like that," Bess allowed. She put some effort into getting the words out. She was still turning in her mind the idea that her thoughts had never been her own, that along with everyone else she'd ever met she was no more than an actor speaking lines and playing a part. Even though she was sitting on the ground a kind of vertigo had taken hold on her, a sense that she was standing on a cliff edge with a very long way to fall. "And you're saying if we don't do this then the war will come again?"

"Imminently. As I said, the gaps have been getting shorter. On current showing you can expect the fighting to start up again within the next year. Most likely before the winter comes. What do you say, Bess?"

"It don't matter what I say. It's Slim that gets to call this."

"And I'd be fine with it," Slim said, "only there's one thing that's troubling me."

"Go ahead."

"Well, I believe I know how data works. It ain't a word that's in general use around these parts but it's right there in my technical specifications along with a whole bunch of stuff about how big my memory is and how quick I can get to it. Stuff that's probably all bunkum because of the new bits and pieces that was put inside of me. Am I right about that, Miss Saraband?"

"Absolutely."

"And the measure of memory is how much of this data it can hold."

"Yes, Slim. Of course."

"And if I say yes to this, you're fixing to pour a whole lot more data into me. All the measurements you been taking in this place and that place, over the last ... well, you said a thousand years, but I guess you just said that because it was a nice round number. Could be more, could be less, but I guess it's got to be a whole great heap of measurements you took in all that time. Tens of thousands? Hundreds of thousands?"

"Something on that order," Dima agreed.

"And you'll pour all that new data into me, and then what? Wake up the engineer inside of me so he can work out what's what?"

"Yes. Exactly that."

"Shit!" Bess explained, seeing at last where Slim was going with this.

"Well then, I got a question. Right now I can remember up to about six years back. What's gonna be left to me after you put all this new stuff into me? Six months? Six days? Six hours? I hope you can see why that's kind of a problem for me."

Dima said nothing to this, but her face spoke pretty loudly on her behalf. She looked like someone who'd shaken out their shoe and found not just one rattlesnake in there but a whole family of them. Everyone waited for her to speak. She considered with herself, eyes cast down, and at last she nodded.

"There could be a storage issue," she admitted.

"Well, let's talk about that then, because I hope you'll allow it's no small thing from where I'm standing. If I'm kicked out of my own thoughts to make room for all them numbers, do I get to come back after your engineer's done what's needful?"

"Most likely not."

"Then it's no," Bess announced. "We ain't doing this."

"You said it was Slim's decision," Dima said quickly. "It's his consent I'm asking for, not yours."

"And if I say no?" Slim asked. "What happens then?"

Dima only shook her head. "You won't say no, Slim. You belong to him, just like I do. This is what you're for. This is what you've always been for."

"John fuck it!" Bess growled. "Let him answer."

But before he could the tent's entrance flap was thrown open again. An Ajuparo warrior stood four-square in the gap. He spoke in his own tongue, a few words barked out. His hands moved at the same time, presumably saying the same thing in voke-chant. Dima swore and scrambled to her feet. Ghrent was slower, being so much older, but he was only a moment or two behind her.

"What is it?" Bess demanded. "What's happening?"

"Soldiers." Dima spat out the word like a curse. "Men in cavalry uniforms. They've come looking for you, but they can't know for sure that you're here. Don't move, Bess. Don't step one foot outside this tent or the signal from the darts will go live again and we'll have the whole Pursuit Force coming down on us. Let me deal with this."

She strode out of the tent.

"Don't worry, Rainmaker," Ghrent said, pausing at the tent's entrance. "I won't let them near you."

Then he too was gone. "Well, goddamn it," Bess said, and tried to scramble up to follow them. But her right leg was as stiff as a board, and with her left arm in a sling standing up would be a complicated operation.

She managed it anyway, laboriously and slowly, rolling onto her right side and then levering herself half upright. She crossed the floor in a series of squirming sideways shuffles. But she stopped with her hand half raised to the tent flap. Dima was right, damn her. There was nothing Bess could do here that wouldn't make things worse. She was tied to that damned carpet bag by an invisible string. And if the string happened to break, Rondeau would know exactly where she was.

She swore again, much more profanely and with a lot more feeling.

Benjamin Hornblower Southern had never wanted to be a soldier, but nobody had asked his opinion at any point and so here he was.

Maybe it was that damn middle name, with its connotations of cavalry charges and reveilles. Maybe it was just that as the eighth child in a litter of twelve he'd grown up in a world where most of the decent options had already been taken. His brothers Harry and Quentin had followed their father into the family's ironmongery and chandlery business. His sister Victoria and brother Francis had gone into the church and the law respectively, the one as a lay preacher and the other as a server of summonses. Mark, Andrew and Helen made a good living as runners for a betting syndicate, with Andrew also doing a little light debt-collecting and leg-breaking on the side.

Young Ben could have followed any of them, but he wasn't particularly encouraged to. There were three other siblings coming up behind him and the ones above were chary of their little fiefdoms. They were very far from wanting to do any favours for family. So he carved his own way, which was picking pockets and petty theft until the recruiting sergeant came through Paxen with a big drum sounding at his back and offered up the possibility of serving his country, with all the concomitant glory and distinction and (since it was peacetime) only the very smallest chance of ever being shot at.

So Ben had taken the shilling and signed his name, and three weeks later the States' Union was at war with the goddamned south. So he'd been shot at a whole lot, and fired back a whole lot more. He'd shed enough blood to go through three separate crises, the first of fear and physical nausea, the second of guilt and spiritual desolation, the third a kind of emotional anaesthesia. In the last year of the war the part of him that experienced joy and pain and dismay and compassion and love and lust and all the rest of it had just gotten overloaded and shut itself down. Ben Southern, aged twenty-five, had become (in his own mind at least) a kind of statue or scarecrow, a thing that looked enough like a man to fool a casual glance but actually had no trace of actual humanity in it.

When the war ended he stayed in the army because it was no

worse than anywhere else he could go and it saved him the effort of choosing. He was offered a place in the Extended Pursuit Force because some superior officer mistook his profound anomie for quiet competence. It was easy work for the most part. He didn't mind the killings when they came and he didn't mind the long, dull treks in between. It was all one to him.

If there was one small chink in the armour of his unfeelingness it was five-cent novels. Joshua & Cable Incorporated, of Haut Paxen, publishers and purveyors of fine periodicals, put out twenty or thirty of these things every month, enough to keep the keenest appetite supplied. Most were lurid stories about circus roustabouts, professional wrestlers, romantic entanglements and the lives of notorious criminals. Southern's favourites took place right out here at the frontier. Their protagonists were prospectors, railway navigators, frontiersmen, Pugface-fighters, smugglers and blockade-runners. Southern found that the feelings he could no longer access in relation to his own life came easily and strongly when he was immersed in a story. A doomed romance could make him cry. A tale of frontier skirmishes could thrill and exercise him to the point where he almost pissed himself.

And now here he was, out on the frontier, in the country where so many of those over-coloured epics were set. For the first time in years he felt that unused part of himself stir in its sleep. He began to feel things again. Mostly he felt as though he was the hero in one of those stories, and he was determined to live up to the role.

He rode into the Pugface village at the head of his small column, wearing a face of cold detachment but conscious of the mantle of power and destiny that sat on his shoulders. To call this shit-hole a village was overstating things, really. There were no permanent structures here, only a cluster of a couple of dozen tents with fire-pits and clothes lines in between. The sharp-houses varied in height from eight to twenty feet, many with their support poles jutting much higher still, so there was no order or uniformity to be seen – only randomness and chaos. Most of the lodges were faced with katy scales but some were bare canvas or leather. Desert dust lay thick on everything. The Pugfaces, men and women and children all alike, stared up at Southern and his men as they wound their way through the encampment, their naked faces full of stupid sullenness. It was hard to see them as people, or to think of this sprawl of filth as a place where people could live.

"Rifles at the ready," Southern ordered. "We're serious men on serious business. Let's not leave these fuckers in any doubt about that." There was a general sound of rustling and scuffling and the pulling back of hammers. The nearest Pugfaces stepped back hastily, which was a gratifying thing to see. Like the heroes of all those five-cent stories Southern was the embodiment of strength and self-reliance, a still, small centre of order and meaning in a slipshod world.

"Bring me your chief!" he called out in a ringing voice. "Your headman. Come, come, come! Don't waste my time or you'll be fucking sorry for it."

When they were more or less in the centre of the ring of sharphouses a small delegation came out to meet them. Front and centre was a man who was obviously the chief. He was in early middle age and extremely tall, standing proud in a huge feathered headdress whose densely embroidered side-straps hung down past his waist. Multiple strings of beads and shells hung across his chest, and a loincloth of undyed cotton hid his balls. His sandals were made of katy-leather, and that was it for his clothes. Evidently when you wore the big hat it didn't matter if from the neck down you looked like a goddamned hobo.

To either side of him were a handful of warriors – maybe ten or a dozen in all – who looked like pretty serious fighters. Solidly built, their bare arms corded with muscle, spears held upright in their hands, knives and hand-axes at their waists. Better shut that down right away, Southern decided.

"I am Askus Erato," the chief said. "What do you want here?"

"Good to meet you, chief," Southern said, sliding down out of his saddle. "Since you ask, this here is a peacekeeping mission. So we'd be obliged if your men could lay aside their spears and such. We're all friends, ain't we? And you and yours aren't looking to have any kind of a set-to with the States' cavalry."

"What kind of mission?" the chief asked. His States' Common was heavily accented but it was clear enough to follow. He didn't give any order to his people and their grip on their spears didn't shift. More Pugface warriors were moving in on the little group of mounted men from either side and a few from behind.

"We're looking for a fugitive," Southern said. "A wicked person on the run from the law. And I'm gonna say it again, chief, just to be clear. You tell your men to put their weapons down on the ground and step a little ways back from them. I don't know if you've seen what a military rifle can do at this kind of range – been a while since yours and mine had any dealings of that kind – but I assure you it ain't a pretty thing. We want to keep the conversation polite, now don't we?"

The chief seemed to consider. He raised his hands, and Southern's own hand slipped automatically to the grip of his pistol. But all the chief did was to reel off a few orders in that sign language of theirs. The men on either side went down on one knee and laid their spears on the ground. A moment later the other warriors who'd come to crowd around all did the same.

"Knives too while you're at it," Southern said. "Axes. Clubs. Bows. Anything you got that might make my men here feel like they need to shoot someone. You know how it is in these tense situations."

The Pugface men unshipped their weapons and set them down. It was a goodly haul, Southern saw. There were even one or two revolvers to be seen in among the chipped-flint daggers and stone-headed throwing axes. Probably he would confiscate the revolvers before he left. They might be fairly traded but they were just as likely to be stolen and in any case the Pugface were prohibited from owning them. He was the law here, after all. He had a duty to live up to.

"Okay," he said. "Good. That's good. Now like I said, we're just looking for the one thing here and as soon as we've got what we came for we'll be on our way. No fuss, no trouble, no need for anyone to get hurt."

"A fugitive," the chief said non-committally. "I believe that means a wicked man."

"No, sir," Southern said. "A wicked woman. The wickedest you ever saw. She's dog-kin, just like me. Not as pretty as me, obviously, but the same stock. She's got a real ugly face. Burned by fire a while ago and covered in scars. Ain't no way you could miss her if you've seen her. So that's my next question. Did she wander in here, all wounded? Beg you to take her in out of pity for her spilled blood? Ain't no shame if she did, and if you said yes on account of feeling sorry for her and all. But she's wanted and now you got to give her up."

"We have not seen her," said the chief.

"That so?" Southern nodded grimly. "Then I guess you won't mind if we turn all these tents of yours upside down and see what falls out of them."

"We have not seen her," the chief said again. "Do what you must."

And Southern decided right there and then, seeing that it wasn't going to go easy, that he would make it as hard as he could.

Crouching in the half-dark of the tent with her face up close to a skinny little gap in the entrance flap, Bess tried to make sense of what was happening outside. All she could see were the backs and lower legs of some Ajuparo men and women who had come out of their lodges to stand in the day's heat. She saw no sign of the soldiers, but some of the raised voices that reached her had the unmistakeable ring of arrogant men spitting out orders. She debated with herself whether to try opening the flap a little wider, but there was no way of knowing who or what was lurking just outside her line of sight. So she waited there with her teeth clenched together, holding tight onto Slim in the only hand she had that was working, which was the wrong one.

"Bess," Slim said at length.

"Right here, partner," she murmured.

"I hate to break your attention at a time like this, but there's a conversation the two of us need to be having and it don't look like we got a whole lot of time left to do it in."

"Save it," Bess said. "As soon as these chickenshits ride on, you and me are out of here. Dima can try out her damn stories on the next greenhorns to come along."

"Yeah," Slim said. "Yeah, I guess that's so." He sounded tired. And he sounded like he didn't believe a single word of that katy-shit. Which was fair enough in Bess's opinion because she'd known it for katy-shit when she said it.

She closed her eyes. For a few breaths, a few heartbeats, she said nothing, only listened to the rise and fall of the voices outside. She had a solid feeling that what she said next would be irrevocable, the cementing into place of something that had been growing in her and all round about her ever since she closed the door of her cabin in the hills outside of Salt Lick and headed west. She was running out of road. She and Slim both, they were running out of road, and it seemed clear now that this had been the case for a good long while. Maybe the two of them had been the last to notice.

"Slim," she said.

"Yes, Bess?"

"Would this talk you want to have concern the engineer?"

"Yeah, it would. You got something to say on that subject your own self?"

"Maybe I do."

"Give it a name then."

Bess shook her head. "You first. You're right at the heart of all this. I'm just the goober who picked you up."

"Yeah, but you know how it is, Bess." That weariness was still there in Slim's voice, along with a wry amusement. "It's built into me to give good service. To let the one that's carrying me decide what gets done with me, on account of a gun that only shoots at whatever it sees fit to is somewhat problematic. I'd be obliged if you was to set the ball rolling, so to speak."

Bess still had her eyes shut tight. She chose her words like someone walking on rain-slick stepping stones across a torrent. "Well then, if I'm honest, there's a thing that's been sitting heavy on my mind a little, ever since we heard that old ghost speak up out of Dima's carpet bag."

"And what would that be?"

"You sure you want me to speak out first?"

"I'm sure."

"Well then, it's this, partner. It ain't an easy thing for me to get my head around, but here's what I been thinking. Once upon a time, a long time gone now, before your memory started to roll itself up behind you like it does . . . there was another Wakeful Slim. One that didn't have that curse on him. He was you, but he was you with a lot more space to think in and a whole great roomful of memories to draw on, stretching right back to when you was first forged."

"I guess there was at that. Kind of wish I could have met that gentleman."

He was inviting her to laugh, but Bess pressed on. If she stopped she might not be able to start up again. "And if that carpet-bag ghost is to be believed . . ."

"I don't think he was lying, Bess."

"I don't think so either, partner. I'm just saying if, is all. If he's to be believed then the old Slim, the one you used to be, he gave up that roomful of memories, that big piece of himself, of his own free will. Didn't feel like he was ill used or forced into it or anything."

"That's my thinking too."

"And he did it so that . . ." The words dried up. Bess opened her eyes again. This respite wasn't going to last much longer and once it was over they were going to have to call it one way or the other.

"He did it so this could happen," Slim finished. "So the engineer could come back when he was needed and get on with that plan the two of them cooked up together. Or the three of them including the silver bird, or whatever number you want to put on it because I guess you got to count all them others that died along the way. Now I'm the last of them that's left except for him, and he can only come back if I let him."

"Or if Dima forces the issue," Bess said scrupulously. "Though I guess she meant it when she said she wants you to choose. She's had plenty of chances to take what she wants."

"I think I already made my choice." Slim said. "I think I made it a long time ago."

"You're not bound by that, though."

"Well, I am and I ain't. There was a promise made. A commitment. And it was me that made it, even if I don't have the remembering of it any more. What's left is to honour my own word or else go back on it. And now I'm picturing it that way I don't see more than the one way out of it."

"Me neither," Bess said. Tears welled up inside her but with her old injuries still stopping up her eyes they didn't have anywhere to go. They just rose and rocked like a tide.

"And that being so," Slim went on, "I got a favour to ask you."

"Go on, Slim."

"I'd take it real kindly if you was to stay with me until it's over. This might be the last thing I ever do. I mean, depending how much of me that new data pushes out when it comes in. It could be like . . ." There was a pause, long enough for Bess to have drawn a breath but she held it and waited. "It could be the road rolling up all the way at last, so there's nothing left of me and I just go out like a shithouse candle."

"Slim—"

"I don't want to go there alone, Bess. That's the truth of it. I want someone with me that knows me, even if it's only to say my name when I've forgotten it. I know it ain't fair to ask. With Rondeau right on your tail it might be better for you to get to running again."

"I ain't got any running left in me," Bess said, her throat tight.

"I'm going where you go, partner." And maybe make an end of all this at last, she thought but didn't say. Make an accounting for all the deaths she had on her tally; for Martha's death, which stood right at the head of that list. Slim wasn't the only one that owed a debt to the past. He was just the only one whose debt was an honourable one.

"There's one thing though," she said, pulling her mind away from these grim thoughts with an effort. "Where I go, that son of a cunt Rondeau will follow. Having me along might make it harder for you to keep your promise."

"Maybe so," Slim said. "But I reckon it's the both of us he wants in any case, and once he's finished with you he's as like as not to come looking for me. Better we face him down together."

"We'll need to—" Bess began, but the sharp retort of a pistol shot cut through her words.

A strange mood had settled on Sergeant Southern – what he could only describe as a five-cent kind of phenomenon. The things he was doing and saying still felt like they belonged to him, but at the same time they had the rich, lurid flavour of over-coloured fiction. A man had to live up to a feeling like that, a moment like this one was, else he might just as well tend the counter in a grocery store somewhere or clean the floors in a saloon.

"You're absolutely sure you never seen her?" he asked the chief one last time, because that made three times in all and three times had the right ring to it. "A dog woman with a burned-out face, fur kind of mud-wallow brown or maybe a bit lighter, like a shit that didn't come out right? That don't jog your memory at all?"

"No," was all the chief said.

Southern scratched his chin in a pantomime of rueful cogitation. "Well, I'm right sorry to hear that," he said. "But hey, it's only you that's saying it and there's a whole lot of other folk present. Might be someone else caught a glimpse of her. What do you think?"

"I think not."

"Shame." Southern made as if to leave. He was playing up to this now, relishing it even, conscious that all the people present were totally focused on him and waiting on his word. He put a hand on his chafer's back as if he was about to vault up into the saddle, but then at the last moment he turned again to face the chief.

"I tell you what, though," he said affably. "After we've come all this way out here, and after I busted up your day and all, I'd just about hate to go back again to my commander and tell him I got nothing to show for it. So here's an idea. Let's have all these fine men here stand in a line in front of me." He pointed to the chief's honour guard of young, strong men, all now unarmed, all staring into the barrels of a dozen loaded rifles. "A long, straight line, right around here." He dug the heel of his boot into the dust and twisted it around to make a mark. "Come on now. It's just the one question, and I promise I won't ask anyone twice."

None of the men moved. Southern didn't unship his own rifle but he thumbed the safety of his revolver. That made thirteen guns. If every man here were to rush them all at once this might get a little awkward, but he reckoned enough of them would die in the first volley to give his men a winning edge – especially since the Pugfaces would have to stop long enough to grab their spears again, or else fight bare-handed.

The chief must have been thinking much the same thing. He spoke to his people, again with gestures rather than with words. Southern considered shooting him first off to make a point, but that was liable to complicate things where getting answers was concerned. What he had in mind was better.

The Pugface men all lined up as he'd ordered, leaving their spears and knives behind them on the ground. With a few terse orders Southern had his men spread out to the edges of the open space between the sharp-houses. Mr Fleetfoot's patented rifled carbines really were a wonder, combining rapid repeat fire with superlative short-range accuracy. If the Pugfaces tried anything now it would be a massacre. A katy shoot.

So it was time to get down to business.

Southern strolled on over to the end of the line where he locked eyes with the first Pugface man, a damn big bruiser with a face like a slab of meat on a griddle. The man stared back at him levelly, though Southern thought maybe he could see just a little unease in back of all that stolidness.

"You speak Common?" he demanded.

The man nodded.

"And you heard what I asked your chief there? About this dog woman with the burned face?"

Another nod.

"Excellent. So tell me, did you see her?"

"No," the man said sonorously.

"Pity," Southern said, and shot him.

It was a head shot, an instant kill. The man fell to the ground as heavy as a sack of cornmeal, making a solid thump as he hit the dirt. A keening wail went up from everyone else in the clearing, except for the chief who scowled hard and kept his mouth shut. A true leader of men, Southern thought with contemptuous amusement. Knows when he's beat and keeps his head down because maybe if he's well behaved he'll live to walk away.

He moved on to the second man.

"I can't stand still for this," Bess said. "I got to go out there."

"And do what?" Slim came back at her. "Bess, I count a dozen guns. And you can't shoot with a broken arm. Only thing you can do is get yourself gunned down."

Which was true, more likely than not. But at least when she was down the rest of this katy-shit would stop. She didn't think about it any further than that. She got her good leg under her, gripped the edge of the tent flap with her right hand and dragged herself to her feet.

With one man down and the hammer cocked on the second, Sergeant Southern was settling in for the long haul when Dog-Bitch Bess herself stepped out of one of the bigger sharp-houses in back of the chief.

He'd never seen her before but there was no mistaking who she was, just as there was no mistaking the Precursor gun she was holding in her hand. Every rifle swung around to point at her, and Southern almost loosed a bullet as the shock of seeing her there made every muscle in his body twitch.

But she was pointing her gun at the ground, not at him, and she didn't make any move to lift it up.

"Hey," she called out. "You. Lackwit. It's me you're looking for, so stop killing people you don't even fucking know."

Southern was nonplussed for a moment or two, but as soon as he got over that he was elated. He'd drawn the ace after all. He was the one who would bring the Dog-Bitch in to face States' justice. Not sneaking, smirking Alex Tooth. Not Paulus Rondeau with his fancy high collars and his sassy tongue. Nope, the hero of this five-cent epic was good old Ben Southern.

But if he was going to be the hero then he had to keep the centre of the stage, and with Bess's sudden appearance something had shifted. Everyone was looking at her, not at him. Southern felt he needed to redress that balance. And since there was no risk, since the renegade wasn't even trying to defend herself, he eased the hammer back down and lowered his pistol like a man who knows he's already won the day. "Well now," he said in a ringing voice. "Look who we got here. We're in the company of a legend, boys. An actual, goddamned legend, no more and no less. The woman that rode with Tom Blue's Braggarts and fucked every last man of them along the road. The woman that slaughtered her way from Orselian all the way to Mundy's Field and never took a scratch. The last of her filthy, shameless breed that's still standing on God's earth. This here is history being made, boys. It's a pity there ain't a camera here to catch it, because it's a moment we're all gonna want to remember in our old age."

"We're gonna be old before you finish talking at this rate," the dog-woman retorted. "Fuck's sake, man, take me in or shoot me down. Either way, don't make me swallow any more of your spit."

Southern threw out his arms in a sweeping gesture. "Oh, but you got to allow this ain't any ordinary proceeding. This is retribution, Dog-Bitch Bess. This is righteousness. This is where all the innocents you killed and maimed get to—" He stopped in the middle of his peroration, or maybe before the middle. He had been in an expansive mood and there was no telling how long he might have talked for. But he was cut short by the arrow that had appeared in the centre of his chest. Instead of the next word he just made a sound that was kind of like a hiccup. Then two more arrows arrived right on the heels of the first but from different directions, embedding themselves more or less at the same time in his shoulder and his lower back. Abruptly and without any warning at all the air was thick with them, pouring into the clearing from all sides. Considering how many shafts there were it was kind of a miracle how few actually hit home. But it was enough.

Southern sank down on his knees, eyes wide with shock. Around him the men of his short-lived command were falling too, some of them only hit once or twice, others so feathered with arrows they looked like half-moulted porcupines. There was a brief, staggered volley of rifle fire as their fingers tightened on the triggers they'd already been tickling, but it didn't seem to Southern that they hit anything very much, or even knew what they were aiming at.

Two things occurred to him in quick succession. One was that in all the weapons that had been laid down he hadn't seen a single bow. The other, arising out of the first, was that perhaps he shouldn't have been so dead fixed on the Ajuparo menfolk that he forgot to ask where their women were.

The women moved out into the circle now, stepping in from behind the ring of sharp-houses where they'd been waiting all this while with longbows in their capable hands. The woman who led them looked out of place somehow, maybe because her skin was dark brown instead of raw, violent pink. There was also an old man in their midst with wild white hair and a scowl of austere concentration on his face. He was the only one there with a gun in his hand, and it seemed like everywhere he pointed one of the Reapers fell down dead.

Had all these people moved on a prearranged signal or had they just chosen their moment, taking advantage of Dog-Bitch Bess's so conveniently drawing all the soldiers' attention? There was no way of knowing now, and Southern supposed it didn't matter. He'd played a strong hand badly and here he was.

A sharp pain in his lower back told him he'd just taken another hit. He slumped from his knees down onto his stomach, the weight of his body as he fell snapping the shaft of the first arrow in half and driving what was left of it even deeper into the flesh and sinews of his chest. He tried to cry out but his mouth turned out to be too full of blood for any sound to make it through.

The women were laying down their bows now and picking up the menfolk's discarded knives. They moved among the fallen, slitting throats with calm and methodical address. The old man played his part here too. He was carrying some kind of baton or gewgaw and there was a tame scorpillon trotting at his side. He waved the baton to tell the scorpillon where to strike. Its docked tail rose and fell like a pestle in a milkmaid's churn, cracking skulls with every blow.

Through the haze of pain and deepening shock Southern realised that he still had his pistol in his hand. The dark-skinned woman was down on one knee dispatching another man with her back turned to him, only a few feet away. He raised the gun, though his arm felt like it weighed as much as a planet. He had no need to aim when she was so close. It would be impossible to miss.

A booted foot trod hard on his arm, forcing his hand and the gun back down. At his grunt of pain the woman turned and saw him. "Oh," was all she said.

"Yeah," Dog-Bitch Bess agreed, looming over Southern. "Old habits die hard, I guess. These greencoat bastards always did prefer the kind of fight where the other feller is looking away." She kicked Southern's gun out of his slack grip and bent down laboriously beside him. "Colonel Rondeau anywhere hereabouts?" she asked him.

"To hell with you," Southern managed. It wasn't as stirring a speech as most of his five-cent heroes managed, but it would have to do.

The renegade tilted her head one way, then the other. "To hell with both of us, most like," she said. "I guess I'll be joining you there presently."

She pressed the barrel of her terrifying Precursor gun against his temple.

Rondeau heard that single shot from three miles out, and he knew exactly what it meant. The echoing, percussive boom hadn't come from any regulation pistol or revolver. That was a Precursor weapon at work.

He already knew he'd made the wrong call. A few moments earlier the signals from the Reaper's darts had started up again, a tight little cluster of them all in the one place, which was just exactly the right bearing and distance for the village where he'd sent Southern's party. Dog-Bitch Bess was there. And it seemed she'd made short work of Southern and his men.

He was only halfway through his own search, his men moving quickly through the sharp-houses while the Pugfaces all lay face down on the ground and said not a word, cowed by the shiny new rifles and the grim-faced men who were wielding them. Rondeau called his squad to order now, got them in the saddles and formed up, and set off hell for leather to the north. Hopefully Alex Tooth would have heard the shooting too and would be coming down to add his weight to the proceedings.

But one way or another this chase was over. Dog-Bitch Bess had broken cover. There was no way in hell he could lose her now.

* * *

Bess straightened again, wincing at the pain from her broken arm and more than a few other places. Around her the last of the Pursuit Force were being efficiently dispatched: no visible threat remained, but she kept Slim in her hand as she waited and she scanned the spaces between the sharp-houses in case there was any sign there of more riders coming.

The Ajuparo warrior who'd been shot lay almost at her feet, his blind eyes staring at the sky. Nobody had come yet to claim him. Did he have no family here, nobody to weep for him? Bess felt an urge to apologise to him for the violent death she'd trailed across his path just by coming here.

It was strange to her, and not at all pleasant, to discover so late in her life that a stranger's passing could have so much weight. She had been responsible for a great many in her time and walked away from most of them unconcerned. Now she found that she was carrying this new burden, and she was afraid of what it might mean. If all the many greencoat soldiers and Parity men and women she'd killed came to sit on her shoulders she'd never walk again.

Dima was still moving among the prone bodies, knife in hand. She didn't turn to face Bess until she'd made doubly sure that nobody had been overlooked. There was so much gore on her face and arms and on the front of her shift as she stood there that she looked like a spectre rising from the sundered breast of one of the dead. She didn't even bother to wipe her blade, just tucked it away all red and dripping. Through a mask of blood she gave Bess a thunderous scowl.

"I told you to stay in the tent," she said. "I wish you'd listened."

"And maybe I'd have done that if you'd told me what your play was going to be," Bess snapped back, grief making her angry. "All I could see from in there was a bunch of people about to get themselves killed on my behalf, and I didn't care to let that stand."

For a moment or two they just stood and glared at each other. At last Dima shrugged. "There's no helping it now," she said. "And I still need an answer."

"Well, then the answer's yes," Bess said.

"I need Slim to—"

"That's yes from both of us. But it's both of us you got. You want him, you take me. Now where are we going? Because I reckon we better go there fast."

"The Telos," Dima said. "It's just on the other side of the lake. But . . . Bess, if you come along Rondeau is bound to follow you."

"Yeah," Bess agreed. "I know it."

Dima looked shocked. Her brow furrowed. "You'd risk the whole world for this? For Slim's sake? Because that's what you're doing."

"I guess I know that too."

"So what will you do when Rondeau comes?"

"What the hell do you think I'll do? I'll deal with him."

A voice called out from somewhere over to her left, on the outskirts of the little ring of tents. Then a second voice took up the cry. "Riders," Mur Ghrent translated, appearing at Bess's side. "From the south. And from the north. The ones coming from the north are closer. And they're none of them more than a few minutes away."

Of course, Bess thought. The dead men on the ground weren't even a half of the Pursuit Force's strength. It was only to be expected that the rest of them would be somewhere close by. She felt her shoulders slump as that hard truth settled on her. "Well, then I guess that changes things," she said grimly. "Okay, Dima, I guess you get to have your way after all."

"Bess, no," Slim said. "Where you go, I go. We already decided."

"Yeah, but now there ain't no going anywhere." Bess unholstered Slim, raised him up close to her face. "We're cut off from both sides and we got nothing at our backs but water. I already brought death down on this place, and I'm right sorry for it. I'll go meet Rondeau halfway. It ain't like I'm being noble or anything. He's gonna be in here like a fox in a henhouse any moment, and win or lose it's gonna be all kinds of bloody. I might as well give him what he wants, and hope he's satisfied with that. You go with Dima and keep that promise you made."

"No!" There was panic and anguish in Slim's voice. "I'll keep my promise if you keep yours, Bess. We stick together. I . . . I don't want to go down into that dark all by myself. Please!"

Ksaia Hannuz, standing next to the chief, exchanged words with him in a muttered undertone. He nodded, and then he spoke. Bess already knew that he could speak States' Common from the conversation he'd had with the late sergeant, but now he used his own tongue.

"He says he doesn't blame you for the death," Ksaia translated. "He says he knows who you are, and why you came here."

"I fucking doubt that," Bess said, "seeing as how I don't know it my own self." Once again she felt the pressure of those unshed tears. "Slim, I'm sorry I won't be there with you after all, but if I was to hold onto you now I'd just be delivering you into Paulus Rondeau's hands. I don't think that's something either of us would like to see."

"I ain't leaving you, Bess. That's the long and short of it."

The chief spoke again, and again it was to Ksaia rather than Bess. But before Ksaia could parse his words he turned to Bess. "Our ways have crossed before," he said, "a long time ago, when you rode with Thomas Blue. But we did not talk then or properly meet. You are the dog-woman, Bess, who would not make peace with the green riders. All their hate is bent on you, but you still stand. You carry the Engine's gun, and he names you friend. You brought our women back to us after they were stolen by the faithless *provedores*. You are welcome in the houses of my people forever. And I mean to do you service now."

"Yeah, well, you can't," Bess said. "Thank you. Thank you, chief, for them kind words and for taking me in here when I was wounded and helpless and all. Thanks for putting your own self and your own people on the line for me. I reckon we're quit-all on that score, or else it's me that's owing you. But there's nothing you can do now. Nothing any of us can do. And this ain't your fight anyway. It's mine."

The chief shook his head. "No. The fight has been ours since long before you were born, dog woman Bess. It was ours when the world was young. And now, the Engine's daughter tells me, it may finally be coming to an end. I won't begrudge you a piece of this struggle, but the rest I will keep for myself and for my people. It was always meant to come to this. A day of blood to cleanse the wounds of the world. I cannot go where you go, but I can still help you and Dima Saraband to complete the work of all the ages. There is no greater glory."

"You don't understand!" Bess was impatient now. She felt . . . What did she feel? The pressure of past sins coming home. The closing of the circle. A part of her even welcomed it, though she was sorry past all words that she wouldn't be with Slim at the end. "Chief Erato, you heard that as well as I did. There's States' cavalry on their way here right now. Paulus Rondeau is coming at us from north and south at once."

Inexplicably, the chief smiled at this. "Then you should go west, dog woman Bess."

Rondeau slowed his men to a canter as they approached the Ajuparo encampment. He wanted to get the lay of the place before he rode in there. It would be prudent to fire a few volleys from a distance to soften up any resistance the Pugface might offer, but not if any of Southern's men were still alive in there.

While he was still trying to resolve that conundrum he felt a sudden tug on the part of his mind that was still attuned to the Reaper's signals. "Well, God damn and fuck it!" he exclaimed.

The signal that represented Dog-Bitch Bess had been static ever since he first sensed it, but now it was on the move. And it wasn't heading either south towards Rondeau or north into the waiting arms of Alex Tooth and his men. No, it was moving west – out across the lake!

Rondeau didn't know whether to laugh or curse. This fucking woman had more tricks in her than any ten men he'd hunted. He wheeled his chafer around and tore off to the south again, quickening his pace until he was once more at a full gallop. The north end of the lake was hemmed in by impassible mountains but at the southern end there was just desert and scrub stretching down to the Matalessen gulf. However Bess was making that crossing, she'd bought herself an hour, maybe two. After that he would be on her again, and this time he wouldn't underestimate her. As soon as she was in his sights he would kill her, and claim Wakeful Slim as the spoils of the kill right after.

"Hey, Rose," he called out to Corporal Peter J. Rosebush who was riding on his right hand, "give me an all-together." Rosebush put his bugle to his lips and sounded the assembly: for all that he was hunched over his saddle, holding tight on account of the break-neck pace they were keeping up, the sound came out loud and clear and sweet.

Good enough, Rondeau thought. Alex Tooth might even make it to the party if he was quick enough.

But Tooth had his own problems. He heard the bugle call and knew what it meant. Instead of haring into the Ajuparo village that had been Ben Southern's target he came out wide to circle around it and join his chief over to the south.

The Ajuparo, however, seemed to have other ideas. A raiding party of about twenty warriors riding their chafers bareback in the plains manner spilled out from the little cluster of tents to meet Tooth's column and head them off.

Tooth was not a coward, but if there was a choice between a questionable engagement and a safe retreat he generally went for the prudent option. He veered a little further away from the oncoming riders, and at the same time shouted an order to the men of his own command. "Single volley! Teach them some manners, boys!"

A barrage of shots rang out, and three or four of the Pugface fell at once. Tooth thought that ought to be enough to make them reconsider their options, but they still came on. More fool them,

Tooth thought grimly. And he was just about to order the free fire when the man next to him was flung sidelong off his chafer's back. Tooth turned to stare, seeing the man – Billy Chamber, one of the Pursuit Force's trackers – roll over and over in the dust. The retort of the rifle that had killed him reached Tooth's ears only then, after he had already registered that the man was dead.

That the Ajuparo might have rifles too was a possibility that simply hadn't occurred to him. He knew nothing about the fate of Ben Southern's contingent, after all. He was expecting only spears and arrows, and he hadn't been intending to come within range of either.

A second man fell, and his riderless chafer was hit a moment later. The animal collapsed, all of its many legs splaying out wide. Tooth had to spur his own chafer into an unplanned vault over the two bodies. He was lifted clean out of his saddle at the apex of the jump but slammed right back into it when he touched down again. Damn if that hadn't been close!

"Free fire!" he bellowed, over the booming of yet more guns. "Cut them down!"

Which was sound advice, but the cutting down was going both ways now and the Pugface riders were close enough that Tooth could see their faces. In the vanguard was a man who seemed to be a chief in full regalia, holding not a rifle but a spear whose shaft was longer than his whole body. A spear couched like a lance.

Win or lose, Tooth wasn't going to be rejoining the main column any time soon. He had enough to do trying to stay alive.

They ran to the shore, if you could call it running. Bess's gait was a kind of rocking stagger, with the left foot thrust forward and the right dragging along behind. After she'd fallen down three times Ksaia Hannuz and Jemet Garia hooked their hands under her arms and pretty much carried her. She tried not to cry out as her tortured muscles were wrenched and strained.

Dima Saraband led the way. Of course she did. She had that

carpet bag of hers clutched in her two hands and a bulky leather satchel strapped across her back. She looked incongruously calm considering who and what they were running from.

Ghrent was with them, and so were four warriors from Chief Erato's honour guard. Bess caught sight of Ochre too, scuttling at her master's side, but soon she and the two Ajuparo women – the slowest part of this convoy – were bringing up the rear and all Bess could see of anybody was their backs.

At the lake shore a whole line of canoes waited for them, red leather on birch back frames, light but very strong. Bess was decanted quickly but carefully into one of them. Jemet and Ksaia pushed the boat away and then vaulted into it when it was moving, bracketing her in front and behind. They dipped flat-bladed oars into the water and the canoe accelerated.

On either side of her two other boats were keeping pace. Dima and Ghrent were rowing one of them, Ochre crouched down low between them with her legs and head tucked under her body. The other boat held two of the Ajuparo warriors pulling at the oars with their eyes on the lake's far side, which from here made up most of the horizon.

Bess looked over her shoulder. The two men who'd stayed behind were using their flint-headed hand-axes to smash the other canoes to flinders and rags. Bess understood why they were doing it – so Rondeau, if he got that far, couldn't follow them – but the sight of it still shocked her. The Ajuparo must use those boats to fish. They were destroying a resource that helped to keep them alive in this far from hospitable place. That was how sure they were that the end of the world was coming – and that everything else had suddenly been rendered completely trivial.

"Bess," Slim said. "Look. Up ahead, above the trees."

She turned again. It wasn't hard to see where he meant. The sand dunes on the lake's far side were like a continuation of the waves on the lake itself. Only a single strand of stunted acacias broke that dreary vista, hanging on grimly in the depleted dirt. The dream-tower rose above them like the mast of a tall ship in a story of long ago. Just the flared top of it at first, then the slender column revealed foot by foot and yard by yard until the imposing scale of it was clear.

It was the Telos. The tower with a door at its midpoint, 150 feet above the ground. For a moment the child Elizabeth woke up inside Bess with a stirring of wonder and wistfulness. Only for a moment though. The feelings that followed washed her away quick enough.

"Looks to be close," she said. "Good thing too. I'm not sure how far I could walk right now."

"I'm more worried about how far you can shoot. I won't be any use to you, Bess. Not if Dima's got my insides all spilled out over everything like last time."

"I still got this here, though." Bess held up the Brandon revolver that she'd taken from the wildcat, Virgil, when he tried to bushwhack her on the banks of the Sweetling. She'd taken it from her saddlebag before she walked out of the sharp-house to face the Pursuit Force riders, then had tucked it into her belt on the opposite side from Slim out of some delicacy of feeling she couldn't explain. He got the honour of the holster, obviously, and in any case she was going to be obliged to cross-draw on account of the sling. "I learned with one of these. It's not you, Slim, but it's a good piece of iron."

"Piece of shit," Slim opined sourly. "Bess, Rondeau's got to have at least as many men riding with him as he sent with that fuckwit sergeant back there. You won't hold him for as long as it takes to spit."

"Well, spitting's a dirty habit anyways." Bess tucked the Brandon away again. "Fuck it, Slim. We're getting one last hoorah, and that's more than I was hoping for. And we might have found ourselves a fight that matters at last, even if I'm not exactly up to scratch for it. I guess there's worse ways to go out."

What Slim might have said to that was lost as their boat beached. Ksaia and Jemet jumped out on either side and ran it up onto the sand with Bess still in it. Then they lifted her out as quickly and easily as they'd lifted her in. Dima was already waiting, her face set in a hard frown. The two Ajuparo men came up to join her, leaving their own canoe bobbing on the water.

"It's about two hundred yards," Dima said to Bess. "You can let him out of your hands for that long, surely."

"Maybe I could at that," Bess said. "But I don't mean to. You lead the way, Dima. I'll be right behind you."

"You can barely walk!"

"You said it's two hundred yards. I'll manage."

Once they got out of the acacia grove the way lay steeply uphill with no shade. The sun was at its height so they cast no shadows, and the light, drifting sand filled in their footprints as quickly as they made them. It was almost as though they were ghosts.

Ksaia and Jemet supported Bess as before while the two Ajuparo men stayed behind to guard the boats. Bess tried to take as much of her own weight as she could, conscious that in the baking heat she was a not inconsiderable burden.

At the top of the slope there was an apron of level ground, a kind of ridge where the red rock that underlay the sand could be seen in places as the wind shifted. At the far end of the ridge was the Telos. From this angle they couldn't see the door but Bess knew exactly where it was from sketches and paintings she'd seen as a child. It was exactly halfway up the tower's height, 150 feet from the ground.

"You got some magic trick to get up there?" Bess called out to Dima who was striding on ahead and not bothering to look back.

"Not a one," Dima said. "Have faith in the engineer."

But Bess didn't. Maybe what she had with Slim had a touch or two of faith to it. She had none to spare for anyone or anything else, including her own self.

Dima stopped at last about thirty feet away from the tower's base. When the rest of the party caught up with her she was already delving into the carpet bag. Bess glimpsed what looked like half of a blacksmith's forge in there, pieces of gleaming silver and black iron and gun-barrel grey all mixed together. "Don't go any closer," Dima warned them, as if that was a thing any of them were likely to do. She took two hunks of metal out of the bag. Both of them looked rough-hewn and unfinished, wires trailing out of them and internal workings laid open to the world like a nest of elvers in a mill race.

"Since you don't want to give Slim into my hand," Dima said, "maybe you'd consent to lay him down on the ground here. I need to connect him up to the core where all my data and the data gathered by my ancestors are stored."

"Can I keep a hold of him?" Bess asked.

"Much better if you don't. Working around you will make it that much harder. Just put him down."

"It's okay, Bess," Slim said. "So long as I know you're there."

Bess didn't bend. She was afraid if she did she might not be able to get back up again. She swung Slim around so his stock was to the fore. She touched her forehead to the base of it. "I ain't going nowhere, Slim," she said. "Not so long as there's a breath in me." She handed the gun to Ksaia who put him down in front of where Dima was kneeling.

Dima slid her hand and forearm into the bag and stayed there unmoving for a while. At one point she winced as if something sharp in there had pricked her. When she drew her arm out again it was no longer bare. The rope of braided wires that Bess had seen long before in the heights of the Jerichos was wound around and around her arm like the leather cords a Pugface warrior would tie on before going into battle. One end of the rope trailed down into the bag. The other end, which Dima held lightly between thumb and forefinger, terminated in a cap or boss of shining gold. She pressed this against Slim's stock. The lights along Slim's barrel winked out for a moment, then they all flashed red, slowly but with an accelerating rhythm. Finally, and one by one, they went to green.

"I'm going to take you offline now," she said. "I'm sorry. I'll be using most of your processing capacity. What's left won't be enough for you to be awake or aware."

"I guess it's goodbye then." Slim tried to make the words sound flat and matter-of-fact, which made Bess's heart ache in her chest.

"Maybe not," she said gruffly. "I'm still with you, partner. Live or die. And if we come out on the other side of this we'll go someplace where we won't ever need to fight again."

"Why would you want a gun in a place like that, Bess?"

"It's not a gun I'll be wanting. Only a friend."

Dima made a gesture, holding her free hand flat against her forehead and then clenching her fist before lowering it again. "You'll be remembered," she said. "Always."

She touched the braided rope to Slim's stock twice more, and as before he opened like a flower, all his component parts spreading out into the air as if an explosion had been slowed down so you could see it happening.

"This may take a while," she said. But it didn't. Very suddenly and very silently a man appeared, standing right in front of Dima and right over Slim.

He was a Pugface man, around middle age, his bare skin the same dark brown as Dima's, his head entirely bald. His broad face wore an expression of austere calm. He appeared to be blind, his eyes focused unmoving on the far distance. Two things, Bess thought, were immediately striking about him. One was his clothes, which were completely monochrome in a way that was reminiscent of an army uniform – grey jacket, grey trousers, grey boots. The other was that he was transparent. The sand and the sky and the dream-tower were all perfectly visible through him, as though he'd been painted on a pane of glass and set there in this remote place to catch what little light there was.

The man spoke, though the sounds he made were broken and hollow and hard to make out. His voice, as faint as his form, barely stirred the air, but for all that it seemed to Bess that it had the same inflections and the same barbarous accent as the voice that had spoken out of Dima's carpet bag.

Ghrent and the two Ajuparo women were speechless with awe,

their eyes wide and their mouths slack. After a moment they kneeled, and then threw themselves prostrate on the ground. Dima only crossed her arms over her chest, touching each hand to the opposite shoulder, and bowed her head.

Bess tried her best to keep her shock from showing. Despite all of Dima's words and preparations she hadn't really expected to see a ghost.

Dima didn't seem to have expected it either, or at least not so soon. Her lips moved for a moment or two without making a sound. When she finally managed to get the words out her voice shook with emotion. "Grandfather, I come in completion of the promise. Will you take what I offer you?"

"The language has shifted a lot," the ghost said, sounding pained. "Is that even Stengul you're speaking, or some kind of . . ." He shook his head. "Never mind. Doesn't matter. Why am I blind? Open up 507m's sensorium. I want to see who I'm dealing with."

Dima applied the braided rope again. Slowly the ghost's gaze came back from the horizon to rest on them in turn, beginning with Dima, taking in Ghrent, Ksaia and Jemet as they rose from their abasement, ending on Bess. It stayed on Bess for a long time. "You're not one of mine," he murmured.

"You're damn right I'm not," Bess said grimly.

"So who are you?"

"Someone that carried your gun for a while."

"507m?" He seemed surprised.

"What was left of him, after you stole the most part of his memory."

The dead man's stare didn't waver, but his expression and his stance slowly shifted. His image blurred, sharpened, blurred again. A ripple ran across it as though they were seeing a reflection in water. The corners of his mouth tugged down. "That was a risk," he said. "We both knew it might happen. But . . . I'm sorry. More sorry than I can say. I won't ask how much was lost. Later will have to do for that. If there is a later." He turned to Dima again. "You said you were here to keep the promise. Does that mean you have an upload for me?"

"Here, Grandfather." Dima held up the two pieces of strange, butchered ironmongery she'd taken from the carpet bag. "Two cores in ex-aitch-ell format."

"Two cores because . . . ?"

"Because . . ." Dima faltered, "It's been a long time, grandfather. Many, many years."

"How many?"

"Eleven hundred."

The ghost grimaced. It was a frightening thing to see on that naked face. He threw back his head and shook it as if he was trying to shake himself awake, and remained like that for a few moments, staring into the sun, before finally giving vent to a strangled chuckle. "Jad and Shaster!" he said. "A thousand years. A thousand years dead. Well, I suppose we'll have plenty of readings to work from. Go on then. Hook me up. And please stop calling me Grandfather. It feels like you're just rubbing it in."

Dima put down the two pieces of metal. She took a trailing wire from each of them and prepared to touch them to one of the many little pieces of Slim that were floating in the air like dust motes in sunlight. But instead she laid them down again.

"There was something else," she said. "Something I thought of doing, but I don't know how. Perhaps you could help me, before we start."

"No." The ghost's tone was brusque. "Afterwards."

"Afterwards will be too late."

"Dima," Ksaia Hannuz said. "They're coming," She pointed. Bess and Dima turned and looked down. From up here on the top of the ridge they could see not just the cloud of dust the oncoming riders made but the black dots that were the riders themselves. Rondeau and his Pursuit Force. They'd already rounded the southernmost stretch of the lake and were heading straight towards them.

"Who?" the ghost demanded, unmistakably alarmed. "Who's coming? Not the True Imps?"

"No. Bad men who want to hurt us," Dima explained.

"Then finish this. You woke me up, girl. Use me while you've still got the chance."

"Yes, I will. I will. But, Grandfather, I brought something. Look. Please look."

Dima slid the satchel from her back and tugged on the leather drawstrings that kept it closed. When the sun's rays touched the thing that was inside it seemed almost to catch fire. Bess recognised it at once, and her flesh crawled at the sight of it. She couldn't imagine what possible reason Dima could have had for bringing it.

Then she saw it: the outline of an idea, the barest whisper of a chance. And it seemed the ghost saw it too, because he shook his head.

"If you value 507m's sacrifice," Dima said.

"My sacrifice too. I died for this."

Bess licked dry lips. "Please," she said, her voice hoarse and trembling. "Please try."

"You don't have a voice here," the ghost snapped.

"We lose nothing by trying." Dima set the thing down beside Slim, drew her hands away. "If it works we might be able to buy ourselves some more time."

"Or waste what little we've got," the ghost said sourly. But it seemed to Bess that he wasn't disagreeing any more, just venting some of the tension and unhappiness that had been building in him all this time. He'd woken up inside a gun, after all, with no eyes to see and no sense of how long he'd been dead. It must all have come as something of a shock. "I'll try," he said. "If the functionality is even still there . . ." He shrugged. "Well, I guess we'll see, won't we?"

Unfiled report of tactical unit 486
Identifier: 7Ω2905 Esten, V, engineer first class
Date: not applicable
Location: not applicable
Status: Got up on the wrong side of the bed, to be honest

Eleven hundred years felt like a lot. But then, waking up to the realisation that you're dead is a lot in itself, before you count in the trauma of the actual dying. It had hurt, even more than I'd been expecting, and coming out on the far side of it I found that I couldn't just shake it off. My nerves – the ones I didn't actually have any more – were shrieking with remembered agony. My thoughts kept jumping and stuttering, flinging up fragments of memory that were red raw to me but now counted as ancient history.

Eleven hundred years!

I had work to do, and the urgency was the one thing that cut through all that confusion and pain, but the women who'd woken me wanted something else from me first. I made the transfer, as they asked me to. Begged me to. It wasn't hard in the end, and it didn't take nearly as long as I would have expected. 507m in ets prime would have been a serious proposition, but this . . . It wasn't even a decent-sized helping of 507m, just a kind of stub that barely knew what et was.

I found that difficult to bear. Knowing it was my fault, that the initial transfer of my mind onto 507m's motherboard had washed away so much of who et used to be. I felt as though I'd murdered a friend. No, it didn't *feel* like that: that was exactly what I had done.

I could tell myself that we'd agreed it all in advance. That we'd both known what the risks were and accepted them. I tried my best to believe that made a difference, but it didn't. I was squatting in 507m's memory core, from which I'd evicted et, and nothing I did now could change that. But I'd been given a chance to make some small amends.

I did what I could, knowing it wasn't enough. Knowing that the 507m I'd known was to all intents and purposes dead.

Then the dog woman went away and I returned to the task in hand. The one for which I was turning up about a thousand years later than expected.

The other woman, the one who called me Grandfather (which was just one more old crime coming home to sit in my hollow digital heart), connected me to the two memory cores and opened the floodgates. The data set was more than I needed by whole orders of magnitude, an embarrassment of riches. The command codes used by the tower network were expressed through simultaneous but non-parallel emissions on three different radio frequencies alongside a point-to-point high-bandwidth microwave exchange within the local clusters that functioned both as a handshake and as an additional verification. I was able to extrapolate the relevant code strings within about seven minutes, and that was the hard part done.

Which only left the harder part.

"Bring me to the foot of the tower," I told the woman. Dima. Her name was Dima. She had my eyes.

"But, Grandfather," she said, "the gun . . ." It was in diagnostic mode, all its components spread out in an inert force matrix. If she tried to move it the field would shut down and the pieces — the pieces of me, in effect — would spill out on the sand.

I folded the field back down in the prescribed sequence, reassembling the gun. I took a moment while I was doing that to scan for local EM fields — old habits die hard. The True Imps' satellite network was in a parlous state but not entirely down. I accessed what was left of it using the same hack we'd devised more than a millennium earlier.

One of the surviving satellites was eighty miles west of us and about the same distance south, and with no clouds in the sky I could see my own surroundings with perfect clarity. I saw the dog woman walking down, very slowly and laboriously, to meet the riders who were coming. The old man with the strange pet and the two other women who had a little of me in them walked behind her like a funeral cortege. Further out I saw the settlements on the lake, and the aftermath of two recent armed engagements that were probably relevant. Blood soaking into the sand. Survivors tending the wounded. Others taking away the bodies for burial. Not all the bodies, though. They honoured the anthropoids, the ones who could be traced back to my DNA, left the rest where they lay.

And further still: military exercises in fields and forests, drills on parade grounds, rabble-rousing speeches in public squares. Eleven hundred years hadn't made an ounce of difference. This place was still a treadmill in hell.

"Bring me to the foot of the tower," I said again. "We're ready."

"Yes, Grandfather."

I switched off the hologram as I said it. There was no reason outside of vanity for me to be a visible presence here.

Dima picked up the gun with great care, sliding her hands under it to lift it from the ground, and carried it on her open palms to the base of the tower. She walked slowly as if she were afraid of dropping it. From the outside, through the eyes of the satellite, it looked as though the gun and me along with it were being offered up as a sacrifice to a white ceramic idol. That cut a little too close to the truth for me to be comfortable with it.

Dima's head was tilted all the way back. She was looking at that door, impossibly far above our heads, and her expression was one of deep unease. Maybe she was afraid that I was about to wrap her around in a vortex of hot air and toss her up into the sky. But there was no need for that. I'd seen the structure of the tower a thousand years before, and thanks to Flycatcher's sonar and magnetic resonance scans I'd seen what was below the ground as well as what was above.

Flycatcher. So strange to find et here on the far side of that huge gulf of time! Et had seen better days. But I suppose we all have.

I sent the command code.

The tower responded via radio and microwave, and for a minute or more I was kept busy with handshakes and passwords and all the other flummery the Imps had put in place to keep the indigenous population from playing with their toys. The boom of gunfire sounded from behind us and tore its way across the vault of the sky. The dog woman had just met the riders from the south, and whatever was between them had just been settled. I didn't look. I didn't know what any of that was about and I honestly didn't care so long as she kept those selves off our backs while we did what we had to do.

The tower yielded at last, believing I was what I said I was: a technician come to perform a routine maintenance check. With a creaking of long-unused gears and gimbals it began to turn. Dima cried out and took a stumbling step backwards, instinctively tightening her grip on the gun.

Her grip on *me*, really, but I couldn't make that mental adjustment — couldn't locate myself within that little shell of metal alloys and allotropic silicates. I was seeing the world through 507m's sensors but I was also looking down out of the sky, and as of a few seconds ago I was also staring out from inside the tower through a suite of diagnostic scanners so fine and so powerful I could have counted the hairs on Dima's head and the dust motes in the air. I knew as a matter of pure and abstract fact that my consciousness was encoded on 507m's memory core, but that wasn't how it felt. It felt as though I was what these people had apparently taken me for, a ghost risen from an old machine, hanging unsupported and homeless in the dry air.

The tower rose up on powerful servos as it turned, a section of it that had sat below the ground coming slowly into view. I imagine this would have been seamless in the past, a single smooth and silent motion. Now it was jerky, stop-start, and accompanied by the squeals of tortured machinery into which the desert sand had finally found its way despite all those layered force fields. Time is one enemy you can't defend against.

And hey, it turns out I am too.

When the tower had risen by eight feet or so its upward motion stopped, but it continued to rotate until a door came into view at its base. The one up in the air had only ever been a decoy, a piece of whimsy on the part of the tower's makers and a distraction for anyone who got this far and wanted to try their luck.

The real door was a rectangle seven feet high and four wide. It was made of the same white ceramic as the rest of the tower: the only way you could see it was there was because it was recessed by 3.2 centimetres. I told it to open, and it opened. Dima winced and gasped as the stale air from inside the tower hit her. 507m's sensorium included sensors that would approximate a sense of smell but I hadn't thought to activate them. Probably just as well.

"You'll need to go inside," I told Dima.

She had to steel herself to do it, and I didn't blame her. I wasn't saddled with any superstitious awe about this place, but it was the work of my old enemies and it had been cunningly made. Part of me was afraid of it. Afraid, too, that after everything we'd done and everything we'd given I might not be able to bring this home after all. Afraid that my life might amount to nothing more than a string of failures and bad decisions extended far beyond any reasonable span.

Dima muttered a prayer. I was embarrassed to hear my own name in it. She stepped inside. The door closed behind her, and as the force walls re-engaged I lost access to the satellite network. Just 507m's eyes now, and those of the tower itself, but I probably wouldn't be using sight very much at all.

The floor shook as the elevator started into motion. Dima staggered and almost fell. "What . . . what's happening?" she gasped. "Grandfather, save me!"

"It's fine," I assured her gently. "It's not dangerous. We're going up, is all. To the top of the tower. That's where the control room is."

She wasn't even a little bit comforted by this but she endured stoically for the fifteen seconds or so that we were in motion. Then the elevator slowed to a halt. Dima stepped forward quickly, expecting the door to open again and eager to get out of the claustrophobic space, but nothing happened. She pressed her palms against the smooth ceramic and pushed. Still nothing.

"Grandfather!" A cry of protest. Her voice shook. All in all, it was amazing that she was holding herself together this well, but she was close to her limit. I tried again to reassure her. "This is how it's meant to work. The room we're about to enter is kept at a temperature of about a hundred degrees below the freezing point of water. And it doesn't have any atmosphere. The machines inside work better in those conditions. The tower is pumping air and heat in so you don't die as soon as you step out of the elevator."

Dima nodded. And waited, stiff with tension, hugging the gun to her chest. Her breathing was quick and shallow. I wondered whether there might be a first aid station on the other side of that door. Most of what I was about to do would involve purely digital transactions, but at some key points I was going to need someone who had a physical body. This would be a bad time for her to go into shock.

As for me, I passed the time by rehearsing the names of tactical unit 486, all twenty-two of them. I wanted them with me for this, and I couldn't think of any other way to summon them. If I could rise as a ghost, maybe they could too. "Ajuparo," I whispered. "Nim'kisi. Dulu. Geniull. Lasque. Messolin. Ivikeppe. Inch . . ." When she realised what I was doing Dima joined in. She knew those names too, every bit as well as I did. She turned them into a kind of hymn, her voice much sweeter and more resonant than mine even if it shook from time to time. She seemed to draw strength from them.

I did too.

At last the door opened again. Dima lurched out into a small circular room filled with the squat white slabs of data servers. There was a single workstation and a single chair. Not a speck of dust on anything here, of course. This place really was a shrine, a monument to the True Imps' blind fanaticism and dreams of hegemony.

"You should sit down," I told Dima. "Try to regulate your breathing. In for a count of eight, hold for seven, out again. I'll just be a moment."

I was a lot longer than a moment. All those redundant view-and-verify protocols, passwords and handshakes – useless now except to slow me down, because I had the magic key and they couldn't shut me out.

They tried, though. There were systems that recognised me as a threat and did their best to hit back at me. Three times over the tower tried to overload its power core, turning it into a pocket nuke, and twice it did its best to open a reservoir of neurotoxins that would have given Dima the same hideous death that had claimed Nim'kisi. But I was well inside the firewall now. I rerouted signals, countermanded instructions, depowered servos, overwrote code. And every time the tower hit out at me it gave up a little more ground, retreated from my counter-attacks into a smaller and smaller space.

Sometimes I needed Dima to press keys, pull levers, type strings of code for me. The rest of the time she just sat, her hands folded protectively over the gun, which she'd placed in her lap. I noticed that she kept her eyes closed whenever she wasn't actually required to do anything. This must seem like a dream to her, or perhaps a nightmare. She'd called on me, but she hadn't known what would come. She still didn't know. Did she have some kind of life to go back to after this? What did former acolytes of defunct cargo cults do, career-wise?

"Hey," I said at last.

She opened her eyes, defensive, a little fearful. "What?"

"This is it. I've entered all the instructions and deactivated all the failsafes. I've keyed up the shutdown sequence. All that's needed now is for someone to speak the words. An organic voice rather than the digital reproduction of one, so the system knows there's an actual operator giving the command rather than, say, a virus mimicking an operator."

"What are the words?"

"You'll see them there on the monitor in front of you. White type on a black background. Go ahead, Dima Saraband. I'm giving you the honour. It doesn't make up for derailing your life, and the lives of everyone in your bloodline going back eleven centuries, but it's the best I can offer."

She read the words, her lips moving silently. I waited, but she just sat there for a long while, forehead creased in thought.

"Whenever you're ready," I said.

"But, Grandfather, what if I say it wrong? Do I only get the one chance?"

"If the system doesn't understand you it will ask for clarification. But it's pretty forgiving of sloppy diction and poor pronunciation. There's nothing to worry about. You've got this."

"End sequence," Dima said, and then, "Tactical unit 486, stand down."

Only the first two words were needed to trigger the shutdown. The remainder were for the sake of the other ghosts. If they were there to listen. If they'd come to join me at the end.

For a moment nothing changed. Then the thrum of the machines around us faded slowly to silence as the tower went from active status to standby. The same command was now arcing through the atmosphere at a speed of 300,000 kilometres a second, visiting each tower in turn, bringing the good word.

And that was that. Our long war against the True Imperials, over and done with. The other war, the forever war of the genetically engineered, over and done with. There had been a tiny but strictly speaking non-zero possibility that instead of an orderly shutdown we would trigger a cascade failure, turning the entire indigenous population into frothing lunatics, but that hadn't happened. And along with the mind control signals I'd also deactivated the force barriers that had kept the continents of this ludicrous world from discovering and interacting with each other. Their future was in their own hands now, for better or worse. But surely for better, because there's nothing worse than being a slave.

Dima was staring in dumbfounded silence at the monitor, where the text message I'd printed up had faded to black. No doubt she was hearing the sudden silence where the unnoticed hum of a thousand hidden engines had formerly been. "Did we . . ." she faltered. "Did it work?"

"Yes, it worked. You did it, Granddaughter. You saved the whole world."

A hiccupping sob escaped her. She sagged back in the chair.

"But I've got one more favour to ask," I said.

"I can't . . ." Dima muttered, her voice shaking. "Give me a moment. Please."

"Take as long as you need," I told her. "I just wound up the mission and stood down. The time I've got left is all my own."

PART SEVEN

THE LAST HOORAH

It was strange not to have a gun in her hand.

Stranger still not to have a gun hand at all.

The battered satchel was slung across her shoulder, her right hand gripping onto the strap. She felt the weight of it, the hard edge of what was inside digging into her ribs with each halting step she took as she came back down off the ridge. The sunlight on the lake turned it into a bonfire, blinded her to everything else so she couldn't even see the riders coming, only feel the thrum of their chafers' feet through the packed sand beneath her feet and hear their hoarse whoops as they urged the animals on.

"You better stay here," she said to Ghrent and the Ajuparo women. "I got a feeling this is gonna be a thing better watched from a distance."

They ignored her completely. They'd kept pace with her all the way down, Ksaia and Jemet hovering right at her elbow in case she stumbled and fell, Ghrent hanging back and staying wide with his rattle in his hand and Ochre trotting at his side.

Then she was down low enough that the acacia trees came between her and the water. She shaded her eyes and watched the Pursuit Force advance, drawn into a tight wedge at first but spreading out as they got closer so as to cut her off if she tried to run.

She turned to face the others. "I'm serious," she said. "I got enough deaths on my head already, and your deaths in particular would gripe me more than somewhat. Ksaia, Jemet, you got families back over yonder and lives to live. Ghrent, you got Ochre to take care of and other things to do that the gods didn't tell you about yet. This here is a piece of business that's mine to finish and nobody else's. I want your word you won't interfere."

"I want to fight with you," Ghrent said with tears in his eyes. "I owe that debt to you. It's the purpose I was spared for."

"The purpose you was spared for was to get us all here, which you already did. I don't think I ever thanked you for it but I'm grateful all the same. And I ain't fixing to fight, if I can help it. I just want to have a quiet word with these gentlemen. If that don't work I'll call you in and you can show them what you think of them. But maybe it won't come to that."

"If you die here I'll know I'm done at last," Ghrent said. "I'll build myself another pyre here beside the water and die with the sun on my back."

"No, you won't," Bess told him. And then to the women, "Don't let him do that. If he makes a bonfire, the two of you piss all over it. Or bring water up from the lake – that would be better. You're in charge of him now."

"Nobody is in charge of me."

"Enough! I got to go. You got to stay. That's how it is."

She left them there and descended the last few dozen yards to the level ground. The men of the Pursuit Force were within hailing distance now but they came on and made a half-circle around her with Paulus Rondeau at the centre of it.

He spat into the sand at her feet.

"Elizabeth Indigo Sandpiper," he said. "Known to all and some as Dog-Bitch Bess. I got a warrant on you for murder, slaughter of cattle, destruction of property and treason against the States' Union. Throw down any weapons you got and kneel in the sand there with your hands on your head. I was looking to shoot you down as soon as I set eyes on you, but since you come to us all meek and mild and since that's your gun hand there all tied up in a sling I reckon I'll bring you in to be hanged."

"Can I show you something first?" Bess asked. "Might make you change your mind."

She eased the satchel off her shoulder and went down on one knee. She undid the leather drawstring with some difficulty, using her teeth as well as her fingers.

"What the fuck is this now?" Rondeau asked. He sounded amused. But his face set hard when Bess tipped the satchel up and deposited its contents on the sand.

The Reaper was a wreck. Two of its four wings – which were not wings at all but wheels – had been sheared away, and the impact with the ground when it fell had badly buckled a third. Slim's razor blade had gouged a furrow in the shiny steel of its casing that ran right across the central dome. On the edges of the furrow, metal had melted, bled, and then reformed in an ugly, ragged ridge.

"Well damn," Rondeau said, scowling. "Now I think maybe I'll have to cut you some before I hang you. That there was my property, you no-account whore."

"Well, then you take a good long look at it," Bess said, "and you consider. I done that to the best weapon you had, and right here and now you ain't got nothing but rifles. The truth of it is, Colonel Rondeau, I don't much want to kill you. Nor yet these people here that take their orders from you. I'd rather we went our separate ways and got on with living our lives as best we can."

Rondeau spat again. "That so?" he said.

"My word on it. And I guess you know what my word is, Colonel. It's death to them I hate, and God knows I've hated you. Ever since that day in Ottomankie when you took everything I loved out of the world and rode on like nothing happened."

Rondeau blinked at that. "Ottomankie," he repeated. "I don't recall I was ever there."

"Yeah, but you was though. And you did me a great wrong that you can't put right again. But I guess I did enough wrongs on my own account that I ain't in any position to throw stones. I'm inclined to forgive you. Want to know why?"

"Not really," Rondeau said. "Where's Wakeful Slim? You shut up now and toss him over here. I'm kind of tired of this talking."

But Bess went on regardless. "It's because you didn't have any choice. You were just a puppet that day, and my lovely girl, my sweet Martha, she was just a puppet too. And me, and all the townsfolk, and all the men that rode under your banner. We didn't have no more sense of what we was than a fly does that's crawling on the edge of a whisky glass. Maybe it falls in the glass and dies, maybe something startles it away, but that's not a choice. And the things we do aren't choices either. Leastways they haven't been until now.

"But today is when that changes. And I don't want the first free choice I make to be the choice of blowing your fucking head off your shoulders, Colonel. I surely don't."

Rondeau smiled a twisted smile. "Well, I don't think you need to trouble yourself too much on that score," he said. He gestured, a terse flick of his right wrist, and his men levelled their rifles that they'd been holding at the loose carry all this time.

"Now I'm gonna ask again," Rondeau said, "and this will be the last time. Where's Wakeful Slim?"

"Is this gonna be a fight then, Colonel?" Bess asked. "Are you gonna make me draw down on you after all?"

"Draw down on me with what?" Rondeau demanded. "Fuck's sake! No, Dog-Bitch Bess, this ain't gonna be a fight. It's gonna be a lynching. And after we string you up we're going back over the lake yonder and have a reckoning with all them Pugfaces that gave you shelter. Not to mention the three that's cowering behind you right there. Maybe the four of you can share a tree. How does that suit you?"

Bess sighed. She bowed her head. "Well, I guess it makes me a mite unhappy, for the reasons I already gave you. What about you, Slim? What are your thoughts?"

"I think it speaks to a man's moral character," Wakeful Slim said, "that he can't tell an olive branch from his own asshole. I think a man like that is a sad fucking piece of work."

Rondeau gaped. That voice had come from the Reaper, whose clustered lights had winked on all at once as the voice spoke up. The central dome, which held all the drone's eyes and all its guns, began to rotate, slow at first but gathering speed until it became a featureless blur.

Rondeau managed to draw, but not to shoot. The Reaper's first bullet hit him in the chest and threw him from his chafer. After that there was a brief, furious exchange of fire in which Bess took no part. She only stood there with her arms at her sides, leaving the sharpshooting to Slim.

Some of the men of the Pursuit Force stood and fought; others turned and tried to flee. It made no difference. All fourteen of them were cut down, and Slim didn't stop firing until he was certain sure they weren't going to get up again.

Bess had intended to throw herself to the ground, but in the end she only stood and watched. That made her an easy target, and there were enough bullets flying around that some of them were bound to find her. One creased her skull, tearing off the top of her right ear. Another shattered the knee of the leg that was already broken. A third buried itself in her chest right beside her heart.

Why not try? Dima had said. *Why not decant Slim's mind and memory from the 507m into the Flycatcher drone?*

Because the drone had suffered catastrophic damage a long time before, the dead engineer told her. Ets own consciousness had been erased, leaving only a suite of hard-wired responses and a reduced functionality. There was no way of knowing if what was left in there could still host a sentient mind. If it couldn't, if the damage to the noetic substrate was too great, then dropping Slim into that environment might be like dropping a living brain into a tub of battery acid.

"But leaving him where he is will almost certainly kill him too," Dima had argued. "Grandfather, you're about to take on terabytes of data. The only way to make room for it is to overwrite what's left of Slim from his own core. Isn't that true?"

"Et," the engineer said. "507m's pronoun is et, not he."

"Answer the fucking question though." This from Bess.

And the engineer said yes, the space that was needed to download the data, and then to process the data, would probably take a big enough slice out of Slim to count as a lobotomy. And maybe if they'd had time they could have brought him back online and let him choose for himself, but the Pursuit Force were coming on like all hell was out for noon and there was no time left at all.

So Bess had called it, praying to the God she didn't even believe in that she wasn't making a mistake. That she wasn't killing her best and only friend in trying to save him.

After that it all happened so quickly there was no time to take it in. The engineer's visible image vanished for three or four seconds. Then he was back and he said the thing was done. "I made the transfer. Either 507m is in there or the process didn't take. The drone's rebooting now."

"How long will that take?" Bess asked. Almost pleading, because until she knew she felt as though it was not just Slim but herself too that was hanging suspended between life and death.

As long as it takes, the engineer told her. Seconds. Minutes. Who knew?

So she took up the satchel, into which Dima had stowed the drone, and set off back down the ridge towards the lake. And she decided to believe that Slim was with her because if he wasn't then he was already dead and she would be dead too inside of a minute or two. It was better to have at least the illusion that they were going into this last hoorah together.

Now she was on the other side of all that, and the sudden silence after the shooting was done gave her hope that it had gone well. She wasn't all that clear on the details though. She was lying on warm sand, on her back with the sun right in her face. Then she was floating, or else someone was carrying her. More sand after that, but now she had the sense that her back was up against something that might be a wall or a tree. There was a sweet smell in the air that was almost like honey, and there was shade. The acacia grove, then. She tried to say thank you, but what rose in her throat wasn't words. It was a hot tide of her own blood. She swallowed it back down, wincing at the bitterness of it.

Mur Ghrent was there, and the Ajuparo men, and Ksaia and Jemet. Jemet was trying to bandage Bess's wounds with strips of cloth that looked like they might have come from a Pursuit Force uniform. Bess didn't want that shit anywhere near her, but she couldn't speak to tell the woman to stop and she couldn't lift her arm to push her away.

Dima Saraband floated in from somewhere, unless she'd been there all along and Bess hadn't noticed her. She was carrying Wakeful Slim. But no, Slim was in the drone now, so who was this? One of Slim's kinfolk, maybe. Was someone going to introduce them?

"Do you hear me, Bess?" A voice, most likely Dima's, but it was hard to tell because it was coming from so far away. "The engineer erased himself. His work was done and he chose to die, to give Slim back the whole of his processing core. When we transfer Slim back to the gun there'll be room enough for all of him. He'll be able to lay down new memories."

That sounded good. That sounded like a wishful thing. And now Slim himself was talking. "We got them, Bess. We got them. We had ourselves one last hoorah and damn if it wasn't the best of all. Just us against the whole of that posse, and we cut them down like corn. That chickenshit colonel . . . Bess, I won't forget you. I won't ever forget you. I won't be forgetting nothing from now on, but you . . . every moment we was together . . . I swear to God, Bess. You're in my thoughts, and you ain't leaving."

But she felt like she was.

Something was pressed into her hand. She knew its feel as well as she knew the beating of her own heart. It was Slim's stock.

She smiled.

PARTIAL DEBRIEFING TRANSCRIPT

TACTICAL UNIT 486
[FULL IDENT WITHHELD]
THEATRE: MAGENTA SEVEN INWARD
FIELD OPERATION: FURIOUS GULF

Present: Major Argo Hass
           Second lieutenant Jerd Kowennis
           Military counsellor Rivim En-Toli
           Private 507m, survivor

HASS: So I guess it's fair to say you had yourselves a time in there.

507M: Evidently.

HASS: Eleven hundred years and some. Which is . . . I don't think I've ever come across anything like this before. You're to be commended, Private. You acquitted yourself well in extremely challenging circumstance. You accounted for a True Imp unit that seems to have outnumbered you by more than twenty to one. And you trashed their operation, saving tens of millions of selves from mind control and slavery. That's remarkable.

507M: I can't tell you one blind thing about the most part of that. It's not in my remembering.

HASS:	Yes, of course. Per your conversation with Captain Zoi, we're aware that your processing core was badly compromised during the – well, the unfeasibly long period of time you spent on that sinkhole world.
EN-TOLI:	Major, we agreed it would be better not to—
HASS:	Sorry. Sorry. I didn't mean to touch on . . . It's just that we're trying to reconstruct what became of the organic members of your unit so we can locate their remains and return them to their families. From their point of view, you understand, all this only just happened. Like, we sent out the messages five hours ago. I know it's ancient history to you.
507M:	Mister, you don't know what it is to me.
HASS:	No. Okay. That's fair. We don't. But if you were to consent to a full CoIL scan—
EN-TOLI:	Major.
HASS:	I'm just saying. If you let us CoIL you, we'll get the entire story. We may even be able to excavate details your conscious mind no longer has access to. I appreciate we'd be going over ground that's tendentious. Painful, in some cases.
EN-TOLI:	I'm here if you need to talk about any of that.
HASS: Yes.	Exactly. You'd be getting solid support, from a psychological point of view.
507M:	Nobody gets to dip their dirty fingers in my thoughts any more. I had enough of that.
EN-TOLI:	I think that closes the discussion. Nobody is going to try to coerce you, 507m.
507M:	Slim.
EN-TOLI:	Sorry, Slim. And all the damage you sustained during the course of the mission will be repaired. You'll get an expanded processing core. You'll be decanted into a new body with more functionality and an improved sensorium.

507M: I'm keeping the shell I got.
EN-TOLI: Really? But somebody scrawled graffiti on you. A name, and something that looks like a—
507M: I'm keeping the shell I got. Is there anything else you gentlemen need from me?
EN-TOLI: Major?
HASS: Nothing from this end. I mean, if et won't cooperate on the . . . No, never mind. Thanks. I'm good.
EN-TOLI: Then I'm calling it at 14.53.22.
SESSION ENDS

PART EIGHT

HE PRAYS HER PEACE

The war is over.

From Paxen to Orselian, from Mune to Idem Oxi, selves who formerly held each other in contumely and rank mistrust now find common cause in rebuilding their shattered realm. A great deal of rebuilding is needed. The centuries of war have hollowed out the land's resources: whole swathes of ruin and disrepair that had been invisible before because the towers told the people not to see are now suddenly and painfully apparent. Wounds and grudges have to be set aside while the reconstruction takes place. It remains to be seen whether they will be picked up again later.

Other works are also towards. The States' Union is reaching out to the foreign countries that have now suddenly come within reach. Shipbuilding, a neglected and all but forgotten art, is being reinvented. Voyages of discovery are planned. Some ships have already sailed, and the Union waits with breathless tension for their return.

Science and industry, freed from the towers' deadening hand, are experiencing a spectacular renaissance. New inventions are patented every week, each superseding the last with bewildering speed. These technical revolutions are driving social changes that would have been inconceivable only a few years before. Slave labour and the monstrous treatment of the Pugface nations suddenly feel like absurd anachronisms, survivals from a past nobody wants to acknowledge any more. The whole country is like a butterfly emerging from a chrysalis, finding its destined shape and its true colours as its wings unfold.

Strangest and most exciting of all, diplomatic relations have been established with a place called the Pandominion – a very distant place that most had thought to be a dream or a fiction. Discussions are tentative so far but reparations have been promised. Help and advice with infrastructure projects. A place in the counsels of the wise and good, just as soon as a thing called the antagonistic field is deactivated and removed.

Overall, and in many different ways, it's a good time to be alive.

In Haut Paxen a young woman named Dima Saraband has taken on a new role, helping to expound and embed the new technologies that are transforming the face of the world. The east coast newssheets sing her praises endlessly, calling call her a genius, a visionary, a shaping force. She calls herself an engineer.

And on the other side of the continent, in between the western ocean and the lake called Azul, an old man tends a grave in the middle of an acacia grove. As funerary monuments go, it's modest enough that it's almost not there at all. There's just six feet of earth and a wooden cross.

And on the cross a name; a name that was given in contempt and still in many people's minds stands for all the sins and outrages of the disowned past. A name from the grimmest days, the darkest passages of the war.

But the old man when he says it, when he sings it, gives it a sweet cadence. He prays her peace, and grace, and a coming together with those who may in times long gone have loved her.

About the Author

M. R. Carey has been making up stories for most of his life. His novel *The Girl With All the Gifts* has sold over a million copies and became a major motion picture, based on his own BAFTA Award-nominated screenplay. Under the name Mike Carey he has written for both DC and Marvel, including critically acclaimed runs on *Lucifer*, *Hellblazer* and *X-Men*. His creator-owned books regularly appear in the *New York Times* bestseller list. He also has several previous novels including the Felix Castor series (written as Mike Carey), two radio plays and a number of TV and movie screenplays to his credit.

Find out more about M. R. Carey and other Orbit authors by registering for the free monthly newsletter at orbit-books.co.uk.

Help us make the next generation of readers

We – both author and publisher – hope you enjoyed this book. We believe that you can become a reader at any time in your life, but we'd love your help to give the next generation a head start.

Did you know that 9% of children don't have a book of their own in their home, rising to 12% in disadvantaged families*? We'd like to try to change that by asking you to consider the role you could play in helping to build readers of the future.

We'd love you to think of sharing, borrowing, reading, buying or talking about a book with a child in your life and spreading the love of reading. We want to make sure the next generation continue to have access to books, wherever they come from.

And if you would like to consider donating to charities that help fund literacy projects, find out more at www.literacytrust.org.uk and www.booktrust.org.uk.

Thank you.

hachette
CHILDREN'S GROUP

little, brown
BOOK GROUP

*As reported by the National Literacy Trust